LOVE ON THE EDGE

STARSTRUCK RECKONING

BOOK 1

Courtney Coleman

Publisher: Courtney Coleman
Distribution: IngramSpark, Barnes & Noble Press

Library of Congress Cataloging-in-Publication Data
Name: Coleman, Courtney, author.
Title: Starstruck Reckoning / Courtney Coleman
Description: First edition. | New York : Barnes & Noble, 2024. |
Summary: A retired athlete, Tyde, recovers from an injury at his farmhouse. Meanwhile, Gia, a journalist seeking career redemption, plans a live NRL all-star event. Unexpectedly, her co-host turns out to be a sports star from her past, adding personal complications to her professional endeavors.
Subjects: Dating Roster, Work Place, Forced Proximity, Stranger to Lovers to Enemies to Lovers

PRINTED IN UNITED STATES

AUTHOR'S NOTE

When I embarked on the journey of writing this book, I allowed my imagination to run wild, embracing the delightful delusions that danced in my mind. As a journalist by trade, armed with the knowledge and skills acquired through my degrees, I found myself naturally drawn to the allure of storytelling. But it was my inherent creativity that truly set the stage for this literary adventure.

It all began with a spark – a brainstorm that ignited a fire within me. From there, I dove headfirst into the vast expanse of Pinterest, immersing myself in a world of inspiration and possibility. Each image, each idea, fueled the flames of my imagination, propelling me forward on this exhilarating ride.

With a heart full of passion and a mind brimming with ideas, I put pen to paper, pouring my soul onto the pages. Every word, every sentence, was a labor of love, crafted with the utmost care and dedication. And as the story unfolded, I couldn't help but think of all my fellow "delulu" girls out there – the ones who dare to dream big and refuse to settle for anything less than extraordinary.

This book is a love letter to all the boss babes who fearlessly chase their ambitions, even in the face of adversity. It's a tribute to the women who refuse to be defined by societal norms and expectations, who carve their own paths and make their own rules. And, let's be real, it's also a cheeky nod to the secret fantasies we all harbor – the ones where a smoking hot NHL player sweeps us off our feet, recognizing the fierce, unstoppable force that we are.

So, to all my "delulu" girls out there, this one's for you. May this book serve as a reminder that your dreams are valid, your desires are powerful, and your potential is limitless. Keep dreaming, keep hustling, and never forget the magic that lies within you. Because when you embrace your inner "delulu," there's no telling where your journey may lead.

Here's to the wild ride ahead, and to the incredible women who inspire me every single day.

SONGS LIST

I Hate You - SZA

Charismatic - Hailey Knox

Fly Girl - FLO ft. Missy Elliot

Through The Night -Maeta

Snooze - SZA

Heartbreak Anniversary - Giveon

After Last Night - Silk Sonic

Pink + White - Frank Ocean , Beyonce

Eyes Off You - PRETTY MUCH

Exes - Tate McRae

#Beautiful - Mariah Carey, Miguel

Billie Bossa Nova - Billie Elish

Bed Chem - Sabrina Carpenter

Poppin Out (Mistakes) - Chxrry22

Houdini - Dua Lipa

On and On - Tyla

Waterfall - Yebba

Come Thru (with Usher) - Summer Walker

CONTENT WARNING

Mental Distress
Insecurity
Toxic Relationships
Parental Issues
Abandonment Issues
Sports Injuries
Vulgar Language
Sexual Content
Anxiety
Drug Addiction
Emotional Trauma

PROLOGUE
Tyde & Gia

I stood there, my heart pounding in my chest, as Tyde's words cut through me like shards of ice. The living room, once our sanctuary, now felt like a battlefield. Shadows danced on the walls, cast by the dim light of the table lamp, mirroring the turmoil within me.

"You don't trust me?" Tyde's voice cracked, a mixture of disbelief and rage. "After everything we've been through?"

I clenched my fists, nails digging into my palms.

"Trust you? How can I when you can't even protect me? Understand me?" The words tumbled out, each one a dagger aimed at the man I thought I knew.

Tyde's eyes flashed, a storm brewing in their depths.

"Protect you? I've given you everything, Gia! My heart, my future—"

"Your future?" I scoffed, the bitterness rising in my throat like bile. "You mean the one I supposedly ruined?"

He stepped closer, his 6'1" frame towering over me at 5'4". I could smell his Roja Dove Enigma Pour Homme cologne, rich with notes of cognac, tobacco, vanilla, and amber. The scent that once comforted me now makes me nauseous.

"Do you have any idea what I've sacrificed for you? I'm a professional hockey player, for fuck sake! Any girl would die to be with me, but I chose you!"

The words stung, each one a reminder of the pedestal he'd placed himself on. I squared my shoulders, refusing to be intimidated.

"Oh, how noble of you," I spat. "Tell me, Tyde, when was the last time you actually cared about what I needed? What I wanted!"

His laugh was hollow, devoid of any warmth. "What you needed? I gave you everything! A home, security, love, the only fucking friendship you have — and what did I get in return? A girlfriend who stopped caring, who stopped showing attention, withdrew from conversations with people around her! Someone who stopped fucking protecting my bloody heart!"

I felt the tears threatening to spill, but I blinked them back furiously.

"Protecting your heart? What about mine? What about those images, Tyde? The ones in our bedroom, at the bar— how do you explain that? We are not fucking Ray J and Kim K."

Tyde's face contorted, a mix of confusion and anger.

"We both know those weren't from our database or security . But how dare you blame me for that! It's probably because of those massive parties you hate so much. The ones where you refuse to socialize, to make any effort—"

"Make an effort?" My voice rose, matching his intensity. "You invite strangers into our home, people I don't know, don't trust. And you expect me to just what? Pretend everything's fine?"

He threw his hands up in exasperation.

"Woman up, Gia! Make your own friends for once! Stop being such a loner and blaming me for your insecurities!"

The room spun around me, his words echoing in my ears. I stumbled back, my hip hitting the edge of the coffee table. The pain barely registered through the emotional turmoil.

"A loner?" I whispered, my voice trembling. "Is that what you think of me?"

For a moment, I saw a flicker of regret in Tyde's eyes, but it vanished as quickly as it appeared. The man standing before me was a stranger, wearing the face of someone I once loved.

I turned, my movements robotic, and walked towards the front door. Each step felt like I was wading through quicksand, the weight of our shattered relationship pulling me down.

"Gia," Tyde called out, his voice a mixture of anger and desperation. "Don't you dare walk out that door!"

I paused, my hand on the doorknob. For a heartbeat, I considered turning back, considered trying to salvage the pieces of us that lay scattered on the floor. But as I stood there, I realized there was nothing left to save.

Without a word, I opened the door and stepped out into the cool night air. The soft click of the latch behind me sounded like a gunshot in the silence. I didn't look back. I couldn't.

As I walked away from the house that was once my home, I felt something inside me break. But with that breaking came a strange sense of freedom. Each step took me further from Tyde, from the life I thought I wanted, and closer to an uncertain future.

The streetlights cast long shadows as I made my way down the empty sidewalk. Somewhere in the distance, a dog barked, the sound echoing in the still night. I wrapped my arms around myself, suddenly aware of how alone I was.

But as I walked, head held high despite the tears now freely flowing, I realized that being alone wasn't the same as being lonely. For the first time, I was making a choice for myself. And despite the pain, despite the fear of the unknown, I knew it was the right one.

I never turned back. I couldn't. The Gia who had entered that house was gone, and I was someone new. Someone stronger. Someone ready to face whatever came next, on my own terms.

Sabrina Grant

SEATTLE, WASHINGTON

The deafening wail of the ambulance siren sliced through the chaos, my heart pounding violently against my ribcage. In the harsh fluorescent glare, Tyde Wright's motionless form seemed almost surreal—the man who'd strutted through locker rooms with a cocky bravado now lay broken, A rich tapestry of chestnut spirals and coils, golden brown eyes shut tight against whatever nightmares plagued his unconscious state. Vivid tattoos trailed down his muscular arms, the only hint of the former NHL star's vibrant persona amidst this sterile, lifeless scene.

"What have we got?" the paramedic barked, his gruff voice cutting through the din.

"Male, early 30s, blunt force trauma to the head. GCS 3, pupils fixed and dilated. BP's tanking."

The lead medic's jaw tightened.

"We've got a sudden and worrisome situation here, team. Mr. Wright needs immediate attention. He's been admitted following a serious accident related to hockey. Let's prepare for complications."

My stomach twisted into knots as we raced through Seattle's rain-slicked streets, the ambulance swaying and jolting. Tyde's face, always so animated, looked utterly foreign in its stillness. The larger-than-life presence that filled every room now seemed impossibly small and fragile against the stark white sheets.

How could this be happening to the most infuriatingly alive person I knew? Tyde was a force of nature, a supernova streaking across the sky. The idea of him just...shutting down? Unthinkable.

At the hospital, a solemn hush blanketed the corridors, the antiseptic smell burning my nose. I hurried through the maze of hallways, my heels clicking a staccato beat against the linoleum. The ICU waiting room was a study in dreary shades of taupe, the outdated magazines and canned muzak doing little to soothe my frayed nerves.

Dr. Evans strode towards me, white coat flapping, his face etched with grim professionalism. I rose to meet his firm handshake, my business facade slipping into place like armor.

"Ms. Grant."

Dr. Evans' voice sliced through my whirling thoughts as we settled in the stark conference room. Fluorescent lights buzzed overhead, casting harsh shadows across the laminate table. "I understand you are Mr. Wright's agent and emergency contact. I'm afraid I have some difficult news."

I clasped my hands together, the metal of my rings biting into my fingers.

"Just give it to me straight, Dr. Evans."

He leaned forward, steepling his fingers.

"Mr. Wright is in a coma—we cannot predict when, or if, he'll regain consciousness. Days, months, years...coma awakenings vary drastically. We've failed to contact any next of kin. Do you know of any parents? Siblings? Anyone close to him?"

The words hit like a sucker punch to the gut, stealing my breath. I managed a jerky shake of my head, Tyde's cocky smirk flashing behind my eyes - a cruel juxtaposition to his current reality.

"To answer your question...no," I croaked, my voice foreign and thready. "He's estranged, severed all ties back in England when he was younger. Whatever family he had has been long gone."

Tyde was a lone wolf, his blustering bravado and endless pranks an entertaining smokescreen. But in the quiet moments, I glimpsed the shadows in his eyes, the unspoken hurts. For all his charm and bluster, Tyde walked through life alone. Until he'd weaseled his way past my defenses with crass jokes and that damnable grin, the infuriating man-child somehow becoming the brother I never asked for.

Reality crashed over me as I sank further into the rigid chair, phone buzzing with updates from Jennifer. Our shared headache, the one who felt more like an authentic family than blood, was lost in limbo while we scrambled for solutions, for anything to drag his ass back to the land of the wisecracking jerks.

"Sabrina? What's the word?"

Jennifer's sharp voice crackled through the speaker, tight with restrained fear and steely determination. An indomitable force, ready to move mountains or wage war for her loved ones.

I white-knuckled the phone, Dr. Evans gave me a moment to speak with Jen. What were the next steps when your proudly reckless client, your pain in the ass brother, hovered between this world and the next? I grappled for my usual clear-eyed pragmatism, that unflappable Agent Grant facade, but it slipped through my fingers like smoke.

One jagged truth crystalized in my mind, cutting through the numbing shock and blistering panic.

Without Tyde's irrepressible spirit, without his life ill-fitting the mundane like a supernova in the suburbs... everything felt dimmer. Muted and gray and suffocating, closing in. Quiet in a way that chilled my bones.

I needed that cackling laughter, those cringe-worthy puns and smirky winks. I needed my friend back, anaconda hug and all.

Failure wasn't an option. Losing him? Unthinkable.

So I gritted my teeth, lifted my chin, and faced the uncertain road ahead. For Tyde.

Gia

PUBLIC TRANSIT - NEW YORK CITY

The jarring newscaster's voice sliced through the morning quiet like shattered glass, the words "breaking news" sending a jolt of adrenaline through my veins. I pricked my ear somewhat listening to the news, not really listening to the details of the accident due to me rushing around trying to get ready for work and get out the door. In a pause turning to the TV just as I see someone…recoiling as the shocking headlines flashed images of a hockey player sprawled lifelessly on the ice. The sickening crunch of his spine and skull against the unforgiving surface audible even through the static-laced audio feed.

"Mother of god…"

The expletive slipped from my lips in a hoarse whisper as I watched the tragic scene unfold in gory detail in slow motion. I resumed getting ready, most of what I heard was - player in a coma from a brutal on-ice accident. The details hardly mattered compared to the visceral horror of witnessing that poor man's life hanging by a thread.

Fingers trembling, I mashed the power button, killing the screen as the newscaster launched into crass speculation about potential long-term injuries. No time to get sucked into the mania—I was already catastrophically behind schedule.

Panic seized my chest as I scrambled around the cramped

studio, the claustrophobic walls closing in with each ominous tick of the antique carriage clock.

"Shit, shit, shit!"

The frantic mantra spilled from my lips as I gulped down the last few scalding swallows of lukewarm coffee sludge and haphazardly stuffed notebooks and camera equipment into my battered satchel. Mascara streaked my pallid cheeks in inky rivulets, mahogany-tinted coil hair in a big puff, stands of my bang hang down in front of my face. A frazzled rat's nest framing my wild-eyed features—it didn't matter, I had to move. Now.

A muffled thump against the thin wall made me jump, the plaster vibrating with the force of my neighbor's irritation.

"Keep it down in there, would ya?" The gravelly voice was muffled but irritated. "Some of us are tryna sleep!"

"Sorry!"

I hollered back, wincing at the bite of acid reflux licking at the back of my throat. The city outside my grimy window buzzed with frenetic energy, no doubt fleeing the crushing weight of the day's fresh tragedy.

"Here goes nothing..."

Throwing open the door, I plunged headfirst into the dizzying morning chaos, recoiling as the thick miasma of exhaust fumes and cigarette smoke replaced the staleness of my apartment. My lungs constricted in protest against the acrid assault as I wove through.

Four stops to the studio, four stops until either salvation or damnation—it all hinged on making it before my tyrannical boss decided my severed head would look fetching mounted on her office wall. I burst from the stifling underground tunnel in a blind sprint, the briny scent of the harbor smacking me in the face like a wet slap from an irate fishwife.

By the time the photography studio's glossy exterior loomed into view, my lungs burned like I'd swallowed shards of glass, screaming for mercy with each ragged inhale. But it didn't matter. Nothing else mattered except clocking in before the devil herself descended to eviscerate me with her razor-sharp tongue for my latest unforgivable transgression.

"Please be in a good mood, please be in a good mood..."

The desperate litany fell from my lips in a breathless pant as I staggered through the streaked glass doors, nearly bowling over a potted ficus as an unholy string of curses spilled forth.

My bag's strap tangled around my elbows as I fumbled with the unwieldy tangle of equipment, shooting panicked looks down the corridor where my boss's domain awaited. Praying to any deity listening that Edith would be in a merciful mood for once…

"How ya going, cunt!"

The mocking lilt cut through the tense silence like a scythe through wheat. Laurie cracked back a laugh underneath his hand.

I very nearly jumped out of my skin, whirling to face my impish friend Laurie slouched against the doorframe in a haze of hairspray and faux nonchalance, the very picture of casual disdain. His expertly plucked blonde brows arched high above glittering blue eyes, pillowy lips twisted into a cat-that-caught-the-canary smirk as he lazily examined his fire-engine red manicure.

"What the hell are you doing lurking in doorways like a creeper?"

I sputtered, still reeling from his jump scare. Rather than wilt under my withering glare, Laurie's grin stretched wider, showcasing a mouthful of blindingly white teeth.

"Oh mate, I've got eyes and ears all over this nuthouse," he crooned in that trademark Aussie drawl, feigning an exaggerated yawn of boredom. "A little birdie told me they caught you trying to sneak in through the back to avoid having your arse handed to you by Edith again."

A leaden weight materialized in the pit of my stomach at the mere mention of our tiny-but-terrifying Editor-in-Chief. Edith Shalom demanded perfection, her signature jet-black, severely slicked-back hairstyle an ever-present reminder that she radiated ferocity and an absolute unwillingness to suffer fools gladly. Success fueled her relentless ambition, a blazing inferno that incinerated anyone foolish enough to cross her path without a protective suit of asbestos armor.

CHAPTER 1
AN UNCHARTED PATHWAY

Tyde

**THE FARMHOUSE - AID ROOM -
SAVANNAH DHU, NEW YORK**

The stench of antiseptic and failure hung heavy in the air, mocking my feeble attempts to reclaim the athleticism that had once pumped through my veins like life itself. Sweat beaded along my brow as tendons protested and lungs seared - my body a shambling wreck, a hollow shell of its former glory.

"What the bloody hell is the point!" The bitter words tore from my lips in a guttural snarl, each razor-edged syllable laced with seething frustration. "I'm never going to make it back to the league."

I whipped my head towards Regina - Ms. Santons professionally, though she insisted I use her first name. She stood unflinching beside me, an immovable bulwark against the raging storm of my anger and self-doubt.

Her brow arched slightly, hazel eyes calm as she met my outburst with infuriating serenity.

"Now, Tyde, let's start from the beginning."

I nearly bared my teeth at her placid tone as she adjusted my posture on the unforgiving therapy table. Her touch held no judgment, no impatience - only that steadfast, maddening determination that grated against my fragile defenses. Those boring hazel eyes seemed to strip away every barrier, seeing straight through to the roiling maelstrom of pent-up rage and shattered dreams within.

"Look at me." The use of my first name dragged me, however reluctantly, back to the present moment. Her voice took on a softer edge. "Progress takes time, Tyde. You've been through hell, but giving up now means you'll never reach your goals. Why did you start this journey in the first place?"

The words sliced through the bitter haze clouding my mind like a solitary ray of sunlight piercing stormy skies. I swallowed hard against the lump in my throat, tearing my eyes from hers to glare at the raindrops trickling down the window - the impassive world continuing its inexorable march onward while I remained trapped, a prisoner of my own limitations.

"To be the best," I rasped, voice little more than a hoarse croak. "To leave it all on the ice with no regrets."

Regina's expression softened further as understanding blossomed. "Exactly. Don't let a few obstacles rob you of that dream."

She pressed on, guiding me through each agonizing

exercise with firm yet encouraging hands, her unshakable belief as maddening as it was inspiring.

"You were at the peak before the accident. You can reclaim that pinnacle, but it won't happen overnight. Patience and tenacity, Tyde."

My jaw clenched as I wrestled with the demons whispering their insidious lies, those traitorous seeds of doubt taking root. Get a grip. I inhaled a ragged breath, squaring my shoulders as I refocused on the arduous path stretched before me.

Regina's voice softened further as she sensed the tempest still raging inside me.

"I know it's brutal," she murmured, "but every small step brings you closer to your goal." Her words wrapped around me like a soothing balm, shielding me from the icy tendrils of pessimism threatening to pull me under once more. "Visualize yourself back on the ice, making those moves you live for. Use that as fuel."

I gave a tiny nod, grudgingly allowing her stubborn optimism to penetrate the walls around my battered spirit. Gritting my teeth, I attacked the next set with everything left in the tank - which wasn't much, if I'm being honest. But that flicker of purpose, that remembered lust for victory that had fueled my meteoric rise, began to smolder in the depths as I pushed through the agony, one grueling rep at a time.

Regina's resolute presence at my side became a talisman against surrender, her unshakable faith offering a solitary seed of truth to cling to as I clawed my way back from the abyss inch by brutal inch.

—

THE FARMHOUSE - LIVING ROOM

The shadows stretched long across my living room, the fading light casting an air of melancholy over the faded trophies and framed jerseys adorning the walls. Relics of a life that seemed to belong to someone else entirely—a man who'd once dominated the ice with effortless grace and fearless bravado. Now, I sat motionless in the growing dimness, a hollow shell haunted by the echoes of my former glory.

"I can do this. One step at a time, mate."

The mumbled affirmation tasted like ashes on my tongue, a desperate incantation to breathe life back into dreams that grew more elusive with every agonizing day.

Restless fingers found my phone, mindlessly scrolling until an old video materialized—a grainy capturing of one particularly stellar game from ages past. There I was, fluid movements and laser-sharp focus, dominating the competition with an ease that now seemed like a twisted joke. Something deep within me stirred as I watched, a smoldering ember flickering beneath the ashes of defeat.

"I won't let this be the end, no way."

The whispered vow hardened my resolve as I pocketed my phone and surrendered to a dreamless sleep. When the first rays of morning light filtered through the curtains, I awoke with a newfound determination blazing in my chest. Screw giving up—giving in. I refused to be consumed by the darkness closing in.

Regina noticed the shift immediately as I strode into the therapy room, shoulders squared and jaw set in a defiant line. A ghost of a knowing smile tugged at the corners of her mouth as she registered the blazing conviction sparking in my eyes.

"That's the spirit, Tyde!" Her voice rang with genuine approval, fueling the raging inferno reigniting within me. "Keep pushing, and you'll surprise yourself."

From rehab to reality. Can I skate again? How well?

The familiar chill of the rink wrapped around me like an icy shroud as I stepped onto the ice, stick gripped white-knuckle tight. This was my arena, my chapel - but as I took those first tentative strides, everything felt drastically, heartbreakingly askew.

Movements that had once flowed with effortless fluidity now felt jarring and hopelessly disjointed. My legs screamed protests with each crossover, my core failing to engage properly. The puck seemed to skitter wildly whenever it struck my blade, refusing to bend to my depleted skill.

But I refused to surrender, pouring every scrap of sheer bullheaded willpower I had into each torturous repetition, each agonizing second that ticked by with cruel indifference. Regina, my physical therapist, remained that steadfast beacon on the boards - a gentle but insistent force urging me onward whenever I teetered on the edge of despair.

I risked a glance up towards the viewing area. There sat Sabrina and Jennifer, two of my oldest friends, their expressions speaking louder than any words. The pity and concern etched across their features lacerated deeper than any check into the boards ever could.

They hid it well enough when I finally stepped off that torturous sheet of ice, sweat-soaked and emotionally drained. But I could see the truth shining baldly in their eyes as I asked the question I already knew the answer to.

"I'm gonna have to pack it in, innit?" The words tasted like ashes on my tongue, my throat threatening to seal shut against them. "Give it to me straight."

Sabrina and Jennifer exchanged a heavy look, seemingly having an entire conversation in the span of a weighted breath. Then, slowly, resolutely, they turned back towards me - and gave a solemn, simultaneous nod.

"You…you were great." They speak at the same time, with the same tone, and try to speak confidently. Jennifer, with no sense of reading the room, harshly says, "It's giving high schooler. Not the NHL. So,Yes."

I wanted to rage, to repeatedly hurl myself against the cold, unforgiving truth until it finally yielded. But their grave expressions told me all I needed to know.

No amount of stubborn persistence could rewrite the harsh reality before me. The game I'd sacrificed everything for, the prowess I'd derived my whole identity from…it was gone. That effortless, divine flow had deserted me, perhaps forever.

I was unmoored, cast tragically adrift. The ice that had once been my bride was now wholly indifferent to my desperate entreaties, my connection to it severed. After pouring my soul into this sport virtually since birth, I was suddenly, devastatingly…obsolete.

As that harsh truth reverberated through my very marrow, I could feel a profound identity crisis looming like a towering tsunami, poised to swallow the only reality I'd ever known. In that endlessly stretching moment, I had no idea who or what I was without the game.

But I knew one thing - I would never again experience that transcendent, incandescent bliss of skating at the peak of my powers. That dream had calcified into dust.

An urgent summons from the NHL Board, their graveled tones somber as they announced their decision over the impersonal Zoom call. Just like that, my career—my life's paramount pursuit—screeched to a halt in a dizzying vortex of corporate jargon and bureaucratic placations.

All the air seemed to vanish from the room as the implications slammed into me like a relentless body check. This was it, the ultimate end of an era. As the shock slowly bled away, a strange sense of resolution settled over me like a weighted cloak. Perhaps this was merely the catalyst for the next, more meaningful chapter.

Straightening my spine, I gathered what tattered remnants of pride still clung to me and made the public announcement that reverberated through locker rooms and arenas nationwide. Tyde Wright was officially retiring from professional hockey.

Regina watched from the sidelines, her expression a portrait of bittersweet pride as she absorbed the magnitude of my decision. Our eyes met in that fragile moment, a lifetime of unspoken understanding and hard-won respect passing between us in perfect silence.

This wasn't the end. Not by a longshot. It was merely the first punishing labor pains of something new being forged from the ashes.

Gia

APARTMENT - BROOKLYN HEIGHTS, NEW YORK CITY

The Brooklyn Heights apartment enveloped me like a warm embrace, a blessed sanctuary from the unrelenting chaos that had become my professional life. Laurie, my closest friend—the one constant through every staggering high and gut-punching low—lounged across from me on the worn couch, eyeing me with a mixture of concern and endless curiosity.

"How ya goin'? What'd the dragon lady have to say?"

The words, innocent enough on the surface, detonated like a grenade in the minefield of my turbulent thoughts. I groaned, raking icy fingers through my disheveled coily hair as the weight of Edith's scathing criticism came crashing back in full force.

"Basically, I am fucked." The bitter admission scorched my tongue like acid as it tumbled past gritted teeth. "She said I have to come up with an inspirational story that pulls in our readers in a big way. Basically told me everything else I presented was shit. Said if I don't produce something great within the next month, I'll be out on the street."

The incredulous outrage blazing in Laurie's gaze was a twisted mirror of the infernal cyclone raging within me. I barked a humorless laugh, the soul-crushing futility of my situation paradoxically granting me a perverse sort of clarity.

"She even had the audacity to compare me to Piers fucking Morgan—that soulless, festering discharge blight upon humankind."

Those last vitriolic words seemed to sap what little strength remained, my body sagging like a crumpled marionette stripped of its strings. I fixed Laurie with a hollow, hopeless stare, shaking my head with leaden resignation.

"I better pull something out of my ass or I'll be fired. And she doesn't know that I've been in a writing slump for some time now. So, I am spiraling!"

There it was, laid bare—the humiliating truth of my impotence, my inability to conjure the inspiration that had once flowed so effortlessly. This stark, damning reality hung in the air like a suffocating miasma as Laurie's eyes widened, the wheels clearly turning behind that impish facade.

Then, her expression shifted, morphing into that unshakable determination that had seen us through so many storms in our unshakable friendship. Leaning forward, she clasped my shoulder, grounding me in that simple, steadfast gesture.

"Fair dinkum, Gia, give it a brisie. It's just a little hiccup, no biggie. I'll give ya a hand, no worries."

My brows knit together as I fixed him with a skeptical squint, the words a derisive scoff on my tongue before they'd even fully formed.

"How?"

But Laurie pressed on, undeterred, those kaleidoscopic blue eyes alight with a fiery conviction that slowly melted my icy defenses.

"To snap you out of your sook, we can put our garbos together. Might be you just need to scratch your chips from somewhere else for a bit." That radiant grin widened, coaxing the first faint ember of hope to flicker in the hollow pit of my chest.

"Let's have a boxer at some fresh ideas, eh? Get those little grays munted and find that ripper spark that made you a top-notch writer from the get-go."

The words washed over me like a soothing balm, temporarily banishing the toxic shadow of self-loathing that had taken up residence in the darkest recesses of my psyche. Laurie's unshakable optimism was an intoxicating tonic, a temporary respite from the relentless grind of despair.

A tremulous exhale stuttered past my lips as I leaned back, letting the rigidity bleed from my shoulders—if only for a fleeting moment.

"Yeah...you're right. I can't let this defeat me."

The words rang with the clarity of a solemn vow, the steel returning to my spine as that flickering spark within me flared with renewed vigor. Laurie grinned, eyes sparking with approval and a touch of mischief as he settled in, ready to plunge headlong into the roiling sea of brainstorming.

"Strewth, you've got it mate! Now let's get stuck into it. What's the fackin' main bark you wanna slam home with this inspirational yarn?"

As the evening hours ticked by in a whirlwind of concepts and half-formed ideas, I felt the invisible vise around my ribs slowly loosening its grip. Laurie's infectious energy proved an unstoppable force, his effervescent enthusiasm stoking the banked embers of my creativity into a roaring blaze.

We fed off each other's fervor, trading pitches and dissecting themes in a dizzying tango fueled by the kind of creative synergy that could only be forged between two kindred, battle-tested spirits. With each meandering conversational detour, I felt myself straying further from that suffocating vortex of insecurity and doubt, propelled by the momentum of our collaboration.

Shattered dreams and looming joblessness were reduced to mere phantoms lurking at the edges of perception, temporarily banished by the feverish brainstorming frenzy. A manic energy thrummed through my veins as fresh inspiration flowed—a torrent that threatened to drown out the leaden shackles of hopelessness that had weighed me down for far too long.

Perhaps there was an invigorating creative rebirth waiting for me just over the horizon…if I could only seize it.

So engrossed was I in this transcendent awakening that I scarcely registered the clink of glass and Laurie's conspiratorial grin as he retrieved the remnants of a 1942 bottle from its dusty repose. Relic of a bygone age, a potent reminder that inspiration could be found in even the most unexpected of vessels.

As the first flames of dawn crept over the Brooklyn skyline, a strange, ethereal shadow loomed over our little sanctuary. My limbs felt deliciously heavy, weighted down by the intoxicating mix of revelation and…well, intoxication. A distant quirk of Laurie's brow pierced the pleasant haze, his raspy voice slicing through the tranquil lull.

"I've got this hankering for a shindig. Maybe cutting loose will help you get your mojo back", alluring in that Aussie suaveness.

In that crystalline moment, reality came crashing back in full, merciless force. Work. Edith's impossible demands. The ever-tightening noose of expectations slithering around my neck with cold inevitability. I blinked slowly, mouth opening and closing in mute protest as Laurie's bleary suggestion sank in with all the grace of a bucket of ice water upended over my head.

"As if I can bounce back like I did in my college days?" The humorless bark of laughter spoke volumes, equal parts self-deprecation and weary resignation. "Yeah, hell no. Thanks for the effort, but I'm already on a buzz and work awaits tomorrow. I'd rather not nurse a hangover in the morning."

Our eyes met in that fragile moment, an entire tapestry of shared history and hard-won camaraderie flashing in those infinitesimal seconds. Laurie's expression softened, lips quaking in that lopsided grin—the universal signal that he knew well enough not to push his luck. With an indulgent shake of his head, he reclined once more, draining the last vestiges of our aged liquid muse.

For now, at least, the intoxicating lure of inspiration would have to suffice as my vice of choice. Come the harsh light of day, there would be ample time to wrestle with looming deadlines and the specter of failure nipping at my heels.

But here, shelled in the ephemeral sanctity of our little world of wordsmithed dreams, I could revel in the freedom to forget, if only for one blissful night.

CHAPTER 2

MANHATTAN COLLISION

Gia

OFFICE - MANHATTAN, NEW YORK CITY

The cacophony of Manhattan's concrete arteries thrummed through the office windows, a relentless metronome underscoring the pulsating urgency pervading every corner of this city that never sleeps. I sat rigid at my desk, a taut wire thrumming with anxious energy as the overflowing inboxes and stacked manuscripts seemed to teeter precariously, ready to bury me beneath their suffocating weight at any moment.

"Gia, we need to talk about the latest project. It's not up to the standards we expect here."

The words detonated like a grenade in the compact office space, their devastating impact sweeping aside all coherent thought. I tore my gaze from the taunting vista of steel and glass beyond the windows to find Edith's imposing silhouette slicing through the chaos, her steely demeanor radiating an impervious poise that I could only fantasize about emulating.

"I...I did my best, Edith." The pathetic whisper scraped past lips rendered dry and cracked by the airless tension permeating every molecule. "I thought I addressed all the concerns we discussed earlier."

A derisive exhalation fluttered the obsidian curtain of her hair as she fixed me with a stare that could peel paint. The city's frantic pulse droned in my ears, a hollow roar rendering her dismissive sigh thunderously oppressive.

"Your best isn't cutting it, Gia." Each razor-edged syllable sliced through my waning bravado like a scalpel through rice paper. "This is a crucial project, and I expected more from you."

The words detonated with earth-shattering finality, the rubble of my professionalism caving inward until all that remained was a visceral, full-body flinch. My throat constricted, robbing me of even the most meager rejoinder as that diminutive titan paced the confines of her gilded arena, eyes narrowing to laser-focused slits.

"It's not just about this project, Gia."

The words lashed out with cruel precision, each lick of the whip stripping away another layer of my flimsy bravado until I sat exposed, raw and flayed to the core.

"I've invested time in mentoring you, and I expected better overall."

The weight of her expectations manifested as an anvil of dread settling in the pit of my stomach—a leaden, inescapable burden. Edith's next question emerged in a tone of scathing finality, the death knell for any remaining delusions of grandeur I may have harbored.

"Are you sure you're cut out for this role?"

The question ricocheted through my skull in endless, torturous cycles. My throat constricted, strangled gasps the only audible feedback as I floundered in a sea of abject humiliation. Edith's glacial stare bored into me with a piercing intensity that rendered the frenetic sounds of traffic beyond a distant murmur.

"I...I believe in myself, Edith." The strangled whisper emerged raw, bleeding with the desperation of a final plea for clemency. "I'll work harder. Please, give me another chance."

For an eternal instant, her expression remained inscrutable—an ancient monument impervious to the ebb and flow of lesser beings pleading at its base. Then the statue's eyes narrowed to slits of polished onyx, and my fragile hopes withered in their frigid glare.

"This isn't just about chances, Gia." The words emerged clipped, precise, devoid of any mercy or compromise. "It's about meeting the expectations of this position. You need to prove you can handle it."

I swallowed hard against the lump of failure lodged in my throat, my fingers digging grooves into the desk's lacquered veneer. The skyline's achingly beautiful grandeur seemed to mock me, the towering icons of success that had once filled me with awe now looming like monolithic reminders of all I wasn't.

But beneath the mantle of dejection and acute self-loathing, an ember of defiance yet smoldered. Straightening my spine, I locked eyes with my diminutive inquisitor, channeling every ounce of bravado and conviction into a response that would decide my fate.

"I'll do whatever it takes, Edith. I won't let you down again."

The declaration hung suspended in the electrified space between us, quavering with a fragile resilience that seemed absurdly insignificant in the shadow of her withering certainty. For a moment, her leonine mask slipped infinitesimally, a micro-expression of...what? Approval? Grudging respect? Whatever it was evaporated with her next words, lancing through the tension with surgical precision.

"We'll see, Gia. We'll see."

With that, she pivoted on her immaculately-heeled loafers and strode from the office, leaving me to contemplate my Sisyphean undertaking once more. Through the glass, the gilded skyline seemed to waver and shimmer in the heat-warped haze, a fleeting mirage of grandeur amidst this churning sea of cut-throats and opportunists.

Sucking in a steadying breath, I refocused on the computer's unblinking cursor--my only present ally in this sprawling arena of tooth-and-claw ambition. The words would come, honed to a razored edge capable of slicing through the maelstrom of doubt. They had to. Too much rode on my ability to conquer the blank page with the sort of resonance that could command even Edith's grudging respect.

No more missed chances. No more excuses. It was do-or-die time in this urban battlescape of power, prestige and cold-blooded scrutiny. I would rise to the occasion, come what may.

The only alternative simply didn't bear consideration. Not from this lofty precipice. Not when I'd sacrificed so much, carved away every ounce of superfluous weakness to elevate myself to this pinnacle. There could be no retreat, no surrender.

Not now. Not when I'd finally grasped the dream that so many claw and scrape for, only to falter inches from the promised land.

Cracking my knuckles, I squared my shoulders and aimed my defiant glare at the demanding expanse of the Great Blank before me.

Game on, New York. Game. On.

CONFERENCE ROOM

The prospect of redemption glimmered on the horizon like a desert mirage, its shimmering promise both tantalizing and potentially ephemeral. In the days following my humiliation at Edith's hands, I wrestled with the thorny tendrils of self-doubt that seemed intent on strangling any fragile seedlings of ambition before they could blossom.

But I was Gia, damn it—a woman forged in the unforgiving crucible of this concrete jungle. Surrendering to the paralytic vise-grip of uncertainty simply wasn't an option, no matter how tempting the siren call of mediocrity might be. With each aimless hour spent pacing my cramped apartment, the ember of determination within me glowed brighter, fanned by desperation's fevered breath.

I was absorbed in my computer screen, the cursor blinking mockingly at me as I struggled to come up with my next article idea. My chestnut hair kept falling annoyingly in my face, and I impatiently tucked it behind my ear for the hundredth time.

The clacking of oxfords against the linoleum floor made me glance up. Laurie was sauntering over, a cocky grin already plastered across his face. He leaned against my cubicle wall, his tie slightly askew.

"Oi, I've got a rippa idea for your next yarn," he said. My hazel eyes narrowed skeptically at his presumptuousness, but he barreled on before I could protest.

"These young fellas playin' hockey' have been gettin' a fair bit of airtime lately - on the tellie, all the sporto shows, you name it. Why don't you do a profile on some of these up-and-comers, ay?"

I tapped my pen against my lips, actually considering his suggestion. The more I turned it over in my mind, the more it appealed to me. My eyes brightened with nascent excitement.

"You know, that's not a bad idea at all, Laurie."

I swiveled eagerly back toward my monitor, fingers flying across the keys as I began scouring the internet for background on the hot new prospects. Interviewing young talent was one of my greatest professional joys - seeing the raw ambition and endless potential shining in their eyes never failed to reignite my own passion.

Laurie grinned smugly, obviously satisfied at having sparked my creative flow again. I was only vaguely aware of him straightening his tie and retreating back to his own disheveled cubicle territory. My mind was already whirring, formulating questions and mapping out angles for this piece.

Then, like a lightning strike illuminating the path ahead, inspiration struck. A bold gambit, one that could potentially salvage my credibility while elevating the magazine to dizzying new heights of relevance and prestige. But the inherent risk was undeniable—put up or shut up time, as they say.

Still, as the scintillating specifics took shape, sharpening into an audacious proposal, I knew there was only one play left to make. Time to go big or go home in a blaze of glory.

I barely registered the humming chaos of the bullpen as I marched through the editorial labyrinth, my singular focus honed with laser-like intensity on the sanctum awaiting at the end. Edith's domain, that hallowed chamber where reputations and careers were just as often cremated as they were minted.

The threshold loomed before me in eerie silence, the sounds of Manhattan's concrete symphony muffled in deference to the sacrosanct air within. Drawing a fortifying breath, I squared my shoulders and rapped my knuckles against the imposing barrier with three percussive strikes.

"Enter."

The curt summons sliced through the tension with all the warmth of a surgeon's scalpel. I turned the handle, pushing through into the lioness' den with what I hoped was the nonchalant swagger of someone supremely confident in the merits of their offering.

Edith glanced up from her computer, one perfected brow arching infinitesimally as her obsidian eyes met mine in a silent challenge. In that transitory instant, the fading afternoon light filtering through the floor-to-ceiling windows cast her imperious visage in stark relief, rendering her every chiseled angle severe and intimidating.

But I was committed now, with no contingencies or safeties to fall back on.

"Edith, what if we host a live NHL All-Star weekend right here in New York? And what if I write about all the up and coming NHL players that everyone can't seem to stop talking about?"

The words burst forth in a breathless torrent, as if giving voice to the sheer insanity of the proposal might somehow diffuse its explosive potential. I pressed on with mounting conviction, the feverish cadences of my pitch accelerating with every passing second.

"We could bring in the biggest stars, create a buzz unlike anything this city has seen, and showcase our brand like never before!"

The declaration hung suspended in the crystalline air, its weight and gravitas radiating outwards like the shockwave from a seismic detonation. Edith regarded me from across the vast, pristine expanse of her desk, her expression unreadable save for the slightest uptick at the corner of her hockey-slashed lips.

For an agonizing heartbeat, the silence stretched taut—a coiled serpent poised to strike at any provocation. Then, with glacial deliberation, those sculpted lips parted to deliver a response that would determine my professional fate.

"Interesting, Gia."

The two words reverberated through my psyche like profane invocations, both a condemnation and a challenge in equal measure.

"Tell me more."

And just like that, I was airborne without a parachute, freefalling into the depths of an audacious gambit whose outcome was as uncertain as the shifting winds howling past the towering monoliths surrounding us.

But for the first time since sealing my own damnation by falling short of Edith's lofty expectations, a sly grin tugged at the corners of my mouth as the first inklings of a grandiose endgame took shape.

Whatever happened next, one thing was certain—it was going to be one hell of a ride.

BOARDROOM - MIDTOWN, NEW YORK CITY

The cavernous boardroom radiated an air of hushed gravitas, the weight of legacies and reputations hanging thick and palpable in the rarefied atmosphere. My knuckles ached from the white-knuckled grip clenched around the smooth wood of the presentation clicker as I strode to the front of the room, each click of my heels reverberating like a judge's gavel across the marbled expanse.

This was it—the apex towards which every sacrifice, every ounce of sweat and sleepless mania had been devoted. All my hopes, my dreams, my very professional future now danced like a marionette at the end of this high-stakes gambit, utterly at the mercy of the four eminences weighing my every move with their soul-stripping scrutiny.

Squaring my shoulders, I pivoted to face the distinguished NHL Board of Governors arrayed before me in all their power-suited impassivity. Edith Shalom was no wilting debutante when it came to command performances—time to show these stuffed penguins how a real ringmaster captivated an audience.

"Ladies and gentlemen," I began in my most resonant tone, inclining my chin a fraction as I met each withering gaze with the scorching intensity of a blast furnace. "As All-Star weekend approaches, the opportunity to host or co-host this prestigious event is before us."

A calculated pause allowed the weight of that tantalizing prospect to percolate and take root before I unleashed the opening salvo of my grand proposition.

"I stand before you today not just as a candidate, but as the embodiment of a vision that transcends the ordinary."

The clicker's plasticky report was the only sound that dared punctuate the weighted stillness as I triggered the first slide. A speculum of visuals burst into radiant beings, their dynamic choreography flooding the chamber with vibrant life and pulsating energy.

As the spectacle played out, I allowed the briefest of smirks to curl at the edges of my painted lips before surging ahead in a cadence that brooked no hint of ambiguity or tepidness.

"This event is more than just a showcase of athletic prowess; it's a celebration of the spirit that binds us all to the heart of the game. Hosting it is not merely about logistics but about creating an experience that resonates with fans and players alike."

The words tumbled forth, precise and impassioned, as I stalked the hardwood stage with choreographed intensity. With each click of the clicker, I unveiled another dazzling component of my grand vision, laying bare the finer intricacies of my meticulously-crafted opus.

"I propose a seamless blend of tradition and innovation, merging the rich history of the NHL with cutting-edge entertainment. From interactive fan experiences to player engagement initiatives, our hosting approach will elevate the All-Star weekend to unprecedented heights."

My voice swelled with escalating fervor, hands slicing through the air in broad, authoritative gestures as the venue's skeletal architecture began fleshing out before the Board's very eyes. They were leaning forward in their wingback chairs now, the barest hints of intrigue disrupting their prudish contours.

"Our partnerships with local businesses and sponsors will not only enhance the event's financial success but also deepen our ties with the community." I allowed myself the most infinitesimal of pauses, letting the implications of that assertion coalesce like a gathering storm front. "This isn't just a hosting opportunity; it's a chance to leave a lasting legacy, showcasing our commitment to the sport and its fans."

With a final decisive click, the grand culmination materialized in all its transcendent glory—a vision of grandeur, ambition, and prestige elevated to the loftiest of pinnacles.

I held the moment in an electrified suspension, allowing the sweeping magnitude of my proposition to penetrate the hidden recesses of each man and woman's avaricious psyche.

Then, when the tension became so taut as to be nearly unendurable, I delivered the coup de grace in a tone bristling with the unshakable confidence of a gambler who knows they're holding the nuts.

"In conclusion, hosting the All-Star weekend isn't merely an honor; it's a responsibility to elevate the NHL's presence. I humbly submit that I am not just ready for this challenge...."

A pause, perfectly calculated to extract maximum impact, and then the final blow to shatter any remaining impediments.

"I am prepared to redefine what it means to host an event of this magnitude."

The silence that followed was deafening, a Canyon of Reverential Awe carved into the stuffy air by the seismic force of my proposition. I drank in the stunned tableau, the boardroom diorama rendered in stark freeze-frame as the consequences of my audacious gambit began taking hold.

In that transcendent pocket of hushed incredulity, I could practically taste the success wafting towards me, the tantalizing ambrosia of a dream coveted, seized, and savored through sheer, indomitable will.

The die had been cast and the gauntlet thrown. Now it remained only to await the verdict as to whether I would bask in the glory of conquest...or writhe in the throes of defeat.

APARTMENT - BROOKLYN HEIGHTS, NEW YORK CITY

The plaintive chirp of my laptop sounded like a thunderclap in the breathless hush of my apartment, each infinitesimal second lingering with the gravid tension of a stormfront about to detonate. It was here—the moment toward which every ounce of my relentless ambition had been feverishly straining.

With trembling fingers, I wrenched open the innocuous-looking email, the words swimming into view in kaleidoscopic bursts as my pounding pulse thrummed a staccato cadence against my temples. This was it, the make-or-break verdict that would either propel me into the stratospheric realm of my dreams or condemn me to the purgatory of the overlooked and undervalued.

"Dear Gia," the impersonal salutation began in that gleaming digital font, each sterile syllable radiating a weight that defied the constraints of mere text on a screen. "We are thrilled to extend an invitation for you to be a host for the upcoming weekend!"

The world around me seemed to dissolve into an ineffable, whitewashed haze as the implications of that tremulous proclamation washed over me in dizzying waves of euphoria. This was no mirage conjured by the cruelest throes of sleep-deprived delirium—this was undeniable validation searing itself into the very fabric of reality.

"Your unique perspective and vibrant energy stood out to us, and we believe you'll bring an extraordinary touch to the event."

The words ignited like an incendiary fuse tripwired to

the deepest wellspring of elation roiling within me. I was...
extraordinary. Extraordinary! Not just a faceless cog in the
machine, not some expendable creative foot soldier toiling in
obscurity—but a singular talent to be coveted and championed
at the highest echelons.

"Oh my god," the rapturous murmur tumbled unbidden
from my lips, more a reverent invocation than a mere platitude.
"This is it!"

Each subsequent line of that sacrosanct digital missive
seemed to shed layer after layer of disbelief and self-doubt
until I was basking in the radiant glory of this pivotal career
breakthrough. The perks, the prestige, the sheer magnitude
of the opportunity stretched out in high-definition splendor
before me, its grandeur matched only by the stratospheric
peak of my ascendant euphoria.

"They want me to host! This is incredible!"

The shrill ping of my phone pierced the sublime reverie,
shattering the ethereal bubble in which I'd found myself
casted. A new notification, the stark legalese and contractual
formalities lending an almost profane gravitas to what had
been, until this point, an utterly transcendent experience.

But no matter. No dense thicket of bureaucratic
minutiae could dampen the blazing intensity of this meteoric
culmination. If anything, the weighty obligations only
reaffirmed that unshakable sense of destiny, of dreams
impossibly manifested into the material plane.

"Thank you! Thank you God! Thank you so much for this
opportunity!"

The exultant cry burst forth in a breathless torrent,

propelled by the manic swells of jubilation crashing through me in relentless succession. Beaming, I leapt from my chair, limbs becoming a whirling dervish of elated motion as the constraints of propriety and rigidity dissolved in the wake of this career-defining tidal wave.

A little happy dance, equal parts undignified and utterly unrestrained in its gleeful expression, as my body moved in effortless tandem with the euphoric oscillations of the soul within. Against the monotonous backdrop of my shabby living quarters, I must have presented a spectacle of unhinged transcendence—but in that eternal instant, I was untouchable, inviolable.

"This is a dream come true!" I crowed to the indifferent heavens, whirling and twirling with reckless abandon. "I can't believe it!"

And in that dizzying, rapturous vortex, the shackles of insecurities and self-doubting whispers dissolved into insignificance, banished from my consciousness by the blazing supernova of yearning actualized. With a breathless giggle, I collapsed back into the chair, my chest heaving with exhilaration and the first tingles of bone-deep fatigue.

As the pulsating thrill show ebbed into a state of quivering anticipation, one thought blazed with meteoric intensity above all others—a new horizon glittering on the edge of perception, rich with the promise of prestige and prosperity that awaited me over the precipice.

All I had to do was spread my wings...and take the leap.

—

The jubilant trill of Edith's specific ringtone on my phone shattered the charged stillness, its effervescent cadence reverberating through the apartment like the first peals of celebratory bells.

"You did it! You got the hosting job for the NHL All-Star weekend! They're going to announce it right away!"

Edith's radiant expression split into a beaming grin as the confirmation crackled through the phone's tiny speaker. "Thank you for the congratulations! I can't believe it!"

The mantra pounded in euphoric counterpoint to the jackhammer cadence of my pulse, every tremor and shudder suffused with the sort of unvarnished jubilation I'd only experienced in the rarest and most transitory of instances.

This was it—the pivotal breakthrough, the seminal milestone that would cement our status as media icons and luminaries. From this dizzying precipice, the possibilities ahead were as abundant as they were limitless. We had thrust ourselves into the spotlight in grand, inimitable fashion and—

The abrupt buzz of my phone slicing through the revelry was akin to an ice-tipped dagger plunging straight into my abdomen, its frigid kiss lancing through the gossamer vestiges of my euphoric high with surgical precision. I blinked dazedly at the notification that had so rudely dragged me back from the rarefied realm of uncomplicated bliss.

My lungs constricted, expelling what little air remained in a strangled wheeze as the insidious implications bloomed into focus with agonizing clarity. There, amid the torrent of elated messages and jubilant hashtags, a single name carved itself into my consciousness like runes inscribed with corrosive acid.

Tyde Wright.

BOARDROOM - MIDTOWN, NEW YORK CITY

The letters burned with the scorching intensity of a solar flare, the memories detonating like seismic detonations ripping fissures in the fragile facade of professional detachment and ambition I'd erected. The shock blossomed into a visceral riptide of resentment crashing over me in suffocating waves.

"No way…" I heard the wispy exhalation as if disembodied from my own numb lips. "Tyde Wright?"

Edith's euphoric chatter came through as an indistinct murmur, the background radiation from some distant cosmos flickering on the periphery of my ensorcelled fixation. Tyde Wright—that arrogant embodiment of every toxic whore womanizing cliche to strut out of the locker room and into infamy. With him in the mix, this event had transformed from a tantalizing milestone into a potential conflagration of tensions and repressed turmoils.

With an abruptness that startled even myself, the bitter pall of resentment crystallized into a hard knot of resentment and resignation.

"Great, just great."

I start to type ferociously on my phone, looking for any little news on Tyde. I'm looking for the latest. And that's when I stumbled upon an article, devastation.

The headline reads, ***"Tyde Wright Career Ending Injury Forced Retirement"***.

"THAT WAS TYDE?", realization screaming in my head.

A quick flashback to a few months ago, realizing now it was Tyde on the news that morning I was in a rush going to work. The horrible video on the ice, bashing his head, spine deformed, knocked out…

With Edith pulling me back into reality with her merry laughter ebbing away with dawning concern. "What's wrong? I thought you'd be thrilled about the news."

I exhaled a harsh, withering sigh, the muscles in my jaw tightening until I could practically feel the ligaments creaking in protest.

"It's just…Tyde is hosting too."

The intonation dripped with such undisguised umbrage that I was mildly surprised the syllables didn't corrode right through the oxygen molecules. But the shock that contorted Edith's angular features was nothing compared to the kaleidoscope of repressed hurts and damage detonating within me.

"Tyde Wright? So?"

I could only try to shake the haze off, the phantoms of a thousand agonies and humiliations raging across the tattered tapestry of our fractured romance in vivid flashes of torment and wasted tenderness.

"That prick," scowling underneath my breath with anger and agony.

Murmuring to myself, "The cheater, the liar, the playboy who broke my heart and ruined everything we had.", each word laced with the precise inflections of a death knell.

The recitation tumbled forth in a cadence utterly devoid of emotion, detached from the turmoil that threatened to unravel me even as I expended every ounce of will to maintain my eroding composure. Edith's eyes widened further, comprehension battling uncertainty as she struggled to grasp the unexpected buckshot blast of revelation.

Edith took this recognition as great competition within the hosting gig, "Gia, do not jeopardize this project for some silly spotlight hungry and egotistical competition you seem to have with whoever this Tyde Wright is…understand!"

Her voice was soft now, the brash Authority Figure dissolving into the guise of a concerned boss in the face of this startling vulnerability. I could only shake my head with a wan smile, bitter resignation painting my features in muted shades of grim inevitability.

"Don't worry Edith. I'm always professional in the face of company. This will be…fun."

The weight of that understatement seemed to hang suspended in the crystalline air, the implications unspoken but undeniably tangible. Edith regarded me from across the infinite span separating us, her expression shifting through a pattern-mirror of emotions in rapid succession before settling into her signature, impenetrable stoicism.

Then, with a decisive nod, the razor edges of her demeanor reformed as she pivoted, immediately relaunching into the controlled frenzy that this eleventh hour upheaval demanded.

As for me, I simply watched her whirlwind acceleration with a carefully detached air, keeping the tumult simmering beneath my rigor mortis veneer in a tenuous stasis. But I could sense its searing presence there, like the blue heart of a flame, growing hotter and more demanding with every jolting second that passed.

Interesting didn't even begin to cover the cataclysm that was brewing on the horizon. I could only gird myself for the reckoning that was poised to consume us both in its searing, uncompromising blaze.

Tyde

TYDE'S PENTHOUSE - CENTRAL PARK WEST, NEW YORK CITY

The plush leather chairs creaked as I shifted my weight, bracing for the impact of my announcement. Jennifer's perfectly arched eyebrow raised in skepticism.

"Tyde, we've been talking about potential opportunities, but hosting the NHL All-Star weekend? That's a whole different ball game."

Sabrina's tight lips pressed into a taut line as she nodded slowly.

"I agree. It's not your usual path post-retirement. We were thinking more along the lines of endorsements or maybe a quick sports appearance gig."

My knee bounced with pent-up energy. A smile tugged at the corners of my mouth - this felt right.

"I appreciate the suggestions, but I've been doing some proper thinking." I paused, savoring the weight of the words. "Retirement hit me harder than I thought. I miss the buzz, the energy of the game, and being part of something bigger. That's why I've decided to co-host the All-Star weekend."

The silence hung thick, Jennifer and Sabrina's expressions frozen masks. I scratched at the back of my neck, the quiet stretching taut between us.

"I need a bit of a change." My fingers drummed against the armrest, desperate to channel the restlessness thrumming through my veins. "I want to be back in the thick of it, but in a different way this time. This feels right."

Jennifer exhaled, raking her perfectly manicured nails through her sleek blonde bob.

"Well, it's unconventional, but if you're sure about it, we'll make it work." A glimmer of determination sparked behind her eyes. "Hosting the NHL All-Star weekend could be… something. Something amazing."

Relief washed over Sabrina's features as she straightened in her chair.

"Let's get to work on the details." A sly smile crept across her face. "This could open up new doors for you."

As their skepticism melted into enthusiasm, anticipation zinged through the air like the sizzle before a lightning strike. I was redefining my path, and the exhilaration of embracing this new challenge flooded my veins with adrenaline. Game on.

—

The sleek granite island gleamed under the warm kitchen lighting as I drummed my fingers against the smooth surface, buzzing with anticipation. Jennifer flashed me a brilliant smile, her perfectly whitened teeth dazzling.

"Tyde, this hosting gig is a fantastic opportunity. We've got everything set up, and it's going to be a game-changer for your post-retirement career."

I couldn't stop the wide grin from spreading across my face.

"Buzzing to get back in the thick of it!" The thrill of the crowd, the roar of the arena, the charged atmosphere - it had been too long since I'd felt that electrifying rush.

But Sabrina's hesitant exhale sliced through my reverie like a cold blade.

"There's one more thing, Tyde. Your co-host is..."

My muscles tensed as the pause stretched agonizingly, bracing for the impact of her words.

"Gia. Gia Clark. GIA CLARK LIKE MY EX! GIA?!"

The name detonated like a bomb in the stylish kitchen, a shrapnel of memories exploding through my mind's eye. Gia's face swam behind my eyes, her signature ruby pout curved in a malicious smile as the lurid headlines bombarded me.

...Multitude of Home Video Scandal Rocks Hockey Star's Personal Life...

...Unauthorized Footage Leaks From Inside Player's Residence...

...Blistering Humiliation Scorches Image of Rising NHL Talent...

The stark white countertop glared, and the air thickened with tension so palpable I could taste it on my tongue - bitter like bile.

"Are you alright, Gia? You winding me up?"

Jennifer's expression softened with sympathy, her voice low and soothing like she was trying to coax a wounded animal from its hiding spot.

"Tyde, we understand it's a sensitive topic. We just wanted to give you a heads up."

But the anger roared through my veins, scalding and all-consuming.

"Right, that's enough of that! Not a peep out of me to anyone. Shut it." The granite shuddered underneath my clenched fists.

I squeezed my eyes shut, struggling to wrestle the inferno blazing inside me.

"Fresh start, mate. Past is in the rearview mirror, no looking back."

The words hung in the tense silence, an ominous vow. No matter how badly they stung, those ghosts would not sabotage my shot at redemption. Not this time.

Gia

OFFICE - MANHATTAN, NEW YORK CITY

The computer screen flickered, bathing my face in its pallid glow as I pored over the coverage surrounding Tyde's transition into hosting. My stomach twisted into anxious knots, nerves sparking like downed power lines.

Edith's warm hand squeezed my shoulder, jarring me from my spiral.

"Gia, I know Tyde's presence might be a concern, but God, don't fuck this up." Her voice rang with conviction. "You need to mingle, get to know your co-workers. It's not just about the event; it's a chance to promote *Incline Media*. I'll do anything to get your name out there."

I exhaled shakily, running my trembling fingers through my coiled hair.

"I get it, Edith. But with Tyde..." Images of salacious headlines and lurid photographs flickered through my mind's eye like damning evidence at a trial. "Our history is complicated."

Resolve hardened Edith's features as she leaned in closer.

"Look, Gia, I don't care about your history with or without Mr. Tyde Wright. The only thing right now that you need to be focused on is this NHL event and pleasing the board. Her dark eyes bored into mine with an intensity that brooked no argument. She says these words like a snake charmer, sickening and fierce.

In the days that followed, a feverish hum of excitement buzzed through the office as the news outlets revealed the hosts. My phone pinged incessantly with notifications - tweets, posts, shares all screaming my name in a digital chorus.

I sucked in a sharp breath, eyes wide. "Edith, look! The buzz is building up!"

With a stoic face she begrudgingly expressed.

"That's amazing, now go promote *Incline Media* and get out my face."

This wasn't just an event - it was a rebirth, a chance to step out from the ashes and let my professional prowess take center stage without interference from the skeletons rattling in my closet. For once, I was the master of my own story.

Little did I know, this was only the opening act. The drama awaiting me in the wings would change everything.

—

BOARDROOM - MIDTOWN, NEW YORK CITY

The weeks leading up to the All-Star weekend were a relentless cyclone of preparations for me. Edith and the Board had meticulously sculpted every detail, guiding me towards the pristine direction they believed would resonate with the audience. As the critical briefing meeting with the Board loomed, the weight of the impending All-Star weekend and game bore down on me like a suffocating blanket.

My hands trembled as I smoothed my skirt.

"I appreciate all the guidance, but I can't shake these

nerves." I swallowed hard, meeting Edith's reassuring but stern gaze. "Speaking to the Board is no small feat, especially with the All-Star weekend just weeks away."

Edith placed a tough yet calming hand on my arm. Creases framed her warm eyes, but her smile radiated confidence.

"You've got this, Gia. Trust in what we've prepared together. Your passion for journalism will shine through."

I drew a steady breath and stepped into the briefing room. Tension saturated the air, palpable and thick, as the Board scrutinized my every movement. Sweat prickled the back of my neck as I launched into the meticulously rehearsed presentation.

"Ladies and gentlemen, thank you for this opportunity." My voice wavered ever so slightly before regaining its strength. "Our program for the All-Star weekend is designed to captivate the audience, blending tradition with innovation. We've curated an experience that—"

A subtle shift in the atmosphere sent a tremor down my spine. It sliced through my fragile concentration like a hot knife. An unexpected presence swept into the room, commanding every set of eyes. My heart thudded as my gaze whipped towards the entrance.

There he was. Tyde.

I leaned towards Edith, stood next to me with an astonished yet serious look on her face. My lips brushed her ear.

"Tyde is here. What's he doing?"

Edith's brow furrowed, confusion flickering across her features.

"Tyde? Gia, he is your co-host. What did you expect? For him not to show up any time during this process? Now, focus on the present, Gia. Snap out of it!" Edith panic whispers. "We can address whatever you have going on internally afterward."

Nodding tightly, I pivoted back to the Board, my pulse thundering in my ears. I pressed on with the presentation, the words flowing from muscle memory while my eyes occasionally darted towards the imposing figure lingering on the sidelines. An uneasy hush blanketed the room as the unexpected visitor's presence sank in.

One of the Board members broke the tense silence, after my presentation was narrowing down and beginning to ask if anyone had any questions for me to answer, but with a voice brimming with his delight.

"Look who it is, one of my favorite players of all time! Tyde, please, come sit."

Tyde & Gia

I'd already claimed my seat, having wrapped up my presentation with efficient brevity. The lone remaining chair, a conspicuous vacancy, taunted from beside me. Tyde's imposing form advanced, an unwelcome encroachment on my hard-won space.

Just as he approached, I saw my chance. With a swift, calculated flick of my foot, the chair shot out, intercepting his stride. A solid thump reverberated as it connected with his leg. Tyde doubled over, gripping his knee, pain etched across his face.

"Ow! You right berk, Gia! What the ruddy hell?" His voice was a low growl, eyes boring into mine with unmasked irritation.

Feigning innocence, I blinked up at him. "Oh, Tyde, I'm so sorry. I didn't see you there." I added a delicate shrug, my lips curving into an apologetic smile. "Must be from the lack of oxygen in the room that you are sucking up."

The room held its breath, the tension palpable as eyes darted between us, capturing the electric moment. Amusement flickered in the expressions of a few board members, lips twitching as they fought to contain their amusement. Tyde's jaw clenched, the muscle ticking with restrained fury as he settled into another chair, nursing his bruised ego.

A low chuckle broke the silence, emanating from one of the board members.

"Well, thank you for joining us, Tyde. We've got more to discuss."

Satisfaction washed over me as the meeting resumed, my small victory a comforting reminder of my control. I masked a smirk, my confidence bolstered by this unexpected twist. Despite the brief disruption caused by Tyde's appearance, I refused to let it undermine my authority.

I watched him out of the corner of my eye, his presence a constant, silent challenge. The years of knowing each other had never prepared us for this side, this new dynamic, where old lovers turned acquaintances was shrouded in unfamiliar hostility. It was as if we were meeting again for the first time, but with a bitter edge. The familiarity was gone, replaced by a cold, hard resolve that neither of us recognized in the other.

For now, I reveled in my small triumph, aware that maintaining control in the face of unexpected obstacles was a skill I had honed to perfection. Tyde's surprise appearance might have rattled me, but I was far from defeated. The battle lines were drawn, and I was ready for whatever came next.

—

SIX YEARS AGO...

FLASHBACK - THE AVIARY NYC

The Aviary NYC, a sleek paradise amidst Manhattan's concrete jungle, became the stage where Tyde and I first collided. The Aviary ambiance—artfully crafted cocktails, innovative culinary delights, and an aura of sophistication—created the perfect backdrop for the unfolding drama.

"In the heart of Manhattan, where dreams meet reality..."

Laurie's delighted squeal pierced the pulsing rhythm of laughter and chatter surrounding our table.

"Fair dinkum, Gia, this place is bonza! Check out the ripper view!"

My gaze followed hers, drawn to the breathtaking panorama unfolding beyond the floor-to-ceiling windows. A prism of glittering skyscrapers, like radiant spires clawing at the inky sky. I basked in the vibrant energy, every fiber of my being thrumming with exhilaration.

Unbeknownst to me, Tyde found himself an island amidst the undulating tide of patrons crowding the bar. Flanked by Jackson Bell and Lorenz Wolf—his closest confidants, brothers-in-arms through life's tumultuous battles. Jackson, all brooding intensity and Latin charm. Lorenz, the golden son of Munich, earnest eyes and an endless well of patience.

They were the pillars anchoring Tyde as he sought solace from the aftermath of his shattered relationship with Charlotte. The path forward remained shrouded, but his friends urged him onward with their steadfast support.

"Buck up, Tyde. Time to get on with your life, eh? Charlotte's yesterday's news."

Listless eyes roamed the room until they locked onto a radiant vision across the writhing sea of bodies. My infectious laughter, the effortless way I commanded the circle of friends—it drew him in like a moth to a flame.

Sparks flew in that electrifying moment as their eyes met. A connection that transcended time and space.

The hours melted away in a blur of stolen glances and charged tension crackling between us. I couldn't tear my gaze from the brooding figure nursing a bourbon at the bar, eyes smoldering with an indescribable intensity. Tyde found himself mesmerized by my natural exuberance, the way I seamlessly captivated those around me.

Eventually, he waded through the crowd, summoning that trademark confidence. After a few stilted moments acquainting ourselves, I introduced him to my circle with a coy smile.

"Tyde. Tyde Wright."

A throat clears harshly and I look beside him to see beautiful, muscular, and tall men. His friends I assume.

He slightly adjusts and gets out of his loving gaze to introduce his friends, "This is my best friends Jackson and Lorenz."

They show dazzling smiles and say hi to me at the same time. They seem nice.

I turn to introduce my friend group.

The two groups merged into a seamless unit, the crackling chemistry between Tyde and myself as we are in our own little world. The inescapable force propelling us forward. We slipped away from the throbbing heartbeat of the lounge, twin celestial bodies caught in one another's orbit.

With a few deft words to the owner, Tyde orchestrated a breathtaking moment under the glittering cosmos of the city skyline.

"This is incredible! How did you manage this?" I gasped, spinning in a slow circle to drink in the panoramic vista unfurling at my feet.

A lopsided grin tugged at the corner of his lips.

"A bit of bodge can work wonders, wouldn't you say? Anything to see that lovely smile."

Enveloped in the warm glow of the Manhattan buildings, we became lost to the world. Basking in the honeyed bliss of rediscovering one another, kindling that smoldering spark. The endless promise of a beginning sparkled on the horizon as our love story started.

"And so, against the backdrop of Central Park and the Manhattan structures, their love story began —a tale of kindled sparks, stolen glances, and the magic of discovering one another in the city that never sleeps.

TWO MONTHS LATER...

TYDE'S HOUSE - SEASIDE HEIGHTS WEST

The credits rolled across the TV screen, casting a soft glow over Tyde and Gia as they cuddled on the couch. The remnants of popcorn and the lingering excitement from the action movie hung in the air.

"Oi, that was proper sick, innit?" Tyde's voice was filled with boyish enthusiasm. "The way he jumped from that helicopter? Bare mad!"

Gia's laughter bubbled up, light and infectious. "I know, right? I thought my heart was gonna explode during that chase scene!"

Tyde glanced down at her, a mix of surprise and admiration in his eyes.

"You're alright, you know that?" he said, his tone softer than usual. "Most girls I've known would be beggin' to watch some soppy romance."

"Oh, don't get me wrong," Gia replied, her eyes twinkling with mischief, "I love a good rom-com too. But there's something about a well-done action flick that just gets my blood pumping."

A grin spread across Tyde's face, transforming his usually tough exterior.

"A girl after my own heart," he murmured. Then, as if struck by inspiration, he added, "Speaking of getting the blood pumping, fancy a round of Street Fighter?"

Gia's competitive spirit flared to life.

"You're on!" she declared, sitting up straighter. "But don't cry when I wipe the floor with you, Mr. Tough Guy."

Tyde's laugh was deep and genuine. "Bring it, love. I've been practicin'."

They untangled themselves from the couch and set up the game console, the air charged with playful competition. As the character selection screen appeared, Gia's fingers flew over the buttons, her focus intense.

"By the way," she said, her eyes never leaving the screen, "I was thinking we could try that new Indian place down the street tomorrow. I'm craving some butter chicken."

Tyde's brow furrowed slightly, his attention divided between the game and the conversation.

"Indian, yeah? Never really given it a proper go. More of an Italian man myself."

Gia's eyes lit up, momentarily distracted from the game.

"Oh, you're missing out! Indian food is amazing. And don't even get me started on Chinese cuisine."

Just then, Gia's character landed a devastating combo, eliciting a groan from Tyde.

"Blimey, you weren't kidding about wiping the floor with me," he admitted ruefully. Then, softening, he added, "But yeah, I'm down to try Indian. Maybe we can do Italian next time? There's this cozy little place that does the best carbonara."

"Deal!" Gia's voice was warm with excitement. "Oh, and there's this Greek place I've been dying to try too. We could make it a culinary tour of the world!"

Suddenly, Tyde paused the game, turning to face Gia fully. His expression had shifted, becoming more serious, almost tender.

"Speaking of world tour," he said softly, "where's your dream holiday spot?"

Gia's eyes widened, a dreamy look overtaking her features.

"Tahiti," she breathed, as if uttering a magical word. "I've always wanted to go there. The clear blue water, the overwater bungalows, the sunsets... It must be like paradise."

Tyde's next words were so quiet, so sincere, that they seemed to hang in the air between them.

"Say the word, and I'll take you there anytime."

Gia's breath caught in her throat. "What? Are you serious?"

"Dead serious," Tyde affirmed, his gaze never wavering. "You and me, Tahiti. Whenever you are ready."

In a burst of emotion, Gia threw her arms around Tyde, nearly knocking him over.

"Oh my god, Tyde! That would be incredible!"

Tyde's arms encircled her, holding her close. His usual bravado melted away, replaced by a gentleness that surprised even him.

"Anything for you, love," he murmured into her hair. Then, lightening the moment, he added, "Now, how about we practice our holiday skills with some karaoke?"

Gia's laughter, muffled against his chest, was music to his ears. She pulled back, her eyes dancing with joy.

"You're on! But fair warning, my rendition of 'I Will Survive' is legendary."

Tyde's grin was back, wide and carefree. "Can't be worse than my 'Livin' on a Prayer'. Let's do this!"

Their laughter mingled as they made their way to the karaoke machine, the video game forgotten. In that moment, lost in each other's company, the world outside ceased to exist. It was just Tyde and Gia, two hearts beating as one, stepping into the sweet, intoxicating dance of new love.

CHAPTER 3
HOSTILE SITUATION

BACK TO REALITY...

NHL HEADQUARTERS - MIDTOWN

MANHATTAN, NEW YORK CITY

The boardroom meeting concluded on a somber note, leaving Tyde and Edith lost in their own spiraling thoughts as we exited into the bustling corridors. Unspoken tension crackled between us, a living force propelling us forward in weighted silence. The cacophony of voices and echoing footsteps filled the air—a symphony of NHL HQ employees eager to escape the confines of their desks and head home for the day.

As the elevator descended, a tide of bodies surged forward, jostling for position. Tyde and I moved at a glacial pace amidst the frenetic crowd, islands amid the churning sea. Edith, her mind still entangled in the intricate web of the meeting, boarded one of the overcrowded cars without a second thought.

"Wait, Gia. This one is way too full. You'll have to catch the next one." Her gentle words halted me in my tracks as the heavy doors slid shut, leaving me marooned.

"Great, just what I needed," I muttered under my breath, expelling a frustrated sigh.

Tyde lingered nearby, a silent observer as I resigned myself to waiting for the next available elevator. A mix of emotions swirled through my mind—irritation at the delay, curiosity about the unresolved tension lingering from the meeting. Tyde's stoic presence radiated waves of contemplation, no doubt dissecting the events that had transpired mere moments ago.

The harsh ding of the arriving elevator snapped me from my reverie. I stepped forward, joining the flow of employees escaping their corporate cages. The doors slid shut with a resonant thud, sealing Tyde in the corridor as the weight of the day's discussions seemed to linger in the stale air.

The hallway hummed with a palpable charge as Tyde approached, our footsteps falling into a discordant rhythm. The atmosphere thrummed with the weight of unspoken words, unresolved emotions crackling between us like invisible lightning. We reached for the down button simultaneously, fingers grazing in an electric spark that shot through my veins with startling intensity.

"Sorry," I murmured, snatching my hand away as though scorched by his touch.

A subtle nod was his only reply as we lapsed into tense

silence, awaiting the elevator's arrival with bated breaths. Fueled by a strange convergence of nerves and boldness, I planted myself directly before the doors, staking my claim.

The harsh ding reverberated through the corridor as the elevator arrived. The heavy doors slid open with a groan, revealing an empty car beckoning us forth. Tyde leveled me with an inscrutable sideways glance before striding into the confined space without uttering a word. I lingered a beat longer before following, the doors sealing us into our metallic tomb with a decisive thud.

Silence hung thick and suffocating as the elevator began its descent. The scant space amplified every measured breath, every infinitesimal shift as unspoken tensions swelled between us. Symphony of unvoiced emotions ricocheted through the stillness in deafening crescendos.

A violent lurch rocked the elevator car, the abrupt motion tearing a cry of indignation from my lips.

"Oh, hell no!"

Tyde, in stark contrast, burst into chuckles at the unexpected development.

"Well, well, well! Didn't see that coming."

I shot him an incredulous glare, irritation pricking my skin.

"What are you laughing about, weirdo?"

A wolfish grin split his features as his gaze roamed our immobile prison. "Just rolling with the punches, life's full of surprises, innit?"

We found ourselves well and truly trapped, entombed together in a limbo saturated with conflicting undercurrents of annoyance and amusement.

"You find joy in everything, don't you?" I muttered, leveling him with a sidelong glare brimming with exasperation.

Forty-five agonizingly slow minutes crawled by in that stifling box. Unsuccessful attempts to summon help and the disheartening realization that rescue wouldn't arrive for another two hours only amplified my restlessness.

"The fastest response time for the fire safety team is estimated to be two hours. We appreciate your patience", says the technician answering from the buzzed emergency button I pressed.

A weary shrug rolled through my shoulders as resignation took hold. "Well, I might as well get comfortable."

I sank to the floor, back braced against the unforgiving wall. After a fleeting moment of indecision, Tyde followed suit. We sat worlds apart in that scant space, bodies separated by a handful of feet yet the emotional distance stretched for infinite miles. Furtive glances ricocheted between us, neither daring to break the uneasy silence blanketing the elevator.

With my phone a lifeless brick thanks to the lack of signal, restlessness gnawed at my bones until I could no longer remain idle. I surged to my feet, determined to find a way to make contact with the outside world—or at least alleviate the maddening stillness, if only for a few moments. A somewhat comical exploration of the elevator ensued as I clambered up the walls, twisted myself into precarious positions, all in pursuit of those elusive signal bars.

"Come on, just a few bars," I muttered under my breath, twisting my body into increasingly absurd contortions.

Tyde lazily looks at Gia with slight interest and admiration, enjoying her struggle.

At long last, three beautiful bars flickered to life on my screen. "Got it!"

I rapidly dialed Laurie's number, praying he could provide some solace—or at the very least, a temporary escape from the awkward tension shrouding the elevator.

"Fair dinkum, Gia, where've ya been? We were meant to be scoffing dinner, weren't we?" Laurie's voice crackled with obvious concern.

"Long story short, I'm stuck in an elevator. Fire safety says they'll be here in two hours," I explained with a roll of my eyes, half expecting his inevitable remark.

"Reckon you and that elevator are best mates, aye? Stuck again?"

"It's not my fault this time!" I bristled defensively. "Anyway, I might be late for dinner. Can you come and rescue me?"

His warm laughter filtered through the speaker.

"How am I supposed to give you a hand from here, love? Bugger all I can do is be there in spirit. And don't go walkabout out of that lift, alright?"

A wry smirk tugged at the corner of my lips. "No promises."

In the aftermath of my call, Tyde shifted—the barest flicker of movement catching my eye. Something dark and turbulent swirled in his gaze, a tempest of half-concealed emotions simmering beneath the surface. A muscle ticked in his chiseled jaw as jealousy reared its ugly head, lashing out in a sudden torrent of vitriol.

"Here we go again! You're like a walking disaster, Gareth!"

His harsh accusation lashed out, leaving me reeling. "It's not like I planned this, Tyde. It's an unfortunate situation."

He scoffed, dismissing my protest with a derisive wave. "Unfortunate?! You muppet! You've knackered my whole day! I've got a million things on, and what about tonight—?!"

The bitter tirade continued to spew forth, fueled by frustration and impatience. Harsh recriminations tumbled from his lips as he berated me for a perceived thoughtless mistake. With every stinging barb, the tension swelled, thickening the air until it felt almost impossible to draw a full breath.

Unnoticed to us an hour later, a team of firefighters outfitted in heavy gear stood poised on the other side of the sealed elevator doors. They observed the heated exchange with calculating eyes, waiting for the opportune moment to intervene before the confrontation could escalate into something more volatile.

"Let's get these doors open."

In a blur of choreographed movement, they sprang into action, prying the stubborn doors wide. The harsh screech of protesting metal rent the air, temporarily drowning out the vicious words slicing between Tyde and me. We whirled toward the unexpected intrusion, momentarily stunned into silence.

"Cheers... I suppose..." Tyde muttered, the fire fleeing his gaze.

"Yeah, thanks guys," I echoed, relief flooding my veins at

the unexpected reprieve.

The firefighters offered tight nods of acknowledgment as we meekly exited our metallic prison, our bitter dispute left behind in the stifling confines of the elevator car. The heavy doors rumbled shut, sealing away the echoes of our caustic confrontation in a resounding finality.

Tyde and I made our way toward the stairwell in silence, both of us inwardly grateful for the timely intervention that had spared us from crossing a line that perhaps neither of us was ready to breach.

Tyde & Gria

The weeks ticked by in a dizzying blur as anticipation for the long-awaited All-Star events reached a fever pitch. The NHL had taken an innovative approach this year, selecting celebrity co-captains to be paired with current professional players, dividing them into four distinct teams.

Fan engagement soared to unprecedented levels as hockey enthusiasts across the globe rallied behind their favorites, a passionate outpouring of excitement that had become a tempest of its own.

The league had successfully secured major cross-industry partnerships—a masterful alignment of broadcasting, merchandising, automotive, tech, beverage, and hospitality brands. Every integral component slotted into place like an intricate puzzle, primed to provide an unparalleled experience that would etch itself into the annals of All-Star lore.

Amidst the whirlwind of preparations, one figure loomed larger than most—Tyde. A tidal wave of nerves roiled through him as the stark reality of his impending debut as both presenter and host came crashing down. The realization that he would be commanding the spotlight at his former league's illustrious event added an exponential weight to the already staggering pressure bearing down on him.

Weeks of meticulous planning and sleepless nights had led him to this precipice, this singular moment where Tyde— once a blazing star careening across the ice—now found himself on an entirely new stage under an entirely different illumination.

"This is it. Hosting an NHL event—never thought I'd be in this position." The internal monologue echoed through the labyrinthine corridors of his mind, each word laden with a turbulent mixture of excitement and trepidation.

"The nerves are real. Presenting anything is one thing, but hosting an event of this magnitude? Crazy." A derisive scoff slipped unbidden past his lips. "And to make things even more interesting, it's my ex-league's All-Star event. Talk about diving into the deep end."

Attired in an impeccably tailored suit, every sharp crease and clean line reflecting the gravity of the occasion, Tyde drew a fortifying breath. With measured strides, he descended into the pulsating heartbeat of the venue, the roar of the crowd and the weight of immeasurable expectation thrumming through the very air he breathed. This was his moment to shine—a new challenge to conquer with the same fierce tenacity that had defined his legendary career on the ice.

As I strode into the vortex of frenetic energy consuming the venue, the spotlight found me with unerring precision, refracting through my being until I became the luminous core around which the entire event orbited. Poised and unphased, an aura of sophistication clung to me like a tailored suit, commanding the unwavering attention of everyone in my orbit.

Tyde, lingering nearby, found himself inexplicably enraptured by my presence. His gaze drank me in with unabashed wonder, as though the relentless march of time had been rewound and he was witnessing my beauty for the first time. A becoming flush crept up the column of his neck as unguarded longing flickered to life in his molten stare.

"Good evening, ladies and gentlemen!" My voice sliced through the cacophony with the practiced confidence of one well-accustomed to orchestrating such events. "I am thrilled to welcome you to the NHL All-Star weekend."

A hushed silence momentarily blanketed the sea of upturned faces as I commanded their reverent attention.

"Get ready for a program that will not only showcase the extraordinary talent on the ice but also provide an unforgettable experience for fans worldwide."

The sheer force of my presence charged the atmosphere until it thrummed with an electric undercurrent of keen anticipation. Tyde remained utterly transfixed, seemingly oblivious to the madness swirling around him. He looked upon me as if beguiled by a vision, an unshakable reminder of that fateful moment when everything had been new, thrilling, and he'd found himself falling—tumbling into the inescapable depths of love.

From the periphery of my peripheral vision, I caught the unmistakable figure of Sandy — program director, producer, and the archangel overseeing every minute detail of the colossal production. She moved with unhurried strides, a vision of composure amidst the controlled chaos as she approached Tyde. The reassuring curve of her smile softened the hard lines etched into his features, no doubt prompted by the sudden swell of ardor he'd found himself swept up in.

"How are we feeling?" The warmth of her tone bled through the terse inquiry, grounding him in the stark reality of the here and now.

Tyde's wistful reverie shattered with an audible crack, the naked yearning in his gaze extinguished in a torrent of nerves.

"Feeling a bit ropey, like I might chuck it up," he admitted, frank and unvarnished.

Sandy's silvery laughter cut through the tension cloaking his shoulders like a weighted mantle.

"Oh, that will go away as soon as we start and you bounce in between your co-host. You can lean on each other." Her palm found the rigid line of his shoulder in a bolstering gesture of reassurance. "I know you've got this."

With those parting words lingering in the air, she turned on her heel and slipped away, a porcelain figurine lost amidst the churning tide of activity. The transient flicker of anxiety dissipated as quickly as it had emerged, replaced by the feverish thrill of anticipation—the adrenaline rush that devoured all in its wake as I prepared to scale the stage.

And then, all at once, she was there, a silent yet towering presence at my side. Gia's unmistakable silhouette loomed in my periphery, the atmosphere charging with the weight of unspoken words, of lingering unresolved tensions reverberating through the stifling veil of quiet from our last encounter in the confines of that elevator. Furtive glances flickered between us in fleeting acknowledgment, a wordless greeting shackled by the burden of unvoiced emotions as she drew nearer still until our elbows grazed with the ephemeral whisper of contact.

A sharp inhale hissed through my gritted teeth at the unanticipated spark of sensation arcing through my veins. Gia seemed similarly affected, her own breath hitching almost imperceptibly before she found her voice again.

"Hey." The extended syllable cracked like a whip in the weighted stillness shrouding us.

"Hey." My own terse response emerged as little more than a grunt, an instinctive reaction mired in residual defensiveness.

I climbed the short staircase, muttering under my breath, (or rather, to Tyde) "Please don't faceplant or suck the life out of this stage."

The announcer rang through the entire arena as the lights dim. "Ladies and gentlemen, please welcome your hosts for the NHL All-Star weekend—Gia Clark and Tyde Wright!"

Permitting the searing brilliance of the spotlight to chase away the last lingering shadows clinging to us.

The roar of the crowd swelled to a crescendo, crashing through me in euphoric tidal waves. This was my stage—my hard-earned moment to command the universe, to shed my corporeal form and become something temporally infinite. Once the opening monologue parted my lips, I would be home. But first, we had to dive into the deep end, Gia and I taking the plunge into the impending All-Star Weekend together.

CHAPTER 4
BREAKING THE ICE

Tyde

As the electric energy of the All-Star weekend reached a fever pitch, Tyde seized the opportunity to proudly announce his two closest friends as co-captains of their respective teams. A brilliant smile split his features as palpable excitement reverberated through every syllable tumbling from his lips.

"Ladies and gentlemen, let's give a roaring welcome to the incredible co-captains of this year's All-Star teams!" The words emerged in a breathless rush, his chest swelling with unmistakable pride. "First up, the man with the moves on and off the ice, leading the 'Black Jackets' with flair—Jackson Bell!"

An exultant roar tore through the venue as Jackson emerged amid the blinding prism of lights and fanfare.

He drank in the thunderous applause, flashing the crowd a roguish grin that no doubt inflamed the ardor of countless besotted fans.

"And now, the man who skates with the grace of a silver wolf, captaining the 'Silver Gems' with style—Lorenz Wolf!"

A fresh swell of cheers crashed over the proceedings like a rogue wave as Lorenz ascended the platform, his posture radiating a serene confidence. The barest hint of a nod acknowledged the crowd's exuberant reception before their captain stood poised, hands tucked behind his back with a soldierly bearing.

The cue was then handed to Gia as she announced the last two co-captains for the teams - the Fierce Pumas captain, Josh Stanford and the Gladiators co-captain, Angel Gonzalez.

In the fleeting respite afforded backstage, Jackson and Lorenz shared a veiled glance freighted with unspoken meaning—a silent acknowledgment of their unique roles as witnesses to the tumultuous love story unfolding between Tyde and Gia. As confidants and brothers-in-arms, they alone possessed insights into the complexities that had brought their closest friend to this pivotal juncture.

Jackson was the first to shatter the weighted stillness shrouding them. "Remember when they were all skookum and shit-eaten grins?" he murmured, a wistful lilt softening his usually hardened features.

A low chuckle rumbled through Lorenz's chest as he reached for his water bottle.

"Yeah, no kidding, who would've thought they'd not end up together." His gaze sharpened with an emotion akin to reproach as he regarded his friend. "But I've always thought Gia was good for Tyde."

Jackson hummed a thoughtful note of accord. "My shoe's untied too, buddy. Maybe this weekend we'll help ol' Tyder put the hop back in his box lackey, eh?"

Jackson and Lorenz share the same reminiscence of their friendship with Gia. It dials them back to the memory of the few days after Gia and Tyde first broke up and it was their first guys night without Gia. The empty space next to them on the couch felt like a void, a stark reminder of Gia's absence. Lorenz's fingers twitched, muscle memory reaching for a controller that wasn't there.

While Tyde just mopes around his apartment, the route from his kitchen to his bed then to his kitchen to his bathroom then to his bed then to the couch. No shave, no shower, just a heartbroken bum. While Jakcosn and Tyde just sit on the couch and their eyes watch his path. The tv watching them not them watching the tv. The sadness not only his Tyde but Lorenz and Jakcson as well.

"Tabarnak, I miss 'er, she was the coolest," Jackson muttered, running a hand through his hair.

Lorenz glanced up from his phone, his brow furrowed. "Gia?"

Jackson nodded. The last guys' night flashed through his mind - Gia's laughter cutting through the chaos of their Twitch stream, her triumphant grin as she landed a perfect combo in Street Fighter. It felt like yesterday and a lifetime ago all at once.

"Tu te souviens how we used to beg 'er to join us?" Jackson

asked, a wry smile tugging at his lips. "And Tyde just sat there, cool as ice, like 'e didn't care either way?"

Lorenz snorted, tossing his phone aside. "Ja, und she'd always say nein at first. She was doing us a favor by finally caving."

The memory stung, bittersweet. Jackson could almost hear her voice, playful and exasperated. "Fine, why not? But if you jerks ruin my K/D ratio, I'm out."

Jackson clenched his fist, anger and frustration bubbling up. Gia wasn't just Tyde's ex-girlfriend. She was family. Their little sister. They thought they were for sure going to get married. And now... now she is gone. Avoiding them at any event that they just so happened to show up at.

Lorenz said suddenly, sitting up straight. "To hell with what Tyde thinks. She needs to know we're still here."

Jackson hesitated, conflict etched across his face. But Lorenz saw the moment he made his decision, determination hardening his features. Lorenz reached for his phone, and Jackson felt a spark of hope ignite in his chest. Maybe, just maybe, they could bring a piece of their family back together.

With the memory dissipating, Jackson snaps back to reality. As the spectacle stretched into its next bombastic act, the two lapsed into companionable silence, each silently rooting for the faintest spark of rekindled romance to ignite between their beleaguered friend and the woman whose fate seemed determined to intertwine with his story.

A weighted sidelong glance in their direction penetrated the muted haze clouding Tyde's features—a steely glint that acknowledged their shared history as privy witnesses to the turbulence between him and Gia.

"Man's ain't feelin' this vibe," Tyde sighed, "It's deep, you get me? Bare stress with all this Gia business."

An audible sigh slipped past his lips as he steeled himself for an admission neither of them was prepared to hear.

Jackson all of a sudden gets a spark of an idea. He has yet to voice it, but a mischievous glint appears in his eye as he contemplates his next move.

Tyde's ears pricked up to what they were saying after texting Sabrina. His head shot up at the realization from Lorenz and Jackson.

"No, no! I know that look," he tells Jackson and Lorenz.

"Oi, listen up, you lot! Sort it out!" Tyde's words emerged in a low rasp, eyes glinting with an unsettling fusion of frustration and stark determination. "No chance in hell I'm getting back with Gia, not even a bleedin' chance, innit?"

The deafening silence cloaking them thrummed with a discordant tension as Tyde plunged recklessly onward, undaunted.

"She's like a walkin' disaster, and everything around her turns into a proper mess. The bird's mad, I'm tellin' ya. She deceived me into thinkin' she was a reliable woman for me."

Jackson and Lorenz exchanged an imperceptible glance weighted with unvoiced reservations before inclining their heads in muted acknowledgment of Tyde's concerns. Utterly unfazed by their muted reception, he pressed on with relentless conviction.

"She's all over the gaff, thick as two short planks sometimes, and I'm done with the drama, you get me?" Each word dripped with caustic disdain as Tyde bared the lingering anguish of past wounds they could scarcely fathom. "No way am I letting her muck up my career, especially after all the graft I've put in."

A pregnant pause reigned as those last damning syllables quivered on the precipice of finality. Tyde's burnished stare found each of them in turn, hardening into impenetrable sheets of flint as the gravity of his confession settled over them like a shroud.

"Look 'ere, if any of you man even think about messin' with what I've built, there'll be bare trouble. You've both been warned, clear as day."

"Holy crap, Tyde. You're being really intense, my guy. Maybe someone will believe your tough talk north of the border, eh?" Jackson teasingly uttered. Lorenz joined in with a chuckle.

"Mein Freund, perhaps you're overreacting a bit, ja?" Lorenz added.

A muscle ticked in Tyde's tensed jaw as his frigid glower lingered, unmistakable conviction blistering from every chiseled line of his face.

"My career's off-limits, no ifs or buts. No one, not even someone I used to be proper soft for, is gonna mess with it. You man understand?"

Jackson smirked, that effortless charisma they'd come to know and begrudgingly admire oozing from his every pore as he nudged Lorenz with his elbow.

"Câlisse, mon gars, you're soundin' like those abandonment issues are givin' you a good gob again, eh?" An impish gleam danced across his rugged features. "But for real, you are no longer caught on a fog over her, are ya bud?"

A low rumble of laughter tumbled from Lorenz's lips.

"Yes, Tyde, we've been through this. You're the retired hockey legend. The last thing you need is to get tangled up in old flames. Blah, Blah, Blah."

Exasperation lent a keen edge to Tyde's response as his brow furrowed into a stubborn v-shape.

"Forget the 'abandonment issues' chat, alright? This is about me lookin' after what I've grafted for." His voice lowered to a resonant rasp, as though imparting a solemn truth too grave to be voiced above a murmur. "Trust me, you don't want to be around when Gia's in the picture."

"At least she is not as schlimm as some of the other Frauen you have had, Kumpel," Lorenz emphasized.

A fraught pause reigned as that ominous edict hovered between them, thrumming with unvoiced implications too dire to fully contemplate. Sensing the inexorable shift in mood, Tyde deftly redirected their attention to more innocuous—yet infinitely more comfortable—terrain.

"Right, that's my two pence." With a self-deprecating chuckle, he waved a dismissive hand. "All eyes on the All-Star weekend now, yeah?"

A grin blazed across his features, the perpetual gleam of boyish mischief rekindled in his gaze as he challenged, "Right lads, Jackson, you gonna smash it out there on the ice, eh? Proper show them your skills! And Lorenz, any dosh on who nicks the MVP this year?"

"Ostie d'câlisse, you know I'm gonna light it up out there,

mon chum!" Jackson exclaimed, his excitement palpable.

"Natürlich, I've got my money on our boy Jackson here," Lorenz added with a grin. "He's going to show them what he's got!"

The transition proved seamless, tension dissipating like a noxious vapor chased away by the balm of camaraderie. Banter flowed easily between them once more, their bonds as brothers forged on the ice transcending any mere human drama as they immersed themselves in the familiar thrill of competition.

For this fleeting instance, the shadow of "that girl" slipped from their midst, banished by the unadulterated excitement of the impending All-Star spectacle.

Gia

Undetected to Tyde, the gossamer-thin partition separating him from the backstage area proved a woefully inadequate barrier. Every caustic syllable—each blistering denunciation of my character slipped past those flimsy walls and burrowed straight into the fragile chambers of my heart like serrated daggers shivered in acid.

Though muffled by plaster and drywall, Tyde's scalding vitriol reached my ears in eviscerating waves. A sickly pattern-mirror of hurt and impotent fury contorted my features as I weathered the bitter deluge crashing over me. With each fresh volley, the onslaught intensified until I could scarcely draw a full breath.

My feet moved of their own volition, propelling me away from that poisoned wellspring with growing urgency. I needed space—distance from the suffocating airlessness swiftly descending. Once the muted rumble of their voices faded into obscurity, I drew an unsteady breath and hugged my arms protectively around my midsection.

"A weak, puny boy playing with my feelings again? Not a chance." The muttered oath slipped through gritted teeth, the grating rasp tasting of bitter vindication. "And as if I'd ever want to date him again!"

The final vehement denial erupted in a scandalized hiss, outrage simmering through my veins at the audacity—no, the unmitigated gall of assuming any lingering ardor endured within me for that wretched creature. These men, with their fragile egos and blisteringly misguided self-assuredness, truly were the scourge of existence.

With a determined pivot of my heel, I stalked away from the noxious epicenter of drama festering in Tyde's wake. My fingers moved with a mind of their own, summoning the worn icon of an all-too-familiar contact as I sought the balm that could soothe even the most excruciating of traumas.

The line scarcely rang before the rich, sympathetic timbre I knew so well filtered through the speaker.

"Laurie, you won't believe what just happened." My anguished declaration sliced through the tranquility cloaking the call like a white-hot blade. "Tyde, my ex? He's out there talking shit about me!"

Laurie's measured breathing—that immutable metronome of steadiness in the eye of the raging tempest—provided the anchor I so desperately clung to as I hurled myself bodily into the churning vortex of exasperated venting. My frustration, my pain, my indignant outrage—it all came spilling forth in a torrential outpouring as Laurie remained the consummate bastion of patient compassion.

"You don't need that shit-fight, darl." The gentle reminder penetrated the feverish haze befogging my senses. "Chuck a thinker on what we've been bunging on about - looking out for ya mug and keeping your head straight, ay? What's the plan of attack?"

A steady inhale expanded my lungs as Laurie's wisdom reverberated through me, grounding me in the stark reality of regained control. The weight I'd born across those merciless miles abruptly lightened as the course ahead revealed itself with searing clarity.

"I'll show him what he's missing, but I won't let him back into my life." The vehement declaration reverberated with the unmistakable ring of conviction tinged by a lingering bitterness. "And that man, can't just talk about me like that."

Laurie's supportive tones washed over me in a soothing balm.

"Exactly. You're in control. Keep your head high and remember your worth." A beat of poignant silence reigned before she continued with a wry chuckle, "And maybe suss out getting a proper mind mechanic on the books, one you can actually shout this time."

A faint smile tugged at the corners of my lips in response to her gentle teasing. With a resolute nod—more for my own benefit than Laurie's—I bade her farewell. This indomitable wellspring of serenity had renewed my sense of self, imbuing me with the resilience to face the looming adversity with an unbowed spine and pride utterly undiminished.

The challenge had been leveled, the gauntlet thrown down before my feet. But this was my story, my narrative to command as I saw fit—and I would not permit any mere mortal to tarnish it with such barefaced audacity. Not Tyde, not his cohorts of blind sycophants, nor any other arrogant wayfarer deluded enough to believe they could unravel the meticulously woven tapestry comprising the sum of my hard-earned contentment.

Fortified by Laurie's wisdom and my own scintillating determination, I strode forward, every footfall resonating with the unyielding cadence of self-assuredness. The path before me twisted and undulated with untold challenges lurking amid the shrouded horizons, but I moved unafraid and undaunted.

This was my moment to seize with both hands—an indelible masterpiece yearning to be inscribed upon the canvas of destiny. And inscribe it I would, without reservations nor concessions to any who dared stand in my way.

—

HALLWAY - MADISON SQUARE GARDEN

I took a deep breath, my nerves buzzing with anticipation as Tyde and I prepared to interview his long-time best friends, Lorenz Wolf and Jackson Bell. These men weren't just NHL superstars; they were living legends, their names etched into the annals of hockey history. As I rifled through my notes, I couldn't help but feel a thrill at the prospect of delving into their incredible careers and uncovering the secrets to their enduring success.

Tyde caught my eye, a knowing grin on his face. "These fellas are the top dogs, but proper down-to-earth as well. You'll feel right at ease with them, no worries."

I nodded, trying to absorb his words, but my mind was already racing ahead to the questions I wanted to ask. How had Lorenz and Jackson managed to maintain such a high level of play for so many years? What drove them to keep pushing themselves, even when their bodies must have been screaming for rest? And perhaps most importantly, what did it take to be a true leader on the ice, inspiring and elevating the players around you?

As we walked into the room where the interview would take place, I felt a rush of adrenaline. This was it - my chance to get inside the heads of two of the greatest players the game had ever seen. I knew that every word they spoke, every anecdote they shared, had the power to ignite a passion for hockey in countless fans around the world.

Lorenz and Jackson greeted with warm smiles and firm handshakes, their easy camaraderie a testament to the bond they'd forged through years of shared triumphs and challenges. As we settled in and the cameras started rolling, I leaned forward, ready to soak up every bit of wisdom they had to offer.

Over the next hour, I listened, rapt, as Lorenz and Jackson painted a vivid picture of life in the NHL. They spoke of the countless hours of grueling practice, the sacrifices they'd made, and the unwavering belief in themselves and their teammates that had propelled them to the top of their game. But more than that, they spoke of the sheer love they had for hockey - a love that had sustained them through the toughest times and made every moment on the ice a gift.

As the interview drew to a close, I felt a profound sense of gratitude and responsibility. These men had entrusted me with their stories, and now it was up to me to share them with the world. I knew that every word I wrote had the power to inspire a new generation of players and fans, to stoke the flames of passion for this incredible sport.

Walking out of the room, my head spinning with ideas and insights, I couldn't wait to get started. This was more than just another story for *Incline Media*; it was a chance to capture the very essence of what made hockey great. And with Lorenz and Jackson's words still ringing in my ears, I knew I had everything I needed to do just that.

Tyde

RESTAURANT LATOUR - NEW JERSEY

The cozy ambiance of the dimly lit restaurant enveloped us in an envelopment of intimate tranquility. Glasses clinked and murmured conversations swirled through the air like fragrant tendrils of espresso as Lorenz, Jackson, and I settled into our usual haunt. An aura of barely contained exhilaration thrummed between us—a scintillating undercurrent born of the impending All-Star festivities.

I couldn't resist flashing my trademark grin as the effervescent energy coursing through my veins found an outlet. "Alright lads, feelin' the buzz in the air? All-Star weekend's here, proper mint!"

Lorenz inclined his head in solemn agreement, lips twitching ever so slightly.

"Absolutely, it's going to be legendär."

Across the table, Jackson's eyes danced with unrestrained glee. "Pumped for the game tomorrow?"

As our server whisked away the remnants of our indulgent meal, my gaze meandered towards the bronzed oak bar dominating the heart of the dining room. A knot of delicately featured beauty queens held court, their painted stares locked onto our table with undisguised intrigue. My lips curved upwards in a wolfish smirk as I recognized the undeniable signs of opportunity presenting itself.

"Well well well, looks like things just got interesting.

Who's gracing us with their intrigue this fine evening, then?"

Lorenz's warm chuckle blended seamlessly with the ambient thrum of conversations cloaking our table. "Aha, I see where this is going."

Jackson, ever the unabashed instigator, leaned across the table with a roguish gleam flickering to life in his gaze.

"Don't tell me you're leaving so soon, Tyde! We just got here, eh?"

A stray wink was my only reply as I hastily polished off the last few bites and drained the dregs of my wine. With a final sweeping glance at my companions, I surged to my feet and smoothed the lapels of my suit jacket—equal parts bravado and preparation.

"I'm outta here! Don't let the dishes pile up, gentlemen." The words slipped from my lips in a dulcet purr rife with devilish promises. "A bit of something to handle, Don't expect me back!"

Lorenz rolled his eyes in a perfunctory display of exasperation even as Jackson shook his head in weary resignation.

"Right on, have a good one, bud!" The familiar platitude drifted from Jackson's lips, utterly devoid of sincerity. "But remember, tomorrow's another day, and that head of yours might not agree, hoser!"

With one final conspiratorial wink, I pivoted on my heel and strode towards the bar with the unmistakable cadence of a born predator homing in on its prey. Their appreciative gazes caressed my sculpted form, drinking in every subtle flourish as I approached. Behind me, the quiet murmurs of my most steadfast cohorts faded into the ambient din.

"Same old, same old." The words reverberated through Lorenz's disembodied sigh as I crossed the point of no return, abandoning all vestiges of reservation in pursuit of the night's indulgences.

Jackson's rich baritone chuckle swirled through my wake. "Leopard can't change its spots, can it? Here's hoping he doesn't cause a scene tonight, bud."

Trouble. The mere concept was as elusive as the lingering vapors of a dream upon waking. Tonight, I moved among the hallowed echelons of debauched immortals—an untouchable demigod traipsing through dens of iniquity, reveling in the sweet descent into deliciously ruinous vices.

Nothing—not admonishments nor providence itself— could dissuade me from the pursuit of tonight's fleeting pleasures. For in these hallowed hours preceding the immense spectacle of the All-Star Weekend, I was simply Tyde. Unbound, unfettered, and gloriously unchained from the shackles of restraint. And the night was still so blissfully young.

Gia

THE GINGER MAN - TRIBECA, NEW YORK CITY

I stepped into the pulsing, sophisticated bar, the day's work at Madison Square Garden finally behind me. Laurie caught my eye from behind the polished oak counter, his hands a blur as he mixed drinks. He flashed me a mischievous grin. I settled onto a stool, the supple leather cool against my skin, and waited.

"Same again, mate?" Laurie materialized before me, eyebrow cocked.

I nodded, watching him pour with deft, practiced movements. The amber liquor swirled hypnotically in the glass as he slid it to me.

"Reckon," he drawled, leaning in conspiratorially, "I got a cracker of an idea to liven up this sheila shindig. Up for a bit of a dare?"

I raised the glass to my lips, the first sip igniting a pleasant burn down my throat. "Oh yeah? What did you have in mind?"

His eyes danced wickedly. "Pash the first ripper bloke who cracks a smile at you tonight? Strewth, right here at the bar?"

I nearly choked on my drink. "Laurie! I can't just –"

"Don't be a drongo, Gia! Get out there and give it a crack!" He winked and spun away to tend to other patrons, leaving me flustered, pulse quickening traitorously at the idea.

Determined to not let Laurie have an upperhand on me at anything. I scanned the night crowd, trying to appear nonchalant. My gaze snagged on Adonis in a crimson shirt at the end of the bar. Expertly styled hair, cheekbones you could cut glass on, a jaw so chiseled it belonged in an art gallery. He oozes sex appeal and confidence. Definitely not my usual type, but...

As if feeling the heat of my stare, he glanced up, molton brown eyes meeting mine. Electricity crackled down my spine. Emboldened by Laurie's dare and the liquid courage warming my veins, I held his smoldering gaze, slowly, deliberately running my tongue along my lower lip.

Surprise flickered across his devastatingly handsome face, followed by unmistakable heat. He rose languidly from his seat and crossed the bar, every movement exuding raw, animal magnetism. My heart hammered against my ribs as he drew near, the spicy scent of his cologne enveloping me.

"Hello gorgeous," he purred, voice smooth as top-shelf whiskey. "I'm Alex. Can I buy you a drink?"

"I'm Gia," I replied, startled by the breathy quality of my own voice. "Actually, I was wondering if you'd like to help me with something..."

I trailed off suggestively, holding his smoldering gaze. A beat passed. Two. Then his full, sensual lips curled in a wolfish grin.

"I'd love to," he murmured, closing the remaining distance between us.

Our lips met, and the world fell away, narrowing to the intoxicating slide of his mouth against mine. He kissed like he moved - confident, skilled, devastating. I melted against him, dizzy with desire...

After long, heated moments, we broke apart, breathing ragged. Over Alex's shoulder, I caught Laurie's eye as he mixed a drink, shooting me a sly grin and an approving nod. Face flushed, lips kiss-swollen, I smiled back, secretly thrilled by my own daring.

Girls' night was definitely off to a spicy start.

Tyde

TYDE'S PENTHOUSE - CENTRAL PARK WEST, NEW YORK CITY

The early morning light seeped through the windows of my penthouse, casting a pale glow over the rumpled sheets and scattered clothes. I stood by the door, arms crossed, glowering at the two girls I had spent the night with. Their names escaped me, not that it mattered.

"Cor blimey, look at the time! We best be off, ladies." I said impatiently, eager to be alone with my thoughts once more.

One of them, a disheveled blonde, looked up at me groggily. "Already? Can't we stay a little longer?" Her voice grated on my nerves.

"No, no, you can't," I replied coldly. "Get your kit on, we're off"

They exchanged confused glances but began gathering their clothes, slipping into skimpy dresses and tugging on high heels. I watched with detached disinterest, my mind already elsewhere.

The other girl, a brunette with smudged mascara, paused as she reached for her purse. "Um, Tyde, do you… would you like to see us again?"

I waved a dismissive hand. "One night stand and all that, don't need names, do we?" he said smugly. "Piss off!"

Hurt flashed in her eyes but I had already turned away,

stalking across the room. They hurried out and I shut the door behind them with a sharp click. The sound echoed in the sudden stillness.

Alone at last, I exhaled and rubbed a hand over my face. Regret panged within me, a familiar ache, but I shoved it aside. What a right muggins I am, bringing them round here? I'd only wanted to clear my head, drown out the unwanted thoughts, but as usual it left me feeling emptier than before.

Unbidden, an image of Gia rose in my mind - her warm smile, the way her eyes sparkled when she laughed. I clenched my jaw and banished the mental picture. She was just a coworker, nothing more. I couldn't afford any attachments, couldn't risk the vulnerability that came with caring.

I repeated the words like a mantra as I went about my morning routine, determined to bury any flickers of longing deep down where they couldn't touch me. Work was the only thing that mattered. Success was all I needed. I wouldn't let anything, or anyone, jeopardize that.

But even as I steeled my resolve, Gia's face lingered in my peripheral thoughts, an enticing reminder of possibilities I didn't dare contemplate. With a low curse, I splashed cold water on my face and headed out to face another day, my armor of indifference firmly in place.

Tyde & Gia

MADISON SQUARE GARDEN

The electric energy thrumming through the venue should have invigorated me, stoking the flames of excitement until I became a blazing beacon commanding the spotlight. Instead, a discordant undercurrent of unease slithered through my veins with each awkward on-screen exchange, each faltering attempt to manufacture the elusive chemistry the director so desperately craved.

Oblivious to the turbulent undercurrent of history surging between Tyde and me, the production team remained frustratingly impervious to the glacial tension saturating the air until, at last, our palpable discomfort could no longer be ignored.

"Alright, Tyde and Gia, we're not quite getting the chemistry we need for the broadcast." The director's sympathetic smile radiated understanding even as her words lanced straight through me.

"We're going to switch things up. Head down to the conference floor for some duo interviews with the All-Stars. Let's see if we can capture that dynamic energy we're looking for. You'll be great!"

I risked the barest of sidelong glances in Tyde's direction, silently acknowledging the monumental discomfort thrumming between us with the subtlest dip of my chin. He mirrored the gesture—a fleeting acknowledgment, an unvoiced treaty to maintain our professional decorum, no matter the strain.

The echoing cadence of our footsteps seemed to ricochet through every crevice as we navigated the labyrinthine corridors toward the conference floor. Tyde's presence loomed in my periphery, an inescapable force both enticing and ominous, awakening ghosts I'd struggled to banish from the innermost chambers of my psyche.

"Alright Gia, ages since we last chinwagged." The words emerged in a strained rush, each syllable clawing its way from his vocal cords like shards of glass being forcibly expelled.

"Yeah, Tyde. Long time." My responding half-truth tumbled into the yawning chasm separating us, ringing with a hollow finality that cleaved the air asunder.

We pressed onward into the fray, enveloped by a churning sea of players and personnel exuding a vibrant energy entirely antithetical to the fraught tensions swirling between us. Microphones in hand, we attempted to project a veneer of professionalism even as the weight of our shared history bore down upon us like an avalanche of bitter memories.

"Seen any of the matches lately?" Tyde's attempt at innocuous small talk sliced through the strained quiet with all the subtlety of a chainsaw.

I shrugged, feigning nonchalance even as resentment sparked embers deep within my soul. "Here and there. Not really my thing anymore."

The loaded implication clung to the words like a noxious vapor. I drew a steadying breath, girding myself against the rising tide of toxic nostalgia as Tyde's brow furrowed.

Our attempts at civility quickly disintegrated into stilted half-truths and evasive deflections as the palpable tension intensified with every passing second.

"Alright, buckle up, this could get sticky," Tyde murmured, lips curving into a tight smirk devoid of mirth as we approached the first player slated for an interview. "Right, let's blag it 'til we make it."

My own smile mirrored his—a rictus grin concealing the roiling tempest within.

"Agreed. We've both been in tougher situations, right?"

Bitter amusement reverberated through the rhetorical inquisition, though from which of us, even I couldn't discern. We brandished our feeble attempt at camaraderie like a tarnished blade as we launched into the first of what was certain to be an interminable string of uncomfortable interviews.

The All-Stars swarmed around us in a speculum of raucous laughter and exuberant energy, blissfully ignorant of the treacherous vicissitudes of history wrapping their suffocating coils ever tighter around us.

For their sake, we crafted a glittering illusion of consummate professionalism and easy banter—a hollow facsimile lacking even a fraction of the authenticity required to truly resonate.

As the endless parade of forgettable faces and rote inquiries trudged onward, I felt myself receding inward, retreating behind the protective battlements of my own formidable psyche. Unbidden, the ghosts of our shared past materialized with insidious inevitability, haunting me with the nightmarish echoes of the confrontation that had eroded the tattered remnants of our romance.

Every agonizing trigger, every brutally severed confidence replayed itself in granular detail through the flickering projector of my memories. The accusations slicing through the fraught airwaves, barbs embedded with dark and unforgivable sins—the gut-wrenching devastation that had shredded the foundations of what I'd once believed was my forever.

Tyde's oblivious presence materialized in my periphery, his focus immutably locked onto the present, onto the charade we were so desperately peddling. A blink rapidly concealed the memory assaulting me in a series of phantasmagoric flashes, only for a new anguish to manifest with merciless immediacy.

The leaked sex tape. God, that damning footage that had so thoroughly eviscerated the tattered remnants of my dignity, my self-worth brutalized beyond recognition. The humiliation, the searing lances of anguish that had pierced straight through my center, leaving a ragged wound that festered endlessly—never quite healing, always aching with a constant throbbing ache.

And Tyde—had he ever truly grasped the titanic devastation that had sundered my entire universe that fateful night? Had he possessed even an infinitesimal inkling of the sheer magnitude of torment I'd endured as the most sacred intimacies of our shared romance were wrenched from their private sanctuary and cast into the harsh illumination for all to gawk and sneer at?

I doubted it. For in that moment, as the roars of riotous joy droned unheeded in the periphery, he seemed so sublimely untouched by the ruinous past clawing at my serenity. He existed in that perfect realm of merciful ignorance, pivoting from player to player with a glib professionalism I could only dream of emulating through sheer force of will.

All around us, laughter and unbridled revelry swelled to deafening crescendos. The bright lights emblazoned every surface, the cacophonous roar of celebration echoed through every shadowed recess and dimly lit alcove. And yet, I found myself retreating inward, the cavernous recess of my heart cloaked in impenetrable gloom as the phantoms of memory swirled through the perpetual darkness without cease.

The unspoken layers of history added a titanic gravity to the simple act of fulfilling our professional obligations. Where Tyde portrayed the consummate image of effortless aplomb, I trailed in his wake as though wading through a dense, obscuring fog—unseen burdens weighing down every faltering footstep, every leaden inhalation.

Our dynamic, which should have radiated with infectious vitality before the revelrous audience, instead sputtered and faltered with each abortive exchange. The heavy silence pulsing through the current between us concealed entire civilizations of unvoiced sentiments—the ruinous aftershocks of lives once inextricably bound, mercilessly torn asunder by fates crueler than either of us could have fathomed.

CHAPTER 5
BLOOMING SYNERGY
Tyde & Gria

MEDIA FLOOR - MADISON SQUARE GARDEN

The interview floor buzzed with a chaotic energy, a whirlwind of questions and answers, laughter and chatter. Amidst the mayhem, Tyde and I gravitated towards each other as if pulled by an invisible force. Our eyes met, and for a moment, the world around us faded into the background.

Laughter spilled from my lips as Tyde cracked a joke, his eyes crinkling at the corners. The shared mirth felt like a lifeline in the midst of the madness. I straightened my shoulders, a sudden surge of determination coursing through me.

"Alright, Tyde, let's wrangle this circus," I said, my voice steady and serious. "I've got an idea to steer this ship in the right direction."

Tyde raised an eyebrow, a glimmer of intrigue in his eyes.

"Carry on, I'm all ears."

I took charge, my focus laser-sharp as I directed the interviews. "We're going to dive deep, get personal. The audience wants more than just stats; they want to know the person behind the player."

Tyde looked momentarily taken aback by my sudden composure, but he quickly adjusted, a smirk playing on his lips. "Right you are, Captain Gia. Onwards to the unknown!"

As the interviews progressed, I felt Tyde's gaze on me, quiet and observant. He seemed to be studying me, discerning the subtle nuances of my personality. I wondered if he noticed the changes in me, the layers I had carefully constructed over time.

"Cor, what a transformation! New aura and all, eh? Most impressive." I heard him mutter under his breath.

I pretended not to hear, but a small part of me was thrilled at his acknowledgment. The past stirred within me, memories of the feelings I once held for him. I pushed them aside, determined to focus on the present.

The arena announcer's voice boomed over the loudspeaker, signaling the end of the interviews. "Ladies and gentlemen, as the interviews wrap up, get ready to embark on your All-Star weekend adventures!"

"Next stop…lunch," I murmured to myself, caught in a swirl of emotions as I glanced at Tyde.

Memories flooded my mind – the enchanting moments we had shared, the laughter and the love. But then the storm hit, the bitter breakup that left us both reeling. I remembered the hate from Tyde's fans, the judgment from those who thought they knew our story.

"Can't escape the ghosts of the past," I whispered, my heart clenching.

The lunch break offered a temporary escape, a brief respite from the chaos. I stood at a crossroads, torn between lingering in the shadows of our history and venturing into an uncertain future. Tyde's presence both comforted and unnerved me, a reminder of what we once had and what we could never reclaim.

With a deep breath, I steeled myself for whatever lay ahead. The All-Star weekend stretched before us, a whirlwind of events and emotions. I could only hope that we would emerge unscathed, our hearts intact and our paths clear.

—

PRESS DINING - MADISON SQUARE GARDEN

I watched Gia from across the lunch table, my gaze fixed on her as she nibbled on her food, lost in thought. Her brow furrowed slightly, and I found myself leaning forward, trying to decipher the emotions playing across her face.

"What was going through her bonce?" I thought, my own mind wandering to places I knew I shouldn't venture.

As if in sync with her movements, I unconsciously mirrored her actions, my own lunch forgotten. The bustling cafeteria faded into the background, and for a moment, it was just the two of us, caught in a bubble of contemplation.

Gia's eyes flickered with a sudden determination, a fire

igniting within their depths.

"Time to break free from the echoes of the past," she murmured to herself, her voice barely audible over the din of conversation.

I leaned closer, straining to catch her words, but the moment was shattered by a playful smack on my shoulder. I startled, my gaze snapping away from Gia as Sabrina and Jennifer plopped down beside me, their laughter ringing in my ears.

"Lost in a daydream, Tyde?" Sabrina teased, her eyes sparkling with mirth.

Jennifer smirked, nudging me with her elbow. "We've been trying to get your attention for a while."

I forced a chuckle, trying to conceal the surprise that still thrummed through me. The lunch table transformed from a realm of quiet contemplation to a lively gathering, the arrival of my friends injecting a burst of energy into the atmosphere.

But even as I engaged in the banter and laughter, my thoughts remain tethered to Gia. She seemed different, a newfound clarity etched into her features. I watched as she sat up straighter, her shoulders squared with determination. She began to type something on her phone. I was unable to understand her liberation from the phone.

"It's time to focus on the present, on me," she declared to herself, her voice carrying a note of finality.

I couldn't help but wonder what had brought about this change, this sudden shift in her demeanor. What was the message of this declaration? Was she finally letting go of our past, of the memories that had haunted us both for so long?

Gia's lips curved into a smirk, a glint of mischief in her eyes. "No more ties, no more looking back," she murmured, her tone laced with a hint of defiance.

I felt a pang in my chest, a mixture of admiration and something else I couldn't quite name.

"Let's see what the world has to offer," Gia grinned, her face alight with anticipation.

I watched as she took a bite of her lunch, a newfound purpose in her movements. The lunch break had become more than just a moment of rest; it had transformed into a turning point, I don't know what for but, it most definitely awoke something.

As the conversations swirled around me, I found myself wondering what the future held, not just for Gia, but for myself as well. The past still clung to me, its tendrils wrapped tightly around my heart, but seeing Gia's new resilience stirred something within me.

I simply watched, captivated by the woman before me, marveling at the strength and resilience that radiated from her very being.

—

THE BULLPEN - MADISON SQUARE GARDEN

The sheets rustled in my hands as I shuffled through them, my eyes scanning the directions for the upcoming segment. Beside me, Gia adjusted her glasses, her gaze focused intently on her own set of instructions. The tension between us had dissipated, replaced by a familiar rhythm of professionalism.

"Right, after the loo break, we're gonna be chinwagging with those newbie superstars, innit?" I asked, my voice casual yet focused.

Gia nodded, her fingers trailing along the details on the page.

"That's correct. We need to keep it light-hearted, get their insights on the season so far, sprinkle in some fun questions. Production wants that camaraderie vibe."

I absorbed her words, mentally noting the key points. "Right, got that lot sussed. Any particular nuggets they want us to drop?"

Gia referred to her notes, her brow furrowing slightly as she sought out the information. "They're emphasizing the community involvement angle. Apparently, fans love hearing about the players giving back."

A smirk tugged at the corner of my mouth. "Alright, I'll bung in a couple of questions about their clobber and what they get up to off the ice. Keep it real, yeah?"

Gia's eyes met mine, a glimmer of understanding passing between us. "Absolutely. And we've got that charity event plugged towards the end."

"Blimey, here we go!" I said, my confidence growing. "No worries, Gia. Easy peasy."

As the break wrapped up, we seamlessly transitioned into the next segment, our practiced professionalism taking center stage. The rookie sensations took their seats across from us, their faces alight with excitement and nerves.

I leaned forward, my elbows resting on my knees as I fixed them with a warm smile.

"Alright lads, welcome! It's great to have you here with us today."

The interview flowed smoothly, Gia and I working in tandem to draw out the players' personalities and experiences. We laughed at their anecdotes, probed for deeper insights, and steered the conversation towards the topics that mattered most to the fans.

Throughout it all, I couldn't help but steal glances at Gia, marveling at the way she effortlessly navigated the interview. Her questions were insightful, her demeanor engaging, and I found myself drawn to the sparkle in her eyes as she interacted with the rookies.

As the segment drew to a close, we seamlessly transitioned to the charity event plug, our voices filled with genuine enthusiasm for the cause. The rookies chimed in, sharing their own experiences and the importance of giving back to the community.

With the cameras cutting, I turned to Gia, a genuine smile on my face. "Cracking interview, that! Another one in the bag, ey?"

She returned my smile, her eyes crinkling at the corners. "We did pretty good, didn't we?"

For a moment, the world around us faded away, and it was just the two of us, caught in a bubble of shared accomplishment and camaraderie. The past, with its complications and heartache, seemed distant, overshadowed by the promise of the present.

As we began to wrap our final segment, I found myself wondering what the future held for us. The spark between us was undeniable, but the weight of our history still lingered, a constant reminder of the obstacles we faced.

But for now, in the afterglow of a successful interview, I allowed myself to bask in the warmth of Gia's presence, the familiarity of our partnership, and the hope that perhaps, just perhaps, we could find something there between us again.

—

END OF DAY 1 - ALL-STAR WEEKEND

As the cameras stopped rolling and the newsroom began to wind down, I turned to Gia, a smile spreading across my face. The day had been a whirlwind of interviews, banter, and unexpected moments of connection, and I found myself pleasantly surprised by how well we had worked together.

"Well, I have to admit, Tyde, I thought today would be a total disaster with you," Gia said, her eyes sparkling with mirth as she rose from her chair.

I feigned offense, placing a hand over my heart in mock hurt. "Right, that's well harsh! Had the exact same thought about you, myself."

Laughter erupted between us, the sound echoing through the now-quiet studio. The camaraderie that had developed throughout the day was evident in our easy banter, a stark contrast to the tension that had hung between us just hours before.

Gia's face softened, sincerity replacing the playful teasing. "But, hey, we did good. First day, and we killed it."

I nodded, a sense of pride swelling in my chest. "Course

we did, didn't we? Bit of a surprise, mind."

The shared moments behind the scenes played in my mind like a highlight reel. The way Gia had effortlessly navigated the interviews, the way our chemistry had sparked on and off camera, the way we had fallen into a comfortable rhythm despite our complicated history.

Gia paused, her eyes distant as she reflected on the day. "Maybe working together won't be so bad after all."

I grinned, the prospect of our future collaboration sending a thrill through me.

"Deffo. Can't wait for tomorrow, innit?"

We exchanged compliments, our voices filled with genuine admiration for each other's skills and professionalism. The success of our first day had ignited a newfound respect between us, a foundation upon which we could build a stronger partnership.

As the All-Star weekend officially began, I couldn't help but feel a sense of excitement for what lay ahead. The challenges, the triumphs, the moments of connection - all of it stretched before us like an unwritten chapter, waiting to be filled with the story of our journey.

I glanced at Gia, taking in the way the studio lights cast a soft glow on her face, the way her eyes shone with a mix of exhaustion and satisfaction. At that moment, I realized that perhaps our past didn't have to define our future, that maybe we could create something new and beautiful together.

With a final nod and a smile, we parted ways, the promise of tomorrow hanging in the air between us. As I stepped out into the bustling streets, the energy of the All-Star weekend pulsing around me, I felt a renewed sense of purpose, a determination to make the most of this opportunity.

The first day had been a success, but I knew that the real test lay ahead. The All-Star weekend would push us to our limits, both professionally and personally, but I was ready to face it head-on.

CHAPTER 6
THE DEVASTATION WALTZ

Gia

LAURIE'S APARTMENT - EAST VILLAGE, NEW YORK CITY

I took a deep breath, my fingers hovering over the keyboard as I stared at the glowing screen of my laptop. The Instagram DM inbox was a minefield of potential dates, each message a ticking time bomb of possibility. My stomach churned.

"Come on, Gia," Laurie prodded, with excitement. "You've got this, mate. It's just a bit of fun, yeah?"

I shot him a glance, taking in his eager grin and the mischievous glint in his eyes. Laurie was sprawled across my bed, his lanky frame at odds with the delicate floral duvet. He'd been my rock since I moved to the States, but right now, I wanted to throttle him.

"Fun?" I hissed, my voice cracking. "This is madness, Laurie. I can't just... just... date multiple guys at once!"

Laurie sat up, his brow furrowing. "Why not? You're single, they're single. It's not like you're making any commitments here."

I turned back to the screen, my chest tight. The cursor blinked mockingly, daring me to make a move. I clicked on the first message, from a guy named Jake. His profile picture showed a chiseled jaw and piercing blue eyes.

"Alright," I muttered, more to myself than Laurie. "Let's do this."

My fingers flew across the keyboard, crafting a response that was equal parts flirty and noncommittal. As I hit send, a jolt of adrenaline shot through me.

"There," I said, my voice shaky. "Happy now?"

Laurie whooped, pumping his fist in the air.

"That's my girl! Now, who's next on this roster of yours?"

I scrolled through the messages, my heart racing. There was Mark, a graphic designer with a dimpled smile. And Carlos, a chef whose bio made me laugh out loud.

"This one," I decided, clicking on Carlos's message. "He seems... fun."

Laurie peered over my shoulder, his breath warm on my neck.

"Ooh, a man who can cook. Fancy that."

I elbowed him playfully, but my hands were trembling as I typed out another message. With each word, the reality of what I was doing sank in. I was actually going through with this crazy plan.

"I can't believe I'm doing this," I whispered, hitting send on the third message of the night. "What if they all want to meet at once? What if-”

Laurie cut me off, his hand warm on my shoulder.

“Gia, love, breathe. You’re overthinking this. It’s just a few dates, not a bloody marriage proposal.”

I leaned back in my chair, closing my eyes. The scent of Laurie’s cologne mingled with the faint aroma of the chai latte cooling on my desk. When I opened my eyes, Laurie was watching me intently.

“I know you want this,” he said softly. “I can see it in your eyes. You’re ready for a change, Gia. Don’t let fear hold you back.”

His words hit home, piercing through the fog of anxiety that had been clouding my mind. I nodded slowly, a small smile tugging at my lips.

“You’re right,” I admitted. “I do want this. It’s just... scary, you know?”

Laurie grinned, ruffling my hair. “Course it is. But that’s what makes it exciting, yeah? Now, come on. We’ve got more blokes to charm.”

As we dove back into the sea of messages, I felt a spark of excitement ignite in my chest. Maybe, just maybe, this crazy roster idea wasn’t so bad after all. With Laurie by my side and a world of possibilities at my fingertips, I was ready to take the leap.

—

Just sparked interest in who was the quickest to respond back to my messages in DMs. The name Mason Jean-Baptiste, sounded glorious and I confirmed the date swiftly. And so did he with the quick back and forth in messages. Mason Jean-Baptiste, a current NHL player, who would be showcasing his skills in the upcoming game.

Sitting on Laurie's couch in his apartment, my heart raced with excitement as I anticipated the night ahead. Laurie with a grin, already pouring drinks as I tell him my plans for tonight.

"Right, chuck it all on the barbie, Gia. What's the goss on Mason?" Laurie asked, his eyes sparkling with curiosity.

I couldn't help but grin, the memory of Mason's charm and prowess on the ice flooding my mind.

"Oh, you're in for a treat. He's got this charm, Laurie. And the way he plays on the field? A total game-changer."

We clinked glasses, laughter filling the room as we dove into the excitement of my impending date. Laurie leaned forward, a smirk playing on his lips.

"Reckon we're talkin' full-on Facebook stalking or just a cheeky Insta peek?"

I nodded, my fingers already itching to scroll through Mason's profiles. "You bet. We're talking deep dives into his social media, his career highlights, the whole nine yards."

We burst into laughter, our phones in hand as we pored over every detail of Mason's online presence. Laurie raised an eyebrow, a hint of concern in his voice.

"See any dodgy vibes or anything suss from Mason?"

I paused, considering his question. My mind wandered to Mason's robust athletic physique, his captivating dark eyes that seemed to draw me in, and the stylish dreadlocks that framed his face, jet black with striking red highlights. His smile alone was utterly mesmerizing.

"Not a single one so far," I replied, my voice thoughtful. "Seems like he's got the whole package."

As we continued our pregame festivities, the room buzzed with anticipation and laughter. The perfect atmosphere for the night ahead.

Mason, ever the man of style, had orchestrated the arrival of a luxurious car, where he patiently waited in the back seat for me. The opulent vehicle would transport me to our designated destination, signaling the beginning of what I fondly termed the "roster dates."

I stepped out of Laurie's apartment, my heart pounding with a mix of nerves and excitement. As I approached the car, nerves kicking, I couldn't help but whisper to myself, savoring the moment.

"Looks like I'm in for a long night."

From his window, Laurie's voice rang out after seeing the car pull up, a playful shout that echoed through the New York streets. "He pulled up in a XL black car! TEEEEEAAAA!"

I rolled my eyes, a smile tugging at my lips as I waved goodbye. The car door opened, and I slid inside, the plush interior enveloping me like a shell. Mason's presence was electric, his charm palpable even in the confines of the vehicle.

As we pulled away from the curb, the city lights blurring past the windows, I couldn't help but marvel at the turn my life had taken. From the tension-filled studio with Tyde to the glamorous world of NHL players and high-profile dates, I was embarking on a journey that promised excitement, adventure, and perhaps even a touch of danger.

But in that moment, with Mason by my side and the night stretching out before us, I felt invincible. The roster dates had begun, and I was ready to embrace every moment, every thrill, and every challenge that lay ahead.

Tyde

DR. RILEY HAMMOND'S OFFICE- THE WATERFRONT, NEW JERSEY

I sank into the plush chair in the quiet confines of Riley Hammond's therapist office, my mind heavy with the weight of my past. Dr. Hammond, who prefers to go by Riley, a seasoned mental health therapist with over 25 years of experience, greeted me with a warm smile and a calming presence that seemed to envelop the room.

As I grappled with the lingering impact of my playboy image and its shadow over my past relationships, a deep yearning for redemption stirred within me. I longed to reshape my approach to dating.

"Right, I feel like I've well and truly nicked a right turn down a dead-end alley. I need a right good shake-up, especially with this... bird... who's just rocked back into my life, and in the most minted way at work of all places!" I confessed, my voice raw with emotion.

Riley leaned forward, his eyes filled with wisdom and understanding.

"Change is possible, Tyde, but it starts with understanding yourself. One step at a time."

His words echoed in my mind, a beacon of hope amidst the turmoil. He urged me to embark on a journey of self-discovery, to delve into the depths of my public persona and identify the aspects that needed alteration.

"Let's start by reflecting on how you see yourself now. What aspects of your public image do you feel need a change?"

Riley prompted, his pen poised over his notepad.

I took a deep breath, the weight of self-reflection pressing down on my shoulders. It was daunting, but I knew it was a necessary step.

"Spot on about the goals. Sounds like a right mare, but let's give it a bash, ey?"

Riley nodded, a smile tugging at the corners of his mouth. "Authenticity is key, Tyde. It's about becoming the best version of yourself, not someone else."

His words struck a chord within me, resonating with a truth I had long ignored. I realized that my transformation had to be rooted in authenticity, in cultivating new skills and enhancing my emotional intelligence.

"I've never been the best at talking, but I'm up for giving it a go," I mumbled, the rawness in my voice catching me off guard a bit. I admitted, the vulnerability in my voice surprising even myself.

Riley's eyes softened, a glimmer of understanding shining through. "Communication is a powerful tool, Tyde. It's about navigating your feelings and those of others with open and sincere dialogue."

As I sat there, absorbing his wisdom, I felt a sense of hope blossoming within me. I knew the path ahead would be challenging, but I was determined to confront the shadows of my past and learn from the behaviors that had tainted my image.

"Opening up to others and seeking feedback will be crucial. It's a collective effort," Riley emphasized, his words a gentle reminder of the support I needed.

My mind drifted to the lingering tape history with Gia, a

knot forming in my stomach.

"Me head's gone and started reminiscing about that right old carry-on with Gia, givin' me a right corker in the gut. We gotta sort this Gia situation, can't keep whackin' it down the road."

Riley nodded, his expression one of understanding and encouragement.

"Addressing it proactively and responsibly is the way forward, Tyde. It's about protecting your energy and letting go of negativity."

As the session drew to a close, I felt a renewed sense of purpose.

"Next time, let's delve into what is causing this hesitance and your delusion to your abandonment issues. It's a crucial part of this puzzle," Riley said, his words a gentle reminder of the layers yet to be explored.

A flicker of pain shot through my chest at Riley's parting words. It wasn't a sharp sting, but a dull ache that settled low in my ribs. I knew better than to take it personally, though. Riley wasn't trying to be cruel. He simply had my best interests at heart, and his comment was likely a reflection of the weariness he'd sensed in my demeanor.

I left the office, my heart lighter yet filled with determination. The uncharted territory of personal change stretched out before me, but I was ready to embark on this journey guided by authenticity, self-awareness, and a steadfast commitment to the love I sought to rekindle.

Gia

LAVO NIGHTCLUB - MIDTOWN, NEW YORK

After a delightful dinner with Mason, we decided to pay a visit to Laurie at one of his many bartending jobs. This particular gig was at "LAVO," a trendy R&B and hip-hop nightclub where Laurie showcased his skills. As we approached the bar, Laurie's eyes lit up with recognition, a smirk playing on his lips.

"Same ol', same ol', Gia?" he asked, his voice laced with a playful undertone.

I couldn't help but smile back. "You got it, Laurie."

Laurie then turned his attention to Mason, his gaze appraising. "Anything for the bloke?"

Mason flashed a marvelous smile that seemed to light up the room. "I will have a Bourbon, thanks."

Laurie grinned right back at us, a mischievous glint in his eyes. He stepped away to start preparing our drinks, leaving Mason and me to face the pulsating dance floor.

"One thing you can say about this place is energy!" I exclaimed, my body already swaying to the infectious beats.

The air was thick with the pulsating rhythm of R&B and hip-hop, the dance floor a sea of energy and movement. Neon lights cast an exchange of colors on the revelers, transforming the space into a vibrant wonderland.

Mason leaned in, his voice raised to be heard over the music. "Laurie sure knows how to keep the vibe alive in here!"

I nodded in agreement, my eyes scanning the eclectic crowd as we waited for our drinks. The anticipation built within me, matching the crescendo of the music that surrounded us.

Laurie returned with our drinks, and we made our way to the dance floor, ready to surrender to the rhythm. As we immersed ourselves in the vibrant atmosphere, our bodies moved in perfect synchronization, our dance a language of its own.

The music wrapped around us like a blanket, and we lost ourselves in the playful and intimate dance. Our movements grew more daring, more uninhibited, as if the crowded room had faded away, leaving only the two of us in our own private universe.

In the midst of the swirling lights and thumping bass, our connection deepened. The outside world ceased to exist, and our dance became a reflection of the chemistry and intimacy that had been building between us.

But as I lost myself in the dance with Mason, a sudden flash of memory struck me. The pulsating beats transported me back to countless nights spent dancing with Tyde in his living room, music blaring, our bodies moving as one, the world outside forgotten.

Mason noticed the shift in my demeanor. "Everything okay?"

I forced a faint smile. "Yeah, I just got lost in a memory for a moment."

The recollection played out like a vivid film in my mind, and I found myself momentarily trapped in the nostalgia of those dances with Tyde. The laughter, the music, the carefree moments—they all came rushing back, slowing my dance with Mason as I relived the emotional echoes of the past.

Suddenly, an unexpected chill ran down my spine. Instinctively, my gaze lifted, and I found myself locking eyes with someone across the room—Tyde.

The intensity of his gaze was like a cold, piercing wind, causing my heart to skip a beat. Time seemed to stand still as the memories of our shared dances collided with the reality of the present, creating a whirlwind of emotions within me.

Tyde retreated into the shadows of the club, and I witnessed the door swinging open forcefully, almost unhinging. In my slightly tipsy state, I glanced at the tumultuous entrance but dismissed it with a carefree shrug.

I returned to the dance floor with Mason, losing myself in the rhythm for one more song before deciding to take a break at the bar.

Seated at the bar with Mason standing protectively over my shoulder, my eyes wandered the vibrant scene. I spotted Laurie hustling and crafting drinks at the other end of the bar, but my attention honed in on the figures standing behind him—Tyde's old teammates.

"They must've told him I was here," I muttered, annoyed.

Mason leaned in, concern etched on his face. "Everything okay, Gia?"

I nodded, my gaze still fixed on the familiar faces.

"Yeah, just vibing." faking a smile to show Mason that I am fine. "Hold on, I recognize one of them, Lorenz." I said his name with a scowl to myself. "Lorenz, the snitch—what the hell is he doing here anyway?"

As Mason immersed himself in the lively atmosphere of the dance floor, I seized the opportunity to confide in Laurie. With my expressions more pronounced in my tipsy state, Laurie noticed my scowl as he approached.

"Fair dinkum, Gia! What's gone on? You look like you've rooted through the lost souls bin!" he said, his brow furrowed.

I leaned in, ensuring my conversation with Laurie remained unheard by Mason. I began explaining the recent encounter with Tyde and the presence of his old teammates, particularly Lorenz, who seemed to have stirred up an unexpected ex-crisis.

As the night with Mason came to a close, I felt a pleasant warmth, but I knew it lacked the electric spark I had once known with "the man who shall not be named." The evening remained sweet and innocent, devoid of any risqué encounters.

When it was time to bid Laurie farewell, he grinned at me.

"Shorter night, Gia, hear me out! This could be a ripper, a grandkids' yarn! Live it up like a top Aussie flick, yeah? Every laugh, stumble, dance - twists in our story. We're the sheilas in charge, chuck 'em a curveball! Unforgettable night, right?"

"Fair suck of the sav, Laurie! Catch ya later." Laurie chuckles at my terrible Aussie accent, funnily mocking him.

But deep down, I couldn't shake the feeling that Mason, though a pleasant companion, wasn't the one who held the key to the deeper connections I sought.

Mason walked over, his eyes soft. "Ready to head home, Gia?"

I nodded, a small smile on my lips. "Yeah, Mason. Let's call it a night."

As Mason escorted me to his luxury car, the prospect of a more intimate connection with him didn't resonate with me. The subtle warmth of the evening didn't ignite the spark I had once known.

When we reached my destination, I bid Mason a cordial goodnight. "Thanks for the ride, Mason. It was a good evening."

"My pleasure, Gia. Sleep well," he replied, his voice warm.

As I stepped out and made my way to my door, I glimpsed Mason climbing into a different luxury vehicle, his path diverging from mine as he headed in the opposite direction.

"Until next time," I whispered to myself.

Unsettled eyes I feel upon the entrance of my space. My eyes drawn to the back of my home finding myself looking at a space of darkness. Assuming my mind is playing games with me. I try to shake off the feeling of someone peeping on me though the window. Forcing my thoughts to drift and reflect on the night.

The pleasant warmth lingered, but the connection with Mason, though enjoyable, didn't carry the weight of a deeper romance. As I pondered the inevitable future encounter with Mason, I acknowledged that he resided on the lower end of the roster in my heart. He would linger in my memory until the next chapter of our story unfolded, each encounter leaving its mark on the evolving narrative of my life.

I stumbled into my apartment, the weight of the night pressing down on my shoulders like a heavy cloak. The door clicked shut behind me, and I slid down its smooth surface, my back pressed against the cold wood. A wave of sadness crashed over me, threatening to pull me under.

"It's just one of those nights," I whispered to myself, my voice barely audible in the stillness of the room.

The drowning feeling crept in again, a relentless force that seemed to consume me from the inside out. I searched the empty space, desperate for solace, for someone to rescue me from the turbulent sea of emotions that threatened to engulf me. But there was no one. Just me and the suffocating silence.

"Pull yourself together, Gia," I muttered, my voice shaky and unsteady.

With trembling limbs, I managed to crawl to the couch, the plush cushions offering little comfort as an anxiety attack gripped me, forcing me to sober up abruptly. The room spun, and I clutched at the fabric beneath me, trying to anchor myself to something solid.

"Breathe, just breathe," I repeated like a mantra, my chest heaving with each labored breath.

The floodgates of tears opened, and I found myself succumbing to the overwhelming emotions that had been building inside me all night. Sobs wracked my body, and I curled into myself, seeking refuge in the sheath of my own misery. I cried until exhaustion claimed me, dragging me into a fitful sleep.

"Why does it hurt so much?" I whispered into the darkness, my voice raw and broken.

In the quiet solitude of my apartment, I surrendered to the vulnerability of the moment. The remnants of the night clung to me like a second skin. My makeup, once flawless, now smudged and streaked across my face. My coily hair, gathered in a tight and high ponytail, had begun to unravel, strands sticking to my tear-stained cheeks. My glasses, perched haphazardly on my nose, felt like a shield against the world, a flimsy barrier between me and the pain that threatened to consume me.

My dress, once a symbol of the evening's promise, had ridden up to my hips, a testament to my wild sleeping habits. I was a mess, inside and out.

"I have to stop…I have to stop…calm," I murmured, my voice thick with emotion and trying to deeply inhale.

One strappy heel clung to my foot for dear life, the other discarded and forgotten in the midst of my emotional turmoil. It was a small detail, but it seemed to encapsulate the chaos of my life, the way things always seemed to fall apart when I least expected it.

"Breath…air," I said, a humorless laugh escaping my lips.

In my restless sleep, I grappled with the echoes of the evening, each detail telling a silent tale of a heart wrestling with the complexities of its own journey. The memories swirled in my mind, a mix of emotions that threatened to overwhelm me.

But even in the midst of the pain, there was a glimmer of hope, a tiny spark that refused to be extinguished. It whispered to me, reminding me that this was just one night, one chapter in the grand scheme of my life. There would be other nights, other moments of joy and laughter and love.

For now, though, I allowed myself to feel the weight of it

all, to succumb to the vulnerability that came with opening my heart to the world. I knew that in the morning, I would pick myself up, dust myself off, and face the day with renewed strength.

But for any and every night, I let the tears fall, let the sadness wash over me like a cleansing rain. Tomorrow will come and make a new day, a new chance to start again. And I would be ready for it, no matter what the future held.

Tyde

OUTSIDE GIA'S APARTMENT - BROOKLYN HEIGHTS, NEW YORK CITY

I cruised through Gia's neighborhood, the streetlights casting long shadows across the pavement. My heart raced, a mix of anticipation and anxiety coursing through my veins. I told myself I was just checking on her after her night out, but deep down, I knew it was more than that.

As I rounded the corner onto her street, a sleek car caught my eye, parked right outside her building. My grip tightened on the steering wheel. Was it her date's car? The thought made my stomach churn.

I found a spot to tuck my car away, hidden in the shadows. And then I waited, my eyes fixed on Gia's front door. Minutes stretched into an eternity until finally, it opened.

My breath caught in my throat as I watched Mason Jean-Baptiste step out. Mason. Of all people. A rage I didn't know I possessed began to build, like a dragon stirring in my chest.

Before I could think twice, I gunned the engine, pulling up to the curb with a screech of tires. "Yo, Mason!" I shouted, my voice rough with anger. "Stay away from Gia, you hear me? Dont' touch her. Don't speak to her. If even her an inkling that you've been in the same space as her, breathing her air. You're dead!"

Mason's head snapped towards me, his eyes narrowing. "The hell you say to me?" he growled, taking a step closer.

I was out of the car in a flash, squaring up to him. We were nose to nose, the air between us crackling with tension.

"You heard me," I spat. "Back off."

"Or what?" Mason sneered, his breath hot on my face. "You don't own her, dude. She can see whoever she wants."

I felt my fists clench at my sides, every muscle in my body coiled tight. We were seconds away from throwing down when a voice cut through the night.

"Aye! Shut the fuck up, both of you!" A neighbor leaned out of their window, face twisted in annoyance. "I'll call the cops if the both of you don't leave!"

Neither of us moved. We stood there, locked in the most intense staring contest I'd ever experienced. I could see the challenge in Mason's eyes, daring me to make a move.

A cruiser rounded the corner, its lights painting the street in red and blue. The wail of a police siren shattered the standoff.

"There's a problem here, gentlemen?" The officer's voice was stern, no-nonsense.

"No," Mason and I answered in unison, our tones dripping with sarcasm.

The cop's eyes narrowed, clearly not buying it. "I suggest you both move along…Now!"

Mason broke first, sliding into his car with one last glare in my direction. I watched him peel away, my heart still pounding.

As I climbed back into my own vehicle, I caught the officer's gaze in my rearview mirror. The look on his face was clear: he was ready to throw someone in lockup tonight if pushed.

I drove off, the adrenaline slowly ebbing from my system. What the hell had just happened? The jealousy that had consumed me moments ago now left me feeling hollow and confused.

As I navigated the quiet streets, my mind raced. Why had I reacted so strongly? Gia and I weren't even together, not even close. But seeing this guy come out of her home, knowing he'd been with her...

I shook my head, trying to clear the jumble of emotions.

Malcolm Smith the Maintenance Man

I crouched in the dank alleyway, my smart goggles humming softly as they captured every detail of Gia's bathroom window. With a beautiful open floor plan and easy to analyze. The night air was thick with the stench of rotting garbage and stale urine, but I barely noticed it anymore. My focus was solely on the sliver of light emanating from her apartment.

"What's she doing now, Malcom?" Charlotte's voice crackled through my earpiece, impatient and demanding as always.

I zoomed in, my breath catching as Gia came into view. "She just got home," I whispered, my heart racing. "Looks like she was out with that guy again. Mason. Mason something, I didn't get the last name."

"Show me," Charlotte snapped.

I blinked, transmitting the images I'd captured earlier that evening. Gia, laughing as she stumbled out of a cab, her arm linked with a tall, dark-haired man. Her cheeks were flushed, her eyes sparkling in a way that made my stomach churn.

"Is he with her now?" Charlotte pressed.

"No," I replied, a mixture of relief and disappointment coloring my voice. "She's alone. Getting ready for bed."

Charlotte's frustration was palpable even through the tinny connection.

"I need more, Malcolm. Something we can use." The line went dead with a sharp click.

I remained perched on my makeshift lookout, a precarious stack of wooden crates and trash bins. My eyes never left Gia as she moved about her apartment, oblivious to my presence. She was so close, yet untouchable. I imagined what it would be like to slip inside, to breathe the same air as her, to—

A shout from the street below shattered my fantasy. "Hey! What's going on out there?"

Panic surged through me. I scrambled down from my perch, nearly losing my footing on the slick metal of a dumpster. My heart pounded in my ears as I hit the ground running, not daring to look back.

The shouts grew louder, footsteps echoing off the brick walls. Voices violent and ready to rage between the men. Over hearing a little of what was said from the men.

"You heard me," the first masculine voice spat. "Back off."

"Or what?" the second masculine voice sneered, his breath hot on my face. "You don't own her, dude. She can see whoever she wants."

I ducked into a narrow passageway, praying the shadows

would swallow me whole. My lungs burned as I gasped for air, pressing myself against the cold, damp wall.

I held my breath, squeezing my eyes shut.

"Not now. Not when I'm so close," murmured to myself.

The image of Gia's smile flashed behind my eyelids, taunting me. I clenched my fists, willing myself to become invisible.

The footsteps drew nearer, then paused.

As my pulse slowly returned to normal, a familiar ache settled in my chest. I'd have to find a new vantage point now. One where I could watch her, undetected. Where I could pretend, just for a moment, that the warmth in her eyes.

I melted into the shadows, already planning my next move. Charlotte would get her information, but Gia... Gia was mine. To worship. To possess.

The night enveloped me as I slipped away, carrying my secrets and obsessions into the darkness.

CHAPTER 7
THE HUNGER OF THREADS
Tyde & Gia

PRESS DINING - MADISON SQUARE GARDEN

Despite the challenges of the previous night—the night out, the meltdown, the anxiety attack, and a bit too much alcohol—I found myself facing another demanding day. The clock ticked away, and responsibilities weighed on my shoulders as I prepared to return to the office.

"One step at a time," I murmured to myself, my voice barely audible.

The morning marked a pivotal moment as I had to clock into the office by 8 AM alongside Tyde, ready to welcome the audience for Day 2 of the All-Star Weekend. Despite not being a "bounce back queen," I summoned my resilience, pushing through the haze of the previous night.

As I stepped into the office, Tyde's gaze landed on me, a smirk playing on his lips.

"Alright? You look like you've been dragged through a hedge backwards!"

I met his gaze with a smirk of my own. The aura of sarcasm in full effect."Oh yeah, I'm doing great. How about you Tyde?"

"Actually, Im…" Tyde began to respond.

My response cut him off, speaking over him with a sarcastic snarl. "Actually, I dont give a damn."

Though I looked pristine, my makeup flawless and my outfit carefully chosen, Tyde could see beyond the facade. He knew me well enough to sense the aftermath of the night's events just by looking into my eyes.

"You were never any good at holding liquor, am I right?" he said, his tone playful yet laced with a hint of concern.

Our shared history spoke volumes, and Tyde's mischievous glint softened into a moment of understanding. Despite my composed exterior, I couldn't hide the weariness, and Tyde acknowledged the unwavering commitment I showed by stepping into the office, ready to fulfill my responsibilities, even in the face of personal challenges. It was a connection that transcended time, a silent understanding between two souls who had weathered storms together.

Tyde couldn't resist asking me about my date, his disapproval evident in his tone.

"Right, what were you thinking bringing Worzel Gummidge home?

I met his gaze defiantly. "You know nothing about him, and you never will."

Tyde, observing my demeanor, remained firm in his

judgment. "Seen enough after last night, ta very much."

I, always one for banter, decided to tease and egg him on, playfully questioning his motives.

"Jealous, Tyde? Why are you so concerned about who I sleep with?"

Tyde's expression shifted, caught off guard by my teasing. The tension between us lingered, unspoken words hanging in the air.

The atmosphere shifted as the director walked into the room, and a wave of work-mode energy swept through the space. Each of us was handed scripts for the day's segment breakdowns, diverting our attention from the dating conversation.

"Alright, everyone, let's focus. We've got a packed day ahead. Here are your scripts for the segment breakdowns," the director announced, his voice cutting through the tension.

The dating conversation faded into the background, and a sense of seriousness settled in. Without missing a beat, we all jumped into action, ready to tackle the day's tasks.

Tyde leans closer to me, voice low. "Right, we'll park that there for now. We'll crack on with it another time."

The air was now charged with a different energy as we delved into our work, leaving the casual chatter behind and getting down to business for the day. I focused on the papers in my hand, my mind already racing with the tasks ahead.

But even as I immersed myself in the work, I couldn't shake the lingering thoughts of the previous night, the weight of my emotions still clinging to me like a second skin. I knew I had to push through, to put on a brave face and carry on with my responsibilities, but it wasn't easy.

I glanced at Tyde, wondering if he could sense the turmoil within me. Our history, the unspoken connection we shared, made it impossible to hide anything from him. He knew me, perhaps better than anyone else, and that knowledge both comforted and unnerved me.

As the day unfolded, I threw myself into the work, determined to prove to myself and everyone else that I could handle anything that came my way. But in the back of my mind, the conversation with Tyde lingered, a reminder of the unfinished business between us.

I knew that sooner or later, we would have to confront the elephant in the room, to address the tension that had been building since forever. But for now, I focused on the present, on the job at hand, and pushed everything else aside.

—

THE BULLPEN - MADISON SQUARE GARDEN

Beneath the weight of my professional obligations, I carried the lingering echoes of last night, a persistent ache resonating deep within my chest. It felt like an enduring discomfort, a subtle nudge hinting at unresolved emotions that refused to be silenced.

"Shake it off, Gia. Focus on work," I whispered to myself, my voice barely audible amidst the bustling office.

But even as I immersed myself in the demands of my responsibilities, I found myself on a quest for personal growth, yearning for a path that could lead to healing from the scars of my past traumas. The realization hit me like a lightning bolt, a sudden clarity that cut through the haze of my thoughts.

It's time to confront the past, time to heal, I thought, the words echoing in my mind like a mantra.

I recognized the profound importance of self-forgiveness as the initial stride towards liberation. Before I could extend forgiveness to others, I knew I had to confront and reconcile with the intricate layers of myself. The wounds of the past, the mistakes I had made, the pain I had endured—they all needed to be addressed, to be acknowledged and embraced.

Forgiveness starts within, I reminded myself, the words a gentle whisper in the depths of my soul.

In this voyage toward self-discovery and healing, I anticipated unraveling the threads of my past, patiently weaving a tapestry woven with threads of strength, resilience, and the eventual embrace of forgiveness. It wasn't going to be easy, I knew that much. But I also knew that it was necessary, that I couldn't keep running from the ghosts of my past forever.

It's a journey, a process. One step at a time, I contemplated, my mind already mapping out the road ahead.

As a crucial step in this transformative process, I acknowledged that it was time to seek therapy. I felt ready to confront the depths of my emotions, to embark on a guided exploration of my inner world. It was a daunting prospect, the idea of baring my soul to a stranger, but I knew it was the only way forward.

I took a deep breath, feeling the weight of my decision settle upon my shoulders. It was a weight I was willing to bear, a burden I was ready to carry in the pursuit of healing and self-discovery.

The office bustled around me, the chatter of my colleagues fading into the background as I focused on the path ahead. I knew it wouldn't be easy, that there would be moments of doubt and fear, moments when I would want to turn back and retreat into the familiar comfort of denial.

But I also knew that I was stronger than that, that I had the courage to face my demons head-on. I had survived so much already, had weathered storms that would have broken lesser people. "I could do this, I told myself firmly. I would do this."

With a newfound sense of purpose, I threw myself back into my work, determined to excel in my professional life even as I embarked on this personal journey. The two were intertwined, I realized, each feeding into the other in a delicate balance of strength and vulnerability.

As the day wore on, I felt a glimmer of hope beginning to take root within me. It was small, fragile, but it was there nonetheless. A promise of a brighter future, a glimpse of the person I could become if I had the courage to face my past and embrace forgiveness.

I smiled to myself, a secret smile that spoke of determination and resilience.

Gia

DR. CELINE DIAZ'S OFFICE - GARMENT DISTRICT, NEW YORK CITY

In the tranquil haven of Celine Diaz's therapist office, I settled into a plush chair across from her, my heart pounding with a mixture of nerves and anticipation. Celine, a seasoned board-certified mental health therapist with a decade of experience in her field, exuded an air of understanding and empathy that seemed to envelop the room. As I sat there, feeling the weight of her gentle gaze upon me, I sensed the safe space she had created, a sanctuary where I could finally unveil the deep-seated turmoil within me.

"So, Gia, your journey can begin anywhere. Just talk to me, casually. Whatever is most comfortable to you," Celine patiently tells me.

"I had a panic attack after my first date in a long time," I began, my voice trembling slightly. "It was the first one since an innocent incident that happened from my past with my ex, Tyde."

Celine leaned forward, her expression one of genuine concern and compassion.

"Take your time, Gia. Tell me more about that."

"The panic attack was nothing new, I get them often," I signed, "But this one hit differently because it was about love and detachment or trying to be detached to someone. Someone who I can't be disattached to at the moment."

I took a deep breath, feeling the vulnerability rise within

me like a tidal wave.

"Tyde was supposed to be my one and only love, to protect me. But he didn't, and now I'm navigating this vulnerability on my own. I just want someone to rely on"

As I laid bare the intricacies of my feelings, Celine offered a supportive presence, her eyes never wavering from mine.

"It's okay to feel vulnerable sometimes, Gia. Healing often begins with acknowledging and understanding our emotions. Also understanding the trauma that you went through, give yourself and Tyde grace. How do you envision moving forward, especially if you have to see him at work?"

I sighed, the weight of uncertainty pressing down on my chest. "I don't know, honestly. I want to move forward, but it feels overwhelming when his presence lingers everywhere. I'm lost on the path of healing from my past."

Celine nodded empathetically, her voice soft and reassuring.

"We'll navigate this journey together, Gia. It's okay not to have all the answers right now."

She paused for a moment, her eyes searching mine, as if sensing the need to explore the root of my struggles.

"Let's delve into the situation with Tyde. Can you share what happened, starting from the beginning?"

I felt a knot form in my throat, the memories rushing back like a tidal wave. I paused briefly, collecting my thoughts, before delving into the night Tyde and I first met. With a heavy heart, I continued to unravel the distressing events that followed months ahead.

"Well, there was this tape that was released by someone.

I don't know who released it," I began, my voice barely above a whisper.

As I continued, the room seemed to shift into the past, enveloped in the haze of an emotionally confusing flashback. I could almost feel the heat of that night, the buzz of alcohol coursing through my veins, the electric touch of Tyde's large hands on my skin.

"Tyde and I had just gotten home from a night on the town, both a bit tipsy. We weren't in the right mindset to think about someone filming us, neither of us. As we stumbled into Tyde's room, things got touchy and feely, and then they escalated from there," I said, my voice cracking with emotion.

Tears pricked the corners of my eyes, an insistent burn I tried desperately to blink away. The memories, so visceral and raw, threatened to drag me under - a riptide of anguish and betrayal. My throat constricted, heart jackhammering against my ribcage as I fought for composure under Celine's watchful gaze.

But then, like a switch flipping, the scene changed. Sadness gave way to exhilaration, hurt morphing into a very different kind of heat. Suddenly, I was back in that room, Tyde's hands branding my skin, his lips searing paths of liquid fire across my body. The arousal hit me like a freight train, sudden and consuming.

Gia

FOUR YEARS AGO…

FLASHBACK - THE TAPE

Colors kaleidoscoped wildly as the drug gripped me in its vise, the world blurring at the edges. Tyde's face, so perfectly sculpted it could make angels weep, drifted tantalizingly close. Oceans of blue bored into me, concern and carnal hunger warring in their depths.

"You okay, babe? Those drinks are hitting you hard tonight."

"Mmm, just tipsy. I'm fine," I managed, voice honeyed and thick. Liquid lust simmered in my blood, every nerve ending screaming for his touch.

We tumbled into the bedroom, a maelstrom of seeking hands and searing kisses. Tyde claimed my mouth like a conquering hero, tongue plundering, teeth nipping. Whimpers caught in my throat as his fingers glided over my fevered skin, igniting blazes in their wake. Desperate, frenzied, we grappled with buttons and zippers until flesh met flesh in a delicious slide of heat.

My nails bit into the marble planes of Tyde's back as he lowered me to the silk ridden bed, muscles rippling sinfully beneath bronze skin. I was drunk on the taste of him, salt and spice and something forbidden. Hips rolling, bodies undulating, we moved together in a dance older than time.

"So beautiful," Tyde moaned, an azure gaze raking over my body, splayed bare and wanton beneath him. Hands calloused from gripping hockey sticks charted every curve and hollow, leaving trails of goosebumps in their wake. Sighs and gasps mingled in a sensual symphony as he mapped and memorized my most intimate terrain.

I was a tuning fork, quivering and ready to shatter at his skillful ministrations. Tyde's wicked mouth traversed the column of my throat, tongue swirling and teeth scraping until I was incoherent with need. He took his sweet time, savoring me like a decadent feast as he ventured lower, lower...

The first velvet stroke of his tongue against my aching center nearly unmade me. Colors burst behind my eyelids. Fingers tangled in silken strands, anchoring him to me as he unleashed his most devastating assault yet. Pleasure mounted, crested, until I shook and shattered with a silent scream.

But even as I drowned in sensation, the drug's fog grew more ominous, smothering. Cold unease slithered up my spine. This spinning, floating feeling verged on terrifying. I was slipping... falling...

Then Tyde rose over me, powerful thighs parting mine, and the world receded. I clung to him, nails scoring his skin as he drove into me, each surging thrust stoking the embers anew. Rational thought splintered, the impending fallout forgotten. There was only this - Tyde moving inside me, filling me, completing me. I surrendered to the dark ecstasy, heedless of the reckoning poised to strike with the rising sun.

I shifted in my seat, thighs clenching as the dull ache between them sharpened to a throb. My skin prickled with awareness, nerve endings sparking to life as if Tyde were still touching me, tasting me. The room dimmed, Celine's concerned face fading into the background as the memory engulfed me.

Phantom hands charted my curves, rough palms igniting shivers in their wake. I could almost feel the rasp of Tyde's stubble against my inner thighs, the delicious stretch as he filled me again and again. A soft moan escaped my parted lips, eyes fluttering shut as I surrendered to the sense memory.

It was wrong, perverse even, to be so turned on by a night that had brought such devastation. But my body didn't care about the context, about the fallout. It remembered only pleasure - white-hot and all-consuming, the kind that obliterated everything else.

I was slipping down the rabbit hole, losing myself to the fantasy. Rational thought receded, overshadowed by baser instincts. I could feel my nipples pebbling against the confines of my bra, my silk thong dampening with each passing second. If I slid a hand beneath my skirt, would I find myself dripping for a ghost? For a man who-

I jolted back to the present, Celine's concerned voice piercing through the haze of arousal. Reality crashed in like a bucket of ice water, dousing the embers of illicit pleasure. Shame slithered through my veins, insidious and sickening. What the hell was wrong with me?

"I'm sorry, I just..." My voice cracked, throat tight with emotion. "Got lost for a moment there."

Celine's eyes held no judgment, only a soft understanding tinged with something uncomfortably close to pity. Celine did not fully understand where my mind drifted off to. She might possibly think I have psychological problems - God forbid. "It's okay, Gia. The mind and body have a way of clinging to intense experiences, both good and bad. What you're feeling is normal. Coming into a space where this is new to you. Don't rush yourself."

Normal. The word tasted bitter on my tongue. There was nothing normal about getting turned on by memories of a night that shattered me, leaving me broken and exposed. I dug crescent moons into my palms, pain grounding me.

"I don't want to feel this icky, sad, and discouraged way," I whispered, a single traitorous tear escaping. "I don't want to be defined by what happened in my past."

Celine leaned forward, gaze gentle yet unflinching. "You aren't, Gia. Your reactions, your emotions - they're a part of your story, but they don't have to control it. You get to choose what defines you."

I wanted to believe her, to trust that I was more than the sum of my traumas. But with phantom pleasure still thrumming through my body, it felt like an impossible feat.

I swallowed past the lump in my throat, meeting Celine's steady gaze. Her presence was a balm, a beacon of safety amidst the tumultuous sea of my emotions. She didn't push or prod, merely held space for me to navigate the painful memories.

Tears welled, hot and insistent. The shame, the violation, the bone-deep ache of betrayal - it crashed over me in relentless waves. But as I sat there, pouring out my broken pieces, a fragile hope took root.

Maybe this was the first step towards healing, towards reclaiming the parts of me shattered that fateful night. And the even more traumatic night of an ignorant young girl before she met Tyde. Maybe, with Celine's guidance, I could begin to put myself back together, to find the strength buried beneath the pain.

As I began to share, voice growing steadier with each word, a profound relief washed over me. Speaking my truth aloud somehow lessened its hold, like lancing a festering wound.

Looking into Celine's compassionate eyes, I knew I was no longer alone in this struggle. I had found a safe haven to be vulnerable, to strip away the masks and begin the arduous journey towards wholeness.

For the first time in forever, a tiny spark of hope flickered to life - small and delicate, but stubbornly persistent.

The road ahead was long and treacherous, paved with painful memories and setbacks. But I refused to let that one night define me anymore. I was more than my trauma, more than what had been taken from me.

I was a survivor. And I would rise from the ashes, forge beauty from the shattered remnants of my old life. One session at a time, one tiny victory after another, I would reclaim my story.

This was only the beginning. But for once, beginnings didn't terrify me. They filled me with tentative hope, fragile but real.

I met Celine's eyes, determination burning bright amidst the tears.

"I'm ready," I said simply. "I'm ready to do the work."

And for the first time, I truly believed it.

Tyde

DR. RILEY HAMMOND'S OFFICE - THE WATERFRONT, NEW JERSEY

The plush leather chair swallowed me whole, comforting a stark contrast to the storm raging inside. Dr. Riley's office, usually a sanctuary of muted tones and calming light, felt like a pressure cooker today. My knuckles were white as I gripped the armrests, the anger threatening to boil over at any moment.

Riley suggested we start with a chapter of my childhood. A chapter for which I wouldn't like to remember, my mother.

"How could she not even ask about Dad?" The words ripped from my throat, a bitter explosion. "She's the one who pushed him and myself away, then scarpered on me too! Right outta order, the whole thing."

Riley's face remained a mask of professional calm, but his eyes held a quiet understanding. He simply nodded,encouraging me to continue, a silent invitation to spill the tempest within.

"Her voicemails are in undetectable state," I muttered, the taste of sour milk clinging to the words. I ran a hand through my cropped hair, the frustration evident in the way it ruffled. "It's like she thinks she can just waltz back in, after all this time. What, just because I have money now?" My voice rose a notch, laced with disbelief.

"And how does that make you feel, Tyde?" His voice, a

gentle counterpoint to my growing agitation, cut through the haze of anger.

I barked out a laugh, a humorless sound that echoed hollowly in the room.

"How does it make me feel? Bloody furious,that's how! It's like… like she's picking at a scab. Just when I think I'm improving my life, she calls, and it's all raw again."

Riley leaned forward, his pen poised over his notepad like a conductor's baton.

"Let's explore that a bit more, shall we? You mentioned your mother's departure was the start of your struggles. Can you tell me more about that time?"

His words were a dam breaking, unleashing a torrent of memories. The stale scent of cigarettes and cheap gin, a constant companion in my childhood home. And that's just the drugs she started with. The sounds of raised voices, muffled by paper-thin walls, a chilling soundtrack to my adolescence.

"It was… chaos," I choked out, the past a bitter pill to swallow. "One day she was there, and the next… gone. Left Dad and me without a second thought."

"And your father? How did he cope?"

A humorless snort escaped my lips, a mixture of anger and a deep-seated pity for the man who raised me.

"Cope? He didn't. Bloke was in pieces. Started drinking, couldn't hold down a job. It was like… like I lost both parents in the quickness, you know?"

Riley nodded, his expression thoughtful. "That must have been incredibly difficult for you, Tyde. How old were you?"

"Twelve," I replied, my voice barely above a whisper. "Old

enough to know everything was going to shit, young enough to think it was somehow my fault."

"And is that when you started…?" Riley left the question hanging, but I knew exactly where he was going.

Shame and defiance warred within me as I nodded. "Yeah. Booze first. Nicked it from Dad's stash. Then… other stuff.Anything to numb it, really."

"What about support systems? Friends, other family members?"

I let out a bitter laugh. "In our town? Everyone had their own problems. And Dad… he was too far gone in his grief of his relationship to notice what was happening with me."

Riley set his pen down, his gaze meeting mine with unwavering sincerity.

"Tyde, what you've been through… it's a heavy burden to carry. But you're here now, trying to work through it. That takes incredible strength."

A lump formed in my throat, unshed tears burning behind my eyes. "Does it? 'Cause most days I feel anything but strong."

"Strength isn't about never falling," he said gently. "It's about getting back up. And you, Tyde, keep getting back up."

There was a long silence in the room, broken only by the rhythmic ticking of the clock. Each second felt like a step forward, a step away from the past and towards… something. Not healing, not yet. But maybe… hope.

"So," I finally managed, my voice rough. "Where do we go from here?"

A small smile played on Riley's lips.

"That, Tyde, is entirely up to you. But I'll be here to help you navigate the path,whatever you choose."

The road ahead was long and undoubtedly difficult, but at least I wouldn't be walking it alone.

"I guess that's why all my relationships have been… interesting, for the most part. Good or bad, I don't know." The only one that has been important to me was Gia.

Tyde

FOUR YEARS AGO...

FLASHBACK - THE TAPE

Gia swayed on her feet, eyes glazed and unfocused as the club's strobing lights painted abstract patterns across her flushed skin. The slinky dress I couldn't wait to peel off her clung to every mouthwatering curve. Something about her seemed off, more than the usual drunk flirtiness, but lust clouded my judgment.

"You okay, babe? Those drinks are hitting you hard tonight."

"Mmm, just tipsy. I'm fine," she purred, words slurring seductively. Heat flared in my core, needing pulsing insistently through my veins.

We stumbled into the bedroom, a fever dream of roaming hands and desperate kisses. I claimed Gia's lush mouth, plundering honeyed depths as needy little whimpers spilled from her throat straight to my aching cock. Clothes disappeared in a flurry until it was just skin, miles and miles of silky skin pressed against my own.

My control frayed as I lowered Gia to the bed, dark coily hair spilling across the pillow in a tousled invitation. Stormy brown eyes, pupils blown wide with want, drank me in hungrily.

"So beautiful," I rasped. Reverent hands skated over dangerous curves, committing every dip and hollow to memory as she shivered and sighed.

I was a man possessed, drunk on the taste of her, determined to worship every inch until she was boneless and pleading. Lips trailed scorching paths down her elegant throat, tongue swirling over the hammering pulse. Further still to lave dusky nipples straining for attention. Gia was a livewire beneath me, writhing and panting, nails scoring my skin in her fevered desperation.

But I took my time, savoring her like the rarest delicacy even as my own need reached a fever pitch. I ventured lower, settling between creamy thighs that parted eagerly for me. The first broad swipe of my tongue through glistening folds had Gia nearly arching off the smooth bed, a choked cry torn from her throat. Ambrosia.

I lost myself in her, relentless licks and deep slow plunges as she shook apart, orgasm cresting over her in dizzying waves. I could have spent hours worshiping at that altar but my body screamed for more, harder, now.

Rising over her, I poised at Gia's dripping entrance, skin slick with sweat and her arousal. With one powerful surge I sheathed myself fully, groaning at the vice-like grip. She clung to me, a drowning woman seeking anchor as I started to move - deep, rolling thrusts that stoked the embers into an inferno.

The world receded until there was only this. Only us. Pleasure built, crested, exploded in a starburst of sensation as we fell over the edge together. I collapsed over Gia, mouthing wordless praise into her damp skin as aftershocks rolled through us both.

If only I'd known what the harsh light of day would

bring. The fallout lying in wait, the reckoning we'd face as our most intimate moments were thrust into the limelight. But in that blissful moment, tangled together in damp sheets, I was oblivious to the brewing storm.

The memory dissipated like morning mist under the sun's glare, Gia's phantom touch still lingering on my sensitized skin. I blinked, disoriented, as the plush leather couch and neutral walls of Dr. Hammond's office materialized around me. The cool, recycled air felt harsh in my lungs after the heat of remembered passion.

Riley watched me, his keen gaze a mixture of understanding and clinical detachment. I shifted uncomfortably, all too aware of the telltale bulge straining against my zipper. Damn inconvenient hard-on.

Casually, I reached for a throw pillow, strategically draping it over my lap in a move I prayed looked natural. The last thing I needed was my shrink psychoanalyzing my physical reaction to a drugged up sex memory.

"Tyde." Riley's voice cut through the charged silence, measured and probing. "Where did you go just now?"

I swallowed against the bitter taste flooding my mouth, a potent cocktail of shame and anger. That night, Gia, the damning video - it all crashed over me in a tidal wave I couldn't seem to outrun.

"Just drifted, sorry." The words felt leaden on my tongue, heavy with unspoken baggage. "Having a bit of a mare with some flashbacks, if you know what I mean."

Riley nodded, infuriatingly calm in the face of my inner turmoil. He jotted something in that ever-present notebook, pen scratching ominously against the page. I had to physically resist the urge to snatch it from his hands, see what dark portents he was scribbling about my fractured psyche.

"These memories, Tyde - they still carry a significant charge for you." It wasn't a question. "The body doesn't forget, even when the mind tries to."

I barked a harsh laugh, the sound grating in the tranquil space.

"Right, a right laugh that was! Like a ferret in a sock drawer in here, ain't it? Sod it, what's done is done. No point flogging a dead horse."

But even as the words left my mouth, I knew it was futile. That night, crystallized in high definition and blasted across the Internet, would haunt me forever - a specter of violation and betrayal I couldn't exercise. It had seeped into my marrow, tainted every relationship, every interaction.

Riley leaned forward, steepling his fingers.

"Healing, it's about integration, acceptance. You need to make peace with your past before it destroys your present."

I met his unwavering gaze, jaw clenched painfully. He made it sound so simple. As if I could vanquish my demons with a few pretty words and a snap of my fingers. But I knew better.

The road ahead was long and treacherous, paved with minefields waiting to drag me back into the abyss. But I couldn't keep running. Couldn't let that one night define me forever.

Riley left me alone in the room and gave me space while he went to talk to his receptionist about setting up my next appointment best fitted for his and my schedules.

The shrill ping of my phone pierced the air, jolting me out of my thoughts. I reached for the device, my fingers swiping across the screen with a sense of trepidation. As I opened the message, I felt my breath catch in my throat, my eyes widening in disbelief.

There, displayed on the screen in vivid detail, was a picture of Gia on a dinner date with a different guy. The image seared itself into my mind, a painful reminder of the distance that had grown between us.

I stared at the screen, my eyes narrowing as I took in the details of the photo. The guy's face was familiar, a nagging sense of recognition tugging at the edges of my consciousness. And then it hit me, like a punch to the gut.

"Is that the geezer, Chris Jennings?" I murmured and eyes seared at the image. "Blimey, Gia! What you playing at?"

The words spilled from my lips, a torrent of confusion and frustration. I couldn't believe what I was seeing, couldn't wrap my mind around the fact that Gia was out there, living her life, while I was stuck in this endless cycle of pain and self-doubt.

A right red mist descended! Furious doesn't even cut it.

"The cheek of her, waltzing on like nothing happened while I'm here like Humpty Dumpty, trying to put myself back together."

I gripped the phone tightly, my knuckles turning white with the force of my emotions. I wanted to scream, to yell, to demand answers from the universe. But I knew that there was nothing I could do, nothing that would change the reality of the situation.

Gia was moving on, and I was left behind, a spectator in my own life. The realization hit me like a ton of bricks, knocking the wind out of my lungs and leaving me gasping for air.

I closed my eyes, trying to block out the image of Gia and Chris together. But it was no use. The picture was burned into my mind, a painful reminder of everything I had lost.

I felt a sense of helplessness wash over me, a feeling of being trapped in a nightmare from which I couldn't escape. I wanted to reach out to Gia and to demand an explanation.

I slumped back in my chair, the phone falling from my grasp and clattering to the floor. I barely noticed the sound, too lost in my own thoughts to care.

How did it come to this? How had I let things get so out of control? I had always prided myself on being strong, on being in control of my own life. But now, faced with the reality of Gia's new reality, I felt like a helpless child, lost and alone in a world that made no sense.

I took a deep breath, trying to steady myself. I knew that I couldn't let this defeat me, that I had to find a way to move forward, to pick up the pieces of my shattered life and start anew.

But even as I tried to summon the strength to carry on, I couldn't shake the feeling of despair that had settled over me like a heavy blanket. I felt like I was drowning, like I was being pulled under by the weight of my own emotions.

I closed my eyes, letting the tears fall freely down my cheeks. I didn't care who saw me, didn't care about the judgment or the pity that I knew would follow. All I cared about was the pain, the all-consuming ache that had taken root in my heart and refused to let go.

And so, with a new sense of determination, I tried to lift my spirits and faced the world once more. I didn't know what the future held, didn't know if I would ever find the happiness that I so desperately craved. But I knew that I had to try, had to keep pushing forward, no matter how hard it might be.

CHAPTER 8
CONSIDERED THE STAR

I found myself on a dinner date with another contender from my dating roster – Chris Jennings, a baseball player who had recently made a career switch. Coincidentally, Tyde, my ex, was an avid fan with multiple signed collector items of Chris, making him more than just a casual interest.

Chris, a well-rounded individual, stood out with his muscular build, though shorter than my usual preference at 5'7". What set him apart was his southern twang accent and proficiency in five languages. Beyond his athletic prowess, he was a family man and a dedicated humanitarian for wildlife.

While Chris might have looked like an excellent catch on paper, the true test lay in whether he could live up to more than just an impressive resume.

We sat across from each other in a cozy restaurant, the atmosphere charged with anticipation. The clinking of cutlery and soft chatter formed a background to our conversation.

I smiled, my eyes sparkling with mischief. "So, Chris, ever been on a date with a woman who has a fan club?"

He grinned, leaning forward with interest. "Honey, bless your heart, I've had my pick of fellas, but a whole fan club? Doggone it, that takes the cake! Now tell me all about it, sugar!"

I couldn't help but smirk, enjoying the playful banter. "You are looking at one of the hosts for the NHL All-Star weekend. So I am quite the hot commodity."

Chris laughed, his eyes crinkling at the corners. "Well bless your heart! That's just tickled pink! Don't you fret none about sharing the spotlight, honey. There's enough sunshine for both of us."

I raised an eyebrow, my lips curving into a smirk. "Sure. It's not like you're a big deal or anything."

He bursts out into laughter. "You sure know how to tickle a fella funny."

I met his gaze, intrigued by his words. "Are you suggesting I'm little bank?"

Chris winked, his southern charm on full display.

"Gia, that ain't no ordinary twist, that's a whole dang rollercoaster ride! Now, sugar, spill the tea about your story."

I leaned back, amused by his boldness. "Oh, I have many stories to tell. I'm not your typical leading lady, though. No damsel in distress here."

He mirrored my posture, his eyes glinting with admiration.

"Well bless your heart, I dig that too. Ain't your everyday hero, that's a fact. But hey, I reckon you can speak five languages, swing a mean baseball bat, and all while helpin' out them critters. That's gotta count for somethin', sugar, don't it?"

I couldn't help but smirk, enjoying the playful exchange.

"It sure does. And the southern twang accent adds a nice touch. So, Chris Jennings, let's see if you're more than just a great catch on paper."

He smiled, his eyes filled with promise. "Hold my sweet tea, Gia! Bless your heart (and buckle up)!"

The restaurant's ambiance hummed with the gentle buzz of conversation and the clinking of cutlery as Tyde and Charlotte Astor entered, a spectacle for the paparazzi stationed at the door. Tyde, exuding confidence and style, seemed almost in competition with the oblivious me and my date, Chris, deeply engrossed in our own world.

I was animatedly talking to Chris, my hands gesturing with enthusiasm.

"It's incredible, Chris, how humanitarian efforts can truly make a difference. Don't you think so?"

He nodded, equally engaged in the conversation. "You preachin' the truth, Gia! Hits you right in the feels, and watchin' things turn around for the better is just pure sugar."

Unperceived to us, Tyde sighed inwardly at our apparent indifference, a self-proclaimed hater on the train of self-sulking. As clicks and clamors from the paparazzi echoed around them, Tyde smirked to himself, thinking they were making quite an entrance.

"Right under their noses," he muttered, a right sour taste in his mouth. "Clueless lot, the bunch of them."

Turning to Charlotte, he whispered, "Alright, let's nick our table then."

Following the hostess through the maze of tables, Tyde and Charlotte settled into their seats, the energy of the restaurant swirling around them.

I continued, unaware of their presence, my focus solely on Chris.

"And the key, Chris, is fostering long-term sustainability in these projects. It's not just about the immediate impact, it's about creating lasting change."

Meanwhile, Tyde and Charlotte shared a moment of quiet as the waiter approached.

Tyde's voice dripped with sarcasm. "Didn't half go down a treat, did it? Our grand entrance proper got clocked."

Charlotte smiled awkwardly, her confidence unwavering. "Babe, I always get noticed."

The evening progressed, revealing the stark contrast between the oblivious couple and Tyde's interactions with Charlotte, weaving an intriguing atmosphere. Charlotte, a 26-year-old Caucasian with strawberry-blonde pinstraught hair and warm autumn brown eyes, stood as Tyde's ex-girlfriend, sharing a meaningful matching tattoo with him. Adding an extra layer of complexity, she was an heiress.

However, despite her privileged background, Charlotte remained a sweetheart who never entertained jealousy, providing a compelling counterpoint to Tyde's occasional exasperation.

As the night unfolded, the tales of these intertwined lives continued to interlace in unforeseen ways, fostering an environment ripe for unexpected revelations and emotional entanglements.

Upon meeting me, Tyde initially spared little mention of Charlotte, giving me the impression that he was eager to move on to what he considered better things – namely, me. As our relationship blossomed, Tyde gradually opened up about the intricacies of his past with Charlotte. One detail he revealed was the matching tattoos they once shared, a significant part of their history.

In the early stages of our relationship, these tidbits served as building blocks, allowing us to better understand each other. As our connection deepened and we officially became a couple, Tyde took a proactive step in moving forward. In a symbolic gesture of commitment and growth, he booked a tattoo cover appointment, choosing to transform a relic of his past into a canvas for a new chapter with me.

Laurie, serving drinks at the bar, noticed Tyde approaching to order drinks for himself and Charlotte. With a dismissive eye roll, Laurie greeted him in a rude tone.

"Whatcha won' then?" Laurie snarled, giving him a fair ropeable.

Tyde, unimpressed, sarcastically reminded Laurie of the importance of proper customer service. "You can't go mugging punters off like that, mate. I could proper get you binned for that sort of cheek."

Laurie fixed up his act, squarin' his munnies and slangin' a smart-arse smirk.

"What'll it be then, mate?"

Tyde, pleased with the change, placed the order with a

touch of impatience.

"Aight, I'll have a gin tom then, and the bird'll have a cosmo. Don't dally about, alright?"

Laurie kept slingin' that smart-arse smirk, firing back, "You got it, bossman. No dramas."

As Laurie shoved off to make the drinks, he muttered a grubby plan under his breath.

"And I'll bung in a special little gobby for the tart. Moll."

Returning with the drinks, Laurie handed them to Tyde, who took advantage of the moment to discuss a more serious matter.

"Oi, can I ask you sumfink serious for a mo?" Tyde said, his tone shifting.

Laurie played along all formal-like, "You know it, your lordship."

Tyde, not having' any of Laurie's lip, got straight to it.

"Aight, cheeky git. Wanna chat about Gia for a tick."

Laurie leaned in, keen as a bean, "Oh yeah? What's the goss on Gia then?"

Meanwhile, Charlotte patiently waited at their table, assuming Tyde was just casually chatting with a random bartender while ordering their drinks. Tyde expressed his concern about Gia's recent behavior.

"What's been goin' on wiv 'er lately? She's actin' proper weird, innit?" Tyde said, furrowin' his brow.

Laurie waved off Tyde's whinge in a stroppy tone, "Pfft, nothin'! She's just out sharkin' around, bein' a single sheila enjoyin' herself. Don't get your nuts in a tangle, Tyde!"

Tyde, not convinced, laid out his observations.

"Look, I know that ain't 'er, she never used to go out datin' n'all like this before. She's a totally different bird than the one I knew."

Laurie slyly suggested another angle, "Well Tyde, people move on, they wanna live large, and find their match eventually, right? Maybe she's just tryin' somethin' new, switchin' up her datin' game."

Tyde's mood brightened, with a shit eating grin as he departed from Laurie and the bar, holding the drinks for himself and Charlotte.

He whispered to Charlotte, his voice filled with mischief.

"Here we go, our bevvies are ere."

Suppressing his grin behind his hand, Tyde approached the table where Charlotte was patiently waiting.

With a charming smile, he presented the drinks.

"Your knight in shining armour returned wiv the elixirs, m'lady."

Charlotte smiled, her eyes twinkling with amusement.

"Cheers Tyde. You always know 'ow to liven fings up, don't ya?"

As Tyde took his seat, he strategically positioned himself to have a clear view of Chris and me. My back was turned to him, and he could fully observe Chris's expressions.

He muttered to Charlotte, his voice low n' conspiratorial.

"Show's about to begin, innit?"

Charlotte remained entirely clueless, engrossed in their conversation.

She chuckled, her curiosity piqued.

"What are you muttering about, Tyde?"

He waved it off, his eyes never leaving our table.

"Just takin' in the vibes, my lovely."

Looking to Charlotte, Tyde relished the unfolding drama before him, convinced that I was none the wiser.

With newfound knowledge of my dating roster, Tyde's interest was piqued, and he contemplated joining the ranks. As he devised a plan to secure a spot on that list, he engaged in an internal dialogue.

Thinking to himself, he mused, "Now I know about Gia's pull-a-bird routine, maybe it's time I joined the lads' club. Gonna need some proper punt for that."

He envisioned proposing a no-strings-attached arrangement, emphasizing the desire for intimacy without the complications of romance or traditional dating.

Muttering to himself, he plotted, "Keep it casual, Tyde. No birds, no lovey-dovey rubbish, just a bit of fancy stuff. We've got wicked chemistry whenever we graft together, so why not explore that connection on the uppers?"

Armed with this plan, Tyde set out to navigate the complexities of proposing such an unconventional arrangement to me, hoping to add a unique chapter to our dynamic.

Chris and I exited the restaurant, greeted by a wall of flashing cameras from the paparazzi.

"Gia, Gia, look this way!" one of them shouted, trying to capture my attention.

"Chris, over here!" another called out, hoping for the perfect shot.

We navigated through the chaos, and a valet pulled up a

sleek custom Ferrari for us.

Chris held the car door open for me, his voice filled with excitement.

"Y'all ready to skedaddle?"

I smiled, sliding into the passenger seat. "Always."

Chris, displaying his skillful driving, maneuvered the Ferrari through the paparazzi frenzy, smoothly escaping the chaos.

He leaned over to me, his eyes sparkling with mischief.

"Want me to crank up the tunes?"

I grinned, reaching for the auxiliary cable.

"Absolutely."

I selected Maeta's soulful tunes, setting a relaxed vibe for the ride.

"Maeta always hits the spot," I remarked, losing myself in the melodies.

Chris nodded, his appreciation evident.

"Good choice, sugar."

Immersed in the music, we enjoyed the ride, finding comfort in the slow jams as we approached my apartment building. Parking the Ferrari, we decided to linger a bit longer inside the car. Lowering the music to a reasonable volume, we engaged in conversation. I sensed a subtle desire from Chris to step inside my apartment. The lingering question hovered in the air. Did I want him to come inside? The moment held a mix of anticipation and uncertainty as we weighed the possibilities.

Feeling a mix of nerves and determination, I decided to invite Chris upstairs. I saw this as an opportunity to overcome my anxieties and prove something to myself.

Smiling nervously, I offered, "You can come inside for a minute if you want."

Chris, eager and perhaps a bit too quick for my liking, responded with enthusiasm.

"Aw shucks, sure thang!"

As we exited the car and headed towards my front door, the rock-solid feeling in my stomach persisted. The music turned off, and we ascended the stairs together. Unseen to Chris, I took a sharp inhale and exhale, marking a significant step in my dating journey. At the front door, I unlocked it for both of us.

Motioning to the living room, I tried to put him at ease.

"Please, make yourself at home."

Gracefully, I removed my shoes, and Chris followed suit behind me. We entered the living room, where I offered Chris a drink.

"Would you like anything to drink? I have some white wine," I said, my voice steady despite the nerves fluttering in my chest.

Chris accepted the offer, making his way to the couch. As he looked around, he complimented me on my place.

"You got yourself a real nice lil' place here." he remarked, his eyes taking in the surroundings.

His gaze settled on a picture hanging on the wall, featuring Tyde and me from our early dating days. I returned from the kitchen, I noticed his attention and felt compelled to explain.

My voice took on a somber tone.

"That's just someone I used to know."

Chris nodded slowly, understanding the implications.

He asked gently, "Special somebody, I reckon?"

Meeting his gaze, I opened up, the words spilling from my lips.

"Yes, I thought he was going to be my forever. Anyway, on to better topics."

I quickly shifted the mood, shaking off the somber atmosphere and steering the conversation towards a happier note.

Eager to shift the conversation to more comfortable territory, I steered it towards Chris's hobbies beyond being a pro baseball player.

"So, aside from dominating the baseball field, what are your hobbies?" I asked, genuine curiosity in my voice.

Chris, downplaying his interests, responded nonchalantly.

"Oh just cookin', tendin' to the garden, advisin' the youngins at the rec club. You know, same ol' same ol'."

Realizing I hadn't explored many hobbies lately, I quickly came up with a fabricated answer.

Smiling, I replied, "I love to cook, and dog walking on the weekends is my thing."

But my internal thoughts betrayed the truth.

"If only he knew the truth—my weekends are all about going on dates when I'm free because work consumes every other hour of my day."

We continued chatting about lighter topics like our favorite shows, making our way through two bottles of wine. With Chris in no condition to drive, the conversation took a more intimate turn. Our hands subtly intertwined as we delved deeper into conversation. Soon, not only our hands but also our legs and arms became entangled.

As the chemistry intensified, we found ourselves making out on my couch, the shared connection evolving beyond surface-level discussions into something more passionate.

Now seated on Chris's lap, I continued our passionate make-out session. However, in the midst of it, I abruptly stopped, sensing that something didn't feel right.

Pausing, I voiced my hesitation.

"Chris, can we slow down a bit?"

Chris, attuned to my discomfort, picked up on my hesitation and reassured me.

"Course, Gia. We can take thangs at whatever pace suits you best, darlin'," he said, his voice gentle and understanding.

Respecting my boundaries, I climbed off his lap, and we transitioned into a more laid-back position on my couch, opting for a comforting cuddle. We spent the rest of the night engaged in light-hearted conversations, steering clear of serious topics.

As the evening unfolded, our chatter continued until the conversation faded into the background, and we both drifted off to sleep on my cozy couch, finding comfort in each other's presence.

As the morning sun painted our content faces with a warm glow, Chris and I woke up, both visibly pleased with the date we shared.

He smiled, his eyes still heavy with sleep.

"Last night was real nice. We ought to do that again

sometime."

I grinned, mirroring his enthusiasm.

"Absolutely, for sure. I had an amazing time."

Chris playfully held me to the promise.

"You can bank on that, sugah."

With that, Chris cheerfully walked backwards over to the front door, disappearing through the door, jogged down the stairs and swiftly entered his car. I remained on the couch, basking in the bliss of the previous night.

Meanwhile, lost in the afterglow, I didn't realize the passing time. The jarring blare of my phone's alarm sliced through the peaceful morning like a hot knife. I jolted upright, disorientation rapidly gave way to a cold slap of realization.

"Shit! Laurie..." I hissed, stomach plummeting as I saw the time glaring in bold, accusatory numbers. Our brunch date - the one he'd been excitedly nattering about for a week - was supposed to start in twenty minutes.

I launched myself up in a flurry of tangled limbs and muttered curses. My head spun as I grabbed wildly for clothes, dressing in a frenetic whirlwind of fabric and panicked gulps of air.

The apartment was a wasteland of clutter and scattered belongings in my haste. I snagged my purse from the floor, its contents spilling all over with a dull clatter as I sprinted for the door. Toothbrush still wedged in my mouth, knotted hair in a disarray, I must have looked utterly debauched to any witnessing neighbors. But there was no time for primping or shame - only the singular drive to make it to the restaurant before Laurie left in an apocalyptic storm of fury.

I bounded down the front steps two at a time, nearly kissing concrete as my ankle rolled precariously. The frantic pounding of blood drowned out all coherent thoughts, reducing my world to a laser-focused quest for transportation and averting total friendship immolation.

My trembling fingers were a blur across the glitching rideshare app as I gulped in precious pints of morning air. The digital countdown mocked me with every agonizing second that ticked by, visions of Laurie's scathing wrath swimming behind my eyes. I had to get there, I had to-

"There ya are, ya galah!"

The familiar voice sliced through my panicked spiral like a bolt of lightning. I whipped around to see the owner striding towards me, arms crossed over his chest in a perfect archetype of annoyed nonchalance. Laurie's piercing gaze raked over my bedraggled appearance as one perfectly sculpted brow arched in silent judgment.

"I...uh...I'm so sorry, I got hung up and completely lost track of..." I trailed off, words failing me as heat flooded my cheeks.

"Uh huh," he deadpanned, clearly unmoved by my embarrassed floundering. "Well now I've tracked down your bogan arse, can we pleeease go get those cinnamon scrolls before they're all gone?"

The familiar spark of our easygoing banter began thawing the icy coils of shame and dread in my chest. A wobbly grin tugged at the corners of my mouth as I straightened, offering my arm with an exaggerated flourish.

"Lead the way, your highness."

As we strolled off towards the brunch rush, I made a silent vow to be more diligent. Laurie's friendship was a precious gem - one I needed to cherish with unwavering commitment. Even if it meant setting a few more alarms from here on out.

CHAPTER 9
BEGIN THE PLAY

Tyde

Charlotte snuggled closer to me on the couch, her head resting on my shoulder as the movie played on the screen. Her hair tickled my chin, and I could smell the faint scent of her vanilla shampoo.

"This is nice, isn't it? Just us, a movie, and some quality time," she murmured, her voice soft and content.

I mumbled a half-hearted agreement, my mind already drifting elsewhere.

"Uh-huh, smashing."

As the movie continued, Charlotte's clinginess became more apparent. She draped her arm across my chest, giggling at every mildly amusing scene. Her laughter grated on my nerves, and I found myself clenching my jaw in annoyance.

"I love this movie. So glad I picked it," she gushed, nuzzling her face into the crook of my neck.

I forced a smile, my voice devoid of enthusiasm.

"Yeah, brilliant. Top notch."

But even as the words left my lips, I couldn't shake the growing sense of unease that had settled in the pit of my stomach. Charlotte's affectionate gestures, once endearing, now felt suffocating. Her presence, once a source of comfort, had become a weight on my shoulders.

As she clung on like a limpet, tracing circles on my chest, my mind went on a right wander. Cast me back to the start of us, when her touch could knock me for six, and her laugh was like the dulcet tones of angels. But now, sat here with her draped around me like a bad case of the 'flu, I couldn't help but ask myself some right corkers.

What was I on about, picking her as me missus? Blinded by the birds, by the way she used to look at me like I was Father Christmas with a bottomless sack of prezzies? Or was I just a right mug, desperate for a bit of company in a world that felt about as friendly as a swarm of wasps? Had I settled for a cup of lukewarm tea when I was after a flaming hot curry?

The questions swirled in my mind, a dizzying whirlpool of doubt and uncertainty. I tried to focus on the movie, on the feel of Charlotte's warm body pressed against mine, but it was no use. The realization had taken root, and there was no going back.

Perhaps Charlotte and I weren't as compatible as I had once thought. Perhaps the spark that had once ignited between us had fizzled out, leaving only the ashes of a once-promising relationship.

I shifted uncomfortably on the couch, suddenly feeling trapped by the weight of Charlotte's expectations, by the way she looked at me with those adoring eyes. I knew I couldn't keep pretending, couldn't keep going through the motions of a relationship that no longer felt right.

But how could I tell her? How could I break her heart and shatter the happily ever after she'd so carefully built?

I closed my eyes, letting out a heavy sigh. The movie continued to play in the background, but I barely noticed. My mind was a tumultuous sea of conflicting emotions, of guilt and regret and a desperate longing for something more.

I knew I had to confront the truth, had to face the reality of our relationship head-on. But for now, I simply sat there, my arm around Charlotte's shoulders, my heart heavy with the knowledge that everything was about to change.

The future stretched out before me, a blank canvas waiting to be painted with the colors of my desires. And as much as it pained me to admit it, I knew that Charlotte was no longer a part of that picture.

I took a deep breath, steeling myself for the difficult conversation that lay ahead. It wouldn't be easy, but I knew it was necessary. I had to be true to myself, had to follow the path that called to me, even if it meant leaving behind the comfort of the familiar.

For in the end, that was all any of us could do. Keep moving forward, keep searching for the love and passion and connection that we all craved. And maybe, just maybe,

I would find it someday, in the arms of someone who set my soul on fire, who made me feel alive in ways I had never thought possible.

But for now, I simply sat there, my mind a whirlwind of conflicting emotions, my heart heavy with the weight of the realization that had finally dawned on me. The future was uncertain, but one thing was clear. It was time for a change, time to take a leap of faith and see where the winds of fate would carry me.

Charlotte's nimble fingers made quick work of my belt buckle, the metallic clink echoing in the charged silence. My breath caught as she popped the button of my jeans, her eyes dark with promise. I knew I should stop this, knew I was treading dangerous waters. But the ache in my body overrode the warning bells in my head.

I watched, transfixed, as she slowly lowered my zipper, tooth by agonizing tooth. The rasp of metal on metal was obscenely loud, a soundtrack to my rapidly fraying control. Charlotte's gaze never left mine, a wicked smile playing at the corners of her painted lips.

With a brazen tug, she yanked my jeans and boxer briefs down in one fluid motion. Cool air kissed fevered skin and I hissed through my teeth. There was no tenderness, no romance in the way she gripped me, stroking with practiced precision. I was just a means to an end, a scratching post for her own desires. The knowledge should have repulsed me. It only inflamed me further.

I surrendered to pure sensation as Charlotte worked me with expert touches, sinking into the mindless oblivion of physical pleasure. But even as my body responded, my heart remained untouched. Numb. This was base gratification, nothing more.

Passion crested, consuming me in a blaze of almost painful ecstasy before receding like a fading ember. Charlotte smirked, triumphant, as she withdrew with a final provocative squeeze. I fought the urge to flinch at the coldness in her gaze. We both knew the score. I was just another notch on her bedpost, a forgettable conquest.

As we righted our clothes in silence, the emptiness came rushing back, a black hole yawning wide in my chest. Shame chased on its heels, acrid and cloying. Using Charlotte, letting her use me – it should have made me feel something, anything. Instead I just felt hollow. Dirty.

With a final empty smile, she sauntered out, hips swaying. The room suddenly felt too small, the air too thin.

I needed a scalding shower. Needed to scrub the evidence of my weakness from my skin until it was raw and aching. But I knew no amount of soap could wash away the bitter aftertaste of self-loathing.

This was what my life had become. A series of meaningless encounters, cheap thrills to numb the gaping void within. I was a ghost, going through the motions, chasing fleeting highs to forget how broken I truly was.

As I sat there, surrounded by the deafening silence of my apartment and Charlotte lazily lying on the couch, the truth hit me like a freight train. I couldn't keep running forever. Sooner or later, I'd have to face the demons nipping at my heels. The question was, would I have the strength to slay them? Or would I let them consume me whole, until there was nothing left but a shell of the man I used to be?

—

Charlotte lingered at my doorstep, her eyes sparkling with contentment as she smiled up at me.

"Thanks for a lovely night, Tyde."

I plastered on a hollow grin, eager to put this awkward evening behind me.

"Yeah, alright. Cheers, see ya.'"

As I walked her to the door, Charlotte leaned in for a parting kiss. I swiftly turned my cheek, her lips grazing my skin in a scorching brand - a stark reminder of my catastrophic lapse in judgment for inviting her over.

The instant she was gone, I made a beeline for the shower. Scalding jets pounded my flesh as I scrubbed away the night's grime and remorse. Yet no amount of searing water could purge the gnawing unease festering in my gut.

The shrill shriek of my phone sliced through the morning quiet. Jackson's name flashed insistently on the screen, and I swiped to answer with an irritated grunt.

"What!"

Jackson's voice crackled with excitement.

"Hey Tyde! How about grabbing some lunch? Just a casual meet, eh?"

I narrowed my eyes, instantly suspicious of his motives. He was undoubtedly fishing for details about the precarious situation with Gia. The notion of being interrogated about my tangled love life added scorching fuel to my already combustible mood.

"Fine, whatever. Where?"

"The usual spot! Let's catch up."

I ended the call with an eye roll. Jackson's intentions were transparent - he'd relentlessly pry until I caved about every torrid, regrettable detail of last night's ill-advised tryst.

"Well Jackson," I muttered, "Charlotte wasn't exactly a highlight reel for my love life."

Later, sprawled across from each other in our usual haunt, Jackson's eyes blew wide as I recounted the sordid events.

"You did what? Charlotte again? Don't tell me you got tangled up with her again, bud," he sputtered in disbelieving accusation.

Defenses flaring, I fired back, "No way, mate! It was just some messed up payback after seeing Gia out with another bloke."

Jackson's jaw went slack. "Gia's dating around now? News to me."

I nodded tightly."Yeah, she's apparently working her way through the whole squad. And I want to be on that list."

A sly grin split his face as the implications sank in. "No way! You want another shot? Count me in - let's get you back in the game!"

Leaning forward urgently, I laid it out.

"We need a plan sharpish. Tomorrow's the big All-Star game after-party, and I need to pull off something massive to get Gia rethinking us."

Jackson rubbed his palms together, eyes glinting with mischief.

"Then let's get you pulling some serious smooth moves, Tyde. It's your best shot to get her interested and back on that roster by the end of the night."

I gave a grim nod, steeling my resolve as the daunting

challenge stretched before me. Little time remained to show Gia I was still the man she deserved. But as Jackson enthusiastically strategized, a pernicious voice whispered doubts.

Was I truly ready to fight for her? Prepared to confront all the stinging mistakes and lingering demons to prove my worthiness? I squeezed my eyes shut, feeling the weight of my emotional baggage crushing down.

"But you gotta give it a go," a voice chimed in.

With a steadying breath, I met Jackson's eager gaze head-on, newfound determination blazing in my veins. "Alright, let's crack on. I'll show up and get myself properly on Gia's roster by tomorrow night."

"Atta boy!" Jackson clapped me on the shoulder, grinning widely. "We've got this covered."

As the details crystallized, a fragile flicker of hope burned through the middle of self-doubt. A chance at redemption, at reclaiming the soul-igniting love Gia and I once shared, not for the hope of love but something else.

The woman who I want to get to know, this new version.

Charlotte

OUTSIDE - TYDE'S PENTHOUSE

I stepped out of Tyde's apartment building, the cool night air a stark contrast to the warmth inside. The city roared with the morning rush. With a sigh, I pulled out my phone and dialed the familiar number. I started to stroll on the pavement to walk through this conversation already assuming to get scolded.

"Charlotte." My father's voice crackled through the speaker, as cold and unyielding as ever. "I trust you have news?"

I rolled my eyes, grateful he couldn't see me. "Yes, Daddy," I drawled, infusing my voice with sugary sweetness. "Your prodigal daughter has been quite busy. Malcolm is developing the images and videos."

"I should hope so," he snapped. "I let you lead this plan because I was sure this will not fall back on me! I didn't raise you to waste time."

I bit back a retort. He hadn't raised me at all – that had been left to an army of nannies and finishing schools. But I knew better than to voice that particular grievance.

"Well?" he demanded. "Don't keep me in suspense."

I leaned against the railing, my manicured nails tapping an impatient rhythm.

"If you must know, I've spent the evening with Tyde Wright."

There was a pause, and I could practically hear the gears

turning in his head. "The athlete?" he asked, a hint of interest creeping into his tone.

"The very same," I purred. "It seems there might be… potential for reconciliation with moving that gold digger out of his life. And you get all of *Incline Medias'* stocks , content library, IP, everything. It's a win-win! Gia will be gone from my life, you will get a son in law. I will get the cover of the magazine, and you will be head of all things *Incline* instead of that freak Edith. This is perfecto!"

"Excellent." The word was clipped, businesslike. "He always was the most suitable of your dalliances. A fine match for the family name."

I closed my eyes, swallowing the bitterness that rose in my throat. Of course, that was all that mattered to him – status, wealth, the almighty family legacy.

"Now listen carefully, Charlotte," he continued, his voice dropping to a conspiratorial whisper. "This is your chance. I want you to secure this relationship, do you understand? Make that boy propose, and do it quickly."

He chuckled, a sound devoid of any real mirth.

"Oh, my dear. And by bringing my *Incline* into the fold, there will be a substantial… shall we say, bonus… waiting for you."

My heart raced at the thought of that money, of the freedom it could bring. But the price… I pushed the doubt aside. This was what I had been trained for, after all.

"Of course, Daddy," I cooed. "I won't let you down."

"See that you don't, Charlotte" he said, his tone leaving no room for argument. "Remember, success is everything for the Astor's. We can't afford any embarrassment to the family."

"I know," I said quietly, my free hand clenching into a fist. "You've made that abundantly clear."

He grunted, satisfied. "Good girl. Keep me informed."

The line went dead, and I was left alone with the city morning and my churning thoughts. This was the game, and I was a master player. With a deep breath, I straightened my shoulders and plastered on a smile. Time to get back to work.

—

NHL ALL-STAR PREGAME PRACTICE

The cavernous arena felt like hallowed ground as Tyde and I took our positions behind the seamless curved glass separating us from the pristine ice. A reverent hush had fallen over the expansive space, the distant murmurs of the gathering crowd muted to a low thrum.

My breath plumed in vaporous bursts, mingling with Tyde's as we checked our camera gear one final time. Excitement crackled between us, a tightly coiled energy ready to detonate at any moment. Tyde's eyes shone with unbridled enthusiasm, gleaming like gemstones freshly plucked from frost-dusted mines.

"This is gonna be mental," he murmured, gaze locked on the yawning tunnel where the players would emerge. "Get sorted."

As if on cue, the first wave of helmeted figures strode onto the rink with purposeful strides. The thunderous cracks of stick against ice reverberated through the barrier, the stinging chill of their exhalations buffeting us in frigid waves. Like an advancing battalion, they took their warm-up laps in a flashing blur of sharpened blades and powerful skating strides.

These were the gods of winter's battlefield - warriors forged in brutal grace and elegance, honed to athletic perfection through relentless sacrifice. Tyde and I moved in synchronized tandem, cameras raised to immortalize every second of their sacred rituals.

One by one, the players peeled off into drills, muscles coiled with intense focus. The air thickened with the metallic tang of frozen sweat and vigorous exertion. Bodies collided and shattered apart in controlled chaos, carving intricate paths with a perpetual teetering between agility and violence.

A rogue puck ricocheted off the glass, its hollow thunk jangling my nerves. I met the wild eyes of a seasoned veteran through the cage of his mask - tanned, weathered face mapped with a crisscross of battle scars. He flashed the barest hint of a savage grin before wheeling off to rejoin the fray.

Despite the punishing toll this unforgiving game exacted, these warriors embodied a pure, childlike joy - the magic of chasing an indelible dream balanced on a blade's edge. In that crackling sphere of sound and fury, I understood the inexplicable lure of this frozen realm. An intricate dance poised between transcendent beauty and sheer violence.

This was more than a game. This was an alchemical ritual where strength, speed and skill were transmuted into something sublime - a sacrament we'd been allowed to document. Tyde and I lost ourselves in capturing their athletic artistry, fingers numbed by the biting chill yet burning with renewed vigor.

When the piercing shriek of a whistle shattered the trance, we were left breathless yet utterly invigorated. Ready to showcase the magic and put the world on notice - the gods had descended to make their opening gambits.

—

BLEACHERS

The chill of the arena seeped into my bones as I sat in the empty bleachers, watching the NHL players finish their morning practice. The scrape of skates on ice and the sharp clack of sticks against pucks echoed through the cavernous space. But as the last player left the ice, leaving nothing but pristine white in their wake, I sensed a presence beside me.

Tyde.

Of all the empty seats in this massive arena, he'd chosen to plant himself right next to me. I studiously ignored him, focusing instead on unwrapping the protein bar I'd brought. From the corner of my eye, I caught the flash of a takeout container as Tyde pulled out a salad.

We sat in uncomfortable silence, the soft crinkle of my wrapper and the quiet clink of his fork against plastic the only sounds. The emptiness of the arena pressed in around us, making the air feel thick and heavy.

"Remember when you used to come to all my practices?" Tyde's voice, low and tinged with nostalgia, broke the silence.

I couldn't help the small smile that tugged at my lips.

"Yeah," I said softly, still not looking at him. "I do."

"I'd always spot you, you know. No matter where you were sitting." There was a hint of that boyish charm in his voice, the kind that used to make my heart skip a beat.

I finally turned to face him, seeing the ghost of a smirk playing on his lips.

"I used to hang out with all the other WAGs," I said, the bitterness I thought I'd buried creeping into my voice.

"They were... nice."

Tyde's smirk faded. "But not after..."

"Not after," I confirmed, my throat tightening. "Once the news broke about us, it was like I'd never existed. Calls, texts – nothing but silence."

Tyde's eyes clouded with regret. He set his salad aside, leaning forward with his elbows on his knees.

"I was a mess after we split, Gia. Threw myself into hockey like a man possessed."

I raised an eyebrow, waiting for him to continue.

"I'd be here until three, four in the morning some days. Pushing myself to the brink, ready to set records left and right." He let out a humorless chuckle. "For what? I told myself it was to be the best, but deep down..."

"You were hoping I'd see you on the news," I finished for him, realization dawning. "That I'd come to a game, maybe."

Tyde nodded, unable to meet my eyes.

I sighed, feeling a complicated mix of emotions swirling in my chest.

"I cut hockey out of my life completely after we ended things. This job with Incline, the NHL partnership – it's the first time I've let myself near the sport since."

The truth of my words hung heavy between us. Tyde's shoulders slumped slightly.

"Maybe," I said quietly, "you weren't trying to prove anything to me at all. Maybe it was always about proving something to yourself."

The words struck home. I saw it in the way Tyde's jaw clenched, in the barely perceptible flinch he couldn't quite hide.

I stood abruptly, needing to escape the suffocating weight of our shared history. Without another word, I strode towards the double doors leading out of the arena. The cool metal of the handle was a welcome shock against my palm as I pushed my way out, leaving Tyde.

Tyde & Gria

Tyde and I came from different places in the building after watching the practice. We found ourselves arriving at the building simultaneously. As our eyes met, an unspoken challenge ignited between us. With a playful glint, we adjusted our steps and began an impromptu race to the entrance to foyer, each trying to outpace the other.

I smirked, my voice laced with determination. "You're not getting there before me, Tyde."

He grinned, his eyes sparkling with cheek. "Oh, we'll see about that."

As one quickened their pace, the other followed suit, creating a comical speed competition. However, the playful race took an unexpected turn. In our haste, Tyde accidentally bumped into me a bit too forcefully, causing me to stumble and land in the nearby bushes.

Annoyed, I glared up at him from my impromptu seat among the foliage.

"Seriously, Tyde?"

Undeterred, Tyde reached the building doors first, opening them with a flourish as if stepping into a royal palace. He glided inside, leaving me in the bushes, amused but clearly unimpressed.

I smirked, sweeping leaves from my tasseled coily hair as I extricate myself from the greenery.

"Smooth, Prince Charming."

With a good-natured grin, I brushed off the remaining twigs, ready to face the day despite the unexpected detour.

Inside the office, Tyde greeted me with a cheeky grin.

"Morning, Gia."

I met his gaze, feeling smug.

"Good morning, Tyde. Feeling victorious today?"

He grinned, waving his script cheekily.

"Always. Just handling my script like a proper pro."

I raised an eyebrow, teasing him.

"Well, I hope you've improved since our last run-in."

Tyde's eyes sparkled with amusement.

"You might be in for a surprise."

As we exchanged playful banter, I couldn't help but notice the way Tyde's gaze lingered on me, as if remembering our recent encounter in front of the building. It added an extra layer of amusement to our morning interactions.

Later, as we prepared for the big show, Tyde turned to me with a smile.

"Ready for the big do?"

I nodded, feeling the excitement building within me.

"Absolutely. Let's make this All-Star broadcast memorable."

We prepped for the day and presented the All-Star program with excellence, creating a captivating broadcast that went off with a bang. As the game approached, we smoothly transitioned to the game presenters, officially signing off.

Tyde leaned back in his chair, a satisfied grin on his face.

"Right, that went a treat."

I sighed with relief, nodding in agreement.

"Agreed. Now, let's enjoy the game."

With the newsroom no longer in production, I kicked off

my shoes, prompting a smirk from Tyde as he noticed. We settled in at the desk, watching the game together through the glass behind us. The atmosphere became nostalgic, reminiscent of old times when we used to cheer for hockey games on Tyde's couch.

Tyde cheered, his voice filled with excitement.

"Go Jackson! Go Lorenz!"

We shared a moment of camaraderie, cheering on our friends just like in the past. I knew Tyde often watched games to study other teams and players' styles, and I couldn't help but admire his dedication.

The game unfolded, and Lorenz's team emerged victorious in the All-Star game, bringing a sense of triumph and celebration. The final buzzer sounded around 6:15 pm.

I grinned, turning to Tyde with excitement.

"What a game! Lorenz nailed it!"

Tyde nodded, a wistful smile on his face.

"He sure did"

But as I watched him, I noticed a distant look in his eyes, as if his mind had wandered elsewhere.

"Something on your mind, Tyde?"

He sighed, his shoulders slumping slightly.

"Just missin' the game, innit? The buzz, the ice, the mateship."

I leaned in, curious.

"You miss playing?"

Tyde nodded, his gaze fixed on the empty rink.

"More than I reckoned, yeah. Watchin' my mates out there, it's rough bein' stuck on the sidelines, even if it's for the telly."

I listened intently, trying to understand the depth of his emotions.

"Wow. Is this the first real conversation we are having? Well…I have to say I empathize."

He opened up, he was a little shocked at how easy it was to do so. But then again, not because it's Gia. His voice tinged with a mix of nostalgia and sadness.

"Uh, Thanks. I realized right before my injury. It ain't just the game itself, is it? It's the bond with the team, the thrill of the scrap. Now I feel like I'm watchin' them live the dream I had to give up."

I reached out, placing a comforting hand on his arm.

"It sounds like you're carrying a heavy load, Tyde."

He smirked, trying to lighten the mood.

"Retirement wasn't exactly on the cards, and it ain't all sunshine and roses like I thought it'd be. But hey, I'm givin' it a go. Maybe it's just a phase, innit?"

I offered a supportive smile, my voice soft.

"You're allowed to miss it, Tyde. It doesn't make you any less of who you are."

Tyde's eyes met mine, a flicker of vulnerability in their depths.

"I appreciate that, Gia. Sometimes it feels like you're the only one who clocks the changes in me."

I squeezed his arm gently, my words filled with understanding. "Change isn't always a bad thing, Tyde. Maybe it's just a different chapter, not the end of the story."

He smiled, genuine gratitude in his expression.

"Cheers, Gia. Means a lot more than you know."

As Tyde opened up about his struggle with retirement and missing hockey, I offered my genuine attention and understanding, creating a space for him to share his feelings. The conversation allowed us to connect on a deeper level, and I could see the wheels turning in Tyde's mind as he pondered whether these changes were for the better or worse in his journey beyond the hockey rink.

Tyde muttered quietly under his breath, "It's not just the hockey I miss, is it?" before clearing his throat. I didn't quite catch his words, and Tyde promptly brushed it off, pretending like he hadn't said anything.

He smirked, trying to change the subject.

"Alright, reckon we should get a move on, eh?"

I nodded, gathering my things.

"Yeah."

Tyde paused, an idea forming in his mind.

"Need a lift home?"

I looked at him, surprised by the offer.

"Oh, you don't have to. I can grab a cab or something."

He shook his head, insisting.

"Don't be daft. My car's parked round the corner. I can give you a kip."

I hesitated, weighing the options.

"Well, if it's not too much trouble..."

Tyde grinned, his eyes sparkling' with something' I couldn't quite suss out.

I smiled, grateful for his kindness.

"Alright then, thanks. I appreciate it."

As we gathered our belongings and observed the departing crowd, I couldn't shake the feeling that Tyde's offer wasn't entirely innocent. While his offer seemed genuine, I suspected that he had an ulterior motive - to be close to me and subtly advance his plan, whatever that might be.

But for now, I decided to accept his offer, curiosity getting the better of me. As we walked out of the building together, I couldn't help but wonder what the rest of the evening had in store for us, and whether Tyde's intentions were as pure as he claimed.

—

As we cruised down the highway, the warm glow of the sunset painted the sky in hues of orange and pink, casting a soft light over the river below. Tyde reached for the radio, his fingers deftly twisting the dial until the smooth sounds of R&B filled the car.

Suddenly, the opening notes of *"Waterfall"* by Yebba floated through the speakers, announced by the DJ with a flourish. I felt my heart skip a beat, recognizing the familiar melody that had once been our song.

I stole a glance at Tyde, wondering if he remembered the significance of the tune. His eyes met mine for a brief moment, a flicker of something unreadable in their depths before he turned his attention back to the road.

As we pulled up to my apartment, Tyde turned off the car, the sudden silence hanging heavy between us. He turned to me, his gaze searching.

"Fancy goin' to the after-do tonight?" he asked, his voice casual yet laced with an undertone of curiosity.

I hesitated, my mind still reeling from the unexpected trip down memory lane.

"I don't know if I'm up for it," I admitted, my voice soft and uncertain.

Tyde raised an eyebrow, a smirk tugging at the corner of his lips.

"Really? Got a corker of a date or somethin'?" ("Shot me a look" for gave me a look, "corker"

I felt a flare of annoyance at his assumption, my defenses rising instinctively.

"No, I just…"

But before I could finish my thought, Tyde leaned in, his eyes gleaming with mischief.

"Come on, Gia, it'll be a right laugh. You deserve a night on the tiles."

I sighed, gathering my things as I prepared to exit the car. The temptation to accept his invitation was strong, but I couldn't shake the feeling that there was more to his offer than met the eye.

"Thanks for the ride, Tyde. I'll consider it," I said, my voice carefully neutral as I opened the door and stepped out into the cool evening air.

Tyde rolled his eyes, a playful grin on his face as he called out through the open window.

"See you later then!"

I shook my head, a smile tugging at my lips despite myself as I climbed the stairs to my apartment. I could feel Tyde's gaze on my back, burning into me like a brand as he drove off into the fading light.

As I fumbled with my keys, my mind raced with the possibilities of the evening ahead. The after party, with its promise of music and laughter and dancing, was tempting. But the thought of facing Tyde again, of navigating the complex web of our past and present, made my stomach twist with nerves.

I pushed open the door to my apartment, the familiar scent of home washing over me like a balm. I kicked off my shoes, sinking onto the couch with a heavy sigh.

The memories of our song, of the countless nights we had spent wrapped in each other's arms, flooded my mind. I closed my eyes, letting the bittersweet nostalgia wash over me like a wave.

But even as I lost myself in the past, I couldn't shake the nagging feeling that Tyde's invitation was more than just a friendly gesture. There was something in the way he looked at me, in the way his voice had dropped an octave when he spoke of the party, that made me wonder if he had ulterior motives.

I groaned, burying my face in my hands. The thought of facing Tyde again, of navigating the minefield of our history, was daunting. But a part of me, a small, traitorous part, couldn't help but wonder what the night might bring.

I stood up, my mind made up.

GIA'S BEDROOM

I glanced at the clock, the glowing numbers staring back at me – 8:45 pm. Sprawled out on my smooth bed, I was engrossed in an episode of Gilmore Girls, a bowl of popcorn nestled beside me and a can of Coca-Cola within reach. The familiar banter of Lorelai and Rory filled the room, providing a comforting escape from the outside world.

Suddenly, the shrill ring of my phone pierced the air, causing me to jump. I reached for the device, my eyes widening as I saw Laurie's name flashing on the caller ID – 9:30 pm. Laurie, my partner in crime and closest confidant, usually preferred texts to calls. The fact that he was ringing me at this hour set off alarm bells in my head.

I answered, my voice tinged with suspicion.

"Hey?"

The background noise of a loud party nearly drowned out Laurie's voice. I strained to hear him, pressing the phone closer to my ear.

"G, you gotta get down here tonight, pronto! The bass is pumpin' and the laughs are ripper!" Laurie shouted, his words barely audible over the thumping bass and raucous laughter.

Intrigued, I sat up straighter, my brow furrowing.

"I can't hear you, Laurie. Find a quieter spot."

There was a rustling sound, followed by the muffled thud of footsteps. I could picture Laurie weaving through the crowd, searching for a quieter corner.

Finally, his voice came through clearly, echoing off the walls of what I assumed was a hallway.

"It's the All-Star wrap-up barbie! Get ya arse over here!"

I blinked, surprised by the invitation. Thinking to myself, the fuck is Laurie doing there?

"No, I'm good. Not feeling it tonight," I said, my voice firm.

But Laurie was persistent, his tone taking on a pleading edge. "Come on, mate! We've been through a fair whack. Time to crack a coldie and celebrate!"

I sighed, my resolve starting to crumble.

Slowly, I got up from the bed, my mind already racing with the possibilities. What would I wear? How would I do my makeup? The questions swirled in my head as I made my way to the closet, my fingers skimming over the hangers as I searched for the perfect outfit.

"Alright, fine. But, just for a little while," I relented, unable to resist the pull of Laurie's enthusiasm.

I could practically hear his grin through the phone as he whooped with joy.

"Sweet! See ya soon, Gia. Don't muck around!"

With that, he hung up, leaving me standing in the middle of my room with a bemused smile on my face.

Despite my initial reluctance, I found myself getting excited as I applied my makeup, the familiar motions soothing my nerves. I lined my eyes with precision, swiped on a bold lip color, and stepped back to admire my handiwork in the mirror.

I looked good, I had to admit. The dress I had chosen hugged my curves in all the right places, and the heels I slipped on added an extra bit of height and confidence to my stride.

By the time I left my apartment and hailed a cab, the clock had already struck 10:20 pm. The city lights blurred past the window as the driver navigated the busy streets, the anticipation building in my chest with each passing block.

I couldn't help but wonder what the night had in store for me. Would I run into old friends, or make new ones? Would there be drama, or would the evening pass in a blur of laughter and good times?

As the cab pulled up to the venue, I took a deep breath, steeling myself for whatever lay ahead. I stepped out into the cool night air, the music already pulsing through the walls and spilling out onto the street.

With a final glance at my reflection in the cab's window, I squared my shoulders and made my way inside, ready to face whatever the night had in store for me.

—

MARQUEE

I had been at the wrap party for a few hours, low-key waiting and hoping for Gia to make an appearance. Positioned at my own VIP table with Jackson and Lorenz, we enjoyed constant bottle service and more. However, I found myself slumped at the table, seemingly babysitting a bottle of champagne, my thoughts consumed by Gia. The music blared, and despite the groupies surrounding the table, I hadn't paid any attention to the girls.

Grumbling under my breath, I muttered, "What's all this about what Gia wants? Blimey, I'm clued up, innit?"

Jackson raised an eyebrow, his voice laced with concern.

"Tyde, you gotta get your act together. Gia won't dig a sloppy drunk."

Lorenz nodded in agreement, his eyes fixed on me.

"Woah, what's going on with you, man? You're not yourself tonight."

I snatched a champagne bottle, my grip tightening around the neck.

"I know exactly what I'm doing, alright?"

In my haste, I accidentally spilled champagne on a girl standing nearby. She shrieked, her eyes wide with disbelief.

"What the hell!?"

I muttered to myself, my voice low and frustrated.

"Fantastic, just fantastic."

The girl stormed off with her friends, their heels clicking angrily against the floor. Jackson pointed at the retreating group, his voice stern.

"Tyde, you gotta ease off a bit, eh? You're hosing yourself down."

Lorenz chimed in, his tone teasing.

"Yeah, and that outfit just got trashed."

I rolled my eyes, my focus unwavering.

"Sod 'em, I don't care about them. Waiting for someone else, anyway."

As if on cue, an emerald jewel walked into the party, catching my eye. Gia made a dazzling entrance, adorned in an emerald mini shimmer dress that hugged her curves in all the right places. She paired it with sleek black lace-up heels and accented the look with silver jewelry that glittered under the lights.

Excitement coursed through my veins as I realized Gia had finally arrived. I knew I needed to sober up quickly to make a good impression.

"Right then! Time to sort yourselves out, lads. Got a lady to impress."

Gia navigated through the lively crowd, her eyes scanning the room in search of Laurie. She tried calling him, but he didn't seem to be answering his phone. Undeterred, Gia took a seat at the bar, ordering a drink while rhythmically swaying to the infectious beats of the reggaeton music.

The bartender approached her, a smile on his face.

"What can I get you?"

Gia returned the smile, her voice warm and inviting.

"A mojito, please."

As the bartender started preparing her drink, Gia muttered to herself, "Where is Laurie when you actually need him?"

She glanced around the party once more, scanning the crowd for any sign of her friend. Sighing, she mumbled, "Always so late, that one."

The bartender placed the mojito in front of Gia, the mint leaves and lime wedge adding a refreshing touch.

"Here you go. Enjoy!"

Gia took a sip, the cool liquid soothing her throat as she continued to scan the room. Suddenly, her gaze locked with none other than mine. At that moment, it seemed as if the entire party faded away, leaving only the two of us.

I teased Gia with a sly finger, motioning for her to join me. She rolled her eyes, mouthing a sharp "No" in response.

I smirked and chuckled, amused by her defiance. Standing up, I adjusted my suit and jewelry, then confidently strode toward the bar where Gia was seated. She was lost in her drink, but I could sense her awareness of my presence behind her.

Taking a seat beside her, I waited as the bartender immediately slid me my usual drink without a word. For a moment, silence hung between us. I broke it with a smug remark, still facing forward.

"So you did decide to show your face after all? What made you change your tune?"

Gia responded without looking at me, her voice cool and collected.

"More like, who changed it?"

Taken aback and slightly irritated, I assumed she had another date.

"Another date, eh? If you don't mind me asking, who's the mug this time?"

Gia caught onto my judgmental tone and swung her chair to face me, her eyes narrowed in a glare.

"Someone you used to know."

Before I could respond, Gia's phone buzzed with a text from Laurie, informing her about a VIP table. She stood up abruptly and headed in that direction. Like a lost puppy, I followed her, my curiosity piqued by her cryptic response.

As we weaved through the crowd, I couldn't help but

wonder who this mysterious person was. A twinge of jealousy tugged at my heart, but I pushed it aside, determined to unravel the truth behind Gia's words.

The party continued to pulse around us, the music thumping in time with my racing heart. I knew I had to play my cards right if I wanted to win Gia over, but the challenge only fueled my determination.

With each step, I drew closer to her, my mind racing with possibilities. Would this be the night I finally make my move? Or would Gia's mysterious companion thwart my plans?

Only time would tell, but one thing was certain – I wasn't going to let Gia slip through my fingers again. Not without a fight.

—

VIP SECTION

I could feel Tyde's presence behind me as I navigated through the crowded party, his footsteps echoing my own. Amusement danced in my eyes as I realized he was following me, unable to resist the pull of our unfinished conversation.

"'Old flame,' more like it," he said sarcastically, his voice cutting through the pulsing music.

I spotted Laurie at his table, surrounded by friends from his job. Their laughter and chatter filled the air, creating a warm and inviting atmosphere. Tyde continued to trail behind me, his agitation growing with each passing moment.

As I approached the VIP section, Tyde stood outside the rope, puzzled and frustrated. He watched as Laurie and I greeted each other warmly, our smiles bright and genuine. Unaware of Laurie's sexuality, Tyde's jealousy consumed him, his mind jumping to the conclusion that I was on a date with my best friend.

I took a seat next to Laurie, perhaps a little too close for Tyde's liking. Unable to contain his annoyance any longer, Tyde rushed into the section, pushing people aside in his haste to squeeze himself between us. The mood instantly shifted, tension crackling in the air like electricity.

"Hey, Tyde. What's got you all worked up?" I asked, trying to diffuse the situation with a light tone.

Tyde grumbled in response, his eyes narrowed and his jaw clenched. I leaned back in my seat, choosing to ignore his childish behavior for the rest of the night. My gaze wandered to the dance floor, watching as bodies swayed and moved to the pulsing beat.

I could feel Tyde's eyes on me, lazily tracing the side of my face. His stare was intense, burning into my skin like a brand. I tried to focus on the music, on the laughter and chatter of the people around us, but his presence was impossible to ignore.

Suddenly, I felt Tyde's warm breath against my ear, his lips brushing the sensitive skin as he whispered, "Fancy a dance?"

Sparks ignited within me, spreading through my body like wildfire. I wanted to resist, to push him away and continue my charade of indifference, but the temptation was too strong..

—

DANCE FLOOR

Just as I was about to reject him, Tyde stood up, his hand outstretched in a silent invitation. The opening notes of *"On and On"* by Tyla filled the air, the sensual melody wrapping around us like a casting.

I hesitated for a moment, my pride warring with my desire. But as I looked into Tyde's eyes, I saw a flicker of vulnerability, a glimpse of the man I once knew and loved.

With a sigh of resignation, I placed my hand in his, allowing him to lead me to the dance floor. As we began to sway to the music, our bodies moved in perfect sync, the tension between us melting away with each beat.

Tyde's hands rested on my hips, his touch sending shivers down my spine. I could feel the heat of his body, the strength of his muscles as he pulled me closer. We moved as one, lost in the rhythm and each other.

The world around us faded away, the people and the noise blurring into the background. In that moment, it was just the two of us, our bodies intertwined and our hearts beating in time.

I closed my eyes, letting the music wash over me. Tyde's scent enveloped me, a heady mixture of cologne and something distinctly him. It was intoxicating, drawing me in like a moth to a flame.

As the song reached its crescendo, Tyde spun me around, his hands guiding my movements with effortless grace. I felt weightless, my troubles and worries melting away in the heat of the moment.

But even as I lost myself in the dance, I couldn't shake the nagging feeling that this was only a temporary reprieve. Tyde and I had a complicated history, a tangle of emotions and unresolved issues that threatened to tear us apart at any moment.

I knew that once the music ended, once the spell was broken, we would have to face the reality of our situation. But for now, I allowed myself to enjoy the moment, to savor the feeling of being in his arms once again.

As the final notes of the song faded away, Tyde pulled me close, his forehead resting against mine. Our breaths mingled, our hearts racing in unison.

"Gia," he whispered, his voice rough with emotion.

I opened my eyes, meeting his gaze with a mixture of trepidation and longing. I knew that whatever happened next would change everything, for better or for worse.

But as I stood there, wrapped in his embrace, I realized that I was ready to face whatever challenges lay ahead. With Tyde by my side, I felt invincible, like I could take on the world and come out victorious.

And so, with a deep breath and a silent prayer, I stepped back into his arms, ready to dance the night away and see where the music would take us.

As the final notes of the song faded away, Tyde and I remained locked in each other's embrace, our bodies still swaying to the lingering rhythm. The heat between us was palpable, a simmering tension that threatened to boil over at any moment. It was as if we were the only two people on the dance floor, lost in a world of our own making.

I looked up at Tyde, my breath coming in short, ragged gasps.

"That was... intense."

He smirked, a glint flickering in his eyes.

"Don't you even know it."

The words hung in the air between us, a promise of something more. I could feel the weight of his gaze on me, the heat of his body pressing against mine. It was intoxicating, a heady rush that made my head spin and my heart race.

Without another word, Tyde took my hand, his fingers lacing with mine. He led me off the dance floor, weaving through the crowded room with a sense of purpose. I followed willingly, my curiosity piqued by the determined set of his jaw and the fire in his eyes.

We walked down a dimly lit hallway, the muffled sounds of the party fading into the background. The air was thick with anticipation, a charged energy that crackled between us like electricity. I could feel the warmth of Tyde's palm against my own, the roughness of his skin sending shivers down my spine.

As we approached the women's restroom, Tyde pulled me into a small alcove, his body pressing me against the wall. His hands found my waist, his fingers digging into the soft flesh as he pulled me closer. I gasped, my breath hitching in my throat as I felt the hard planes of his body against mine.

Tyde's eyes bore into me, a silent question hanging between us. I knew what he wanted, what we both wanted. It was a dangerous game we were playing, a tightrope walk between desire and reason. But in that moment, with the heat of his breath on my skin and the pounding of my heart in my ears, I couldn't bring myself to care.

I reached up, my fingers tangling in the soft strands of his curly hair. I pulled him closer, my lips parting in a silent invitation. Tyde groaned, a low, guttural sound that sent a bolt of heat straight to my core.

His lips crashed against mine, a bruising kiss that stole the breath from my lungs. I kissed him back with equal fervor, pouring all of my pent-up frustration and longing into the press of our mouths. It was a battle of wills, a dance of tongues and teeth that left me dizzy and aching for more.

Tyde's hands roamed my body, skimming over the curves of my hips and the swell of my breasts. I arched into his touch, my skin burning with each brush of his fingers. I wanted him, needed him with a desperation that scared me.

But even as I lost myself in the heat of the moment, a small voice in the back of my mind whispered a warning. This was Tyde, the man who had broken my heart and left me to pick up the pieces. The man who had hurt me in ways I never thought possible.

I pulled back, my chest heaving as I fought to catch my breath. Tyde's eyes were dark with desire, his lips swollen from our kisses. He looked at me with a question in his gaze, a silent plea for more.

Laurie

VIP SECTION

My gaze as it drifted across the pulsing dancefloor, where Gia was spinning in a whirl of sequins and laughter. The bass thumped through my chest, each beat a reminder of why I loved these nights out. But as I turned back to my mate, I noticed a feeling of someone staring at me.

My own eyes wandered, drawn like a magnet to the bar. And there they were.

Our gazes locked, and the world fell away. The strobing lights, the press of bodies, the deafening music - it all faded to a distant hum. There they were.

They were propped against the bar, one elbow resting on the sticky surface, a half-empty glass dangling from their fingers. Dark hair tumbled over their shoulders in messy waves, and even from here, I could see the glint of mischief in their eyes.

I couldn't look away. Didn't want to. The spark between us was electric, crackling across the crowded room.

"Oi, Laurie!" Stephanie's voice broke through my trance. "You gonna stand there gawking all night, or what?"

I blinked, dragging my attention back to my mates. Steph was grinning, her eyebrows waggling suggestively. Next to her, Jasper snorted into his beer.

"Reckon our Laurie's found himself a bit of eye candy,"

Jasper drawled, elbowing me in the ribs.

I felt my cheeks flush.

"Piss off," I muttered, but there was no real heat behind it.

Steph leaned in, her breath warm against my ear as she shouted over the music.

"Go on then! Chat them up!"

I hesitated, my gaze drifting back to the bar. They were still there, still watching me. A slow smile spread across their face, and my heart did a little stutter-step.

"I dunno," I hedged, suddenly unsure. This wasn't like me. I was Laurie the larrikin, always up for a laugh, always the life of the party. But something about this person made me feel something... more.

Jasper clapped me on the shoulder, nearly sending me sprawling.

"C'mon, mate. You're not gonna let a little thing like nerves stop you, are ya?"

I straightened, squaring my shoulders. He was right. This was my night, my moment.

"Wish me luck," I said, flashing them a grin.

As I wove through the crowd, my heart pounding in time with the music, I couldn't shake the feeling that everything was about to change. The party boy might be ready to hang up his dancing shoes, all for a person whose name I didn't even know.

Yet.

Gia

WOMEN'S RESTROOM

The restroom door slammed shut, the sound reverberating through the charged air as it sealed us away from prying eyes. The distant pulse of music thrummed through the walls, a sensual heartbeat to the electrifying tension that crackled between our bodies. Gia's eyes glittered with unbridled desire, pupils eclipsing the stormy gray and betraying the barest hint of trepidation.

"Tyde, what are we doing?" The words left her lips in a breathless whisper, a question that demanded no answer.

Drawn by the irresistible magnetism of her presence, I closed the remaining distance, invading her space until we shared the same air. The atmosphere thickened, grew heavy with the weight of unspoken hunger.

"Let's just see where it goes, eh?" I murmured, my lips a hairsbreadth from hers, the promise of sin and salvation.

And then I was claiming her mouth, a bruising clash of lips and teeth and tongues. The simmering attraction that had haunted our every interaction ignited into a raging inferno, consuming rational thought. Gia melted into me, her lush curves fitting perfectly against the hard planes of my body as if we were made to interlock.

Greedy hands explored with abandon, mapping the dips and hollows, committing every inch to memory. Gia was an intoxicating paradox - silk and steel, fire and ice - awakening nerve endings I'd long thought deadened. Desperation colored our movements as we sought to eliminate every millimeter of space, to fuse our flesh until we couldn't tell where one ended and the other began.

Nimble fingers attacked the barrier of clothing with clumsy urgency, buttons scattering in their wake. The first brush of skin against heated skin tore a guttural groan from my throat, Gia's nails branding delicious trails down the newly bared expanse of my chest. Possessed by the need to have her, I hoisted her up, relishing the way her legs instinctively wrapped around my hips as I pinned her against the wall.

Our kisses grew filthy, a tangle of biting nips soothed by clever tongues. I rocked into the cradle of her thighs, dizzy with want at the breathy keen that escaped her kiss-swollen lips. She was a goddess incarnate and I a mere mortal, aching to worship at the altar of her pleasure, to bury myself in her molten heat until the outside world crumbled to dust.

The last scraps of fabric fluttered carelessly to the floor until there was nothing but miles of bare skin, flushed and hungry. Gia arched into my reverent touch, head thrown back in ecstasy, an offering too tempting to resist. I ventured lower, painting a path down her throat with lips and teeth and tongue, feeling her pulse jump and flutter. The first taste of her, slick and scorching, nearly unmade me.

When I finally sheathed myself in her silken depths, twin groans of completion filled the air. It was coming home and seeing the face of the divine, a union so profound it defied articulation. We moved together, a sinuous dance of give and take, each undulation stoking the flames higher. Breathless pleas and declarations fell from our lips, a litany of encouragement and praise.

Release hit with the force of a tsunami, pleasure cresting and breaking, bodies shaking apart only to fuse back together in the aftermath. I peppered Gia's face with gentle kisses, marveling at the vulnerability, the raw openness in her blissed out expression. She clung to me, trembling through the aftershocks, and for a suspended moment, the fractured pieces of my world rearranged and locked into place.

Come morning, the harsh fluorescents of reality would cast unflattering shadows on our stolen paradise. The tangle of consequences and complications would rear their ugly heads, poised to shatter this fragile connection. But ensconced in our hideaway of cool tile and warm skin, I drank in the fleeting perfection, content to exist in the now.

For in Gia's arms, I'd caught a glimmer of what could be in the lucid mindset- a glimpse of the man I wanted to become, whole and unafraid. And though the path ahead promised to be littered with landmines, I clung to that image, that intoxicating potential. A touchstone to guide me through the darkness.

CHAPTER 10
DANCING WITH SHADOWS

Tyde & Gia

We stood in the bathroom, our chests heaving as we tried to catch our breath. The air was thick with the scent of sex and sweat, a heady mixture that made my head spin. I could feel the heat of Tyde's body, still pressed against mine, as we hurried to clean ourselves up and make ourselves presentable.

The banging on the door intensified, a harsh reminder that our little tryst had not gone unnoticed. The occupied status of the restroom was no longer acceptable, and we needed to make a hasty exit before someone decided to take matters into their own hands.

"We should probably get out of here," I whispered, my voice still raw from the passion that had consumed us moments before.

Tyde pulled me close, his arms wrapping around my waist in a possessive embrace. I could see the satisfaction in his eyes, the smug grin that tugged at the corners of his mouth. But there was something else there too, a flicker of uncertainty that made my heart skip a beat.

"Right good that was," he said, his voice low and rough. "We should do more stuff together, yeah? Not just the... rumpy pumpy bits, you know what I mean?"

I felt my breath catch in my throat, my eyes widening in surprise. Of all the things I had expected Tyde to say in the aftermath of our encounter, this was not one of them. The idea of spending more time with him, of exploring a relationship beyond the physical, was both thrilling and terrifying.

"Tyde, I... I don't know," I stammered, my voice trembling with uncertainty. "This is... unexpected."

I could see the hope in his eyes, the way he clung to the possibility of something more. But as I struggled to find the words to express my own conflicted emotions, I could see that hope begin to dim, replaced by a flicker of disappointment.

"No rush, love," he said, his voice soft and understanding. "Just thought it could be more than a one-night stand, is all."

I nodded, my heart racing as I tried to process the implications of his words. A part of me wanted to say yes, to throw caution to the wind and explore the possibility of a future with Tyde. But another part of me, the part that still bore the scars of our tumultuous past, held me back.

We left the women's restroom, our heads held high as we tried to ignore the judgmental stares and whispers of the people waiting in line. I could feel their eyes on us, could hear the speculation and gossip that followed in our wake.

But as we walked away, Tyde's hand firmly clasped in mine, I couldn't bring myself to care. In that moment, all that mattered was the connection we had shared, the raw and primal passion that had consumed us both.

And yet, even as I reveled in the afterglow of our encounter, I couldn't shake the feeling of unease that had settled in the pit of my stomach. Tyde's proposition had caught me off guard, had forced me to confront the tangled web of emotions that I had been trying so hard to ignore.

I knew that I needed time to think, to sort through the conflicting desires that warred within me. But as I looked at Tyde, his eyes still shining with the hope of something more, I knew that I couldn't keep him waiting forever.

Whatever happened next, I knew that it would change everything between us. And as we walked back into the party, the music and laughter washing over us like a cleansing wave, I couldn't help but wonder what the future held for us both.

"What now?" I whispered to myself, my voice barely audible over the pounding of my own heart.

The question hung in the air, a silent plea for guidance in a situation that felt impossibly complex. I still couldn't wrap my mind around the idea of something more with Tyde, couldn't fathom the possibility of a future together after all that we had been through.

I glanced at Tyde, taking in the strong lines of his jaw and the intensity of his gaze. He looked like a man on a mission, a man determined to fight for what he wanted. And in that moment, I realized that I had no idea what I wanted.

Did I want to take a chance on Tyde, to risk my heart on the possibility of something more? Or did I want to run, to put as much distance between us as possible and never look back?

The questions swirled in my mind, a dizzying array of possibilities and potential outcomes. I knew that I needed time to think, to sort through the tangled web of emotions that had taken root in my heart.

But even as I grappled with my own indecision, I could feel the weight of Tyde's gaze on me, and could sense the silent plea for a chance to prove himself.

And so, with a deep breath and a silent prayer for strength, I turned to face him, my eyes locking with his in a moment of unspoken understanding.

"Tyde, I..." I started, my voice trailing off as I struggled to find the right words.

He shook his head, a small smile tugging at the corners of his mouth.

"No worries, Gia. I get it's a lot to process. Just... just promise me you'll give it a mull, alright?"

I nodded, my heart clenching at the vulnerability in his voice.

"I will. I promise."

And with that, we stepped back into the party, the music and laughter washing over us like a tidal wave. But even as we lost ourselves in the crowd, I couldn't shake the feeling that something had shifted between us, that the events of the night had set us on a course that we couldn't turn back from.

Whatever happened next, I knew that it would be a journey, a path that we would have to navigate together. And as I looked at Tyde, his hand brushing against mine in a silent gesture of support, I couldn't help but feel a flicker of hope ignite in my chest.

Maybe, just maybe, we could find a way to make this work. Maybe, in the end, all of the pain and heartache we had endured would be worth it, if it meant a chance at something real and lasting.

But for now, all I could do was take it one step at a time, one moment at a time. And as we walked back into the fray, the uncertainty of the future hanging heavy in the air, I knew that I was ready to face whatever lay ahead, as long as Tyde was by my side.

Laurie

BAR

I made my way to the bar, heart thrumming against my ribs. The tantalizing stranger I'd been eyeing all night was just a few feet away. I had to make a good impression.

I caught the bartender's eye and gave a subtle nod. No words needed - he knew my usual.

"I'm Tyson," a smooth voice said beside me. I turned, coming face to face with the object of my desire.

A smirk tugged at my lips as I sized him up.

"Laurie," I purred, leaning in close. "Pleasure."

The bartender slid my drink across the polished wood. I wrapped my fingers around the cool glass, never breaking eye contact with Tyson.

We fell into easy banter, the tension between us crackling. I inched closer, letting my knee brush against his. Tyson's eyes darkened as he mirrored my body language.

The world around us faded away. There was only the heat of Tyson's gaze, the curve of his smile, the tantalizing closeness of his lips.

I'm not sure who moved first. One moment we were talking, the next his mouth was on mine. The kiss was electric, passionate, leaving me breathless and wanting more.

I pulled away, relishing the dazed look in Tyson's chestnut eyes.

"Reckon I'll rack off now", I murmured, trailing a finger down his chest.

"Wait," Tyson said, reaching for me. "Can I get your

number?"

I flashed him a coy smile.

"Bet we'll cross paths again, mate." With that, I sauntered away, feeling his eyes on me until I disappeared into the crowd.

Gria

LAURIE'S TABLE

I made my way back to Laurie's table, my heart still racing from the encounter with Tyde. The music pulsed around me, the beat matching the pounding of my own heart. I could feel the heat of Tyde's gaze on my back as I walked away, and could sense the unspoken longing that hung in the air between us.

But even as I tried to focus on the path ahead, I couldn't shake the feeling of Laurie's eyes on me, taking in every detail of my appearance. I knew that he would notice the changes, the rosy flush of my cheeks and the slightly disheveled state of my knotted hair.

As I approached the table, Laurie's eyes lit up with excitement, a knowing grin spreading across his face.

"Crikey! Fair dinkum? Looks like someone had a night to remember!" he exclaimed, his voice rising above the din of the party. Hit me with the goss, G!"

I felt my cheeks flush even deeper, my eyes darting away from Laurie's eager gaze. I wasn't ready to have this conversation, not in the middle of a crowded party with prying eyes and ears all around us.

"Laurie, not now," I said, my voice firm but gentle. "It's not the right place for this conversation."

But Laurie was undeterred, his smirk growing wider by the second. He leaned back in his chair, his eyes sparkling with mischief.

"Alright, alright, settle down, Sheila." he said, his voice

dripping with sarcasm. I'll wait. But you'd better cough up the whole story later, yeah?"

I rolled my eyes, but I couldn't help the small smile that tugged at the corners of my mouth. Laurie was my best friend, the one person who knew me better than anyone else. And even though his teasing could be infuriating at times, I knew that he only wanted the best for me.

As the night wore on, the party began to wind down. The music grew softer, the lights dimmer, and the crowd started to thin out. Laurie and I found ourselves drawn to the dance floor, our bodies moving in sync to the rhythm of the music.

I could feel Tyde's eyes on me from across the room, could sense the admiration and longing that radiated off of him in waves. But even as I lost myself in the music, I couldn't shake the feeling of uncertainty that lingered in the back of my mind.

What did the future hold for Tyde and me? Could we really make this work, after all the pain and heartache we had endured? The questions swirled in my mind, a dizzying array of possibilities and potential outcomes.

But as I danced with Laurie, our laughter mingling with the music and the chatter of the crowd, I knew that I couldn't dwell on the future forever. For now, all I could do was live in the moment, to embrace the joy and the excitement of the night and let the rest fall into place.

And so, as the party began to wind down and the last few stragglers made their way out into the night, I found myself walking arm in arm with Laurie, a sense of contentment settling over me like a warm blanket.

We made our way out into the cool night air, the stars twinkling overhead like a million tiny diamonds.

To take each moment as it came, to embrace the joy and the pain and the love that life had to offer. And as I walked into the night, Laurie by my side and Tyde's eagerness lingering, I knew that I was ready for whatever lay ahead.

I felt my phone buzz in my pocket and pulled it out to see a text from Edith. My heart raced as I read her message congratulating me on finishing my deal with the NHL and submitting my report for *Incline Media*'s upcoming issue. She said I had done a great job, but I still couldn't quite believe it was real.

Weeks of tireless work - interviewing rookies and veterans, attending practices and games, delving into the lives and motivations of these incredible athletes - it had all led to this moment. And now, my story would be featured in one of the most prestigious media publications out there, putting a spotlight on the NHL's rising and enduring stars alike.

I thought back to my interviews with Lorenz Wolf and Jackson Bell, two legendary players dominating on the ice. Their hard-earned wisdom and infectious passion for the game had struck me to my core. Through them, I gained a profound respect for the grit, resilience and sheer love for hockey that propelled these veterans to keep pushing themselves to greatness.

But it wasn't just the established stars that captured my imagination. The hungry rookies, with their wide-eyed ambition and raw talent, were equally fascinating. Tyde and I had spoken to so many of them, hearing in their voices an unwavering determination to carve out their own legacies.

In the end, that was the heart of the story I wanted to tell the indomitable spirit of these athletes and the sport they dedicated their lives to. With every word I wrote, I aimed to transmit that passion, encouraging people from all walks of life to tune into the NHL and experience the rush for themselves.

Gazing at Edith's text, it finally sank in that I had done it. Exhaustion and elation washed over me in equal measure. I knew the road ahead would bring new challenges, but for now, I let myself bask in the hard-won satisfaction of telling the stories that mattered to me and, hopefully, making a real impact. With a deep breath, I stepped forward into a thrilling new chapter.

—

LAURIE'S APARTMENT - EAST VILLAGE, NEW YORK CITY

I woke up slowly, my senses gradually coming alive as I drifted out of a deep, dreamless sleep. The first thing I noticed was the scent, a tantalizing aroma that wafted through the air and tickled my nostrils. It was a mix of freshly brewed coffee, sizzling bacon, and something sweet and buttery that I couldn't quite place.

I sat up, rubbing the sleep from my eyes as I tried to get my bearings. It took me a moment to realize that I was on Laurie's living room couch, the soft cushions cradling my body like a gentle embrace.

As I stretched my arms above my head, I heard Laurie's voice floating in from the kitchen, warm and inviting.

"Good mornin', sunshine! Brekkie's nearly on the barbie."

I couldn't help but smile at the sound of his voice, the familiarity of it washing over me like a comforting blanket. Laurie had always been an early riser, the kind of person who greeted the day with enthusiasm and energy.

I followed the tempting scent into the kitchen, my stomach growling in anticipation. Laurie stood at the stove, a spatula in one hand and a plate of pancakes in the other. He looked up as I entered, his eyes crinkling at the corners as he smiled.

"You're a lifesaver, Laurie. Thanks," I said, my voice still rough with sleep.

Laurie handed me a plate piled high with a hearty breakfast, the steam rising from the food in tantalizing tendrils. I took a seat at the kitchen table, my mouth watering as I dug in.

For a few moments, the only sound was the clinking of silverware against plates, the sizzle of bacon in the pan, and the quiet hum of the refrigerator. But as I savored each bite, I could feel Laurie's eyes on me, could sense the curiosity that burned behind his casual demeanor.

Finally, he spoke, his voice casual but laced with an undercurrent of excitement.

"Alright, come clean. What went down after you and Tyde did a runner from the dance floor last night?"

I nearly choked on my food, my eyes widening as the memories of the previous night came flooding back. The heat of Tyde's body pressed against mine, the taste of his lips on my skin, the way he had made me feel alive in ways I hadn't thought possible.

I cleared my throat, putting down my fork as I tried to gather my thoughts. My cheeks burned with a mixture of embarrassment and excitement, the heat spreading across my face like wildfire.

"Uh, well... I hooked up with Tyde in the bathroom," I said, my voice barely above a whisper.

Laurie's eyes widened in surprise, his mouth falling open in a perfect "o" of shock. But just as quickly, his expression shifted to one of pure, unadulterated excitement.

"Fair suck of the sav, you did not!" he exclaimed, his voice rising an octave in his enthusiasm. Spill, G, what happened in that dunny?"

I felt my blush deepen, my heart racing as I hesitated for a moment. But as I looked into Laurie's eyes, I saw nothing but love and support, a silent encouragement to share my story.

And so, with a deep breath and a nervous smile, I began to recount the thrilling events of the previous night. I told him about the way Tyde had looked at me on the dance floor, the heat of his gaze burning into my skin. I described the way he had pulled me into the bathroom, the urgency of his touch as he pressed me against the wall.

I could see Laurie's eyes widening with each detail, could sense the excitement and the joy that radiated off of him in waves. He listened intently, hanging on my every word as I relived the most intense, most passionate moments of my life.

And as I spoke, I could feel the weight of the previous

night's events lifting off of my shoulders, could sense the clarity and the peace that came with sharing my story with someone I trusted.

For in the end, that was what friendship was all about. The ability to share our deepest, darkest secrets with someone who loved us unconditionally, who supported us through the good times and the bad.

And as Laurie and I sat there, laughing and talking and savoring the delicious breakfast he had prepared, I knew that I had found that kind of friendship in him. A bond that could weather any storm, a love that would last a lifetime.

Laurie

I pushed my plate away, not a crumb left in sight. Gia did the same, and we both leaned back in our chairs, the satisfaction of a good meal settling over us. The morning sun streamed through the kitchen window, casting a warm glow on the wooden table.

I took a deep breath, running a hand through my messy hair. It was time to spill the beans.

"Oi, Gia," I started, with nervousness. "Reckon I've got somethin' to tell ya."

Gia's dark eyes widened, curiosity sparking in their depths.

"What's up, Laurie?"

I launched into the story, words tumbling out in a rush.

"So, ya know that wrap party last night? Well, I met this bloke named Tyson."

Gia's eyebrows shot up, but she stayed quiet, letting me ramble on.

"We were at the bar, right? And next thing I know, we're havin' a proper pash. It was bloody electric, I tell ya."

I could see Gia practically vibrating with excitement, but she bit her lip, holding back her questions.

"Here's the kicker," I continued, a grin spreading across my face. "I didn't give him my number or anythin'. Just racked off with a cheeky 'See ya 'round.'"

Gia's jaw dropped.

"Laurie, you didn't!"

I nodded, feeling rather pleased with myself.

"But get this - the drongo found me on Insta. We've been messagin' all night."

That was it for Gia. She leapt from her chair, her curls bouncing as she jumped up and down.

"Oh my God, Laurie! This is huge!"

I chuckled, standing up to gather our plates.

"Easy there, sheila. It's not serious... yet."

Gia's laughter filled the kitchen as I made my way to the sink, plates in hand. The ceramic clinked against the stainless steel, a counterpoint to Gia's excited chatter.

"Not serious, my ass," she exclaimed.

"You're blushing and eyes glazed!"

I turned on the tap, warm water cascading over my hands and the dishes.

"Yeah, well," I mumbled, feeling a blush creep up my neck. "We'll see where it goes, yeah?"

Gia's reflection grinned at me from the window above the sink.

"Oh, we'll see alright. I've got a good feeling about this one, Laurie."

I just shook my head, focusing on the dishes. But I couldn't quite hide the smile tugging at the corners of my mouth. Maybe Gia was right. Maybe Tyson is something special. Only time would tell.

Tyde

TYDE'S PENTHOUSE

I woke up with a satisfied grin plastered across my face, my mind already drifting to my new favorite pastime—daydreaming about Gia. The memory of the previous night's bathroom escapades had me feeling lighter than air, a pep in my step as I moved through my penthouse.

I cranked up the music, the pulsing beat filling the space as I started whipping up breakfast in the kitchen. The sizzle of bacon and the aroma of freshly brewed coffee mingled with the lively tunes, creating a perfect symphony of morning bliss.

As I flipped pancakes and scrambled eggs, my phone buzzed with an incoming Facetime call. I glanced at the screen, seeing Jackson and Lorenz's names flashing insistently. With a swipe of my finger, I answered, propping the phone up against the fruit bowl.

"Tyde, what's got you in such a great mood?" Lorenz asked, his brow furrowed in confusion. "Did you win the lottery or something?"

I couldn't help but smirk, a right cheeky grin spreading across my face.

"Nah, something a bit more special, like."

As I continued to cook, Lorenz and Jackson shared puzzled glances through the screen, both clearly clueless about the reason behind my cheerful demeanor. I could practically see the gears turning in their heads as they tried to piece together the puzzle.

Lorenz, ever the curious one, decided to probe further.

"Seriously, spill it, man. What's making you this happy?"

I chuckled, enjoying the way they squirmed with anticipation.

"Oh, you lot haven't a clue."

Jackson and Lorenz exchanged a look, their eyes widening as realization dawned on them. They knew me well enough to recognize that I hadn't been this happy since my relationship with Gia, and the pieces were starting to fall into place.

Unable to contain my excitement any longer, I decided to put them out of their misery.

"Alright, alright, settle down. Gia last night, right? Well, let's just say it was... a right palaver. To put it mildly."

Jackson and Lorenz leaned forward, their faces filling the screen as they hung on my every word. They were expecting some typical Tyde-style story, a tale of conquest and charm that would leave them equal parts impressed and envious.

"Spill the beans, man. What went down?" Jackson urged, his voice laced with anticipation.

I grinned, the memory of Gia's body pressed against mine sending a shiver down my spine.

"Let's just say I pulled out all the stops with Gia, and it went down a treat."

Lorenz and Jackson's jaws dropped in unison, their eyes wide with shock and disbelief. They had known Gia and I had history, but they never expected me to actually make a move, let alone succeed.

"Even with a skinful on me, I sobered up sharpish. It was a right cracker of a night, that's for sure." I continued, relishing the way their expressions morphed from surprise to amusement to a grudging respect.

I left out certain details, of course. Gia was a lady, and I wasn't about to kiss and tell. But the broad strokes were enough to paint a picture, to let them know that I had pulled off the impossible.

As I regaled them with the story, I could see the wheels turning in their heads, and could practically hear the gears clicking into place. They knew that this was more than just a one-night stand, more than a fleeting moment of passion.

This was a turning point, a shift in the tides that had the potential to change everything. And as Lorenz and Jackson shared a look of amused disbelief, I knew that my triumphant night with Gia had become a legendary tale in our friendship, a story that would be told and retold for years to come. I'm a man who can get anyone to come crawling back.

Or am I the one that is going crawling back?

But even as I basked in the glow of their admiration, I couldn't shake the feeling that this was just the beginning. That the road ahead was filled with twists and turns, with challenges and obstacles that I couldn't even begin to imagine.

And yet, as I looked out over the city skyline, the sun rising in a blaze of orange and gold, I knew that I was ready for whatever lay ahead. That with Gia by my side, I could face anything, and could overcome any obstacle that stood in our way.

And as I ended the call with Lorenz and Jackson, their laughter still ringing in my ears, I knew that I was ready to take that chance, to see where this crazy, beautiful journey would take us.

Jackson & Lorenz

I hung up the phone, Tyde's words still echoing in my ears. The glow of the screen illuminated my dimly lit room as I immediately dialed Lorenz. My fingers drummed an impatient rhythm on the desk while I waited for him to pick up.

"Yo, Jackson! What's the deal, eh?" Lorenz's voice crackled through the speaker, his German accent.

"Bud, you're not gonna believe this," I said, leaning back in my chair. "Just got off the horn with Tyde. The man's gone and decided to give it another go with Gia. Can you believe it?"

Lorenz let out a low whistle.

"Ach du lieber! No strings attached, I bet?"

"Bang on, my friend. Our boy thinks he's being slick, but we both know how this song and dance goes."

There was a pause, and I could almost see Lorenz's gears turning.

"So, what's the play here, Jack? We're just gonna sit back and watch this gong show?"

I snorted, shaking my head even though he couldn't see me.

"As if. Nah, I'm thinking we need to get our hands dirty on this one. Those two knuckleheads need all the help they can get."

"Jawohl! Operation Lovebirds is a go, then?" Lorenz's enthusiasm was infectious, and I found myself grinning.

"You got it, bud. Time for doofus one and doofus two to

work their magic."

We spent the next hour bouncing ideas back and forth, each one more outlandish than the last. Lorenz suggested everything from skywriting to carrier pigeons, while I lobbied for a more subtle approach involving strategic text messages and "accidental" run-ins.

"Hold up," I said, a lightbulb moment striking. "What if we set up a fake emergency? Get them both to show up at the same place, you know?"

Lorenz's laughter boomed through the phone.

"Brilliant! We could pretend one of us is in hospital or something. They'd both come running!"

I chuckled, shaking my head. "Maybe dial it back a notch, bud. We don't want to give anyone a heart attack."

As the night wore on, our plan began to take shape. It wasn't perfect – far from it – but it was a start. We'd nudge Tyde and Gia together, create opportunities for them to reconnect beyond the physical. It was meddling, sure, but it came from a place of love.

"You think this'll work?" Lorenz asked, a rare note of uncertainty in his voice.

I sighed, running a hand through my hair. "Honestly? I don't know. But they're both too stubborn to figure it out on their own. Sometimes you gotta give love a little push, you know?"

"Ja, I hear you," Lorenz replied. "Well, here's to Operation Lovebirds. May we not royally screw this up."

Tyde

TYDE'S PENTHOUSE

The number on the screen burned a hole into my retinas. It was my estranged mother, Elle's number, the one etched into my voicemail log, a constant reminder of the gaping chasm in my life. My thumb hovered over the dial button, a nervous tremor coursing through it. This was it. The moment I'd both dreaded and craved for years.

With a deep breath, I punched in the digits, the dial tone a shrill scream in the otherwise silent room. Two rings. My heart hammered a frantic tattoo against my ribs. Chicken out, a voice whispered in my ear. Just hang up and pretend this never happened.

But another voice, stronger and laced with a desperate yearning, drowned it out.

"Don't be a bitch Tyde!" It's time.

Steeling myself, I hit redial. This time, the wait stretched into a torturous eternity. Four rings. Five. Just as I was about to give up, a sound crackled through the receiver – a low, ragged breath. It was her.

"Hello?" The voice was barely a whisper, yet it sent a jolt through me, a potent cocktail of emotions warring within.

"Hi, Elle," I managed, my voice thick and unfamiliar. "It's me, Tyde."

Silence stretched, so long I thought the call had dropped. Then, a gasp, a choked sob. My name, a broken melody on her lips. Relief washed over me, mingled with a pang of guilt.

"Oh, Tyde! I... I can't believe it's you!" Her voice, once strong and vibrant, was now raspy, tinged with an underlying tremor. A deluge of questions tumbled out, each one laced with a desperate need. "How are you? What have you been up to? What does your life look like now?"

The barrage caught me off guard. Years of resentment bubbled up, threatening to spill over. But seeing the raw vulnerability in her voice, the barely concealed hope, I forced it down.

"I'm doing alright," I mumbled, my answers clipped and unenthusiastic. It wasn't a complete lie, but it wasn't the whole truth either.

The conversation flowed, or rather, it sputtered along. Hours bled into night, a tapestry woven with awkward silences,tentative questions, and unspoken apologies. We skirted around the past, a minefield too dangerous to navigate. Instead,we clung to the present, a fragile bridge over a chasm of years.

As dawn painted the horizon with streaks of orange and pink, exhaustion finally claimed us. We said our goodbyes,promises of future calls hanging heavy in the air. I cradled the phone, a strange sense of emptiness washing over me.

The conversation hadn't healed the wounds of the past, not by a long shot. But it had been a start, a tentative step towards a semblance of reconciliation. And as I stared out the window, the first rays of sunlight warming my face, a sliver of hope,fragile as a butterfly's wing, flickered to life within me.

Gia

GIA'S APARTMENT - BROOKLYN HEIGHTS, NEW YORK CITY

I sat alone in my apartment, the silence pressing in on me from all sides. The only sound was the gentle hum of the refrigerator, a constant reminder of the emptiness that surrounded me. I stared at my phone, the screen glowing softly in the dimly lit room.

A text from Laurie flashed across the screen, his words casual and lighthearted.

"Listen up, G, just chuckin' a thought your way 'cause you're a top mate. Maybe keep it cranky with Tyde, could save you a world of heartache down the track. "

I read the message over and over again, my eyes tracing the words until they blurred together in a haze of confusion and uncertainty. Casual. The word tasted bitter on my tongue, a reminder of all the times I had tried to keep things light and breezy, only to have my heart shattered into a million pieces.

Could I do it? Could I keep things casual with Tyde, knowing the history we shared? The weight of my past heartbreak lingered, a heavy burden that I carried with me every day. It was a constant reminder of the pain and the hurt that came with opening myself up to someone, with letting them see the vulnerable parts of me that I kept hidden away.

I closed my eyes, my mind drifting back to the last time I had let myself fall for someone. It had been a whirlwind romance, a heady mix of passion and excitement that had swept me off my feet. But in the end, it had all come crashing down, leaving me broken and alone, my heart in tatters on the floor.

I couldn't go through that again. I couldn't bear the thought of putting myself out there, of taking that risk, only to have it all fall apart once more. The fear gripped me like a vice, squeezing the air from my lungs and leaving me gasping for breath.

But even as I tried to push the thoughts away, I couldn't shake the memory of Tyde's touch, the way his hands had felt on my skin, the way his lips had moved against mine. It was a feeling I had never experienced before, a connection that went beyond the physical, beyond the superficial.

I wanted more. I wanted to explore that connection, to see where it could lead. But the fear held me back, the weight of my past mistakes pressing down on me like a heavy blanket.

I stared at my phone, my finger hovering over the screen as I tried to decide what to do. Should I take Laurie's advice? Should I keep things casual, play it safe and protect my heart from the inevitable pain that would come with letting someone in?

Or should I take a chance? Should I throw caution to the wind and see where this crazy, beautiful journey with Tyde could take me?

I took a deep breath, my mind racing with the possibilities. I knew that whatever I decided, it would change everything. That the road ahead was filled with twists and turns, with challenges and obstacles that I couldn't even begin to imagine.

But even as the fear threatened to consume me, I couldn't shake the feeling that this was a chance worth taking. That the connection I had felt with Tyde was something special, something rare and precious that I couldn't let slip through my fingers.

And so, with a shaking hand and a pounding heart, I typed out a response to Laurie's text.

"I appreciate the advice, but I think I need to see where this goes. I can't let my past hold me back forever."

I hit send before I could change my mind, the weight of my decision settling over me like a heavy cloak. I knew that I was taking a risk, that I was opening myself up to the possibility of heartbreak and pain.

But I also knew that I couldn't live my life in fear, couldn't let the ghosts of my past dictate my future. And as I sat there in the silence of my apartment, the glow of my phone the only light in the darkness, I knew that I was ready to face whatever lay ahead.

Laurie's message pinged back, "Understood, love. But just chuck a shoey on Tyde, alright? Bloke's a bit of a galah."

For in the end, that was what life was all about. Taking chances, risking everything for the chance at something real and lasting. And as I closed my eyes and let the memories of Tyde wash over me, I knew that I was ready to take that leap, to see where this crazy, beautiful journey would take us.

—

DR. CELINE DIAZ'S OFFICE - GARMENT DISTRICT, NEW YORK CITY

I walked into Celine's office, my heart heavy with the weight of the past few weeks. The room was warm and inviting, with soft lighting and comfortable chairs that seemed to beckon me to sit down and unburden myself. I took a seat, my hands clasped tightly in my lap as I prepared for our session.

Celine greeted me with a warm smile, her eyes filled with compassion and understanding.

"Hello, Gia. It's good to see you again. How have things been since our last session?"

I sighed, the sound escaping my lips like a deflating balloon.

"It's been a rollercoaster, Celine. So much has happened."

And so I began, the words tumbling out of me like a waterfall. I told her about my date with Chris Jennings, the way he had made me feel safe and cherished. But even as I spoke of the joy and excitement of that night, I couldn't shake the memory of my unexpected encounter with Tyde in the women's bathroom at the All-Star weekend wrap party.

Celine listened attentively, her brow furrowed in concentration.

"It sounds like there's been a lot on your plate. Tell me more about how you're feeling about these experiences."

I paused, my mind racing with the possibilities.

"Well, about Tyde, I'm considering dating him and multiple other men. All at the same time. I;ve already created a roster, so why not. Right? You know, giving him another chance possibly?"

Celine nodded, her eyes searching mine.

"Um. Okay Gia, I want to explore this dating roster idea a little more with you. Are you comfortable with it, especially considering your past dealing with men around certain situations?"

I hesitated, the weight of my past pressing down on me like a heavy blanket.

"I'm not sure, Celine. At first it started off as an unserious thing between myself and Laurie, my best friend. But now I'm actually considering taking this roster dating situation seriously and really finding someone. It's a way for me to have some control over my life again, but I know it might not be the healthiest approach to anyone but…"

Celine sensed there was more to the story, her voice gentle and encouraging.

"Tell me about your anxiety. In what way do you feel anxious and can you tell me the things that may trigger this. Why do you think it manifests in certain situations?"

I took a deep breath, the memories flooding back like a tidal wave.

"It started one night when I was 20. I came home, and there was a man in my apartment. A random drifter who managed to go unnoticed by everyone in my building. I had just moved to the city, didn't have friends or a boyfriend at the time – it was all pre-Tyde, pre-Laurie. He abused me, badly, and I didn't tell anyone for a long time, not even my parents. You're only the third person to know."

Celine listened attentively, her eyes filled with empathy

and understanding.

"Thank you for sharing that with me, Gia. It takes courage. We can work through this together."

And so we delved into the darker corners of my mind, the places I had kept hidden for so long. Celine guided me through the pain and the trauma, her voice a soothing balm to my battered soul.

But even as we explored the heavy topics, Celine knew when to shift the conversation to a lighter note.

"Now, Gia, let's focus on some strategies to help with your anxiety. Have you tried any techniques during those difficult moments?"

I shook my head, my voice small and uncertain. "I've tried deep breathing and laying down, but it doesn't always work."

Celine nodded, her eyes sparkling with encouragement.

"Let's explore some alternatives. Have you considered mindfulness exercises? They can be effective in grounding you during anxious moments."

I leaned forward, my interest piqued.

"I haven't tried that. What should I do?"

Celine smiled, her voice calm and reassuring.

"Start by focusing on your breath. Inhale deeply, counting to four, and then exhale slowly. Pay attention to the sensations, the rise and fall of your chest. Let your thoughts come and go without judgment. It takes practice, but it can help bring you back to the present."

I closed my eyes, following Celine's guidance. I felt the air filling my lungs, the gentle rise and fall of my chest. For a moment, the world seemed to fade away, leaving only the sensation of my breath and the sound of Celine's voice.

When I opened my eyes, I felt a sense of calm washing over me, a newfound sense of peace and clarity. Celine smiled, her eyes filled with pride.

"Great job, Gia. Remember, it's okay to ask for support when you need it. You don't have to face everything alone."

I nodded, my voice filled with gratitude.

"Thanks, Celine. I'll give these a try."

As the session drew to a close, Celine's words echoed in my mind.

"You're making progress, Gia. I'm here to support you. Take these strategies with you, and use them whenever you need. Best of luck, and we'll reconvene in our next session."

The tools Celine had given me felt like a lifeline, a way to navigate the choppy waters of my anxiety and emerge stronger on the other side.

As I walked down the street, my head held high and my heart filled with hope, I knew that I was one step closer to becoming the woman I had always dreamed of being.

—

GIA'S APARTMENT

I stood in front of the mirror, my eyes critically appraising my reflection as I smoothed the fabric of my dress. The elegant outfit hugged my curves in all the right places, the deep blue hue complimenting my chestnut skin tone and making my eyes pop. I had spent hours getting ready, carefully selecting each piece of clothing and accessory, determined to make a lasting impression on my date for the evening.

Dylan Morneo, the Brazilian futebol star, was a name that had been on everyone's lips lately. Rumors swirled about his playboy reputation, his penchant for breaking hearts and leaving a trail of devastated women in his wake. But as I applied a final touch of perfume to my wrists and neck, I couldn't help but feel a flicker of excitement at the prospect of getting to know the man behind the headlines.

"Alright, Gia, time to give Dylan a chance," I murmured to myself, my voice barely audible over the pounding of my heart.

I took a deep breath, steadying my nerves as I grabbed my clutch and headed for the door. The apartment was quiet, the only sound was the soft click of my heels against the hardwood floor. I couldn't shake the feeling that this night would be different, that something momentous was about to happen.

As I approached the door, I heard a sharp knock, the sound echoing through the stillness of the room. My heart skipped a beat, my palms suddenly clammy with anticipation. I took a moment to compose myself, smoothing my coily hair to the best of my ability and straightening my shoulders before opening the door.

And there he was, Dylan Morneo in the flesh. He was even more stunning in person, his jet black curly hair tousled just so, his eyes sparkling with mischief and charm. I couldn't help but let my gaze wander over his muscular frame, taking in the way his suit clung to his broad shoulders and narrow waist.

"E aí, Gia! You're killing it, hein?" he said, his voice warm and inviting. His smile was infectious, his dimples making an appearance as he looked me up and down appreciatively.

I felt a blush creep up my neck, my cheeks heating under his intense gaze.

"Thank you, Dylan! You're not looking too bad yourself."

We exchanged pleasantries, the conversation flowing easily as we made our way out of the apartment building. Dylan offered his arm, his touch sending a jolt of electricity through my body. I couldn't help but feel a sense of anticipation, a thrill of excitement at the thought of what the evening might hold.

As we stepped out into the crisp night air, I couldn't shake the feeling that this was the beginning of something special. Dylan's presence was intoxicating, his charm and charisma drawing me in like a moth to a flame. I knew that I should be cautious, that I should guard my heart against the rumors that swirled around him.

But as we walked arm in arm down the bustling city street, the lights of the city twinkling above us like a thousand stars, I couldn't help but feel a sense of hope, a flicker of possibility that this night might be the start of something wonderful.

I glanced at Dylan, taking in the strong lines of his jaw, the way his eyes crinkled at the corners when he smiled. He was a mystery, a puzzle waiting to be solved. And as we made our way to the restaurant, the anticipation building with each step, I knew that I was ready to unravel the secrets that lay beneath his charming exterior.

For in the end, that was what dating was all about. Taking

a chance, opening yourself up to the possibility of something new and exciting. And as I looked at Dylan, his hand warm and solid in mine, I knew that I was ready to take that leap, to see where this crazy, beautiful journey might lead.

—

SALA ONE NINE

As we stepped into Sala One Nine, I couldn't help but be impressed by the ambiance. The soft lighting, the elegant decor, the gentle murmur of conversation - it all combined to create the perfect atmosphere for a romantic evening. I felt a thrill of excitement run through me as Dylan guided me to our table, his hand warm and solid on the small of my back.

With a flourish, he pulled out a chair for me, his manners impeccable. I couldn't help but smile at the gesture, a flicker of warmth spreading through my chest. It was a small thing, but it spoke volumes about his character, about the kind of man he was beneath the surface.

"I hope you like this place. It's one of my favorites," Dylan said, his voice low and intimate as he took his seat across from me.

I met his gaze, my heart skipping a beat at the intensity I saw there.

"It's lovely, Dylan. Thank you for bringing me here."

As we perused the menu, I couldn't help but let my mind wander to the rumors I had heard about Dylan's personal life. The whispers of infidelity, the tales of broken hearts and shattered dreams of the women he has dated. I knew that I shouldn't let them color my opinion of him, but I couldn't shake the nagging sense of unease that had settled in the pit of my stomach.

Taking a deep breath, I decided to broach the subject head-on.

"I've heard some murmurs of drama, Dylan. About your personal life. Mind sharing a bit?"

Dylan's eyes met mine, a flicker of vulnerability passing across his face.

"Olha, Gia. The rumors, some true, some not. But tonight, I want you to know the real me."

And so, as we talked, Dylan began to open up, to share the parts of himself that he kept hidden from the world. He told me about his philanthropic work for cancer research in Brazil, about the way he advised the youth in the fútbol community, about the countless hours he spent helping the homeless whenever he could.

I listened, my heart swelling with admiration and respect. This was a side of Dylan that I had never seen before, a glimpse of the man behind the headlines and the gossip columns. And as he spoke, I could see the passion and the compassion that drove him, the desire to make a difference in the world and leave a lasting impact.

"That's incredible, Dylan. I'd love to hear more about your passions," I said, my voice soft and sincere.

And so, as the evening progressed, I found myself drawn deeper and deeper into Dylan's world. He was a complex man, a puzzle waiting to be solved. But with each passing moment, I could feel the walls between us crumbling, the barriers that we had both erected to protect ourselves from hurt and heartbreak.

There was a vulnerability to him, a rawness that I had never seen before. And as we talked and laughed and shared our hopes and dreams, I couldn't help but feel a sense of connection, a spark of something that went beyond mere attraction.

I knew that there was still so much to learn about Dylan, still so many layers to peel back and secrets to uncover. But as I sat there, lost in the depths of his eyes and the warmth of his smile, I knew that I was willing to take that journey with him, to see where this crazy, beautiful thing between us might lead.

For in the end, that was what dating was all about. Taking a chance, opening yourself up to the possibility of something real and lasting. And as I looked at Dylan, his hand reaching across the table to grasp mine, I knew that I was ready to take that leap, to see where the road ahead might take us.

The evening was far from over, and I knew that there would be twists and turns along the way. But for now, in this moment, I was content to bask in the glow of Dylan's presence, to let myself be swept away by the magic of the night and the promise of what lay ahead.

Gia

The glittering lights of the Upper East Side sparkled like scattered diamonds as Dylan's strong hand guided me into his boss's opulent rental apartment. Dylan rarely visits New York, so he doesn't feel the need to get a place of his own. Floor-to-ceiling windows revealed a breathtaking view of the inky water, the night sky an endless expanse above. Anticipation tingles through my veins, mixing headily with the champagne buzz.

Dylan's heated gaze raked over me, sending delicious shivers racing across my skin. He moved with the lethal grace of a panther stalking its prey, all coiled power and raw magnetism. I was ensnared, willingly captured.

"Gia," he murmured, voice low and rough with desire. Long, deft fingers brushed my cheek, tilted my chin up."Você é um arraso."

Then his lips claimed mine in a searing kiss and coherent thought scattered. His wicked tongue delved deep, tasting, teasing, igniting an inferno in my core. Calloused hands slid over my curves, mapped the contours of my body like he was committing them to memory.

We tumbled onto the smooth, silky bed in a tangle of limbs, a frenzy of grasping hands and urgent kisses. He took his time, worshiping every inch of my flushed skin with lips and teeth and tongue until I was writhing, pleading, desperate for more.

When he finally joined his body to mine, I arched into him with a strangled cry, nerve endings singing with molten bliss. He moved over me, inside me, stoking the flames higher and higher until release crashed over us both and the world shattered into stained-glass ecstasy.

Afterwards, he gathered me close, strong arms banded around me as if shielding me from everything beyond the refuge of rumpled sheets. Fingers carded gently through my coily hair, soothing now rather than inflaming. My racing heart gradually slowed.

Drowsy and sated, my mind drifted to the whispers I'd heard of this man's prowess, on and off the field. The rumors were clearly true - Dylan's mastery of a woman's body was unparalleled.

Well, almost unparalleled. Unbidden, an image of Tyde rose in my mind's eye. Piercing golden brown eyes, wicked smile, clever hands that never failed to play my body like a virtuoso. A familiar ache bloomed in my chest.

No, nobody could surpass Tyde when it came to pleasuring me, body and soul. What he and I had was singular, transcendent.

As sleep stole over me, I pushed aside the treacherous thoughts of my ex-lover. Tonight had been a thrilling diversion, nothing more. For now, I would bask in the afterglow of skilled lovemaking and let tomorrow worry about itself.

CHAPTER 11
UNEXPECTED INVITATIONS

**TYDE'S PENTHOUSE - CENTRAL
PARK WEST, NEW YORK CITY**

Those goddamn paparazzi photos burned into my retinas, searing my vision with images of Gia and Dylan cuddled up together like lovesick teenagers. My jaw clenched until it ached, molars grinding against the bitter taste of jealousy scorching my throat.

This simmering green monster inside me wasn't rational - it was an all-consuming inferno threatening to reduce me to ashes. How could she look at him that way, with those soft bedroom eyes that used to be reserved for me? It's like our history, our connection, meant nothing to her now.

I slammed my fist against the desk, pain blossoming across my knuckles. I couldn't stand the thought of losing her, of that blazing fire we once shared dwindling to cold, dead embers. Gia was the one who used to understand me, accepted me at my most raw and real. Without her, I'd be adrift, a lone skyscraper slowly succumbing to the decay of neglect.

I paced my flat, frustration and determination warring within me. The walls seemed to close in, echoing my tumultuous thoughts.

"She deserves better," I growled through gritted teeth, the sting of failure pricking my eyes. "Proper better than I've been lately. I gotta up my game."

My phone felt heavy in my hand as I fired off a group text to Jackson and Lorenz. The lads had always been there for me, through thick and thin. If anyone could help me sort this mess, it was them.

The response was almost immediate. My phone buzzed with incoming messages, a rapid-fire exchange that made me smile despite myself.

Jackson's Canadian drawl practically leapt off the screen: "Bud, you gotta wine and dine her! Show her you're not messin' about this time."

Lorenz chimed in, his German accent somehow evident even in text: "Ja! Take her somewhere special, mein Freund. Somewhere that means something to both of you."

I froze, their words triggering a cascade of memories. The Aviary. It hit me like a lightning bolt, vivid and electrifying. That first night, when everything had changed.

I closed my eyes, letting the recollection wash over me. The warm glow of fairy lights, the gentle clinking of glasses, and the intoxicating scent of lavender in the air. But most of all, I remembered Gia.

She'd been radiant that night, her laughter like music cutting through the din of the crowded bar. I'd spotted her across the room, and it was like the world had tilted on its axis. Everything else faded away – the posh crowd and there was only her.

I remembered the way my heart had raced as I approached her, how my palms had gone sweaty as I fumbled for something clever to say. But then she'd smiled, and suddenly, words didn't matter anymore.

We'd talked for hours that night, losing track of time as we discovered shared passions and dreams. It was more than just attraction; it was a connection that ran soul-deep. For the first time in my life, I felt like I'd met someone who truly saw me – not the athlete, not the party boy, but the real me underneath it all.

As the memory faded, I found myself grinning like a right muppet. This was it. This was how I could show Gia that I was serious, that what we had was worth fighting for.

I quickly typed out a response to the lads: "You beauts are bloody brilliant! I know just the place."

Jackson's reply came through almost instantly: "Attaboy! Go get her, Tiger!"

Lorenz added: "Viel Glück! Don't cock it up this time, ja?"

I chuckled, shaking my head at their enthusiasm. But as I set my phone down, a wave of nerves washed over me. This was my chance – maybe my last chance – to make things right with Gia.

Within minutes, plans were scribbled across my notepad as the vision took shape. I'd transform that cozy space into an intimate paradise, all aglow with faux candlelight glow and rose petals scattered like velvet gemstones. The gentle thrum of our favorite jazz record would provide the soundtrack for a romantic evening sealed with lingering kisses and whispered endearments.

My hands trembled with manic determination as I made arrangements, an obsessive need to craft the perfect atmosphere pounding through my veins. This had to be flawless - no, mind-blowingly spectacular. A romantic tour-de-force to sweep Gia off her feet and remind her why we belonged together.

I'd never been more certain of anything in my life. Gia would become my beginning and end, the air I breathed. And I would move heaven and earth to prove my devotion and win back the woman I loved.

—

GIA'S APARTMENT - BROOKLYN HEIGHTS, NEW YORK CITY

My phone buzzed with an incoming message, the screen lighting up in the dimness of my apartment. I reached for it, my heart skipping a beat as I saw the words "Unknown Number" flashing across the display. Curiosity piqued, I swiped to open the text, my eyes widening as I read the mysterious instructions.

"Sort yourself out by 9, look mint. - Ty"

A smile spread across my face, a flicker of excitement igniting in my chest.

"What's Tyde up to now?" I murmured to myself, my mind already racing with possibilities.

I leapt to my feet, rushing to my closet with a newfound sense of urgency. My fingers trembled as I dialed Laurie's number, my heart pounding with anticipation as I waited for him to pick up.

"Laurie, guess what? Tyde just texted me to be ready by 9 pm. Something's up," I blurted out, the words tumbling from my lips in a breathless rush.

Laurie's voice crackled through the speaker, his tone laced with curiosity.

"C'mon, Gia, fess up! What's the goss?"

I shared the mysterious message with him, my voice rising with each word.

"What should I wear, Laurie? I want to look amazing, but not too over the top."

Laurie's response was immediate, his excitement palpable even through the phone.

"Chuck on that frock we snagged last month! He'll be flippin' his lid. Fair dinkum."

I grinned, my mind already conjuring up images of the dress in question. It was a stunning creation of black lace and silk, the kind of dress that made a woman feel like a goddess. I knew that Tyde wouldn't be able to resist me in it, knew that it would be the perfect weapon in my arsenal of seduction.

With a newfound sense of purpose, I hung up the phone and set to work. I spent the next hour primping and preening, my hands steady as I applied my makeup and styled my rust-tinted coils. I wanted to look perfect, wanted to take Tyde's breath away the moment he laid eyes on me.

As the clock ticked closer to 9 pm, I slipped into the dress, the fabric skimming over my curves like a lover's caress. I added a pair of sky-high heels and a spritz of my favorite perfume, the scent lingering in the air like a promise of things to come.

With a final glance in the mirror, I grabbed my clutch and headed for the door. My heart raced with anticipation as I locked up my apartment, my mind already spinning with possibilities of what the night might hold.

As I stepped outside, I was greeted by the sight of a sleek black car idling at the curb. A driver stood beside it, his face impassive as he opened the door for me.

"Good evening, Ms. Clark. Mr. Wright sends his regards. Please, step in," he said, his voice a low rumble in the stillness of the night.

I slid into the back seat, my skin tingling with excitement as the car pulled away from the curb. The city lights blurred past the window, a chromoscope of color and motion that only added to the sense of anticipation building within me.

I didn't know where Tyde was taking me, didn't know what surprises he had in store. But as I sat there, my heart racing and my blood singing with desire, I knew that I was ready for whatever lay ahead.

For in the end, that was what love was all about. Taking a chance, stepping into the unknown with the one person who made your heart skip a beat and your soul come alive.

And as the car wound its way through the city streets, carrying me closer and closer to my destiny, I couldn't help but feel a sense of exhilaration, a thrill of adventure that set my pulse racing and my skin on fire.

Tyde had always been a mystery to me, a puzzle waiting to be solved. But as I sat there, my body thrumming with anticipation, I knew that I was ready to unravel the secrets that lay ahead, to discover the man behind the enigma and claim him as my own.

The night stretched out before me, a blank canvas waiting to be painted with the colors of passion and desire. And as the car drew closer to its secret destination, I couldn't help but feel a sense of excitement, a certainty that this was the beginning of something truly special.

THE AVIARY NYC

I leaned back against the plush leather seat, my eyes drifting closed as I savored the smooth ride down the familiar road. The anticipation was like a living thing, a flutter of wings in my stomach that grew with each passing mile. I couldn't shake the feeling that something big was about to happen, that Tyde had a surprise in store that would change everything.

As the car wound its way through the city streets, I found myself lost in memories of the past, of all the moments that had led me to this point. Tyde and I had always had a complicated relationship, a push and pull of attraction and frustration that had left me breathless and aching for more.

But as the car slowed to a stop and I opened my eyes,

all thoughts of the past vanished like smoke on the wind. Because there, looming before me like a beacon in the night, was The Aviary.

Suddenly, it all clicked into place. Tyde's mysterious message, the secrecy surrounding our destination - it all made sense now. This was the place where we had first met, the place where that initial spark of attraction had ignited into a flame that had never quite gone out.

Excitement bubbled up within me, a giddy rush of adrenaline that made my heart race and my skin tingle. I stepped out of the car, my heels clicking against the pavement as I moved towards the entrance.

The driver, ever the gentleman, offered me a courteous smile.

"Ms. Clark, I hope you have a wonderful evening. Mr. Wright has everything arranged for you."

I returned his smile, my voice warm with gratitude.

"Thank you so much. I appreciate it."

As I walked through the doors of The Aviary, I was greeted by the owner and hostess, their faces alight with welcoming smiles. They guided me towards the elevator, their voices low and conspiratorial as they spoke of the surprise that awaited me.

"Enjoy your evening, Ms. Clark," the hostess said, her eyes twinkling with mischief. Leaving me at the last exit before the rooftop entrance.

I nodded my thanks, my heart hammering in my chest as I began to climb the stairs. Each step was a journey, a path that led me closer and closer to the man who had captured my heart and refused to let go.

But even as the excitement coursed through my veins, I couldn't shake the hint of suspicion that niggled at the back of my mind. Tyde was a man of many secrets, a master of the grand gesture that always seemed to come with a catch.

What did he have in store for me tonight? What surprise lay waiting at the top of these stairs, ready to sweep me off my feet and leave me breathless with desire?

I didn't know the answer, but as I climbed the few steps, the anticipation building with each passing second, I knew that I was ready to find out.

Because in the end, that was what love was all about. Taking a leap of faith, stepping into the unknown with the one person who made your heart race and your soul come alive.

And as I reached the top of the stairs and pushed open the door to the rooftop, I knew that whatever lay ahead, I was ready to face it head on.

And as the cool night air hit my skin and the city lights twinkled below, I couldn't help but feel a sense of excitement, a certainty that this was the beginning of something truly special.

The rooftop stretched out before me, a blank canvas waiting to be painted with the colors of passion and desire. And as I stepped forward, ready to embrace whatever surprises the night had in store, I knew that I was exactly where I was meant to be.

THE AVIARY - ROOFTOP

The space on the rooftop had been transformed into a romantic haven, a sea of candles flickering in the gentle breeze. Peony petals created a path that led to a table draped in a crisp white cloth, and there, standing beside it with a warm smile on his face, was Tyde.

"Alright, Gia, you made it," he said, his voice soft and inviting.

For a moment, I was struck speechless by the sheer beauty of the scene, by the effort and thoughtfulness that had gone into creating this intimate setting. But even as my heart swelled with emotion, I couldn't shake the lingering hesitation that came with our complicated history.

"Tyde, this is... incredible," I managed, my voice guarded. "But we have a history, and if you're going to start taking the leap into new territory for our relationship, you'll have to take things slow."

Tyde nodded, his expression understanding. He knew the weight of my caution, the fears and doubts that had plagued us both for so long. But there was a determination in his eyes, a sincerity that made my heart skip a beat.

"I hear you, Gia. I just want a shot at showin' you things can be different, yeah?" he said, his words a promise and a plea all rolled into one.

We shared a smile, a tentative truce in the face of the unknown. Cautiously, I approached the beautifully set table, my heart pounding with a mix of excitement and trepidation.

As I took in the romantic rooftop setting, I couldn't help

but question Tyde about the unexpected rendezvous.

"Tyde, what are we doing here?"

He met my gaze, a sincere smile playing on his lips.

"Our story wasn't finished, Gia, just on hold for a bit."

With a gentle motion, he guided me to my side of the table. "Do us a favour, sit down."

Intrigued and cautious, I settled into my chair, watching as Tyde took his place across from me.

"Now, let's see what this Aviary lark's all about tonight," he grinned, his eyes sparkling with mischief.

As if on cue, a waiter appeared, bearing a spread of appetizers that made my mouth water. Calamari, mushrooms with melted mozzarella, caesar salad - all of my favorites, laid out before me like a feast fit for a queen.

"I was hopin' you'd like this. Is it alright?" Tyde asked, his voice tinged with a hint of nervousness.

I nodded eagerly, my earlier hesitation melting away in the face of such thoughtfulness. Tyde chuckled, relief and joy mingling in his expression.

"Shall we tuck in, eh? Grace has already been said."

We joined hands, a moment of silent gratitude passing between us. As I closed my eyes, I could feel the spark of connection that had always been there, the undeniable pull that drew us together time and time again.

The evening unfolded in a delightful dance of flavors and conversation, the renewed connection between us growing stronger with each passing minute. Tyde's laughter mingled with mine, his stories and jokes making me feel lighter than I had in years.

But even as we lost ourselves in the magic of the moment, I couldn't shake the feeling that this was just the beginning. That the road ahead would be filled with twists and turns, with challenges and obstacles that we would have to face together.

For now, though, I was content to bask in the glow of Tyde's presence, to savor the delicious food and the warmth of his smile. Because in the end, that was what mattered most - the connection we shared, the love that had never truly died.

As the night wore on and the candles burned low, I found myself leaning closer to Tyde, my heart full to bursting with the joy and the hope that he brought into my life. And when he reached across the table to take my hand, his fingers lacing with mine, I knew that I was exactly where I was meant to be.

And as we sat there under the stars, the city lights twinkling below, I couldn't help but feel a sense of excitement and imagine our future that stretched out before us.

A future filled with love and laughter, with challenges and triumphs. A future that we would face together, hand in hand, heart to heart.

And as I looked into Tyde's eyes, I saw the same promise reflected back at me. The promise of a love that would never die, a connection that would only grow stronger with each passing day.

—

As the night wore on, Tyde and I found ourselves drawn to a cozy spot on the rooftop, the twinkling city lights stretching out before us like a sea of stars. The gentle hum of the nightlife below mingled with the soft strains of music drifting up from the boats on the river, creating a perfect backdrop for our evening.

I leaned against the railing, my eyes drinking in the breathtaking view of the skyline, the bridge, and the shimmering water below.

"This is amazing, Tyde. Thank you for all of this."

Tyde's voice was soft, filled with a tenderness that made my heart skip a beat.

"Anything for you, love."

We fell into easy conversation, the words flowing between us like a gentle stream. It was as if no time had passed at all, as if we were picking up right where we had left off all those years ago.

"It's crazy how much has changed since we were last really talking," I mused, my eyes meeting his. "Tell me, Tyde, how's life for you now?"

Tyde's expression turned reflective, his gaze distant as he considered my question.

"Tell you what, telly's got its good bits and bad bits. Jackson and Lorenz are alright, still my best mates."

I smiled, warmth blooming in my chest at the mention of our old friends.

"I'm glad to hear they're doing well. I miss...our conversations."

"Same here, Gia," Tyde grinned, his eyes sparkling with mischief. "What about Laurie?"

I laughed, shaking my head at the thought of my snarky

best friend.

"Laurie's doing Laurie things, still snarky as ever. He wishes you the best, you know."

Tyde's eyebrows shot up, his expression flabbergasted.

"Laurie's wishing me well? Blimey, that's a surprise after the last row we had."

I frowned, my curiosity piqued.

"What conversation?"

Tyde's lips twitched into a right cheeky grin, his eyes full of secrets.

"Nothin' much, just that Laurie gives me a right dodgy vibe."

"Well that could be because he's jealous of our situation or past situation," I teased, my heart fluttering at the thought.

Tyde's forehead creased in confusion, his eyes searching mine.

"Why would he be?"

I couldn't help but laugh, the sound echoing across the rooftop.

"Oh, Tyde, darling. Laurie is into men too. You're just that irresistible."

Tyde's jaw hit the floor, his eyes like saucers.

"Hold on, Laurie fancies blokes too?"

I nodded, my laughter mingling with his as we shared in the absurdity of the moment.

"Duh, Tyde. You've got that effect on people... I guess."

As we lost ourselves in the laughter and the easy banter, the night became a canvas for rediscovering our connection. The rooftop ambiance was elevated as we delved into a feast of some of my favorite dishes, bolognese, panzanella, baked salmon, stuffed peppers, and caprese salad.

I savored each bite, my taste buds singing with delight.

"Tyde, this is amazing. You know all my favorites."

Tyde's gaze was fixed on me, his expression soft and admiring as he watched me enjoy the meal. I caught his eye, a playful smile tugging at my lips.

"Are you just going to stare, or are you going to eat?"

Tyde smirked, shaking his head in denial. But as I fixed him with a mock glare, he relented, picking up his fork and maintaining eye contact with me as he took a bite. The air between us crackled with electricity, the sparks of connection shooting back and forth like fireworks.

We ate in comfortable silence, the only sound the clink of silverware and the distant hum of the city below. As the plates cleared, a satisfied quiet settled over us, the connection between us palpable and undeniable.

"That was incredible. Thank you," I murmured, my voice soft and sincere.

As if on cue, music began to drift up from the boats on the river, the gentle strains of a romantic melody filling the air. Tyde's eyes lit up, a mischievous grin spreading across his face as he rose to his feet and extended his hand to me.

"Fancy a boogie?"

I couldn't help but be impressed, my heart swelling with delight as I accepted his offer. We swayed under the stars, our bodies moving in perfect sync as the jazz music from the boats became the soundtrack to our intimate dance.

The night unfolded, filled with unspoken connections

and shared moments that would be etched into my memory forever. As I lost myself in Tyde's arms, the rest of the world faded away, leaving only the two of us and the magic of the moment.

And as we danced, our hearts beating as one, I knew that this was just the beginning. That the road ahead would be filled with twists and turns, with challenges and triumphs that we would face together.

But for now, in this moment, I was content to bask in the glow of Tyde's presence, to savor the connection that had never truly died. Because in the end, that was what mattered most - the bond that had brought us together time and time again.

TYDE'S PENTHOUSE

As our connection deepened on the rooftop, Tyde and I made the decision to continue our night back at his penthouse. The anticipation hung heavy in the air as we made our way through the city streets, our hands intertwined and our hearts beating in sync.

When we entered Tyde's home, I found myself once again in awe of the atmosphere that greeted us. The space was awash in the soft glow of candlelight, the flickering flames casting dancing shadows on the walls. It was as if the rooftop had been transported indoors, the same romantic ambiance enveloping us in its warm embrace.

"Alright Gia, get yourself comfy. Anything you fancy?" Tyde asked, his voice low and inviting.

I met his gaze, my lips curving into a soft smile.

"Wine, please."

Tyde nodded, disappearing into the kitchen and returning moments later with a bottle of the finest red wine and two glasses. As he poured the ruby liquid, I took a slow look around the penthouse, drinking in the elegance and sophistication that surrounded me.

"This is incredible, Tyde," I murmured, my voice filled with admiration.

Tyde handed me a glass, his fingers brushing against mine and sending a shiver down my spine. We settled onto the couch, the plush cushions enveloping us in their softness. The glow of the candles bathed the room in a warm, intimate light, and I found myself reaching for the remote to turn on the projector.

As the movie began, we sipped our wine slowly, savoring each taste and letting the rich flavors dance on our tongues. Tyde's arm slipped around my shoulders, drawing me closer until I was nestled against his side. The heat of his body seeped into mine, warming me from the inside out.

The dim lighting and the ambiance set the mood for a relaxed and intimate evening, and as the movie played on, I found myself getting lost in the moment. Tyde's fingers traced lazy patterns on my skin, his touch feather-light and electrifying all at once.

In the midst of the movie, the sensual touches began to intensify. Tyde's hand slid down my arm, his fingers lacing with mine as he brought our joined hands to his lips. The soft brush of his mouth against my knuckles sent a jolt of desire through me, and I found myself leaning closer, my body aching for more.

The room was filled with the soft sounds of the movie, the flickering of candles, and the quiet exchanges between us. Whispered words and gentle sighs mingled with the dialogue on the screen, creating a symphony of intimacy that wrapped around us like a casting.

As the connection between us deepened, the simple movie night transformed into something more. Something memorable and intimate, a moment suspended in time that belonged only to us.

Tyde's lips found the sensitive spot behind my ear, his breath hot against my skin as he murmured words of affection and desire. I turned my head, capturing his mouth with mine in a kiss that was both tender and passionate.

We lost ourselves in each other, the movie forgotten as we explored the depths of our connection. Hands roamed and hearts raced, the heat between us building until it was a palpable force that filled the room.

And as we surrendered to the moment, to the magic of the night and the love that flowed between us, I knew that this was just the beginning.

I was content to bask in the glow of Tyde's presence, to savor the intimacy and the connection that we had rediscovered. Because in the end, that was what mattered most - the love we shared, the bond that had brought us together time and time again.

We gravitated from the plush couch to my massive bedroom, the low murmur of a forgotten movie fading into background static from the living room. Gia's body pressed against mine, the heat of her skin searing through the denim barrier. Slowly, deliberately, I traced a finger up the silken expanse of her arm, reveling in the goosebumps left in my wake. She shivered, head lolling back against the cushions, an open invitation.

Unable to resist, I leaned in, ghosting my lips along the column of her throat. Gia's breath hitched, fingers tangling in my coily hair as she guided me lower. I obliged, worshiping the hollow of her clavicle, tongue darting out to taste the salt of her skin. She was an oasis and I was a man dying of thirst, desperate to drink my fill.

Clothes were shed with fumbling urgency, a trail of fabric breadcrumbs leading to my bed. The sight of Gia sprawled across my silk sheets, an offering of cognac limbs and flushed skin, stole the air from my lungs. I crawled up her body, mapping every curve and valley with reverent hands, determined to commit every inch to memory.

When our lips finally met, it was a crash of teeth and tongues, weeks of pent-up longing pouring out in a frenzy of grasping hands and rolling hips. I swallowed Gia's moans, relishing the vibrations against my mouth as I explored the honeyed recesses of her body. She arched into my touch, a bowstring pulled taut, begging for release.

I took my time, lavishing attention on every freckle, every sensitive spot that made her gasp and writhe. Gia's nails scored delicious paths down my back, urging me on with breathless pleas and whispered encouragement. The world narrowed to the slide of sweat-slicked skin, the symphony of sighs and groans, the intoxicating scent of our combined arousal.

When I finally surged forward, burying myself in her welcoming heat, it was like coming home. We moved as one, give and take, push and pull, climbing higher and higher until the coil of tension snapped. Ecstasy crashed over us in waves, bodies shaking, souls shattering and reforming in the afterglow.

I gathered Gia close, pressing soft kisses to her damp brow as our racing hearts gradually slowed. She burrowed into my embrace, fitting perfectly against my side as if she'd always belonged there. In that moment, with the candles burning low and the first tendrils of sleep beckoning, I knew I'd found something rare and precious.

This wasn't just a physical connection, but a meeting of kindred spirits. Two fractured halves discover their perfect match again. As I drifted off, Gia's steady breaths ghosting across my chest, I allowed myself to hope. To believe that this could be the start of something real and lasting.

Morning would bring its own challenges, but covered in the warmth of tangled sheets and Gia's sweet weight, I pushed those thoughts aside. For now, I would savor this blissful interlude, storing up every sensation, every sigh. A talisman against the trials to come.

—

I woke up slowly, my senses gradually coming alive as I drifted out of a deep, dreamless sleep. The first thing I noticed was the warmth of Tyde's body pressed against mine, his arms wrapped around me like a protective encasement. I snuggled closer, savoring the feel of his skin against my own.

"Good morning," I whispered, my voice still rough with sleep.

Tyde's eyes fluttered open, a slow smile spreading across his face as he looked down at me.

"Alright, gorgeous. Morning to you."

We lay there for a moment, lost in the intimacy of the moment. Soft kisses were exchanged, gentle caresses that spoke of the joy and contentment we found in each other's arms. It was the start of something new, a new chapter in our lives that held the promise of something beautiful.

But as we basked in the warmth of Tyde's bed, our phones simultaneously started buzzing, shattering the peaceful silence. I groaned, reluctantly untangling myself from Tyde's embrace to search for my phone on the floor. Tyde reached for his dresser across the room, his brow furrowed with concern.

"Hello?" I said, wrapping the covers around my naked body as I walked into the living room.

Edith's voice crackled through the speaker, her tone all business.

"Gia, it's Edith. The NHL reached out. They want you to host another event... with Tyde. This upcoming week."

I felt a flicker of excitement, even as a sense of unease settled in the pit of my stomach.

"Oh, that's fantastic news! Of course, I'll do it. Thanks for letting me know."

As I ended the call, I heard Tyde's voice drifting from the bedroom, the door closing behind him as he took his own phone call. I busied myself in the kitchen, preparing coffee and trying to ignore the nagging feeling that something was off.

Tyde emerged a few minutes later, his expression unreadable.

"Fancy some brekkie?"

I nodded, forcing a smile.

"Definitely."

We moved around each other in the kitchen, Tyde cooking while I prepared the coffee. The morning unfolded with a blend of shared moments and a touch of uncertainty, the easy intimacy of earlier replaced by a subtle tension that hung heavy in the air.

Tyde moved effortlessly around the stove. The sizzle and pop of eggs hitting the hot pan filled the sunlit space. He looked unfairly good for this early in the morning, all tousled curly hair and lean muscles. My traitorous heart stuttered.

With a flourish, Tyde slid the fluffy scrambled eggs onto two waiting plates. Then he reached for the ketchup bottle and my brow furrowed. What was he up to?

I watched, curiosity mounting, as he carefully squeezed out lines and curves on my plate, tongue caught between his teeth in concentration. When he finished, he stepped back with a satisfied grin, gesturing grandly at his handiwork.

"Voila!"

I moved closer, peering down at the message scrawled in red. 'Be mine?' My stomach dropped even as my pulse kickstarter into overdrive.

"Tyde..." I began, scrambling for the right words.

His eyes, those magnetic blue pools I'd lost myself in countless times, sparkled with hope and excitement.

"We said casual, yeah, but Gia, this feels, well, mint. We click right together. Let's be a thing, officially."

I swallowed hard, staring at the plate to avoid his earnest gaze. Memories swirled in my mind - whispered locker room talk I wasn't meant to overhear, memories of his playboy ways, my own determination to keep my walls firmly in place this time. I couldn't comprehend fall again, even though my body was saying one thing and my mind another.

"I... I need to think about it," I managed, hating the way his face fell.

"Alright. Course. No sweat." He aimed for nonchalance but the tightness in his voice betrayed him.

Guilt wormed through me but I pushed it down. This was self-preservation. I had to prove, to him and to myself, that I could keep things casual, keep my heart safely locked away. Tyde Wright would be just another name on my roster, a fun distraction and nothing more.

I forced a breezy smile.

"Come on, these eggs are getting cold. Let's eat."

He nodded, jaw clenched, and slid into his seat. The scrape of forks against plates filled the strained silence as we ate. I kept my eyes on my food, my appetite long gone.

I knew I was hurting him but it was for the best. Easier this than risking another devastating heartbreak. Still, as I chewed mechanically, my chest ached hollowly.

If casual was what I wanted, why did it feel so wrong?

As we finished breakfast, I knew I couldn't stay any

longer. The uneasy feeling in my gut had grown, a sense of foreboding that I couldn't shake.

"Anyways, I should get going," I said, my voice soft and hesitant.

I gathered my things, preparing to leave Tyde's place. He walked me to the door, the atmosphere heavy with unspoken thoughts and lingering doubts.

As I went to grab the handle, Tyde's hand shot out and grabbed my arm.

"Gia, hold on a sec."

He pushed me gently against the door, his lips finding mine in a kiss that was both passionate and graceful. It was a bittersweet goodbye, a moment suspended in time that held the promise of something more, even as it acknowledged the uncertainty that lay ahead.

"Have a smashing day, G," Tyde murmured, his forehead resting against mine.

I left, my heart pounding and my mind racing with the memory of that lingering kiss. As I stepped out into the hallway, I couldn't shake the feeling that something had shifted between us, that the events of the morning had set us on a path that we couldn't turn back from.

Behind me, I heard the door close, the sound echoing in the stillness of the penthouse. And as I walked away, my steps heavy with the weight of my thoughts, I couldn't help but wonder what the future held for Tyde and me.

Little did I know that behind that closed door, Tyde was grappling with his own emotions, his heart pounding with an unexpected realization.

"Sweet on Gia, am I?" he whispered to himself, the words hanging in the air like a confession.

The penthouse fell silent, my thoughts echoing louder than the distant hum of New York City traffic below. I stood by the floor-to-ceiling windows, the twinkling lights of the skyline blurring as I lost myself in contemplation. The weight of my feelings for Gia pressed down on me, as tangible as the cool glass beneath my fingertips.

My phone buzzed, shattering the stillness. I hesitated for a moment before grabbing it, my fingers hovering over the screen. With a deep breath, I opened our group chat and fired off a message:

"Lads, I'm in deep. Need your wisdom. What's the next move with Gia? How do I get her to ditch that bloody roster?"

The response was swift, my phone lighting up with rapid-fire replies.

Jackson's message popped up first, his Canadian enthusiasm practically leaping off the screen, "Bud! You gotta go big or go home, eh? Send her something special – flowers, maybe? Or one of those fancy paintings she likes!"

Lorenz chimed in, his words tinged with German practicality,"Ja, Jackson's got the right idea. Something personal, something that shows you've been paying attention."

I ran a hand through my hair, conflicted. Their suggestions were solid, but a nagging doubt gnawed at me.

"I dunno, boys," I typed back. "Ain't that a bit much? Don't want her to think I'm pushin' too hard, yeah?"

There was a pause, and I could almost hear them thinking across the miles.

Jackson replied first, "Come on, man! You can't play it too safe. Gotta show her you're serious!"

"Genau," Lorenz agreed. "But perhaps something smaller to start? A book she mentioned, or tickets to that gallery opening she was excited about?"

I paced the length of the penthouse, their words swirling in my mind. The lads meant well, but they didn't understand the delicate balance I was trying to maintain with Gia. One wrong move, and I could send her running for the hills.

"Thanks, mates," I finally responded. "But I reckon I need to take this slow. Don't want her to pull back, you know? Gotta play this smart."

I could practically hear their collective sigh of frustration through the phone. But they knew me well enough to respect my decision.

"Alright, alright," Jackson conceded. "But don't wait too long, eh? Someone else might swoop in and steal your girl!"

Lorenz added a string of encouraging emojis, followed by, "We believe in you, mein Freund. Just don't overthink it, ja?"

I smiled despite myself, grateful for their unwavering support. "Cheers, lads. I'll keep you posted."

As I set the phone down, my gaze drifted back to the city sprawled out before me. Somewhere out there was Gia, probably unaware of the turmoil she was causing in my heart. I had to find a way to show her how I felt without scaring her off.

—

GIA'S APARTMENT

The shrill ping of my phone pierced the morning stillness, jolting me out of my thoughts. I reached for the device, my brow furrowing as I saw an unfamiliar name flashing across the screen, Paul Winnipeg. The name rang a distant bell, a vague recollection of a Canadian hockey player I had heard mentioned in passing.

I hesitated, my finger hovering over the screen as I debated whether to open the message. The memory of last night with Tyde was still fresh in my mind, the magic of the rooftop date lingering like a warm embrace. I could still feel the touch of his lips on mine, the way his hands had roamed my body with a reverence that left me breathless.

But curiosity got the better of me, and I swiped to open the text, my eyebrows shooting up in surprise as I read the words that greeted me.

"Hey Gia! Your name's been popping up everywhere, eh? All good things, for sure. Up for grabbing some grub together tonight?" - Paul

I bit my lip, my mind racing as I contemplated the invitation. A part of me wanted to decline, to hold onto the memories of last night and the promise of something more with Tyde. But another part of me, the part that craved adventure and excitement, whispered that there was no harm in keeping an open mind.

Before I could second-guess myself, I typed out a quick reply, hitting send before I could change my mind.

"Sure, dinner sounds good. See you tonight." - Gia

As the message whooshed away, I felt a flicker of uncertainty, a nagging feeling that I was making a mistake. But I pushed it aside, determined to approach the evening with a sense of nonchalance.

I moved through the motions of getting ready, my mind only half-focused on the task at hand. I couldn't shake the memory of Tyde's touch, the way he had made me feel cherished and desired in a way I had never experienced before.

But even as I slipped into a dress and applied my makeup, I knew that I couldn't let myself get too caught up in the magic of last night. Tyde and I had a complicated history, a tangled web of emotions and unresolved issues that threatened to trip us up at every turn.

And so, as I stepped out into the evening air, ready to meet Paul for our date, I tried to keep my expectations in check. I knew that I wouldn't easily let someone take Tyde's place, that the connection we shared was something rare and precious.

But I also knew that I had to keep an open mind, to give myself the chance to explore other possibilities and see where they might lead. Because in the end, that was what life was all about - taking chances, embracing the unknown, and seeing where the journey might take you.

The insistent buzz of my phone sliced through the tension hanging heavy in the air. I glanced down, my stomach tightening as Tyde's name flashed across the screen.

Suddenly, I was overwhelmed by the enormity of what I was about to do. Could I really go through with this...date? Risk jeopardizing everything Tyde and I had rebuilt with such painstaking effort? The memories of our magical rooftop rendezvous were still so viscerally fresh - the warm flicker of candlelight gilding his chiseled features, the gentle sway of jazz mingling with our breathy whispers of affection.

My finger hovered over the message, suspended in that molasses-thick moment of indecision. Some deep-rooted part of me still nostalgically clung to the dream of Tyde and I made it work against all odds. But another piece, my fiercely independent soul, craved the electrifying uncertainty of exploring new connections.

With a steadying breath, I typed back a maddeningly vague reply about "having plans." I knew it would fan the flames of Tyde's jealousy and stir up that tornado of insecurities he worked so hard to contain. But this one night was about indulging my own wants, not contorting myself to soothe his perpetual doubts.

I was doing this for me.

The delicate ping of my rideshare notification jerked me back to the present moment. I blew out a resolute breath and grabbed my purse.

No matter what lay ahead this evening, I refused to bloat it with expectations or "what-ifs." I was a woman in full control of her own destiny, no longer the insecure girl who fumbled her way through situationships and disappointments. Paul was an unanticipated detour on my journey, one I could embrace with open arms or merely smile and walk away from.

Whatever happened would simply be another brilliant thread woven into the ornate tapestry of my life. With one last cleansing exhale, I spun on my heel and strode out into the inky evening, my future awaiting like an electrifying promise over the horizon.

—

Paul, at 6'3", with honey-hued rippling mane and striking blue eyes, embodied the very essence of Canadian charm.

As I approached, Paul's face lit up with a warm smile. He greeted me with a hug, his strong arms enveloping me in a brief but friendly embrace. We made our way to our table, the conversation flowing easily as we settled in.

"So, Gia, spill the beans about yourself. What's life like in the big smoke, eh?" Paul asked, his eyes sparkling with genuine interest.

I laughed, the sound bubbling up from my chest.

"It's a whirlwind, but I love it. Working in TV keeps things interesting. How about you? How's life in Canada?"

As I spoke, I couldn't shake the lingering magic of the night spent with Tyde. The memories danced at the edges of my consciousness, threatening to pull me back into the enchantment of that rooftop encounter.

But I pushed them aside, determined to give Paul my full attention. He was charming and engaging, his easy manner putting me at ease even as my heart remained guarded.

As the night unfolded, we traded stories and laughter, the conversation flowing like a gentle stream. But even as I enjoyed Paul's company, I couldn't help but feel a subtle undercurrent of tension, a sense that something was holding me back.

And then, as if reading my thoughts, Paul leaned forward, his expression growing serious.

"Gia, I hope you don't take this the wrong way, but Jackson and Lorenz rave about you. Heard whispers about your history with Tyde, and totally get it if you don't wanna dish on that. Your private life is your business, end of story," he said, his voice sincere.

I felt a flicker of surprise, followed by a rush of gratitude. It was a relief to know that Paul understood that he wasn't going to push me for details I wasn't ready to share.

"Thanks, Paul. I appreciate your understanding. Jackson and Lorenz are good friends, and, well, life happens. So, what did they say about me?" I asked, a smile playing at the corners of my mouth.

Paul grinned, his eyes crinkling at the corners.

"Oh, just good stuff, I swear. They think you're unreal. Figured I'd shoot my shot and see if we could click as mates, or maybe somethin' more down the road, who knows?"

I giggled, the sound ringing out in the quiet restaurant.

"Well, I appreciate the honesty, Paul. Friends sounds like a great start."

He nodded, his expression warm and open.

"Mates it is then. Lookin' forward to gettin' to know ya better, Gia."

As we clink our glasses together in a toast to new beginnings, I felt a sense of ease wash over me. Paul was a good man, someone I could see myself becoming close with over time.

But even as we chatted and laughed, my mind kept

drifting back to Tyde. The memory of his touch, the way he had looked at me with such intensity, refused to fade.

I knew that I couldn't let myself get too caught up in the past, that I needed to keep an open mind and an open heart. But as the evening wore on, I couldn't shake the feeling that something was missing. Which I begrudgingly know why - because these men aren't him, they aren't Tyde. The connection I share with Tyde was something rare and precious.

As we said our goodbyes outside the restaurant, Paul pulled me in for a hug. His arms were strong and comforting, but they didn't ignite the same fire in my veins that Tyde's touch had.

I walked away from the restaurant, my mind swirling with conflicting emotions. I was grateful for Paul's niceties, for the chance to start fresh with someone new.

And as I climbed into bed that night, silk bonnet on, my heart heavy with the weight of the unknown, I knew that I had a choice to make. I could cling to the past, to the memories of what had been. Or I could embrace the future, the possibilities that lay ahead.

And as I drifted off to sleep, my mind filled with dreams of penthouse kisses and whispered promises, I knew that whatever choice I made, it would change everything.

GIA'S APARTMENT

The sharp knock at my door startled me out of my TV-induced stupor. I wasn't expecting company, not after the friendly date I'd endured earlier. Frowning, I padded to the entryway and peered through the peephole.

A delivery guy stood, a tower of takeout bags obscuring his face. Baffled, I opened the door. The savory aroma of Indian spices wafted in, making my mouth water and my stomach growl traitorously.

"Gia Clark?" the guy asked, thrusting the bags toward me.

"That's me, but I didn't order-"

"Already paid for. Enjoy." With that, he turned and strode off, leaving me gaping after him.

Curiosity piqued, I carried the food to the kitchen counter and began unpacking cartons. Butter chicken, lamb rogan josh, palak paneer, garlic naan... all my favorites from my go-to Indian place. There was enough to feed a small army.

Realization dawned and I couldn't suppress a small smile. Tyde. He was the only one who knew my order by heart, the only one I'd mentioned my dinner plans (or lack thereof) to earlier.

Something warm and fluttery unfurled in my chest as I imagined him placing the order, picking out all the dishes he knew I loved. It was thoughtful, sweet even. Not at all in line with the player persona he cultivated so carefully.

I knew I should be annoyed at his presumption, but I was too charmed (and ravenous) to summon any irritation. Grabbing a fork, I dug in, letting the complex flavors burst across my tongue.

As I ate, my mind drifted to Tyde, picturing the cocky grin he'd no doubt be sporting if he could see me now. The man was insufferably sure of himself, secure in the knowledge that no one could measure up to him in my eyes.

If I was being honest, he wasn't entirely wrong. Tonight's "date" had been a prime example - nice enough guy, but no real spark, no zing. Not like the electricity that crackled between Tyde and me whenever we shared the same space.

But I couldn't let myself dwell on that, on him. We worked together, and had a long, complicated history. Keeping him firmly in the friend zone was the smart play, no matter how my traitorous heart raced at the mere thought of him.

My phone lit up with a new text and I smiled in spite of myself.

"Tuck in, G! Can't wait to see you tomorrow, sleep tight." - Ty

I typed back a quick thanks, wishing him good night, then set my phone aside and refocused on the mouth watering spread before me.

As I polished off the last of the naan, I reflected that maybe having Tyde Wright as a friend wasn't the worst thing in the world. Especially if it came with surprise deliveries of my favorite comfort foods.

I fell asleep that night with the phantom taste of spices on my tongue and luscious brown eyes dancing behind my lids, full, content, and cautiously optimistic about what tomorrow would bring.

Malcolm Smith

The memory of that first contact with Charlotte burned in my mind like a brand. I was slouched in my dingy apartment, surrounded by the soft glow of computer screens, when my phone buzzed. An unknown number. I almost ignored it.

"Malcom Smith?" The voice was crisp, authoritative. Familiar.

I sat up straighter, suddenly alert. "Yes, who's this?"

"Charlotte Astor. You worked in my father's building downtown."

My heart raced. Charlotte Astor. Daughter of mogul Derek Astor. I'd seen her striding through the lobby, all power suits and clicking heels.

"I remember," I managed to croak out.

"Good. I have a... job opportunity for you." The way she paused made my skin prickle.

I swallowed hard. "What kind of opportunity?"

"The kind that requires discretion. And your particular skill set." Her voice lowered. "You've worked in tech before, haven't you?"

I glanced at my array of gadgets, a graveyard of half-finished projects.

"Yeah, I have."

"Excellent. I need a camera. Small. Undetectable. Something that can be placed... incognito."

My pulse quickened. This wasn't legal territory we were treading.

"Where exactly would this camera be going?"

"That's not your concern," Charlotte snapped. Then, softer: "Let's just say it's somewhere no one will notice for a long time."

I hesitated, weighing the risks. Then my phone pinged. A notification from my bank app.

Charlotte's voice dripped with satisfaction. "That's just a down payment. There's more where that came from."

I stared at the screen. $40,000. My rent was due. My fridge was empty.

"When do you need it?"

We arranged to meet the following week. A busy café downtown. I arrived early, nerves jangling, the tiny device burning a hole in my pocket. I spotted Charlotte immediately. She sat alone, sipping a latte, looking for all the world like a busy executive on a coffee break.

My heart hammered as I approached. One smooth motion. That's all it would take. I brushed past her table, my hand darting out. The camera slid from my fingers, landing silently next to her cup. I kept walking, not daring to look back.

"Well done," her voice purred in my phone. I allowed myself a small smile as I exited the café.

Days passed. I tried not to think about where the camera might be, what it might be recording. Then Charlotte called again.

"I need the footage, I have enough to use," she demanded. No pleasantries. No explanation. " I'm going to need more cameras soon."

I complied, of course. The money was too good to ask questions. But curiosity gnawed at me. Late that night, after sending Charlotte the files, I couldn't resist. I opened a copy.

The screen flickered to life. A bedroom came into focus. Tasteful decor, luxury, muted colors. And then... her.

She entered the frame, and my world stopped spinning with her giant cinnamon-hued spiral hair, dreamy brown eyes that seemed to pierce right through the camera. She moved with a grace that made my breath catch.

I leaned closer, drinking in every detail. The curve of her neck as she tilted her head. The way her fingers absently twirled a strand of hair as she read. The soft sound of her laughter drifting through my speakers.

I was transfixed. Obsessed. I had to know everything about her.

Her name was my first discovery. Gia. It rolled off my tongue like a prayer. I dug deeper. Social media accounts. Public records. Each new piece of information was a treasure, carefully cataloged in my mind.

I told myself it was harmless. Just curiosity. But deep down, I knew. This was something darker. Something dangerous.

As the sun rose, painting my cluttered apartment in shades of black and green, I finally tore myself away from the screens. But Gia's face lingered in my mind, a ghost I couldn't shake.

I collapsed onto my bed, exhausted but wired. Sleep eluded me. All I could think about was her. Gia. And how I could see her again.

Little did I know, this obsession would lead me down a path from which there was no return.

CHAPTER 12
DEAD RECKONING

Tyde & Gia

NHL DEAL ZONE SET - DAY 1

I arrived at the set for the NHL Trade and Draft Coverage, my heart racing with a mixture of nerves and excitement. The atmosphere was electric, the air buzzing with anticipation as the crew hustled to get everything in place. I glanced over at Tyde, his presence a reassuring constant amidst the chaos.

"Ready for another weekend of trade and draft action?" I asked, my eyes scanning the script in my hands.

Tyde grinned, his eyes sparkling with mischief.

"You said it. Let's cause a right kerfuffle!"

We were handed our scripts, lines, and sides for each segment of the program. The aesthetic of the show was dynamic and engaging, reminiscent of the popular sports show First Take. I could feel the energy thrumming through my veins, the thrill of being a part of something big and exciting.

As I flipped through the pages, my eyebrows shot up in surprise.

"We've got some controversial takes lined up, especially with your predictions, Tyde."

He laughed, his voice rich and warm.

"Can't help myself, love, it's in my blood to wind people up a bit."

The cameras rolled, and Tyde launched into his first bold prediction, urging a recently retired star veteran to make a comeback. I chimed in with my own insights on the emerging talents and potential team destinations, our voices blending together in a perfect harmony.

"Tyde, you're not making any friends with those predictions," I smirked, my eyes dancing with amusement.

He grinned, his face alight with joy.

"Even if we're just mates, it's all a bit of a giggle, innit?"

As the show progressed, our chemistry shone through, our banter and controversial takes capturing the attention of the audience. The energy in the room was palpable, the excitement building with each passing minute.

I could feel the adrenaline coursing through my veins, the rush of being in the moment, of being a part of something bigger than myself. Tyde and I worked seamlessly together, our years of experience and natural rapport evident in every word and gesture.

As the day wore on, the show gained momentum, our takes and predictions going viral on social media. The buzz was electric, the audience hanging on our every word.

I glanced over at Tyde, my heart swelling with pride and admiration. He was in his element, his passion and knowledge shining through in every moment. I couldn't help but be drawn to him, to the way he commanded the room with his presence and his words.

As the cameras stopped rolling and the crew began to pack up, I felt a sense of accomplishment wash over me. Day one had been a resounding success, unscathed by problems or setbacks.

I turned to Tyde, a smile playing at the corners of my mouth.

"We did it. Another successful day in the books."

He grinned, his eyes locking with mine.

"We're a right good team, wouldn't you say?"

I nodded, my heart skipping a beat at the intensity of his gaze.

"The best."

As we made our way out of the studio, the energy of the day still buzzing in our veins, I couldn't help but feel a sense of excitement for what lay ahead. The weekend was just beginning, and I'm starting to believe with Tyde by my side, anything was possible.

We stepped out into the bright sunlight, the sounds of the city enveloping us like a warm embrace. I took a deep breath, savoring the moment, the feeling of being alive and in the thick of things.

And as we walked side by side, our shoulders brushing and our laughter mingling in the air, I knew that this was just the beginning. That the adventures and challenges that lay ahead would only serve to strengthen the bond between us, to deepen the connection that had been forged in the heat of the moment.

For now, though, I was content to bask in the glow of our success, to savor the feeling of being a part of something special. And as I looked over at Tyde, his face alight with joy and excitement, I knew that I was exactly where I was meant to be.

Ready to take on the world, one bold prediction at a time.

NHL DEAL ZONE SET - DAY 2

I walked into the office with Tyde, our steps in sync as we prepared for another day of coverage. The excitement from the previous day still lingered in the air, a palpable energy that crackled like electricity. But as we made our way through the hallways, I couldn't shake the feeling that something was off.

The weight of suspicious glances from our colleagues bore down on us, their eyes following our every move. I glanced over at Tyde, my brow furrowed in confusion. He met my gaze, his own expression mirroring my perplexity.

"What the blazes is going on here?" he muttered, his voice low and tense.

I shook my head, just as clueless as he was. The odd atmosphere hung heavy in the air, a suffocating blanket of unease that threatened to smother us both.

Tyde's jaw clenched, his eyes narrowing as he pulled out

his phone. I watched as his face contorted with rage, his fingers gripping the device so tightly I thought it might shatter. But even in his anger, he held it in, his professionalism a thin veneer masking the storm that brewed beneath the surface.

With a discreet motion, he tilted the phone towards me, his expression grim. I cupped the device in my hands, my eyes widening in horror as I took in the images that filled the screen.

Scandalous paparazzi photos, the very ones we thought we had left behind, stared back at me. The world seemed to tilt on its axis, the ground beneath my feet giving way as the reality of the situation crashed down upon me.

"No..." I whispered, my voice trembling with a mixture of fear and disbelief.

Tyde's hand clenched into a fist, his knuckles turning white with the force of his grip. I could see the tension coiled in his muscles, the barely contained fury that threatened to explode at any moment.

I passed the phone back to him with shaking hands, my mind reeling as I tried to process the magnitude of what we were facing. Our past had come back to haunt us, the resurfaced tape and paparazzi photos now circulating among our colleagues like a virus.

I felt the walls closing in around me, the air growing thick and heavy with each passing second. I couldn't breathe, couldn't think, couldn't move. The weight of the world pressed down on my chest, crushing me beneath its unrelenting force.

And then, without warning, I was running. My feet carried me out of the building, my heart pounding in my ears as I fled from the suffocating atmosphere that threatened to consume me whole.

I could hear Tyde calling after me, his voice desperate and pleading. But I couldn't stop, couldn't turn back. The need to escape, to put as much distance between myself and the nightmare that had just unfolded, was too strong to resist.

I ran until my lungs burned and my legs ached, until the world around me blurred into a hazy mess of colors and shapes. And then I collapsed, my body giving way to the exhaustion and the pain that consumed me.

I sat there on the ground, my back pressed against the rough brick of a building, my chest heaving with each ragged breath. Tears streamed down my face, hot and stinging as they carved paths through the makeup I had so carefully applied just hours before.

I didn't know how long I sat there, lost in the swirling vortex of my own thoughts. But eventually, I heard footsteps approaching, the sound of someone drawing near.

I gathered myself as quickly as I could. And got out of there as fast as I could. Just imagining the enclosed wall of my home at this moment and how fast can I get there.

Charlotte Astor

FOUR YEARS AGO...

FLASHBACK - SURVEILLANCE ROOM

In the dimly lit security room, a bank of monitors cast an eerie glow across my face as I leaned forward, eyes narrowed in concentration. The CCTV cameras, silent sentinels with their unblinking autumn brown lenses, tracked every movement on the pulsing dance floor below. Amidst the writhing mass of bodies, two figures in particular commanded my attention.

Tyde and Gia, oblivious to the watchful gaze of the cameras, moved as one to the hypnotic beat. Their bodies were so close, skin glistening with a sheen of sweat, as if they were trying to meld into a single entity. Gia's head fell back, exposing the smooth column of her throat as she lost herself to the primal rhythm, heedless of who might be observing her uninhibited display.

I zoomed in, fingers flying across the control panel with practiced ease. The high-definition feed revealed every flickering emotion that danced across their faces - the undisguised hunger in Tyde's eyes, the wanton abandon in Gia's parted lips. They were so wrapped up in each other, in the magnetic pull that seemed to draw them inexorably closer, that the world around them ceased to exist.

A smirk tugged at the corner of my mouth as I watched them, a predator surveying its unsuspecting prey. They had no idea that their every move, every stolen caress and heated glance, was being immortalized on the unforgiving digital eye of the cameras. That someone was privy to their most intimate moments, a voyeuristic intruder in their private universe.

Anticipation coiled in my gut, a serpentine twist of perverse glee. This was only the beginning, a tantalizing glimpse of the power I held over them. They were marionettes, dancing on strings they couldn't even see, and I was the puppet master lurking in the shadows.

I leaned back in my chair, the worn leather creaking under my shifting weight. The fluorescent overhead light buzzed, casting harsh shadows across the planes of my face. In the reflected glow of the screens, my eyes glinted with malicious intent, a shark scenting blood in the water.

Tyde and Gia thought this night was about them, a stolen moment of passion in the anonymous crush of the club. But they were merely pawns, unwitting players in a game far bigger than their petty desires. A game in which I held all the cards.

My gaze flicked to the frozen image on the central monitor, their faces caught in a moment of unbridled ecstasy. A cruel chuckle escaped my lips, the sound swallowed by the whirring of computer fans and the distant thump of bass.

They had no idea what was coming, the storm that was about to break over their unsuspecting heads. But I did. And I relished every second of it.

Let them have their fleeting happiness, their illusion of control. Soon enough, the truth would come crashing down, shattering their world like a house of cards in a hurricane. And I would be there to watch it all unfold, savoring every delicious moment of their destruction.

After all, that was the true thrill - not the act itself, but the inevitable fallout. The devastation left in its wake.

And Tyde and Gia? They were just the latest in a long line of victims, lambs led willingly to the slaughter.

They had no idea who they were dealing with. But they would learn.

Oh, how they would learn.

Tyde & Gia

CLUB BAR

The dimly lit nightclub pulsed with energy, the beat of the music thrumming through my veins as Tyde and I wove through the crowded dance floor.

As we reached the bar, Tyde leaned in close, his breath hot against my ear.

"Just popping to the loo, love." he murmured, his voice barely audible over the pounding bass.

"Don't go anywhere."

I nodded, my skin tingling where his lips had brushed against my cheek. As he melted into the crowd, I turned back to the bar, my fingers curling around the cool glass of my drink. I swirled the liquid absentmindedly, my thoughts drifting to the events of the past few days.

I was so lost in my own thoughts that I didn't notice the stranger sliding up beside me, his charming smile glinting in the dim light.

"Hey there, beautiful," he purred, his voice smooth as silk. "Mind if I join you?"

I blinked, caught off guard by his sudden appearance. But politeness won out over caution, and I found myself nodding.

"Um, sure."

We exchanged pleasantries, the conversation flowing as easily as the drinks. But as we talked, I couldn't shake the feeling that something was off, that there was more to this stranger than met the eye. But I don't judge a book by its cover.

A figure slipping up behind Gia, pretending to order a drink but surreptitiously adding a substance to her cocktail.

Tyde finally arrived back, his presence a comforting warmth at my side.

"Alright, what's going on here?" he asked, his brow furrowed with concern.

I forced a smile, trying to mask the unease that had settled over me.

"Yeah, everything's fine. Just making a new friend."

Tyde's eyes narrowed, his gaze flicking between me and the stranger. I could see the suspicion in his expression, the protective instinct that drove him to keep me safe.

But he had no idea of the true danger that lurked, of the sinister plot that was unfolding right under our noses.

The stranger who had added the substance to my drink exchanged a knowing glance with his accomplice, a subtle nod passing between them. Tyde, sensing something was amiss, shooed away the flirtatious stranger, his arm wrapping around my waist in a possessive gesture.

"You alright, love?" he murmured, his voice low and urgent. "You sure that bloke wasn't giving you any grief, were you?"

I waved off his concern, taking a sip of my drink to relax.

"Nah, I'm good. Just enjoying the night."

But even as the words left my lips, I felt a twinge in my senses, a slight haziness that crept over my mind. I brushed it off, too caught up in the moment to realize the danger that lurked in my glass.

And so I drank, unaware of the poison that coursed through my veins, of the trap that had been set for me in the heart of the nightclub.

Little did I know that this was only the beginning, that the true horror of the night was yet to come.

But for now, I was lost in the music, in the heat of Tyde's touch and the buzz of the alcohol. Oblivious to the danger that stalked me, to the eyes that watched my every move.

Waiting for the perfect moment to strike.

PRESENT DAY

GIA'S APARTMENT

I couldn't let the tears fall, not until I was safely within the confines of my own home. The weight of the world pressed down on my shoulders, threatening to crush me beneath its unrelenting force. But I refused to break, refused to let them see the cracks in my armor.

It wasn't until I stepped through the threshold of my apartment, the door clicking shut behind me with a sense of finality, that I allowed myself to crumble. The sobs tore from my throat, raw and agonized, as I sank to the floor in a heap of despair.

I couldn't bear to face the outside world, couldn't stomach the thought of their prying eyes and whispered judgments. So I did the only thing I could think of - I turned off my phone, blocking out the relentless attempts to contact me.

But even in the silence of my self-imposed exile, I couldn't escape the old echoes of hated voices.

Tyde's desperate pleas filled Gia's voicemail.

"Gia, come on... I'll sort this, we'll sort it. This ain't like before, alright? I'm here now, a better bloke, standing by you through this, promise." he promised, his voice cracking with emotion.

But how could he fix this? How could anyone undo the damage that had been done, the scars that had been ripped open for all the world to see?

Laurie tried to reach me, my parents too. But I couldn't face them, couldn't bear to see the pity and the concern in their eyes.

And I don't want to hear the words they always say, "You should've been paying attention... Why do you feel like you should be hanging around those types of people?... Look at what has happened... Hanging around the wrong crowd of people?...We would never criticize who you are as a person but we know who we raised and we don't see her."

So I retreated further into myself, curling up on the cold tile of my bathroom floor as the mascara streaks flowed down my cheeks in an inky river of despair.

I cried until there were no tears left, until my body was wracked with silent sobs and my eyes burned with the salt of my own misery. And then, exhausted and hollow, I let the darkness take me, drifting off into a fitful sleep that offered no respite from the pain.

Miles away, on the set of the show that had once been my life's blood, Tyde felt the weight of my absence like a physical ache. As they came back from a commercial break, he faced the camera with a smile that didn't quite reach his eyes, his gaze flicking to the empty chair beside him. Prickles all over his skin, he begins the broadcast hiding his real emotions with the facade of being okay.

"Ladies and gentlemen, thank you for joining me today," he began, his voice steady despite the turmoil that raged within him. "Well, you may notice the absence of my co-host, Gia. Regrettably, she's unable to be with us today."

But as he delved into the first segment of the show, the words felt hollow, the script a flimsy facade that couldn't hope to mask the truth. And so, in a moment of uncharacteristic candor, Tyde made a decision that would change everything.

He cut the teleprompter dialogue, impulsively trying to put out the fire and eyes locking onto the camera with a fierce intensity that sent shivers down the spines of all who watched.

"Life throws right wingers at you sometimes, and today's been a real doozy for both me and Gia," he said, his voice all choked up. "Just wanna get somethin' off my chest, you know?"

And so he did. He spoke of his feelings for me, of the time we had spent together and the bond that had forged between us. He spoke of standing by my side through thick and thin, of being there for me no matter what challenges we faced.

And then, with a conviction that left no room for doubt, he addressed the recent exposure, the violation of our privacy that had rocked us to our core.

"For those who choose to expose the personal lives of others in a disheartening light, remember, there are always consequences," he warned, his voice low and dangerous. "But sod that, let's move on from the bad vibes. Focus on the good stuff, yeah?"

As he turned back to the camera, his eyes softened with a tenderness that made audiences everywhere swoon. Everyone could understand this heart ache, knowing that his next words were meant for Gia and Gia alone.

"Gia, if you're watching this, I just wanna say I'm right behind you, now and always. Wish you were here, squashed beside me, but we'll sort this out together, eh, love?"

The audience was left with a moment of silence, the weight of Tyde's sincerity hanging heavy in the air. And as he continued with the rest of the show, his words echoing in the hearts and minds of all who listened.

—

GIA'S APARTMENT - MORNING AFTER

My falsely grip the cold flood as a tremor of dread flooded my veins. The shadowy lobby beckoned, but felt disturbingly familiar - like hunted prey scenting danger on the wind. I willed my leaden feet forward, the sickly yellow overhead lights casting macabre shadows that seemed to reach for me with gnarled fingers.

A tall silhouette lurked near the stairwell, unmoving. A strangled gasp lodged in my throat as he turned, those cruel eyes piercing me like icy daggers of recognition. Analyzing him for two seconds, I could only make out from the moonlight beaming his name badge…*Mac.*

No…it couldn't be. Not him. Never again.

Bile scorched the back of my tongue as terrifying memories came crashing down. The brutal slaps and chilling taunts, bones crunching under relentless blows, haunting me from the deepest recesses of my mind. My pulse thundered like a wardrum in my ears as his lips curled into that signature sadistic sneer.

"Leaving so soon, pet? We're just getting started."

The gravelly timbre of his voice lacerated through me, ripping open freshly scabbed wounds with surgical precision. This was no lucid dream...this was the re-living of my personal purgatory.

As his hulking form advanced, I wanted nothing more than to flee, to run until my lungs burned and my legs gave out from under me. But some deeper, primal instinct took over, holding me paralyzed in the vortex of his scrutinizing stare. I was reduced to a trapped animal again, weak and vulnerable.

No matter how many nights I spent carousing just to numb the pain, no matter how much feverish scrubbing to scour away the phantom ache of his ruthless hands...his unrelenting malice would forever be seared into the fabric of my soul.

My personal demon had returned to make me relive the traumatic hell he so savored putting me through. And this time, there was no waking up to escape the brutal onslaught about to be unleashed. And so I thought, my mind was on my side for once.

I woke up in a frightful sweat, shaking myself off the dream, and reluctantly peeling my body off the cold, unforgiving bathroom floor. Every muscle aches, every joint creaked in protest as I slowly made my way to the living room. The weight of the world pressed down on my shoulders, threatening to crush me beneath its unrelenting force.

I sank into the couch, my body melting into the soft cushions as I sought refuge from the harsh reality that awaited me beyond the walls of my apartment. I couldn't bear the thought of turning on any electronic device, couldn't stomach the idea of facing the world and all its judgments.

So I sat there, lost in my own thoughts, my mind a tangled web of emotions that I couldn't even begin to unravel. The silence was deafening, the emptiness of my apartment a stark reminder of the loneliness that threatened to consume me whole.

And then, without warning, a loud bang echoed through the stillness, startling me from my reverie. I dragged myself up from the couch, my heart pounding in my chest as I made my way to the front door.

I glanced through the peephole, my breath catching in my throat as I saw Laurie standing there, his expression a mix of determination and impatience. For a moment, I hesitated, my hand hovering over the doorknob as I debated whether to let him in.

But in the end, I knew I couldn't turn him away. Not when he had been there for me through thick and thin, not when he was the one person I could always count on to have my back.

With a shaky breath, I opened the door, my eyes widening as Laurie rushed in, his arms laden with bags of food.

"Front door, Gia! Delivering some nosh to cheer you up. Chinese, your all-time favorite," he boomed, striding to the dinner table like he's on a mission.

I watched in silence as he unpacked the bags, the scent of spices and warmth filling the air. He moved with a sense of purpose, his hands deftly preparing our plates and ensuring that we had equal servings.

We ate in silence, the only sound was the clink of silverware against plates. I was grateful for Laurie's presence, for the way he respected my need for solitude even as he refused to let me wallow in my own misery.

But as the meal drew to a close, I could see the tension building in his shoulders, the words he was desperate to say bubbling up inside him like a volcano ready to erupt.

And then, without warning, he handed me his phone, his eyes locked onto mine with an intensity that took my breath away.

I glanced down at the screen, my heart skipping a beat as I saw Tyde's face staring back at me. It was a video, a recording of the heartfelt message he had delivered on live TV.

As I watched, my eyes filled with tears, a mix of emotions swirling inside me like a tempest. Gratitude, love, fear, and a desperate longing for the man who I've grown to love.

Laurie's voice went all soft and gentle, like he was talkin' to a spooked horse.

"Just sayin', Gia, there's a heap of support out there for you and Tyde. Most people are on your side, not much hate goin' around from what I've seen."

"Let me see," I said, my voice trembling as I held out my

hand for Laurie's phone. He passed it over reluctantly, teeth worrying his lower lip.

I could feel his eyes boring into me as I began swiping through the endless feed of apps and websites - Twitter, Instagram, TikTok, TMZ, CNN, NHL Network, ESPN. Each new screen delivered a fresh gut-punch of violation and shame.

There were the photos I'd trusted to remain private, splashed across the internet in tawdry high definition - my bare breasts, my most intimate areas exposed for the world's depraved scrutiny. I felt utterly debased, stripped of my last vestiges of bodily autonomy and dignity.

The dehumanizing comments started flooding in, a torrent of cold, razor-edged judgments slicing through my brain:

"Typical slut, always desperate for attention."

"She was just asking to be leaked, posing like that."

"How much for a personal photo shoot? Name your price, whore."

"No Surprise! She's a druggie."

"So, she likes coke and I don't mean the soda."

I squeezed my eyes shut, bile rising in my throat, but the words kept screaming through my mind in that endless, contemptuous loop. No matter how successful I became, it seemed I could never escape society's compulsion to diminish me to just a body, a piece of meat for consumption.

As a public figure and wealthy, I knew cruel objectification was practically inevitable. But having such deeply personal, deeply private pieces of myself seized and sensationalized...it felt like the most searing violation imaginable.

Hot tears scorched my cheeks as the onslaught continued - strangers shredding my character, speculating crudely about my anatomy, cold-bloodedly assigning numerical "ratings" to my physicality as if evaluating a side of beef. Their heartless objectification made me feel less than human.

Laurie remained silent and still beside me, sensing I needed to confront this injustice at my own pace. His steady presence was paradoxically grounding, a reminder that I wasn't just these lurid photos - I was a whole, inviolable person worth far more than my physical form.

Still, I couldn't shake the bone-deep disgust, the visceral sense of personal desecration. Having my boundaries and privacy so callously invaded felt like being robbed of my very identity, my right to self-determination.

As the gravity of that profound betrayal kept crashing over me, one furious resolution took hold - I would fight with every fiber of my being to regain control.

I couldn't speak, couldn't find the words to express the depth of my emotions. But Laurie seemed to understand, his hand reaching out to give mine a gentle squeeze.

"I know things seem crook right now, but you're not in this alone, love," he mumbled, his voice a right soother for your worried mind. "You got people who love ya, who reckon you're the real deal. And we're gonna get through this as a team."

I nodded, the tears spilling down my cheeks in silent rivulets. And as I sat there, lost in the warmth of Laurie's presence and the love that radiated from every pore of his being, I knew that he was right.

That even in the darkest of moments, there was still hope. That with the support of the people who loved me, I could weather any storm, overcome any obstacle that stood in my way.

And so, with a shaky breath and a trembling hand, I reached for my phone, turning it on, ready to face whatever lay ahead.

Because I knew that I wasn't alone. That I had Tyde, and Laurie, and a world of people who believed in the power of love and forgiveness.

—

DR. RILEY HAMMOND'S OFFICE - THE WATERFRONT, NEW JERSEY

I stepped into the therapist's office, my heart heavy with the weight of the past few days. The room was warm and inviting, with soft lighting and comfortable chairs that seemed to beckon me to sit down and unburden myself. I sank into the plush cushions, my body feeling like it was made of lead.

Riley greeted me with a warm smile, his eyes filled with a mix of compassion and understanding. He had been there for me through some of the darkest moments of my life, a steadfast beacon of support and guidance in a world that often felt like it was spinning out of control.

"Tyde, what you did on the broadcast was a significant step forward," he said, his voice filled with pride. "You're making positive changes, not just for your public image, but for yourself too. Without ego."

I felt a flicker of warmth in my chest, a glimmer of hope that maybe, just maybe, I was on the right path. But even as I basked in the glow of Riley's praise, I couldn't shake the nagging sense of unease that had settled in the pit of my stomach.

Riley must have sensed my inner turmoil, because he shifted the conversation to Gia, his voice gentle and probing.

"Have you seen her since the 'disaster'?"

I gave my head a wobble, throat suddenly tightening up like a drum.

"Nah, haven't spoken to her yet. Don't know if she even wants to see me, or how she's feeling after all this kerfuffle."

Riley nodded, his expression thoughtful.

"It's crucial to find a common ground, something that respects her boundaries but also shows your genuine desire to be there for her. Take it slow, see what her headspace is like after the event, and find comfort in each other."

I let his words wash over me, a balm to my battered soul. I knew that he was right, that I needed to approach the situation with sensitivity and patience. Gia had been through hell, and the last thing I wanted was to add to her burden.

But even as I nodded in agreement, I couldn't shake the feeling of helplessness that had settled over me like a heavy blanket. I wanted to be there for Gia, to support her in any way I could. But I also knew that I had to give her the space she needed to heal, to process the trauma that had been inflicted upon her.

Riley must have sensed my inner struggle, because he

leaned forward, his eyes locking with mine.

"Tyde, it's been a productive session. I can see the progress you're making, and it's commendable. Keep going in this direction, and remember, it's a journey. You're on a stairway to progress. Take it one step at a time."

As I left the office, I couldn't help but feel a sense of determination washing over me. I knew that the road ahead would be filled with challenges, with obstacles that would test me in ways I had never been tested before.

But I also knew that I had the strength to face them head-on, to keep pushing forward even when the world seemed to be crumbling around me. And with Riley's words echoing in my mind, I felt a renewed sense of purpose, a drive to be the best version of myself that I could be.

For Gia, for myself, and for the future that lay ahead.

Gia

GIA'S APARTMENT

The doorbell trilled, a jarring sound that shattered the fragile peace I'd carved out for myself. I sank deeper into the plush cushions of the sofa, burying my face further into the well-worn copy of "Brown Sugar." Who the hell could be visiting at this ungodly hour? Ten past nine at night was strictly reserved for takeout, reruns of "Living Single," and drowning my sorrows in the comforting embrace of black sitcoms.

With a sigh, the migraine, a constant reminder of distancing myself from Tyde. It felt like a lifetime ago, yet the sting of his words lingered, a bitter aftertaste on my tongue. The "drama," as I watch Max and Kyle go back and forth about whatever drama they have going on in their lives at the time.

I shuffled to the door, the foyer an unnervingly dark expanse bathed only in the faint glow of the television. Peeking through the peephole, I saw a cardboard monstrosity dwarfing my front porch. A gift basket. My heart lurched. It could be anyone, but the sinking feeling in my gut told a different story.

Twisting the lock, I threw the door open, bracing myself. There stood a giant teddy bear. A card, propped precariously inside the bear's arms, a box overflowing with gourmet chocolates.

My breath caught. A bear? This man needs to give me

time!

Anger bubbled hot within me, threatening to spill. I slammed the door shut, the bear tumbling down the front stairs.

But even as the anger burned, a tiny, traitorous ember of hope flickered to life in the cold recesses of my heart. Maybe, just maybe, this extravagant display was a sign.

The gift basket, a symbol of his hope for the future, sat at the bottom of my doorstep, a silent challenge.

—

NEXT WEEK

CENTRAL PARK

I walked slowly through Central Park, my feet dragging against the pavement as if weighed down by invisible chains. The world around me was a blur, a prism of colors and sounds that I barely registered. All I could feel was the heaviness in my chest, the dull ache that had taken up residence in my heart since the disaster that had turned my life upside down.

My head hung low, my eyes fixed on the ground beneath my feet. The music in my ears was a somber soundtrack to my thoughts, a melancholy melody that seemed to echo the pain that consumed me.

I was so lost in my own world, so consumed by the weight of the past two days, that I almost didn't notice the little girl approaching me. But as she drew closer, her small hand outstretched, I found myself stopping in my tracks.

She looked up at me with wide, innocent eyes, a single

lavender daisy clutched in her tiny fist. I blinked, surprised by the unexpected gesture. But before I could say a word, she pressed the flower into my hand, a sweet smile spreading across her face.

I stared down at the delicate petals, my heart swelling with a sudden rush of emotion. And then, as if materializing out of thin air, a little boy appeared beside the girl, another lavender daisy in his hand.

I glanced up, my eyes searching for an explanation. And there, standing a few feet away, was a woman holding a bouquet of the same flowers. She smiled at me, her eyes filled with a warmth that I hadn't felt in days.

I took the lavender daisy bouquet from her, my hands trembling slightly as I cradled them against my chest. And that's when I saw it - a small note tucked among the blooms.

With shaking fingers, waiting for the heartbeat to normalize, I pulled it free, my heart pounding as I unfolded the paper. And there, in Tyde's familiar handwriting, were the words that I hadn't even known I needed to hear.

"My Dearest Gia," I read aloud, my voice barely above a whisper.

"This whole storm that's blown up out of nowhere, well, I just want you to know my love for you is rock solid, no matter what. You've been a right trooper through all this, and it makes me admire you even more, the amazing woman you are."

I felt a lump rising in my throat, a mixture of emotions flooding my heart. Tyde's words were like a balm to my battered soul, a reminder that even in the darkest of moments, I wasn't alone.

"The world might feel a bit scary right now, but don't forget you're not on your own. I'm right here beside you, love, ready to face whatever comes our way. The way you're bouncing back from all this is bloody inspiring, Gia."

A small smile tugged at my lips, a flicker of warmth spreading through my chest. Tyde had always had a way with words, a talent for making me feel seen and understood in a way that no one else could.

"You're not defined by what other people do or this rubbish we're dealing with. You're all about the love and kindness you show everyone, and the way your spirit shines even when things are dark."

I clutched the lavender daisies closer, breathing in their sweet scent. Tyde's words were like a lifeline, a reminder that even in the midst of the chaos and uncertainty, there was still beauty to be found.

"Take a breather, feel the warmth of our love, and remember how strong you really are. You're my personal highlight reel, turning even the most ordinary moments into something unforgettable. There's just something about you that goes beyond the everyday, leaving me in awe of how I ever let this beautiful masterpiece go. As we sail these rough seas, know I'm here to support you, love you, and pick you up whenever you need a boost."

I felt the emotions welling up inside me, threatening to spill over in a flood of tears. But I blinked them back, determined to finish reading Tyde's message.

"In the quiet times, the crazy times, and through the love that holds us together, we'll find peace. We can face anything as long as we're together. Our love is unbreakable, and so are you. "

"All my love, Ty."

I caressed the note, my fingers tracing the familiar curves and lines of Tyde's handwriting. And then, as I took in the somewhat messy scrawl, I couldn't help but chuckle softly.

"God, his handwriting still looks like chicken scratch," I murmured to myself, a smile spreading across my face.

It was a bittersweet moment, a reminder of the quirks and idiosyncrasies that made Tyde who he was.

As I stood there in the middle of the park, surrounded by the lavender daisies and the warmth of Tyde's words, I felt a tear escape from the corner of my eye. But it wasn't a tear of sadness or despair.

It was a tear of hope, of love, of the unbreakable bond that Tyde and I shared.

—

DR. CELINE DIAZ'S OFFICE - GARMENT DISTRICT, NEW YORK CITY

I stepped into Celine's office, my heart heavy with the weight of the past few days. I sank into the plush cushions, my body feeling like it was made of lead, and lifting my head begrudgingly to look at her eyes.

"Hello, Gia," Celine greeted me, her voice soft and soothing. "How have you been since our last session? Please, take a seat, and let's catch up."

I took a deep breath, trying to gather my thoughts.

"Well, it's been a treturus, Celine. You won't believe what has happened since I've last seen you."

Celine leaned forward, her eyes filled with compassion and understanding.

"I'm here for you, Gia. Tell me everything. How are you feeling?"

I sighed, the sound escaping my lips like a deflating balloon.

"Honestly, Celine, it's been tough. The broadcast disaster, the paparazzi, the leaked photos... It feels like the world's turned upside down. But you know what? Tyde has been surprising me."

Celine raised an eyebrow, curiosity flickering in her gaze.

"Oh? In what way?"

I felt a flicker of warmth in my chest, a glimmer of hope that maybe, just maybe, things weren't as bleak as they seemed.

"First, he declares his love on live TV, and then today, he sent me a bouquet of lavender daisies with a heartfelt note confessing his love, sincerely! In Central Park, of all places!"

Celine nodded, her expression thoughtful.

"That's quite a gesture. How does that make you feel?"

I hesitated, trying to put my swirling emotions into words.

"It's... It's complicated, Celine. I love him, too. And seeing him take steps to show his affection publicly is making me reconsider caring about what others think. Maybe I can do the same."

Celine smiled, her eyes crinkling at the corners.

"Love is a powerful force, Gia. It's clear there's a deep

connection between you two. How do you want to move forward?"

I felt a rush of determination wash over me, a sense of clarity that had been missing for so long.

"I want to embrace it, Celine. I want to stop letting external opinions dictate my happiness. If Tyde can be bold about his feelings, maybe I can, too."

Celine listened attentively, her presence a steadying force in the midst of the chaos that had consumed my life. She guided me through my emotions, her questions and insights helping me navigate the intricate journey that lay ahead.

I felt a sense of relief wash over me, a weight lifting from my shoulders as I poured out my heart to Celine. She had a way of making me feel seen and understood, of helping me find the strength and resilience that I didn't even know I had.

As we talked, I found myself opening up more and more, sharing the fears and doubts that had plagued me for so long. Celine listened without judgment, her eyes filled with compassion and understanding.

And as the session drew to a close, I felt a sense of hope blooming in my chest, a flicker of light in the darkness that had consumed me for so long.

I knew that I had the tools and the support to navigate it all, to find my way through the darkness and into the light.

Tyde

The bustling energy of Fifth Avenue enveloped me as I strode down the sidewalk, my mind preoccupied with the day's upcoming meetings. The sun glinted off the storefronts, casting a dazzling array of reflections that danced across the pavement. Lost in thought, I barely registered the click of high heels rapidly approaching until a familiar voice cut through the din.

"Tyde! Tyde, wait!"

My stomach clenched, a sinking feeling of dread washing over me as I turned to face the source of the commotion. Charlotte, my ex, stood before me, her perfectly manicured hands reaching out in a desperate plea.

"Tyde, hey! Hey, please, can we talk? I miss you so much, baby. I know we can make this work," she begged, her voice trembling with emotion.

I took a step back, putting distance between us as curious onlookers began to slow their pace, eager to catch a glimpse of the unfolding drama.

"Charlotte, we've been down this road, haven't we? It's kaput. There's no point flogging a dead horse."

But she wasn't deterred. In a shocking display, Charlotte dropped to her knees, oblivious to the dirty concrete beneath her designer jeans. Sobs wracked her body as she clasped her hands together, mascara-streaked tears cutting paths down her cheeks.

"Please, Tyde! I can't live without you. We belong together. You know it, and I know it. Just give me another chance!"

Mortification burned through my veins as I watched the pathetic spectacle, acutely aware of the growing number of smartphones pointed in our direction. The last thing I needed was this humiliating scene splashed across social media.

"Get a grip, Charlotte," I hissed under my breath, my eyes scanning the room like a hawk. "You're making a right mug of yourself, and dragging me down with you. This is a right palaver."

But she remained on the ground, her sobs growing louder, snot mingling with the ruined remnants of her carefully applied makeup. The secondhand embarrassment was palpable, the air thick with a mixture of pity and morbid fascination.

After what felt like an eternity, Charlotte finally staggered to her feet, her once-immaculate appearance now a disheveled mess. She wiped at her face with the back of her hand, smearing the inky streaks across her porcelain skin. Her autumn brown eyes are slightly sparkling.

"You think you're too good for me?" she spat, her voice dripping with venom. "You'll never find anyone better, Tyde. I'm the best thing that ever happened to you, and you're too stupid to see it!"

I shook my head, a hollow laugh escaping my lips.

"See ya later, Charlotte. Look after yourself, yeah?"

With that, I turned on my heel and walked away, ignoring the string of expletives and insults she hurled at my retreating back. The curious onlookers parted like the Red Sea, their whispers and pointed stares following me as I made my way to my car.

As I slid behind the wheel, the engine roaring to life, I caught a final glimpse of Charlotte in the rearview mirror. She stood frozen on the sidewalk, a look of utter disbelief etched across her face, before storming off into a nearby shop, the door slamming shut behind her with a resounding bang.

I exhaled slowly, my grip tightening on the steering wheel as I pulled out into the unforgiving traffic of the city. The confrontation had left a bitter taste in my mouth, a reminder of the toxic past I so desperately wanted to leave behind.

The road ahead was uncertain, but one thing was crystal clear - Charlotte was a chapter I'd finally closed, a mistake I slightly repeat. But I will never do it again. And as I navigated the concrete jungle of the city, I couldn't help but feel a sense of liberation, a weight lifting from my shoulders with each passing block.

CHAPTER 13

HOPE IN THE RUBBLE

Tyde

TYDE'S PENTHOUSE - CENTRAL
PARK WEST, NEW YORK CITY

I paced around my penthouse, my heart racing and my mind whirling with a thousand different thoughts. The city lights twinkled below, a sea of glittering jewels that stretched out as far as the eye could see. But even their beauty couldn't ease the ache in my chest, the loneliness that had settled over me like a heavy blanket.

I couldn't shake the image of Gia from my mind, couldn't stop thinking about the way her eyes had sparkled when she laughed, the way her smile had lit up the room like a beacon in the darkness. I missed her with an intensity that took my breath away, a desperate longing that consumed me from the inside out.

I knew that I couldn't go on like this, couldn't keep

pretending that everything was okay when my heart was shattered into a million tiny pieces. I had to do something, had to take matters into my own hands and fight for the woman I loved.

With a sudden burst of determination, I grabbed my phone, my fingers trembling as I scrolled through my contacts. I hesitated for a moment, my thumb hovering over Laurie's name. I knew that he was Gia's best friend, that he would do anything to protect her from anything.

But I also knew that he was my only hope, the one person who might be willing to help me win her back.

I took a deep breath, my heart pounding in my chest as I pressed the call button. The phone rang once, twice, three times, each shrill tone sending a jolt of anxiety through my body.

And then, just when I thought all hope was lost, I heard Laurie's voice on the other end of the line.

"Yeah?" he said, all shifty-eyed and on his guard.

I gulped, my throat suddenly parched as I fumbled for the right words.

"Laurie, it's Tyde. I need a favour."

There was a long pause, a moment of heavy silence that seemed to stretch on for an eternity. I could almost hear the gears turning in Laurie's head, could sense the hesitation and the doubt that must have been swirling through his mind.

But then, to my surprise and relief, he spoke again.

"What's up?"

I felt a flicker of hope ignite in my chest, a tiny spark that grew into a raging inferno with each passing second.

"...I need to see Gia. I need to talk to her face, tell her how much I love her and that I want to be with her properly."

Laurie sighed, the sound heavy and weary.

"Tyde, I dunno if that's a cracker of an idea. She's copped a fair whack lately, and the last thing she needs is more aggro and heartbreak."

I nodded, even though he couldn't see me.

"I know, Laurie, believe me, I do. But I also know I can't live without her, that I'll do anything to mend things between us."

There was another long pause, a moment of tense silence that seemed to stretch on forever. And then, finally, Laurie spoke again.

"Alright, alright, Tyde. I'll chuck you a bone. But you owe me big time. Promise me you won't string her along again, that you'll do your best to make her happy as a lark."

I felt a rush of gratitude wash over me, a sense of relief that was almost overwhelming.

"I promise, Laurie. I swear on my life I'll never let her down again."

And with those words, I knew that I had taken the first step towards winning Gia back, towards proving to her that our love was strong enough to weather any storm.

I lingered on the call, my heart racing with a mix of excitement and nerves.

As I stood there in my penthouse, the city lights twinkling below and the promise of a brighter future stretching out before me, I knew that I was ready to take that leap of faith.

Ready to fight for the love that I knew was worth fighting for.

Laurie

LAURIE'S APARTMENT - EAST VILLAGE, NEW YORK CITY

I had seen the way Tyde looked at Gia, had watched as their relationship had blossomed and grown over the years. I knew that he loved her with a fierce intensity that took my breath away.

"Fair dinkum, the heart wants what the heart wants," I said, my voice all gentle and whatnot. "So, what's the game plan?"

Tyde hesitated for a moment, as if searching for the right words.

"I was thinkin'... I gotta see her. How about a clandestine meeting somewhere real romantic? Brooklyn Botanic Garden at night, perhaps?"

I raised an eyebrow, impressed by his choice. The Brooklyn Botanical Garden was a place of breathtaking beauty, a lush oasis in the heart of the city. At night, it would be transformed into a magical wonderland, the perfect setting for a romantic rendezvous.

"Ooh, a bit different! I dig it," I said, my grin getting even wider. "What's next on the agenda, then?"

Tyde's voice grew more animated, his words tumbling out in a rush of excitement.

"And from there, we'll just see where the night takes us, maybe the Brooklyn Bridge. You know, fairy lights, a bit of magic, what do you reckon?"

I couldn't help but chuck a sneaky laugh out, my voice

laced with a bit of mickey.

"Tyde, you're a right softie at heart. But I'm on board, mate. Let's bloody well do it!"

I could almost hear the relief in Tyde's voice, the gratitude that poured out of him like a flood.

"Cheers, Laurie. I owe you one, big time."

I shook my head, even though he couldn't see me.

"Just make it a cracker of a night, Romeo. Good on ya."

We exchanged a few more details, finalizing the plan and ironing out the logistics. And then, with a final goodbye, we hung up, the weight of what we were about to do settling over me like a heavy blanket.

I leaned back against the couch, my mind racing with a thousand different thoughts. I knew that what we were doing was risky, that there was no guarantee that Gia would even show up, let alone be receptive to Tyde's advances.

But I also knew that I had to try, that I couldn't stand by and watch as two people who were meant to be together drifted further and further apart.

Because in the end, that was what friendship was all about. Being there for the people you loved, even when things got tough. And as I sat there in the darkness, the TV still flickering in the background, I knew that I was ready to do whatever it took to help Tyde win Gia back.

My phone buzzed against my thigh, jolting me from my daydream. I fished it out, heart skipping as I saw the Instagram notification. Tyson. He'd found me.

I swiped open the app, fingers trembling slightly. There it was - his profile, that cocky grin beaming up at me. I tapped 'follow' without hesitation, then dove into my DMs.

His message set my pulse racing:

"Quick question: On a scale of not at all to fantasizing, how many times have you thought of me?"

Heat bloomed in my cheeks. I bit my lip, thumbs hovering over the keyboard. How to play this? Coy? Bold? My mind raced with possibilities.

I settled on flirty honesty, "Hmm... somewhere between 'constantly' and 'is there anything else worth thinking about?'"

The moment I hit send, butterflies erupted in my stomach. I stared at the screen, willing those three dots to appear.

They did. My breath caught as I read his reply, "Funny, I've been having the same problem. Care to help me focus on something else for a while?"

And just like that, we were off. Messages flew back and forth, each one more charged than the last. We traded quips and innuendos, flirting shamelessly. I found myself laughing out loud, grinning at my phone like an idiot.

Hours slipped by unnoticed. The sky outside my window darkened, then lightened again. Still, we talked. About everything and nothing. Our hopes, our fears, our wildest dreams. With each message, I felt myself falling deeper.

As dawn broke, exhaustion finally caught up with me. But I couldn't bring myself to say goodnight. Not yet. Not when every new message felt like unwrapping a gift.

So I kept typing, fighting heavy eyelids, savoring every moment of this unexpected connection. Morning could wait. Right now, there was only Tyson, me, and the electric buzz of possibility.

Tyde

BROOKLYN BOTANICAL GARDEN

I stood in the middle of the Brooklyn Botanical Garden, my heart racing with a mixture of nerves and excitement. The soft glow of the bulb string lights cast a magical atmosphere over the lush greenery, transforming the space into an enchanted wonderland.

The air was thick with the scent of blooming flowers, their delicate petals dancing in the gentle breeze. I inhaled deeply, letting the sweet fragrance wash over me like a soothing balm.

But even as I took in the beauty of my surroundings, I couldn't shake the anxiety that thrummed through my veins. My eyes darted around the garden, searching for any sign of Gia's arrival.

I had spent hours planning this moment, carefully selecting the perfect location and setting the stage for what I hoped would be a night to remember. But now, as I stood there waiting, I couldn't help but wonder if it had all been for nothing.

What if she didn't show up? What if she had moved on, leaving me behind in the dust of our shared past? The thought made my stomach churn, bile rising in the back of my throat.

I closed my eyes, taking a deep breath to steady my nerves. I had to believe that she would come, that the love we shared was strong enough to overcome any obstacle.

I pictured her face in my mind, the way her eyes sparkled

when she laughed, the way her smile could light up even the darkest of rooms. She was my everything, the missing piece that made my life complete.

As the minutes ticked by, I found myself pacing back and forth, my hands clenched into fists at my sides. The anticipation was killing me, each second feeling like an eternity.

And then, just when I thought I couldn't take it anymore, I heard the soft crunch of footsteps on the gravel path. My heart leapt into my throat, my pulse pounding in my ears.

I turned slowly, afraid to get my hopes up. But there she was, walking towards me like a vision from a dream. Gia looked breathtaking in a beautiful dress, her stretched afro billowing with pillow soft curls.

For a moment, I couldn't breathe, couldn't move. It was as if time had stopped, the world falling away until there was nothing left but her.

She came to a stop in front of me, her eyes searching mine with a mix of uncertainty and longing. I wanted to reach out and touch her, to pull her into my arms and never let go.

But I knew that I had to take things slow, to earn back the trust that had been shattered by my past mistakes. So instead, I offered her a tentative smile, my voice soft and gentle as I spoke.

"Gia, cheers for coming. I know I messed up big time, don't deserve another go or anything, but I'm hoping you might give me a chance to make things right."

She looked at me for a long moment, her expression unreadable. And then, to my surprise and relief, she nodded, a small smile tugging at the corners of her lips.

"I'm here, Tyde. Let's talk."

And with those simple words, I felt a flicker of hope ignite in my chest, a tiny spark that grew into a raging inferno with each passing second.

We walked deeper into the garden, the string lights casting a warm glow over our faces. And as we talked, the words pouring out of us like a dam had burst, I knew that this was just the beginning.

Tyde stretches out of anxiety, that crooked smile playing at the corners of his mouth.

"Right then, listen up. I gotta tell you the whole story, the real reason behind this whole plan, babes."

Tyde drew a deep breath, squaring his broad shoulders. When he spoke, his voice resonated with raw emotion, dripping with vulnerability and regret.

"Gia, I've got to come clean. My intentions when I first started sniffing around you again were...less than pukka." He cringed, raking a hand through his tousled chocolate hair. "It started off as some daft ego trip - a laugh to see if I still had enough chat to get an ex back on the pulls, no strings and all."

My stomach twisted with disbelief and hurt. So that's what I was to him? Just another notch on his bedpost? I opened my mouth to berate him, but the anguished look in his steel-blue eyes stopped me.

"But over time..." He hesitated, choosing his words carefully. "Working cheek-by-jowl with you again during the NHL All-Star bender, seeing how much you've grown up and changed in the last four years - it opened my eyes wide. You're in a totally different gaff now, Gia. And so am I."

Tyde stepped closer, his arm extending imploringly. His tongue darted out to wet his lips.

"The therapy, the self-work I've done...it made me clock how deeply I still care for you. How brassed off I am about the pain I caused you before."

He dropped to one knee, tears shining in his eyes.

"I'm down on my hands and knees groveling here, baring my soul, because I need you to know the truth. I don't want some meaningless knee-trembler." His voice dropped to a hoarse whisper. "I want to be part of your life again, for real this time. Please, just give us another chance."

I could feel his raw anguish like a tidal wave crashing over me. Part of me wanted to turn away from the searing honesty in his gaze. But a larger part felt that soul-deep connection we once had, still smoldering underneath the rubble of our past.

Could I really trust him after his initial deception? Did I have the courage to open myself up to that level of vulnerability again? As I stared into the endless depths of Tyde's eyes, I knew I might never forgive myself if I didn't at least try.

I crossed my arms, eyes narrowed. Part of me was bracing for some over-the-top romantic drama only Tyde could concoct. The other part felt a reluctant twinge of curiosity locked in a battle with dread.

My eyebrows shot up as heat rushed to my cheeks.

"You're unbelievable..."

Tyde sighed, looking weary.

Disgust and anger swirled like a volatile storm inside me. So he just viewed me as another notch for his bedpost? This arrogant, childish man-child actually thought elaborate schemes would make me swoon?

I opened my mouth to tell him off proper, but Tyde put his hand up to stop me.

"Jackson and Lorenz were like bouncers for my stupid ideas. Every dodgy plan I came up with to win you over, they shut it down."

A startled laugh escaped my lips before I could stop it. Leave it to Tyde to recruit his friends to vet his ridiculous schemes like researchers in a monumental scientific study.

As irritation faded, it gave way to an odd sense of gratitude. Ridiculous or not, he'd put real thought and effort into his pursuit of me. Not many men would go to those lengths just for a fling.

Tyde's face softened as he looked at me seriously.

"It turned into something more for me. A deep longing, like a missing piece."

The raw sincerity in his voice enveloped me like a warm blanket. Tendrils of contentment unfurled inside me. This relentless, harebrained man had jumped through endless hoops, all to slowly chip away at the walls around my heart.

I was the cannonball he'd been aiming for all along, shattering his defenses in that sneaky, inimitable way of mine. And somehow, despite his dubious methods, I found that possibility more exciting than insulting.

—

GIA'S APARTMENT

I stood in front of my mirror, a critical eye assessing my

reflection as I smoothed the fabric of my dress. It was a casual number, perfect for a laid-back night out with my best friend. I had spent the last hour on the phone with Laurie, discussing outfit options and laughing at inside jokes that only we understood.

"Laurie, are you ready? I'm heading out now," I said, a smile playing at the corners of my lips.

His voice crackled through the speaker, filled with an enthusiasm that was infectious.

"Fair suck of the sav, I'm on me way! Can't wait to see ya!"

I grinned, my heart swelling with affection for my partner in crime. Laurie had always been there for me, through thick and thin. He was the one person I could always count on, the one who understood me better than anyone else.

With a final glance in the mirror, I grabbed my purse and headed for the door. The city streets were alive with energy, the warm summer air filled with the sounds of laughter and music.

As I walked, my mind drifted to the evening ahead. Laurie had been uncharacteristically secretive about our plans, dropping hints and clues that only served to pique my curiosity. But I trusted him implicitly, knew that whatever he had in store would be an adventure worth having.

Little did I know just how right I was.

Miles away, in his own apartment, Laurie hung up the phone with a chuckle. He leaned back in his chair, a mischievous glint in his eye as he pictured the surprise that awaited his unsuspecting friend.

He had spent so much time planning this moment, carefully orchestrating every detail to ensure that it was perfect. And now, as he sat there in the dimly lit room, he couldn't help but feel a sense of excitement building in his chest.

Laurie knew that Gia was still hurting, still reeling from the pain of her past. He had watched her struggle and suffer, and had seen the toll that heartbreak had taken on her once vibrant spirit.

But he also knew that she was strong, that she had a resilience and a fire within her that refused to be extinguished. He knew that Gia was in for the surprise of her life, that the evening ahead would be filled with laughter, tears, and with joy.

BROOKLYN BOTANICAL GARDEN

I stepped out of the cab, my heart racing with excitement as I thanked the driver. The night air was cool against my skin, the soft glow of the city lights casting a warm halo over the streets. I climbed the steps to the entrance of the Brooklyn Botanical Garden, my heels clicking against the concrete with each step.

As I pushed open the heavy wooden door, I felt a rush of anticipation wash over me. I had been looking forward to this night for weeks, a chance to spend some quality time with my best friend and forget about the stresses of everyday life.

But as I peered into the garden, my breath caught in my throat. There, standing amidst the lush greenery and twinkling lights, was Tyde. He looked back at me with an affectionate smile, his eyes sparkling with mischief.

Tyde smirked, a hint of red creeping into his cheeks as he realized that the surprise had been unveiled. I felt a flicker of happiness ignite in my chest, even as my mind raced with questions. Despite my initial confusion, I was thrilled by the unexpected twist. Laurie had always been a master of surprises, but this one took the cake.

"Oh, revenge is coming for Laurie, but I'm glad to be here with you, Tyde. What's the plan for tonight?" I asked, my voice playful and light.

Tyde grinned, his hand reaching out to take mine. His touch was warm and familiar, sending a shiver down my spine.

"Tonight's all about getting that spark back, yeah? Let's see where the night takes us," he said, gazing into my eyes.

As he led me deeper into the garden, I felt a sense of anticipation building in my chest. The past few weeks had been a whirlwind of emotions, a rollercoaster ride that had left me feeling lost and confused.

But here, in this moment, with Tyde by my side, everything felt right. The world seemed to fade away, leaving only the two of us and the magic of the night.

We came to a stop at a picturesque bench, nestled amidst a sea of blooming flowers. Tyde gestured for me to sit, his eyes never leaving mine.

"Gia, these past few weeks have been a right nightmare. I've missed you more than words can say," he said, his voice gentle and genuine.

I felt a blush creep into my cheeks, my heart skipping a beat at his words.

"Tyde, it's been hard for me too. I didn't realize how much I needed you until you weren't around."

He grabbed my hand, his fingers intertwined with mine.

"Gia, I can't bottle it up any longer. I love you, alright? Always have, even when things got messy."

Tears pricked at the corners of my eyes, my vision blurring with emotion.

"Tyde, I… I love you too. More than words can express."

He pulled me into a warm embrace, his arms wrapping around me like a protective shell. I melted into his touch, my head resting against his chest as I breathed in his familiar scent.

"Gia, you light up my world. I want to be with you, no matter what we have to face. Let's take it on together," he whispered, his lips brushing against my fluffy afro.

I smiled through my tears, my heart swelling with love and gratitude.

"Yes, Tyde. Together. I'm ready for this journey with you."

BROOKLYN BRIDGE

As we walked across the Brooklyn Bridge, the city lights shimmered below us, casting a magical glow over the night. The air was thick with emotion, a mix of hope and fear, of love and vulnerability. I could feel Tyde's hand in mine, his touch a reassuring presence that anchored me to the moment.

"You know, Tyde, there are parts of my past I've never

shared with anyone," I said softly, my voice barely above a whisper. "It's scary, but I want you to understand me."

Tyde squeezed my hand, his eyes locking with mine in a gaze that was both tender and intense.

"Always there for you, Gia, you know that."

I took a deep breath, steeling myself for the words that were about to come. It was a story I had never told before, a painful memory that I had buried deep within myself for years.

But as I spoke, the words pouring out of me like a torrent, I felt a sense of relief wash over me. Tyde listened attentively, his emotions ranging from anger to empathy as I recounted the painful tale of my encounter with a streetwalker.

"Can't imagine how rubbish that must have been for you," he said softly, his voice full of empathy. "But I'm here for you now, alright? Always."

We reached a standstill on the bridge, leaning against the railing as a contemplative silence enveloped us. The city stretched out before us, a glittering tapestry of lights and shadows that seemed to mirror the complexity of our own emotions.

Tyde took a deep breath, his eyes fixed on the distance as he spoke.

"Been carrying this burden for ages, Gia. It's a part of me, but I want you to see the real me."

I nestled closer to him, my head resting against his chest as I listened to the steady beat of his heart. As he opened up about his struggles with abandonment, stemming from his relationship with his mother, I felt a sense of understanding wash over me.

We were both broken, both carrying the weight of our past like a heavy burden. But in that moment, as we stood there on the bridge, our hearts laid bare before each other, I knew that we were also stronger together.

"Tyde, I understand now," I said softly, my voice filled with emotion. "I never meant to hurt you in any way. I'm so sorry."

He stroked your cheek, the touch sending shivers down your spine.

"We've both been through a right mess, haven't we? But maybe, just maybe, we can turn those scars into something strong. Together."

I looked up at him, my eyes shining with tears. At that moment, I knew that he was right. We had both been through hell, both carried the scars of our past like badges of honor.

But we had also found each other, and had discovered a love that was strong enough to weather any storm. And as we stood there on the Brooklyn Bridge, united by a shared commitment and a deep understanding of each other's pain.

As the night wore on and the city lights twinkled above us, I felt a sense of peace wash over me. For the first time in a long time, I knew that I was exactly where I was meant to be.

I took a deep breath, my heart pounding against my ribcage. The space felt smaller suddenly, as I faced Tyde. His golden brown eyes, usually so warm, now held a storm of emotions I couldn't quite decipher.

"Tyde," I began, my voice barely above a whisper. "We need to talk about what happened."

He nodded, his jaw clenching.

"I'm listening, Gia."

I swallowed hard, trying to find the right words.

"We've been at each other's throats for too long. This... this recording, it's torn us apart. But it's not about us versus each other anymore. It's us against whoever invaded our privacy."

Tyde's brow furrowed.

"You're right. We don't even know who could've done this to us."

"Exactly," I said, taking a step closer to him. "We said things... horrible things that cut deep. But that's in the past now."

He reached out, his fingers grazing my arm.

"We've both grown, haven't we?"

I nodded, feeling a lump form in my throat.

"Yes, we have. Let's never fight like that again, okay."

He slowly breathes in and heart thumping slowly.

"Okay, love."

Without thinking, I say...

"I love you."

I feel him smile and his posture straightened, saying...

"I love you too."

GIA'S APARTMENT

As the night wore on, Tyde and I made our way back to my apartment, our hearts full and our spirits light. The journey had been a whirlwind of emotions, a rollercoaster ride that had taken us from the depths of despair to the heights of joy. But as we stepped through the door and into the warmth of my living room, I knew that we had finally found our way home.

We settled onto the couch, our bodies nestled together like two puzzle pieces that had finally found their perfect fit. The movies played softly in the background, a gentle hum that filled the air with a sense of comfort and familiarity.

"This has been such a magical night," I said, a smile playing at the corners of my lips.

Tyde grinned, his eyes twinkling with mischief and fondness.

"Couldn't have said it better myself."

As the night stretched on, our laughter and shared moments filled the room, a symphony of joy that drowned out the rest of the world. We were lost in each other, in the magic of the moment that had brought us together.

But even as we reveal ourselves in the warmth of each other's company, I could feel the tug of fatigue at the edges of my consciousness. My eyelids grew heavy, my limbs languid with the weight of the day's events.

"Your bed is looking right inviting," Tyde whispered, his breath warm against your ear.

I couldn't help but smile, a playful glint in my eye.

"Well, it's about to get cozier."

We made our way to the bedroom, the soft glow of the city lights peeking through the window and casting a gentle ambiance over the room. As we slipped beneath the covers, our bodies intertwined like vines, I felt a sense of peace wash over me.

Here, in the safety of Tyde's arms, I knew that I was exactly where I was meant to be.

Some mindless rom-com played on the TV, but I couldn't focus, not with Tyde's heartbeat thrumming steadily beneath my cheek, his fingers tracing lazy patterns on my skin.

"Gia," he murmured, and you tilted your head up to look at him. Those bright blue eyes, usually full of mischief, were soft and serious. "Tonight was mint. Being with you is just perfect."

I hummed in agreement, pressing a kiss to his jaw.

"It really was. I wish it never had to end."

"What if we didn't have to end this?" The words came out hesitantly, a big change from his usual confident self.

I pulled back slightly, searching his face.

"What do you mean?"

He took a deep breath, like he was getting ready for something.

"Move in with me, G. Let's wake up next to each other every day, fall asleep in each other's arms every night. I want to share everything with you, build a life together."

Tears pricked at the corners of my eyes and I blinked them back, heart soaring and stomach swooping.

"Tyde, are you sure? It's a big step..."

His hand cupped your cheek, his thumb wiping away a stray tear.

"Never been more certain about anything in my life. I love you, Gia Clark. Completely and utterly, forever. Please say yes."

I gazed at him, this beautiful, complicated, wonderful man who held my heart in his hands. The man I'd loved for longer than I cared to admit, the man I couldn't imagine my life without.

"Yes," I whispered, half-laughing, half-crying. "Yes."

His answering smile was blinding, joyous, and then his mouth was on mine, stealing my breath and pouring out every ounce of his love, his elation, his devotion. I kissed him back just as fiercely, tangling my fingers in his hair, molding my body to his.

In between kisses, whispered words of love and promises of forever filled the scant space between us. The movie droned on, forgotten, as we lost ourselves in each other, celebrating this new chapter, this thrilling culmination of our journey.

As we drifted off to sleep, limbs entwined, I marveled at the twists and turns that had brought us here, to this perfect, shining moment. Moving in with Tyde was a big step, a leap of faith, but I knew, with bone-deep certainty, that there was no one else I'd rather take that leap with.

My last thought before slumber claimed me was that I couldn't wait to begin this new adventure, to build a beautiful, messy, extraordinary life with the man I loved. The future had never looked brighter.

As the night gave way to dawn and the first rays of sunlight began to peek through the curtains, I knew that I had found my home. Not in a place, but in a person.

In Tyde, the man who had stolen my heart again and shown me the true meaning of love.

—

TYDE'S PENTHOUSE

Unsettled and gathering the timeline in my head with Gia moving in very soon. I paced around my luxurious penthouse, frustration simmering in my veins as I spoke to the private investigator, Scout Walker. I'd hired to unravel the tangled mystery of who had leaked the intimate details of my and Gia's relationship.

"I need to find out who's behind this!" I growled into the phone, my voice tense with barely controlled anger. "Who's been prying into my life and Gia's? This invasion of privacy is completely unacceptable."

"I understand, Tyde," private investigator Scout Walker replied, his tone level and professionalism. "I've been combing through your list of suspects, but this seems more complex than we initially anticipated."

The investigator continued his update, each word stoking the flames of my outrage higher. He delved into the convoluted details of the ongoing investigation.

"It's possible this wasn't a solo act," he said slowly. I could hear him choosing his words with care. "There are indications that multiple individuals might be involved. The leak seems... coordinated."

I clenched my jaw so hard pain shot through my skull. I struggled to process this new information as the red haze of fury threatened to choke me. The possibility of a conspiracy, of multiple betrayals, added another sickening layer to an already intolerable situation.

"More than one person..." I forced the words out through gritted teeth. "Can't believe people would stoop this low. Feels like I'm surrounded by bloody snakes!"

"We're doing our absolute best to trace the source back," Scout assured me. "It might take some time, but I'll keep you informed the moment we have any significant developments."

As the call ended, my mind raced, churning with dark thoughts of who could be behind this ultimate betrayal. Suspicion and paranoia crashed over me in unrelenting waves. The investigation had only just begun, and the answers I desperately needed seemed shrouded in a tangled web of secrecy and lies.

But I was determined to protect my privacy, to salvage what I could of my relationship with Gia. I would do whatever it took. Squaring my shoulders, I steeled myself for the challenges ahead, for the brutal battle to reclaim control over my own life. They had no idea who they were messing with. I would make them regret ever crossing me.

CHAPTER 14

THE HUNTER BECOMES THE HUNTED

OFFICE - MANHATTAN, NEW YORK CITY

My phone buzzed insistently as I wove through the bustling city streets, heading towards my off-site interview. Fishing it out of my pocket, I glanced at the screen. Laurie. My brows furrowed.

"Hey, what's up?" I answered, dodging a harried-looking woman with an oversized briefcase.

"G, it's all gone pear-shaped here." Laurie's usually cruisy voice was tense as anything. "Edith's gone off her rocker. Got everyone running around like chooks with their heads cut off, reckonin' we gotta 'lift our game' and 'wow the bigwigs.' It's bonkers, mate."

I frowned, sidestepping a gaggle of tourists gawking at a window display.

"That sounds like her. I mean, she's tough, but this seems

excessive."

"You're telling me," Laurie grumbled. "Stuck in a bloody staff meeting right now. Blabbering on about big shake-ups coming. And get this - had to chuck a sickie on my bar shift tonight. The one that was gonna be a cracker. All because Her Majesty decided we gotta do extra hours."

Unease prickled down my spine. Something wasn't adding up.

"Do you think something's going on with her? Something we don't know about?"

"Dunno for sure, but I copped an earful of some whispers. Rumour mill's churnin' that she might be getting the sack. But that's been a rumour forever."

I exhaled slowly, my mind racing. A sinking feeling settled in my gut. Her sudden crackdown, the paranoid micromanaging - it was all starting to make a twisted kind of sense.

"Keep your ear to the ground," I murmured, lowering my voice instinctively. "If she's trying to control us, there's got to be a reason. And I have a hunch it's nothing good."

"Sweet as, will do. Keep your head down out there, G. Something's crook at Incline, and I don't want you caught in the crossfire."

We said our goodbyes and I slipped my phone back into my pocket, mind churning. Edith was hiding something, that much was clear. And whatever it was, it had her spooked enough to whip the entire office into a frenzy.

Well, *Incline Media* was practically choking on the fumes, figuratively. It was only a matter of time before the flames burst through, consuming everything in their path.

Scout Walker

SCOUT'S OFFICE - CHINATOWN, NEW YORK CITY

I stared intently at the cork board, my eyes boring into the headshots of Jackson Bell, Lorenz Wolf, Charlotte Astor, Edith Shalom,and Laurie Payne. The faces seemed to mock me, each one a potential suspect in this tangled web of deceit. I narrowed my eyes, muttering under my breath as I tried to piece together the puzzle.

"Alright, let's break this down," I murmured, my voice low and focused. "Jackson Bell and Lorenz Wolf seem to have clean records, both singing Tyde's praises online and in person. They're best friends. Gia's not making an appearance on their socials, though. For relationship comfortability, understandable."

I scrutinized each face, my gaze lingering on Charlotte Astor's headshot. The wealthy heiress with a matching tattoo certainly fit the bill for a potential suspect. Old flames had a nasty habit of reigniting old grudges. The thought made my jaw clench.

My eyes shifted to Edith Shalom's picture, and I felt a flicker of suspicion.

"Edith Shalom, the high-strung Editor-in-Chief, keeps tabs on Gia's career. Might be more to this boss-employee relationship than meets the eye. At least from Edith's point of view. "

Laurie Payne's image caught my attention next, but I dismissed him with a shake of my head.

"Laurie Payne, Gia's best friend, what would be his feelings towards Tyde?"

Walking over to his file and research gathered about Laurie.

"He is great friends with Gia and has a quite close relationship. Although I won't count them out, they don't seem to hold any hate for the couple."

I took a deep breath, the musty air of the room filling my lungs as I steeled myself for the task ahead. I was determined to unravel this mystery, to expose the snake in the grass before they could strike again.

Preparing to divulge into their lives and more than research, see who might have a motive.

"This snake won't slither away for long," I declared, my voice echoing in the quiet intensity of the room.

The hunt was just beginning.

—

A week later, I sat in my car, parked discreetly nearby, my eyes glued to Charlotte's every move as she went about her day in town. The leather seat squeaked beneath me as I shifted, trying to find a comfortable position for what I knew would be a long and tedious surveillance.

"This better be worth the trouble," I muttered to myself, my voice low and gruff in the confines of the vehicle.

I stayed persistent, tailing Charlotte with the skill and discretion that came from years on the job. She led me on a merry chase, but I never lost sight of her, not even for a moment. When she finally arrived at Edith's upscale condo, clutching a confidential envelope in her perfectly manicured hands, my suspicions skyrocketed.

"What's going on in there, and why is it taking them all day?" I whispered, my brow furrowing as the minutes ticked by with no sign of either woman.

As night fell, I remained vigilant outside the building, my curiosity gnawing at me like a hungry beast. I was determined to uncover the details of this extended meeting between Charlotte and Edith, no matter how long it took.

Finally, I couldn't take it anymore. I had to know what was happening behind those closed doors. I made my way inside the building, only to be met with resistance from the desk attendant and security. They eyed me with suspicion, their bodies tense and ready for a confrontation.

But I was undeterred. I flashed my badge, my voice low and insistent.

"Look, it's imperative that I see what happened up there. Lives may be at stake."

It took some convincing, but eventually, I gained access to the CCTV footage. I scrutinized the screen, my eyes narrowing as I watched Charlotte enter the private elevator to Edith's apartment, alone. And then I saw it - an envelope with Gia Clark's name on it, clutched tightly in Charlotte's hand.

"Gia Clark? Now, this just got interesting," I murmured, my mind racing with the implications.

The security guard took note of my interest and captured a screenshot of the footage for me. Armed with this new piece of the puzzle, I exited the building, my steps quick and purposeful. I was more determined than ever to unravel the mystery involving Charlotte and Edith, to discover what secrets that envelope held and how it all tied back to Gia Clark. The game was on, and I was ready to play.

—

I sat in my car, parked discreetly, my eyes glued to the glowing screen of my phone as I scrolled through Charlotte's social media. The soft tapping of my fingers against the glass filled the silence, punctuated only by the occasional hum of a passing car.

"Charlotte's putting on quite a show on socials, but the insecurity is hard to miss," I muttered to myself, my voice rough with exhaustion. I'd been at this for hours, trying to piece together the puzzle that was Charlotte Astor and her connection to the leak. "Why is Edith tangled up in this mess? Charlotte's a typical heartbroken ex, but Edith's involvement adds another layer."

I rubbed my eyes, feeling the grit of too many sleepless nights. This case was consuming me, body and soul. But I couldn't give up. Not now. Not when I was so close to the truth.

"Time to get closer to Charlotte and see what connects her to Edith," I said, my jaw clenching with determination.

I put my phone away and started the car, the engine rumbling to life like a beast awakening from slumber. I pulled out onto the street, my eyes scanning the sidewalks for any sign of Charlotte. I had to be careful, and had to stay invisible. If she caught wind of my presence, it could all fall apart.

The city passed by in a blur of neon and concrete as I tailed Charlotte, my mind racing with possibilities. What was she hiding? What secrets lurked beneath that polished exterior? And how did Edith fit into the picture?

I knew I wouldn't rest until I had the answers. Until I'd unraveled the tangled web of lies and deceit that surrounded Tyde and Gia. It was more than just a job now. It was personal.

So I kept driving, kept watching, and kept digging. I'd follow Charlotte to the ends of the earth if that's what it took. Because in this game of shadows and secrets, the truth was the only thing that mattered. And I wouldn't stop until I had it in my grasp.

LANTERN'S KEEP

The sophisticated cocktail lounge hummed with a relaxed energy, the soft clink of glasses and murmur of conversation filling the dimly lit space. I sat at a distant table, my autumn brown eyes locked on Charlotte as she sipped her mojito, completely unaware of my presence.

I watched her for a few minutes, taking in every detail - the way her perfectly manicured nails tapped against the glass, the slight flush in her cheeks as the alcohol worked its magic. She looked relaxed, carefree. But I knew better. I knew the secrets that lurked beneath that polished exterior.

I decided to play a subtle game, to see if I could get her to let her guard down. I signaled to the waiter, slipping him a few bills and murmuring instructions. He nodded, a slight smirk on his lips, and made his way over to Charlotte's table.

"Compliments of the gentleman at the bar," he said smoothly, setting a fresh mojito in front of her. "He wishes you a fantastic evening."

Charlotte looked puzzled but intrigued, her eyes darting around the lounge as she tried to identify her secret admirer. I caught her gaze from across the room, subtly tipping my glass toward her in a silent toast. The alcohol was already working its magic, and I could see the thrill of the unknown lighting up her face.

I seized the opportunity, rising from my seat and making my way over to her table. I slid into the chair across from her, my movements smooth and confident.

"I hope you don't mind the intrusion," I said, my voice low and smooth. "But I couldn't resist the chance to buy a drink for a beautiful woman."

Charlotte smiled. a hint of flirtation in her eyes.

"Well, how could I say no to such a charming offer?"

I signaled to the waiter, ordering another round of drinks. The night was young, figuratively, and I could sense that there was an opportunity here - a chance to gather the information I needed to crack this case wide open.

So I settled in, ready to play the long game. Ready to charm and flatter and cajole until Charlotte spilled her secrets. It wasn't going to be easy, but I was up for the challenge.

—

The dimly lit bar pulsed with energy, the chatter of patrons and the clinking of glasses creating a cacophony that filled my ears. I sat across from Charlotte, watching as she swayed in her seat, her words slurring together in a drunken jumble.

I leaned in, a smile playing at the corners of my mouth.

"You know, Charlotte, secrets have a funny way of finding their way out. Why don't you tell me about Edith's next move?"

Charlotte laughed, the sound harsh and grating.

"Oh, Edith, that conniving witch! She's planning more! Something big, real big." She hiccuped, her hand sloshing her drink precariously. "But I don't care," she hiccups. "I don't care anymore."

I raised an eyebrow, my interest piqued.

"So, Charlotte. What's her plan?"

She giggled, her eyes unfocused.

"You're smart, too smart. She's...uh...something about... betraying Gia. Yeah, that's it! First she wants my men to set up cameras everywhere Gia frequents. She wants any bad image of her out there. And I.... I hired someone. He was homeless and willing."

I sat back, my mind racing. Betrayal from Edith? That was a bold move for Edith, especially with her having *Incline Media* to lose.

And Charlotte hired someone? Who did she hire?

"Plotting on Gia, huh? Interesting. By chance who... who was the man hired?"

Charlotte scoffed and on the verge of falling asleep at the table, "His name... He's... the maintenance man."

"Okay, Thanks for your time Charlotte. I will definitely be seeing you later."

I stood up abruptly, leaving her disoriented and confused at the table. I signaled to the waiter, slipping him a few bills.

"Make sure she gets a cab home. She's had enough for tonight."

As I walked out of the bar, my mind was already spinning with possibilities. Edith was planning something big, something that could destroy Gia. I needed to find out what it was, and fast.

I stepped out into the cool night air, the sounds of the city washing over me. I had a lead now, a thread to follow. And I wasn't going to stop until I unraveled the whole damn thing.

I lit a cigarette, the smoke curling around my face as I walked down the street. The game was on, and I was ready to play. Edith thought she could outsmart me, but she had no idea who she was dealing with.

SCOUT'S OFFICE - CHINATOWN, NEW YORK CITY

I stood in my dimly lit office, the city's orange glow seeping through the venetian blinds. The evidence was spread before me on my worn desk, a puzzle I was determined to solve. My eyes darted from photo to photo, document to document, piecing together the fragments of this twisted case.

Charlotte and Edith. Their names echoed in my mind as I traced their movements. They'd been meeting at Edith's building, plotting their next move against Gia and Tyde. But why? What was their endgame?

I grabbed my tumbler, the whiskey burning my throat as I swallowed. The ice clinked against the glass, a jarring sound in the otherwise silent room. My head throbbed with unanswered questions.

A name caught my eye on one of the documents. Malcolm. Who the hell was Malcolm? Charlotte had hired him, but for what? My gut twisted. This guy was the key, I could feel it.

I paced the length of my office, the floorboards creaking beneath my feet. The weight of the case pressed down on me, suffocating. I needed answers, and I needed them now.

My phone rang, piercing the silence. I snatched it up, hoping for a break.

"Scout," I barked into the receiver.

"I've got something for you," a familiar voice rasped. My informant, always lurking in the shadows.

"Speak," I demanded, my free hand clenching into a fist.

"Word on the street is Charlotte and Edith are planning to plaster Gia and Tyde's information and sexual content everywhere. Soon."

My heart raced.

"Revenge porn? When exactly?"

"That's the million-dollar question, isn't it?" The line went dead.

I slammed the phone down, frustration coursing through me. I needed more. I needed to find this Malcolm character, to unravel the web of lies and deceit that surrounded him.

My mind raced, connecting dots, forming theories. Who else might know something? Who else was tangled up in this mess?

Dandi Ray. Edith's assistant. The name floated to the surface of my thoughts like a corpse in a river. She might know something, might be the weak link I needed to crack this case wide open.

I grabbed my coat, the leather creaking as I shrugged it on. The day was young, and I had work to do. I'd shake down every lowlife, every connection I had until I got the answers I needed.

As I stepped out into the bright morning, the city's pulse thrumming around me, one thought consumed me: I'd uncover the truth, no matter the cost. The game was on, and I was playing for keeps.

CHAPTER 15
NOWHERE TO RUN

Scout's face filled the screen, his expression grim and serious. I could feel the tension radiating through the phone as Tyde and I huddled together, our faces tight with worry.

"I've got updates on Charlotte and Edith," Scout said, his voice low and urgent.

Tyde's jaw squared off, his miff clear as day.

"Alright, what's going on?"

Scout took a deep breath, his eyes locked on ours.

"Charlotte gave me a lead. Edith's planning something big against Gia."

My heart stopped, my breath catching in my throat.

"What? Edith? My boss? Why would she do that?" The words tumbled out of my mouth, disbelief coloring every syllable.

Scout's expression softened, his voice sincere.

"Sometimes enemies are where you least expect them. It's a tough pill to swallow, Gia."

Tyde flashed me a sorry look, his eyes full of regret.

"Gia, I'm sorry about this. I had no idea Charlotte would drag you into this whole kerfuffle."

Anger flared inside me, hot and bright.

"Our past keeps haunting us, Tyde. I never thought Edith would turn out to be an enemy." My voice shook with emotion, the betrayal cutting deep.

Scout leaned forward, his voice calm and assured.

"I understand this is difficult, but we need to focus. Tyde, you too. This is about Edith's motives, not just the past."

Tyde's face screwed up in frustration, his fists clenched tight.

"Another bit of old business coming back to haunt me, brilliant. Thought I'd seen the last of that..." He takes a deep breath. Carries on, voice calmer but firm. "Guess I was wrong."

I could feel the tears burning behind my eyes, the realization that my boss, someone I had trusted and looked up to, had been working against me. It was a blow I hadn't seen coming, and it left me reeling.

Scout's voice cut through the heavy silence, resolute and determined.

"I'll keep digging into Charlotte and Edith. We need to find out the extent of their plans and how deep this betrayal goes."

The room fell into a heavy silence, the weight of the revelation pressing down on us like a physical force. I could feel Tyde's arm around me, his touch a small comfort in the face of such a shocking betrayal.

But even as the pain and anger swirled inside me, I knew we couldn't give up. We had to face this head-on, to unravel the tangled web of lies and deceit that had been woven around us.

So I took a deep breath, squared my shoulders, and prepared myself for the challenges ahead. Whatever Edith and Charlotte had planned, we would be ready. We would fight back with everything we had.

And we would win.

Tyde's email to his lawyers:

Subject: No Quarter for Case

Representation,

Right, let's get this straight. I won't stand for no messing about, no cop-outs, or any pathetic attempts to play down the right monstrous wrongs done to Gia and me by your lot, Charlotte Astor and Edith Shalom. The charges they're facing - stalking, nicking our privacy, threats and bad-mouthing - are about as low as you can go. Demanding proper punishment ain't just my right as the victim, it's my bloody duty to see justice served.

So forget any tired old sob stories about them being "young and daft" or having a "tough time at work" to make Astor and Shalom seem like they didn't know any better. That 24-year-old leech, Astor, deliberately terrified us with her ever-escalating, tech-savvy stalking designed to make us feel unsafe and like we couldn't trust anyone. What she did weren't just silly mistakes, they were carefully planned attacks by a right nutter, no two ways about it.

And Shalom? Being 30-something with a posh career doesn't excuse the vile lies and trash talk she spread about us like confetti. Mindlessly throwing around nasty lies from her position of privilege wasn't some "emotional overreaction." It was the manipulative, sociopathic behaviour of a right wrong'un who cares more about hurting people than being decent.

I don't just want to see them punished for these disgraceful crimes - I want them to feel the full force of the consequences they deserve. The 18-year sentences shouldn't be some kind of favour, they should be the least they get, not some harsh punishment you'll try and weasel out of.

So go on, trot out your pathetic excuses about outside pressures, mental problems, momentary lapses - whatever rubbish you think will make people feel sorry for them. We both know the truth. Astor and Shalom are deranged predators who planned and carried out a systematic campaign of terror, invasion, and ruining people's reputations. Crocodile tears in court and fancy lawyer tricks won't get them off the hook.

When the gavel comes down, no amount of clever lawyer stuff will stop your heartless clients from finally facing the music for the lives they've maliciously messed up with stalking, harassment, lies, and mental torture. Justice has been a long time coming, but it's coming in full force.

The victims deserve proper payback, not to be kept on edge by your clients' convenient lies. I expect my lawyer to go after them with everything they've got, legally speaking, until

Astor and Shalom face the right sort of serious consequences they've earned.

No messing. No delays or empty excuses. Just the scales of justice tipping the right way, weighing up the awful damage your clients caused - and a bloody great big ton of accountability finally being served.

Time's up for messing around.

Tyde Wright.

Scout Walker

SCOUT'S OFFICE - NEW YORK CITY

I hung up the FaceTime call with Tyde and Gia, the screen going dark as their faces disappeared. Determination surged through my veins, a fire that couldn't be quenched. I rolled up my sleeves, the fabric of my shirt stretching tight across my forearms as I got back to work.

The room was a chaos of information, photos, and notes scattered across every surface. A corkboard loomed on the wall, strings connecting the dots in a tangled web of conspiracy. I stood at the center of it all, my mind racing as I tried to piece together the puzzle.

"I can't let emotions cloud my judgment," I muttered to myself, my voice low and gruff. "Charlotte and Edith are planning explicit content for both of them."

I scanned through the documents, my eyes darting from surveillance photos to hastily scribbled notes. The hum of computers filled the air, punctuated by the occasional tap of my fingers on the keyboard. I was a man possessed, driven by the need to uncover the truth.

The phone rang, and I snatched it up, pressing it to my ear.

"I need every detail on Edith's recent activities. No stone unturned." My informant's voice crackled through the receiver, promising to dig deeper.

"I'll expose their plan, whatever it takes," I vowed to myself, my jaw clenched tight.

The room was a flurry of activity, papers flying and coffee cups piling up as I worked tirelessly to unravel the threads of deception and conspiracy. The investigation was intensifying, the stakes rising with every passing moment.

But I remained resolute, my focus unwavering.

—

INTERROGATION ROOM

The atmosphere crackled with tension as I stared down Edith's executive assistant, Dandi Ray, a timid slip of a girl with nervous eyes and fidgeting hands. I could practically taste her fear, the acrid tang of it hanging heavy in the air between us.

"You've been Edith's right-hand for a while, haven't you?" I asked, my voice low and intimidating. I leaned forward, invading her space, watching as she shrank back in her seat.

"Yes, but I don't know anything about her personal affairs," she stammered, her words tumbling out in a rushed jumble.

I grinned, a predatory flash of teeth.

"Funny how personal affairs often find their way into the professional world. Let's talk about what you might have overheard."

The assistant squirmed, her anxiety written all over her face. She looked like a trapped animal, desperate for escape but knowing there was nowhere to run.

I leaned in closer, my voice dropping to a sly whisper.

"You know, people like Edith tend to forget the walls

have ears. What have you heard? Anything about Gia, Tyde, or Charlotte?"

She swallowed hard, her voice barely audible.

"I hear everything. Every argument, every secret call."

I raised an eyebrow, my interest piqued.

"And what are they arguing about?"

She glanced around nervously, as if afraid Edith might materialize at any moment.

"It's mainly about Charlotte being on the cover of the magazine. Edith wants a fair partnership from Charlotte's dad."

I smiled, a slow, knowing curve of my lips.

"Money and power, the age-old motivators. What else?"

The assistant's voice dropped even lower, a terrified whisper.

"Edith doesn't care who she crushes for a story. Gia is just collateral damage. And Tyde's story was right there."

My ears pricked up at that.

"Tyde's story? What's that about?"

She looked like she might bolt at any moment, her fear palpable.

"A recently retired NHL player. He suddenly decided to become a reporter. And just her luck it was Gia's Ex. It's the perfect situation for Edith. And Charlotte made promises of more security and legacy to Ediths' *Incline Media*. Edith signed documents."

I smirked, triumph singing in my veins.

"Promises and documents, huh? Get me those documents, and you might just save yourself a lot of trouble."

The assistant hesitated, her eyes darting back and forth like a trapped rabbit. But then she nodded, visibly frightened. With shaking hands, she pulled out her phone, logged into her work database with Edith's password, and started downloading the incriminating documents.

I watched her work, my smirk growing wider by the second.

"Send them to me, now."

As the documents pinged into my inbox, a sense of triumph washed over me. The pieces of the puzzle were falling into place, the picture becoming clearer with every passing moment. Justice was on the horizon, and I was the one who would bring it crashing down on their heads.

—

I leapt from my chair, the address burning a hole in my pocket. My fingers closed around the cold metal of my car keys, and I was out the door before I could second-guess myself. The familiar smell of leather and stale coffee greeted me as I slid into the driver's seat, my heart pounding with anticipation.

The streets of the Bronx blurred past my windows, a gritty kaleidoscope of urban decay. I pulled up to the curb, killing the engine but leaving the key in the ignition. Malcolm's supposed address loomed before me, a dingy apartment complex that had seen better days. Peeling paint and boarded-up windows told a story of neglect and desperation.

I waited, my eyes never leaving the entrance. Minutes stretched into what felt like hours, the tension coiling in my gut like a spring. And then—movement. A figure emerged from the shadows of the lobby, and I knew instantly it was him. Malcolm.

My hand was on the door handle before I could think, and I found myself striding towards him with false confidence. His eyes widened as I approached, wariness etched into every line of his face.

"Hey there, buddy!" I called out, plastering on my best 'long-lost friend' smile. "Fancy running into you here!"

Malcolm's brow furrowed, confusion wrestling with suspicion on his features.

"I'm sorry, do I know you?" he asked, his voice tight with barely concealed anxiety.

I laughed, the sound hollow even to my own ears.

"Come on, man, it's me! Scout! We met at that thing last month, remember?"

His eyes narrowed, and I saw the moment recognition dawned. Not of me, but of the danger he was in. Malcolm's muscles tensed, ready to bolt—but it was too late.

Two burly men materialized from the shadows, moving with a speed that belied their size. Before Malcolm could utter a sound, they had him. One meaty hand clamped over his mouth, muffling his protests as they efficiently manhandled him towards my waiting car.

The trunk popped open with a soft click, and Malcolm disappeared inside, his eyes wide with terror. The lid slammed shut, and just like that, it was over. The whole thing had taken less than a minute.

My hands shook as I slid back behind the wheel,

adrenaline coursing through my veins. I took a deep breath, trying to steady myself. This was just the beginning.

The interrogation room was a stark contrast to the grimy streets we'd left behind. Harsh fluorescent light bounced off the bare walls, leaving nowhere to hide. I could feel the weight of unseen eyes behind the two-way mirror, and knew the cops were watching our every move.

Malcolm sat across from me, his earlier bravado shattered. Sweat beaded on his forehead, and his eyes darted around the room like a cornered animal.

I leaned forward, my voice low and intense.

"Let's cut the crap, Malcolm. We know Charlotte hired you. We know you've been stalking and possibly assaulted Gia. What I want to know is why."

He flinched at Gia's name, and I knew I had him.

"I-I don't know what you're talking about," he stammered, but the lie was weak, unconvincing.

I slammed my hand on the table, making him jump.

"Don't bullshit me!" I snarled. "We've got Charlotte in custody. She's already singing like a canary. This is your one chance to come clean."

The fight seemed to drain out of him all at once. Malcolm's shoulders slumped, and when he spoke, his voice was barely above a whisper.

"I love her!" he said. "Gia. I'm in love with her."

I leaned back, disgust churning in my gut.

"And Charlotte? How does she fit into all this?"

Malcolm's eyes hardened, a spark of defiance flaring to life.

"Charlotte started it all," he spat. "She hired me, showed me that video she took of Gia and Tyde. But after that... It was all me. I couldn't help myself. I had to know everything about her."

The words poured out of him now, a torrent of obsession and justification. He rattled off Gia's favorite flowers, her go-to comfort food, her route home from work, the dream vacation she'd always wanted to take. With each revelation, I felt my skin crawl.

I didn't need to look at the mirror to know the cops had heard enough. The door burst open, and two officers strode in, their faces grim.

As they cuffed him, reading him his rights, Malcolm's eyes locked onto mine.

"Tell her I love her," he pleaded. "Tell Gia I did it all for her."

I watched as they led him away, revulsion and pity warring within me. The door closed behind them with a final-sounding click.

"Yeah, sure," I muttered to the empty room, my voice dripping with sarcasm. "I'll tell her. And Tyde too."

I pushed myself to my feet, bone-weary and soul-sick. This case was far from over, but at least we had Malcolm.

Tyde & Gia

I thought back to the moment Scout had burst into our apartment, his face alight with triumph as he waved a stack of incriminating documents in the air.

"We got 'em," he crowed, his voice ringing with satisfaction. "Charlotte and Edith, they're going down. We've got enough evidence to put them behind bars."

The next few weeks had been a whirlwind of legal proceedings, endless meetings with lawyers and detectives. But through it all, Tyde had been my rock, my unwavering support. He had held my hand through every court appearance, every tearful breakdown. And now, as we sat together on our new sofa, in our new home, it felt like we had finally emerged on the other side.

I turned to face him, my eyes locking with his.

"Thank you," I whispered, my voice thick with emotion. "For everything. I couldn't have gotten through this without you."

Tyde grinned, his hand cupping your cheek.

"No need for thanks, Gia. You know I love you, always have and always will. You can rely on me, no matter what."

I leaned in, capturing his lips in a soft, tender kiss. The world fell away as we lost ourselves in each other, the past fading into nothing more than a distant memory.

—

I sank into the plush cushions of our new sofa, Tyde's arm draped comfortably around my shoulders. The TV flickered in front of us, the news anchor's voice filling the room with a sense of finality.

The harsh glare of the television screen illuminated my face as I sat transfixed, the news anchor's somber voice filling the room with a palpable tension. My heart hammered against my ribcage, a sickening mixture of anticipation and dread churning in my gut as I leaned forward, hanging onto every word.

"Breaking News: Billionaire's Daughter and Editor of Notable Media Outlet Sentenced up to 25 Years for Crimes Against Hockey Star and Reporter"

"We have breaking news to report. Charlotte Astor, daughter of multi-billionaire Derek Astor, has been found guilty and sentenced to 18 years in prison. Astor was found guilty of multiple charges for concocting a plan of revenge exposure, including criminal solicitation , bribery, invasion of privacy, and first-degree stalking of retired hockey player Tyde Wright and his girlfriend, reporter Gia Clark.

"Malcolm Smith, recently arrested for multiple charges, has been revealed to have deeper connections to the Astor case than previously thought,"News Reporter Janis Fox continued, her blue eyes boring into the camera.

"Sources close to the investigation have confirmed that Smith was posing as a maintenance man hired by Charlotte Astor through bribery."

"Smith is now facing additional charges of assault, stalking, and invasion of privacy of reporter Gia Clark."

The charges also include leaking unauthorized personal information and first-degree assault by threat. In a related development, Edith Shalom, Astor's alleged co-accomplice and Clark's former boss at Incline Media, faces similar charges, along with additional accusations of defamation.

We'll bring you more details on this shocking story. Stay tuned."

The words hit me like a physical blow, the air rushing from my lungs as if I'd been sucker-punched. Charlotte Astor and Edith Shalom, two names that had haunted my waking moments and plagued my nightmares for weeks, were finally facing the consequences of their actions. Up to 25 years behind bars, a fitting punishment for the hell they'd put Gia and me through.

Memories flashed through my mind in a dizzying montage - the invasive pop-ups, the unauthorized leaks of our most intimate moments.

Edith, with her vicious lies and carefully crafted defamation, had sought to destroy our reputations, our very identities.

My gaze drifted back to the television where Charlotte and Edith's mugshots now filled the screen. Their faces, once so smug and self-assured, were now haggard and defeated, the weight of their crimes etched into every line and shadow.

A part of me wanted to feel sorry for them, to find some shred of empathy for the broken women they had become.

Charlotte and Edith may have stolen our past, but they would not define our future. That was up to us, and us alone.

Tyde

DR. RILEY HAMMOND'S OFFICE - THE WATERFRONT, NEW JERSEY

I sat across from Riley, a smile tugging at the corners of my mouth. The late afternoon sun slanted through the windows of his cozy office, bathing everything in a warm, golden glow.

"Taking the plunge on the engagement ring soon," I said, buzzing with excitement. "Think I'm ready to pop the question to Gia."

Riley's face lit up, his eyes crinkling at the corners as he beamed at me.

"That's fantastic, Tyde! I'm genuinely happy for you."

I felt a rush of warmth at his words, a sense of gratitude washing over me. This man had been my rock, my guide through some of the darkest moments of my life. When everything had felt like it was falling apart, when the weight of my past mistakes had threatened to crush me, he had been there to help me pick up the pieces.

"Your advice has been a right lifesaver, Riley," I said, my voice choked up. "Couldn't have got this far without you."

And it was true. When I first walked into his office, I was a mess. Plagued by guilt, haunted by the ghosts of my past. But through our sessions, through the hard work and the tears and the painful self-reflection, I had slowly begun to heal.

I thought back to the early days of my relationship with

Gia, how I had been so afraid to let her in, to let her see the broken parts of me. But with Riley's help, I had learned to open up, to trust in the strength of our love.

And now, as I sat across from him, the future stretching out before me like a shining path, I knew that I was ready. Ready to take that next step, to make Gia my wife.

I could picture it so clearly in my mind - the way her eyes would widen in surprise, the way her mouth would curve into that beautiful, radiant smile. I could imagine slipping the ring onto her finger, watching as it sparkled in the light.

It was a future I had never dared to dream of, a happiness I had once thought was beyond my reach. But with Gia by my side, with the love and support of the people around me, I knew that anything was possible.

I looked back at Riley, my heart fit to burst.

"Cheers," I said, my voice barely a whisper. "For everything."

He smiled, his eyes shining with pride.

"You did the work, Tyde. You fought for your happiness. And now, you're ready to claim it."

I nodded, a sense of peace settling over me like a warm blanket. I was ready. Ready to start this new chapter, to build a life with the woman I loved more than anything in the world.

Gia

GIA'S FLOWER SHOP - NOLITA, NEW YORK CITY

I moved through my flower shop with a sense of purpose, my hands deftly arranging bouquets and tending to the vibrant blooms that filled every corner of the space. The air was heavy with the heady scent of roses and lilies, the delicate perfume of jasmine and gardenia.

It had been a long road to get here, a journey filled with twists and turns and unexpected detours. But as I looked around at the thriving business I had built from the ground up, I couldn't help but feel a sense of pride and accomplishment.

A customer approached me, a smile lighting up her face as she took in the riot of color and beauty that surrounded us.

"Your flowers are stunning, Gia. This place is amazing!"

I felt a rush of warmth at her words, a sense of gratitude washing over me.

"Thank you so much! It's been a dream come true."

And it was true. Ever since I was a little girl, I had dreamed of owning my own flower shop. Of spending my days surrounded by beauty and life and the simple joy of bringing a little bit of brightness into people's lives.

But for so long, that dream had felt like just that - a dream. Something distant and unattainable, always just out of reach. I had struggled and fought and clawed my way through life, always searching for that elusive sense of purpose and fulfillment.

And then I met Tyde. Tyde, with his kind eyes and his gentle smile, his unwavering support and his boundless love. He had been my rock, my anchor in the storm. And with him by my side, I had found the courage to chase my dreams.

It hadn't been easy. There had been long nights and early mornings, endless hours spent pouring over business plans and financial statements. There had been moments of doubt and fear, times when I had wondered if I was crazy for even trying.

But through it all, Tyde had been there. Cheering me on, wiping my tears, holding my hand every step of the way. And now, as I stood in the middle of my very own flower shop, I knew that it had all been worth it.

I looked around at the customers milling about, their faces alight with joy and wonder as they took in the beauty that surrounded them. I watched as they carefully selected their bouquets, their eyes shining with anticipation and excitement.

And I knew, in that moment, that this was where I was meant to be. This was my calling, my purpose in life. To bring a little bit of beauty and joy into the world, one flower at a time.

I turned back to the customer, my smile widening.

"Is there anything in particular you're looking for today?"

And as I listened to her describe the perfect bouquet for her mother's birthday, I felt a sense of contentment wash over me. This was my dream, my passion. And I was living it, every single day.

Life was good. And with Tyde by my side, I knew that it

would only get better from here.

—

DR. CELINE DIAZ'S OFFICE - GARMENT DISTRICT, NEW YORK CITY

I sat across from Celine, a smile playing at the corners of my mouth. The afternoon light filtered through the curtains of her cozy office, casting a warm glow over everything.

"I think Tyde and I are ready for the next step," I said, my voice barely containing my excitement. "Marriage might be on the horizon."

Celine's face lit up, her eyes shining with pride.

"Gia, you've grown so much. I'm thrilled to see the strength of your relationship with Tyde."

I felt a rush of warmth at her words, a sense of gratitude washing over me. Celine had been my guide, my confidante through some of the toughest moments of my life. When I first walked into her office, I had been a shell of myself; broken, lost, haunted by the ghosts of my past.

But through our sessions, through the hard work and the tears and the painful self-reflection, I had slowly begun to heal. I had learned to love myself again, to trust in the strength of my own resilience.

I thought back to the early days of our relationship, how I had been so afraid to let him in, to let him see the broken parts of me. But with Celine's help, I had learned to open up, to trust in the power of love.

And now, as I sat across from her, the future stretching

out before me like a shining path, I knew that I was ready. Ready to take that next step, to build a life with the man I loved more than anything in the world.

I could picture it so clearly in my mind - the way Tyde's eyes would light up when he saw me walking down the aisle, the way his hand would feel in mine as we exchanged our vows. I could imagine the laughter and the tears, the joy and the love that would fill every moment of our life together.

EPILOGUE
Tyde & Gia

I stepped out into the backyard, my breath catching in my throat as I took in the scene before me. The entire space had been transformed into a romantic haven, bathed in the soft glow of twinkling bulb string lights. The air was heavy with the sweet scent of lavender daisies, their delicate petals covering the ground like a magical carpet.

And there, in the middle of it all, stood Tyde, a nervous smile playing at the corners of his mouth as he put the final touches on a beautifully set table.

"Alright, Tyde, you're sorted," I heard him murmur to himself, his voice barely audible over the pounding of my own heart.

I took a step forward, my eyes wide with wonder.

"Tyde, this is... breathtaking!"

He turned to face me, his eyes sparkling with a mix of

excitement and jitters.

"Thought we could do something special. Dinner's sorted. Shall we tuck in?"

I followed him to the table, my heart fluttering in my chest as I took in the soft glow of the lights, the warm ambiance that seemed to envelop us like a cozy blanket.

"So, what's the occasion?" I teased as we sat down, my eyes sparkling with mischief. "Did you become a secret gourmet chef when I wasn't looking?"

Tyde chuckled, his laugh sending a right tingle down my spine.

"Maybe. Or perhaps I just wanted an excuse to have a posh nosh with the most gorgeous bird in the world."

I felt a blush creep up my cheeks, my smile widening.

"Smooth, Tyde."

As we dug into the delicious steak dinner, the conversation flowed effortlessly between us, filled with laughter and love. But even as we talked and joked, I couldn't help but notice the nervous energy that seemed to radiate off of Tyde, the way his hands shook slightly as he reached for his glass.

"What's going on in that mind of yours, Tyde?" I asked teasingly, my heart racing with anticipation.

He took a deep breath, his gaze meeting mine.

"Well, what I was thinking is... I've got something rather important to ask you."

And then he was standing up, taking my hands in his and guiding me to my feet. I watched in disbelief as he dropped to one knee, my heart skipping a beat as I realized what was happening.

"Is this really happening?" I whispered to myself, my voice trembling with emotion.

Tyde's voice was low and passionate as he spoke, his eyes never leaving mine.

"Gia, love, you're the sunshine of my life, my rock, and my everything. Will you do me the greatest honour and become my missus?"

Tears of joy filled my eyes as I nodded ecstatically, my voice barely above a whisper.

"Hell yes!"

And then I was jumping into his arms, knocking us both over as laughter and kisses filled the air. We lay on the flower-covered ground, surrounded by the scent of lavender daisies and the twinkling of the lights above us.

"I love you, Gia," *Tyde murmured, his voice thick with emotion.*

I grinned, my heart bursting with happiness.

"And I love you, Tyde."

We stayed like that for a long time, staring up at the stars and basking in the magic of the moment. And as I lay there in Tyde's arms, I knew that this was just the beginning of our forever. A forever filled with love, laughter, and endless adventures.

END OF BOOK 1

CHAMPIONSHIP OF THE HEART EXCERPT
PROLOGUE

Christian Nuku

ACCOR STADIUM - SYDNEY, NEW SOUTH WALES, AU
GRAND FINAL

The roar of the crowd was deafening as we ran out of the tunnel and onto the field, a surge of adrenaline coursing through my veins. I led the charge as captain of the Stallions, my heart pounding with anticipation for the championship match ahead. The stadium lights glared down, illuminating the field and the frenzied faces of the fans.

"Fair dinkum, the mob that fights the hardest deserves the cup come sundown!", the announcer's voice boomed over the loudspeakers. A shiver ran down my spine.

This was it - the biggest game of our careers. Months of

grueling practices and hard-fought victories had led to this moment.

The referee's whistle pierced the air and the game kicked off with a thunderous rumble from the crowd. I launched the ball downfield, but to my dismay, it was a bad kick.

The Jaguars' Tyler Harper leapt up and swatted it down effortlessly. In a flash, the Jaguars capitalized and scored. 4 to 0, just like that. My stomach dropped as Christopher Nelson knocked through a field goal, stretching their lead to 6. We were in for a long, intense battle.

Gritting my teeth, I huddled the team and called for composure. On the ensuing drive, I connected with Xavier Latu who dished it to Finn Williams.

Finn bulldozed through a wall of Jaguar defenders and stretched the ball just over the try line as he was gang-tackled to the turf. Erupting with a primal yell, I kicked the conversion to claw us back to 8-6.

The Jaguars still clung to the lead, but we had life.

"Only forty ticks left to see who's king of the hill!", the announcer called out as play resumed.

Suddenly, Jonah Miro exploded through a gap, leaving defenders grasping at air as he blazed in for a sensational try.

The Jaguars struck back with a field goal to make it 10-8, but I responded in kind to wrestle back the lead at 12-8 going into the half. We jogged to the locker room with a slim advantage, but the game hung in the balance.

Anything could happen in the final 40 minutes...

The second half started with a bang as Christian Nuku gashed through the defense.

Just when it looked like he would score, he dished to a streaking Miro for a brilliant try, his hat trick. I converted again and we surged to a 24-8 lead.

The championship was within reach, but the Jaguars refused to go quietly.

Lucas Thompson linked up with Khalil Hussain for a critical try, then drilled the field goal to pull within 10 with just 16 minutes remaining.

"Can the Panthers pull off the sickest fightback ever in a Grand Final? Let's throw another shrimp on the barbie for that!", the announcer wondered aloud.

Thompson was a man possessed, orchestrating another try with pinpoint passes to Hussain and Harper before Christopher Nelson stiff-armed Latu and dove across the line.

In a blink, our lead had evaporated to 24-20.

Hearts racing, lungs burning, we battled for every inch. Sean Murphy beat Nuku but was tackled just short by Parker. The Jaguars recycled and spread it wide to Thompson who dove into the corner to tie it up at 24-24.

I could barely watch as he lined up the go-ahead conversion. The ball sailed through the uprights and the Jaguars stormed ahead 26-24 with precious seconds remaining.

We launched one final desperate attack but the Jaguars defense held firm. The final whistle sounded and I collapsed to the turf, exhausted and gutted. The Jaguars had done the impossible, winning their 5th championship.

Through tears, I watched them celebrate and hoist the trophy. Thompson was named player of the match and graciously acknowledged our efforts, calling Miro a "freak".

As the stadium emptied, I sat on the field with my teammate Spencer, staring blankly at the jubilant Jaguars fans. My almost 2-year-old daughter Maia toddled over and plopped into my lap.

Cradling her, a sad smile crossed my face. We had given everything and come up agonizingly short. But as I held Maia and watched the stadium lights dim, I knew we would be back. This loss would drive us. The Stallions' time would come.

Wordlessly, we boarded the bus to head home. Fans pounded the sides, their cheers fading into the night as we pulled away. It was a somber ride back, each of us alone with our thoughts. The lights of the stadium disappeared in the rearview mirror. Next year, I vowed, it will be our turn to bask in their glow as champions.

ALSO BY COURTNEY COLEMAN...

LOVE ON THE EDGE SERIES
A series of interconnected standalones
Starstruck Reckoning
Championship of the Heart

What's Next For the Rekindled Series?
"*Championship of the Heart*" follows NRL star Christian as he balances his team's quest for glory with the complexities of his personal life, including a troublesome ex and a budding attraction to Talula, a new American sports photographer on the Stallions' media team. As Christian and Talula's playful teasing evolves into genuine feelings, they must navigate the challenges of their professional lives and past relationships to find a path to love.

ACKNOWLEDGEMENTS

I would like to express my deepest appreciation and sincere thanks to all those who have been unwavering in their support throughout my writing journey. Your encouragement and belief in my work have been the driving force behind my continued efforts, and I am truly grateful for each and every one of you. Please know that this is just the beginning, and there are many more exciting projects on the horizon. I would like to give a special mention to Delilah Salazar, who has been an exceptional one-woman promotional powerhouse and an invaluable source of support.

ABOUT THE AUTHOR

When she's not busy making characters fall in love, Courtney Coleman is out there living her own rom-com life! This whirlwind of creativity founded 1607 Studios (because why settle for one passion?), launched PHENOM magazine (as if being phenomenal wasn't enough), and snaps award-winning photos that'll make your heart skip a beat.

Courtney's words have danced across the pages of Fashion School Daily and 180 Magazine, proving she's as fabulous with a pen as she is behind a camera. With a toolbelt full of talents and a head full of dreamy stories, this young adult author is ready to sweep you off your feet and into her next adventure. Hold onto your bookmarks, folks – Courtney Coleman is here to steal your heart, one page at a time!

**Keep in Touch with
Courtney**

Website:
https://hoo.be/1607.studios
Instagram:
@courtney.coleman_